Books by Rick Riordan

The Percy Jackson series
PERCY JACKSON AND THE LIGHTNING THIEF*
PERCY JACKSON AND THE SEA OF MONSTERS*
PERCY JACKSON AND THE TITAN'S CURSE*
PERCY JACKSON AND THE BATTLE OF THE LABYRINTH*
PERCY JACKSON AND THE LAST OLYMPIAN*

THE DEMIGOD FILES
CAMP HALF-BLOOD CONFIDENTIAL
CAMP JUPITER CLASSIFIED

PERCY JACKSON AND THE GREEK GODS
PERCY JACKSON AND THE GREEK HEROES

The Heroes of Olympus series
THE LOST HERO*
THE SON OF NEPTUNE*
THE MARK OF ATHENA
THE HOUSE OF HADES
THE BLOOD OF OLYMPUS

THE DEMIGOD DIARIES

The Kane Chronicles series
THE RED PYRAMID*
THE THRONE OF FIRE*
THE SERPENT'S SHADOW*

THE KANE CHRONICLES SURVIVAL GUIDE
BROOKLYN HOUSE MAGICIAN'S MANUAL

The Percy Jackson and Kane Chronicles Adventures
DEMIGODS AND MAGICIANS: THREE STORIES FROM THE
WORLD OF PERCY JACKSON AND THE KANE CHRONICLES

The Magnus Chase series
MAGNUS CHASE AND THE SWORD OF SUMMER
MAGNUS CHASE AND THE HAMMER OF THOR
MAGNUS CHASE AND THE SHIP OF THE DEAD

HOTEL VALHALLA GUIDE TO THE NORSE WORLDS
9 FROM THE NINE WORLDS

The Trials of Apollo series
THE HIDDEN ORACLE
THE DARK PROPHECY
THE BURNING MAZE
THE TYRANT'S TOMB
THE TOWER OF NERO

Also available as a graphic novel

THE TRIALS OF APOLLO

THE TOWER OF NERO

RICK RIORDAN

PUFFIN

PUFFIN BOOKS

UK | USA | Canada | Ireland | Australia
India | New Zealand | South Africa

Puffin Books is part of the Penguin Random House group of companies
whose addresses can be found at global.penguinrandomhouse.com.

www.penguin.co.uk   www.puffin.co.uk   www.ladybird.co.uk

First published in the USA by Disney • Hyperion, an imprint of Disney Book Group,
and in Great Britain by Puffin Books 2020

002

Text copyright © Rick Riordan, 2020

The moral right of the author has been asserted

This book is set in Danton, Gauthier FY, Roundhand/Fontspring,
Goudy Old Style, Goudy, Sabon/Monotype
Designed by Joann Hill

Printed and bound in Great Britain by Clays Ltd, Elcograf S.p.A.
A CIP catalogue record for this book is available from the British Library

INTERNATIONAL PAPERBACK
ISBN: 978–0–141–36408–7

All correspondence to:
Puffin Books, Penguin Random House Children's
One Embassy Gardens, 8 Viaduct Gardens, London SW11 7BW

To Becky,
Every journey leads me home to you

1

Two-headed snake dude
Jamming up my quiet ride.
Also, Meg's shoes stink.

WHEN TRAVELLING THROUGH WASHINGTON, DC, one expects to see a few snakes in human clothing. Still, I was concerned when a two-headed boa constrictor boarded our train at Union Station.

The creature had threaded himself through a blue silk business suit, looping his body into the sleeves and trouser legs to approximate human limbs. Two heads protruded from the collar of his shirt like twin periscopes. He moved with remarkable grace for what was basically an oversize balloon animal, taking a seat at the opposite end of the coach, facing our direction.

The other passengers ignored him. No doubt the Mist warped their perceptions, making them see just another commuter. The snake made no threatening moves. He didn't even glance at us. For all I knew, he was simply a working-stiff monster on his way home.

And yet I could not assume . . .

I whispered to Meg, 'I don't want to alarm you –'

'Shh,' she said.

Meg took the quiet-car rules seriously. Since we'd boarded, most of the noise in the coach had consisted of Meg shushing me every time I spoke, sneezed or cleared my throat.

'But there's a monster,' I persisted.

She looked up from her complimentary Amtrak magazine, raising an eyebrow above her rhinestone-studded cat-eye glasses. *Where?*

I chin-pointed towards the creature. As our train pulled away from the station, his left head stared absently out of the window. His right head flicked its forked tongue into a bottle of water held in the loop that passed for his hand.

'It's an *amphisbaena*,' I whispered, then added helpfully, 'a snake with a head at each end.'

Meg frowned, then shrugged, which I took to mean *Looks peaceful enough*. Then she went back to reading.

I suppressed the urge to argue. Mostly because I didn't want to be shushed again.

I couldn't blame Meg for wanting a quiet ride. In the past week, we had battled our way through a pack of wild centaurs in Kansas, faced an angry famine spirit at the World's Largest Fork in Springfield, Missouri (I did not get a selfie), and outrun a pair of blue Kentucky drakons that had chased us several times around Churchill Downs. After all that, a two-headed snake in a suit was perhaps not cause for alarm. Certainly, he wasn't bothering us at the moment.

I tried to relax.

Meg buried her face in her magazine, enraptured by an article on urban gardening. My young companion had grown taller in the months that I'd known her, but she was still compact enough to prop her red high-tops comfortably on the seatback in front of her. Comfortable for *her*, I mean, not for me or the other passengers. Meg hadn't changed her shoes since our run around the racetrack, and they looked and smelled like the back end of a horse.

At least she had traded her tattered green dress for Dollar General jeans and a green VNICORNES IMPERANT! T-shirt she'd bought at the Camp Jupiter gift shop. With her pageboy haircut beginning to grow out and an angry red zit erupting on her chin, she no longer looked like a kindergartener. She looked almost her age: a sixth-grader entering the circle of hell known as puberty.

I had not shared this observation with Meg. For one thing, I had my own acne to worry about. For another thing, as my master, Meg could literally order me to jump out of the window and I would be forced to obey.

The train rolled through the suburbs of Washington. The late-afternoon sun flickered between the buildings like the lamp of an old movie projector. It was a wonderful time of day, when a sun god should be wrapping up his work, heading to the old stables to park his chariot, then kicking back at his palace with a goblet of nectar, a few dozen adoring nymphs and a new season of *The Real Goddesses of Olympus* to binge-watch.

Not for me, though. I got a creaking seat on an Amtrak train and hours to binge-watch Meg's stinky shoes.

At the opposite end of the car, the amphisbaena still made no threatening moves . . . unless one considered drinking water from a non-reusable bottle an act of aggression.

Why, then, were my neck hairs tingling?

I couldn't regulate my breathing. I felt trapped in my window seat.

Perhaps I was just nervous about what awaited us in New York. After six months in this miserable mortal body, I was approaching my endgame.

Meg and I had blundered our way across the United States and back again. We'd freed ancient Oracles, defeated legions of monsters and suffered the untold horrors of the American public transportation system. Finally, after many tragedies, we had triumphed over two of the Triumvirate's evil emperors, Commodus and Caligula, at Camp Jupiter.

But the worst was yet to come.

We were heading back to where our troubles began – Manhattan, the base of Nero Claudius Caesar, Meg's abusive stepfather and my least favourite fiddle player. Even if we somehow managed to defeat him, a still more powerful threat lurked in the background: my archnemesis, Python, who had taken up residence at my sacred Oracle of Delphi as if it were some cut-price Airbnb.

In the next few days, either I would defeat these enemies and become the god Apollo again (assuming my father Zeus allowed it) or I would die trying. One way or the other, my time as Lester Papadopoulos was coming to an end.

Perhaps it wasn't a mystery why I felt so agitated . . .

I tried to focus on the beautiful sunset. I tried not to obsess about my impossible to-do list or the two-headed snake in row sixteen.

I made it all the way to Philadelphia without having a nervous breakdown. But, as we pulled out of Thirtieth Street

Station, two things became clear to me: 1) the amphisbaena wasn't leaving the train, which meant he probably wasn't a daily commuter, and 2) my danger radar was pinging more strongly than ever.

I felt *stalked*. I had the same ants-in-the-pores feeling I used to get when playing hide-and-seek with Artemis and her Hunters in the woods, just before they jumped from the bushes and riddled me with arrows. That was back when my sister and I were younger deities and could still enjoy such simple amusements.

I risked a look at the amphisbaena and nearly jumped out of my jeans. The creature was staring at me now, his four yellow eyes unblinking and . . . were they beginning to glow? Oh, no, no, no. Glowing eyes are never good.

'I need to get out,' I told Meg.

'Shh.'

'But that creature. I want to check on it. His eyes are glowing!'

Meg squinted at Mr Snake. 'No, they're not. They're *gleaming*. Besides, he's just sitting there.'

'He's sitting there suspiciously!'

The passenger behind us whispered, 'Shh!'

Meg raised her eyebrows at me. *Told you so.*

I pointed at the aisle and pouted at Meg.

She rolled her eyes, untangled herself from the hammock-like position she'd taken up and let me out. 'Don't start a fight,' she ordered.

Great. Now I would have to wait for the monster to attack before I could defend myself.

I stood in the aisle, waiting for the blood to return to my numb legs. Whoever invented the human circulatory system had done a lousy job.

The amphisbaena hadn't moved. His eyes were still fixed on me. He appeared to be in some sort of trance. Maybe he was building up his energy for a massive attack. Did amphisbaenae do that?

I scoured my memory for facts about the creature but came up with very little. The Roman writer Pliny claimed that wearing a live baby amphisbaena around your neck could assure you a safe pregnancy. (Not helpful.) Wearing its skin could make you attractive to potential partners. (Hmm. No, also not helpful.) Its heads could spit poison. Aha! That must be it. The monster was powering up for a dual-mouthed poison vomit hose-down of the train car!

What to do . . . ?

Despite my occasional bursts of godly power and skill, I couldn't count on one when I needed it. Most of the time, I was still a pitiful seventeen-year-old boy.

I could retrieve my bow and quiver from the overhead luggage compartment. Being armed would be nice. Then again, that would telegraph my hostile intentions. Meg would probably scold me for overreacting. (I'm sorry, Meg, but those eyes were *glowing*, not gleaming.)

If only I'd kept a smaller weapon, perhaps a dagger, concealed in my shirt. Why wasn't I the god of daggers?

I decided to stroll down the aisle as if I were simply on my way to the restroom. If the amphisbaena attacked, I would scream. Hopefully Meg would put down her magazine long enough to come rescue me. At least I would have forced the inevitable confrontation. If the snake didn't make a move, well, perhaps he really was harmless. Then I *would* go to the restroom, because I actually needed to.

I stumbled on my tingly legs, which didn't help my 'look casual' approach. I considered whistling a carefree tune, then remembered the whole quiet-car thing.

Four rows from the monster. My heart hammered. Those eyes were definitely glowing, definitely fixed on me. The monster sat unnaturally motionless, even for a reptile.

Two rows away. My trembling jaw and sweaty face made it hard to appear nonchalant. The amphisbaena's suit looked expensive and well-tailored. Probably, being a giant snake, he couldn't wear clothes right off the rack. His glistening brown-and-yellow diamond-pattern skin did not seem like the sort of thing one might wear to look more attractive on a dating app, unless one dated boa constrictors.

When the amphisbaena made his move, I thought I was prepared.

I was wrong. The creature lunged with incredible speed, lassoing my wrist with the loop of his false left arm. I was too surprised even to yelp. If he'd meant to kill me, I would have died.

Instead, he simply tightened his grip, stopping me in my tracks, clinging to me as if he were drowning.

He spoke in a low double hiss that resonated in my bone marrow:

> *'The son of Hades, cavern-runners' friend,*
> *Must show the secret way unto the throne.*
> *On Nero's own your lives do now depend.'*

As abruptly as he'd grabbed me, he let me go. Muscles undulated along the length of his body as if he were coming to a slow boil. He sat up straight, elongating his necks until he was almost noses-to-nose with me. The glow faded from his eyes.

'What am I do–?' His left head looked at his right head. 'How . . . ?'

His right head seemed equally mystified. It looked at me. 'Who are –? Wait, did I miss the Baltimore stop? My wife is going to kill me!'

I was too shocked to speak.

Those lines he'd spoken . . . I recognized the poetic metre. This amphisbaena had delivered a prophetic message. It dawned on me that this monster might in fact be a regular commuter who'd been possessed, hijacked by the whims of Fate because . . . Of course. He was a snake. Since ancient times, snakes have channelled the wisdom of the earth, because they live underground. A giant serpent would be especially susceptible to oracular voices.

I wasn't sure what to do. Should I apologize to him for his inconvenience? Should I give him a tip? And, if he wasn't the threat that had set off my danger radar, what was?

I was saved from an awkward conversation, and the amphisbaena was saved from his wife killing him, when two crossbow bolts flew across the coach and killed him instead, pinning the poor snake's necks against the back wall.

I shrieked. Several nearby passengers shushed me.

The amphisbaena disintegrated into yellow dust, leaving nothing behind but a well-tailored suit.

I raised my hands slowly and turned as if pivoting on a

land mine. I half expected another crossbow bolt to pierce my chest. There was no way I could dodge an attack from someone with such accuracy. The best I could do was appear non-threatening. I was good at that.

At the opposite end of the coach stood two hulking figures. One was a Germanus, judging from his beard and scraggly beaded hair, his hide armour, and his Imperial gold greaves and breastplate. I did not recognize him, but I'd met too many of his kind recently. I had no doubt who he worked for. Nero's people had found us.

Meg was still seated, holding her magical twin golden *sica* blades, but the Germanus had the edge of his broadsword against her neck, encouraging her to stay put.

His companion was the crossbow-shooter. She was even taller and heavier, wearing an Amtrak conductor's uniform that fooled no one – except, apparently, all the mortals on the train, who didn't give the newcomers a second look. Under her conductor's hat, the shooter's scalp was shaved on the sides, leaving a lustrous brown mane down the middle that curled over her shoulder in a braided rope. Her short-sleeved shirt stretched so tight against her muscular shoulders I thought her epaulettes and name tag would pop off. Her arms were covered with interlocking circular tattoos, and around her neck was a thick golden ring – a torque.

I hadn't seen one of those in ages. This woman was a Gaul! The realization made my stomach frost over. In the old days of the Roman Republic, Gauls were feared even more than the Germani.

She had already reloaded her double crossbow and was

pointing it at my head. Hanging from her belt was a variety of other weapons: a gladius, a club and a dagger. Oh, sure, *she* got a dagger.

Keeping her eyes on me, she jerked her chin towards her shoulder, the universal sign for *C'mere or I'll shoot you.*

I calculated my odds of charging down the aisle and tackling our enemies before they killed Meg and me. Zero. My odds of cowering in fear behind a chair while Meg took care of both of them? Slightly better, but still not great.

I made my way down the aisle, my knees wobbling. The mortal passengers frowned as I passed. As near as I could figure, they thought my shriek had been a disturbance unworthy of the quiet car, and the conductor was now calling me out. The fact that the conductor wielded a crossbow and had just killed a two-headed serpentine commuter did not seem to register with them.

I reached my row and glanced at Meg, partly to make sure she was all right, partly because I was curious why she hadn't attacked. Just holding a sword to Meg's throat was normally not enough to discourage her.

She was staring in shock at the Gaul. 'Luguselwa?'

The woman nodded curtly, which told me two horrifying things: first, Meg knew her. Second, Luguselwa was her name. As she regarded Meg, the fierceness in the Gaul's eyes dialled back a few notches, from *I am going to kill everyone now* to *I am going to kill everyone soon.*

'Yes, Sapling,' said the Gaul. 'Now put away your weapons before Gunther is obliged to chop off your head.'

2

Pastries for dinner?

Your fave Lester could never.

Got to pee. Later.

THE SWORD-WIELDER LOOKED DELIGHTED.
'Chop off head?'

His name, GUNTHER, was printed on an Amtrak name tag he wore over his armour – his only concession to being in disguise.

'Not yet.' Luguselwa kept her eyes on us. 'As you can see, Gunther loves decapitating people, so let's play nice. Come along –'

'Lu,' Meg said. 'Why?'

When it came to expressing hurt, Meg's voice was a fine-tuned instrument. I'd heard her mourn the deaths of our friends. I'd heard her describe her father's murder. I'd heard her rage against her foster father, Nero, who had killed her dad and twisted her mind with years of emotional abuse.

But when addressing Luguselwa, Meg's voice played in an entirely different key. She sounded as if her best friend had just dismembered her favourite doll for no reason and without warning. She sounded hurt, confused, incredulous – as if, in a life full of indignities, this was one indignity she never could have anticipated.

Lu's jaw muscles tightened. Veins bulged on her temples. I couldn't tell if she was angry, feeling guilty or showing us her warm-and-fuzzy side.

'Do you remember what I taught you about duty, Sapling?'

Meg gulped back a sob.

'Do you?' Lu said, her voice sharper.

'Yes,' Meg whispered.

'Then get your things and come along.' Lu pushed Gunther's sword away from Meg's neck.

The big man grumbled 'Hmph', which I assumed was Germanic for *I never get to have any fun.*

Looking bewildered, Meg rose and opened the overhead compartment. I couldn't understand why she was going along so passively with Luguselwa's orders. We'd fought against worse odds. Who *was* this Gaul?

'That's it?' I whispered as Meg passed me my backpack. 'We're giving up?'

'Lester,' Meg muttered, 'just do what I say.'

I shouldered my pack, my bow and quiver. Meg fastened her gardening belt around her waist. Lu and Gunther did not look concerned that I was now armed with arrows and Meg with an ample supply of heirloom-vegetable seeds. As we got our gear in order, the mortal passengers gave us annoyed looks, but no one shushed us, probably because they did not want to anger the two large conductors escorting us out.

'This way.' Lu pointed with her crossbow to the exit behind her. 'The others are waiting.'

The others?

I did not want to meet any more Gauls or Gunthers, but Meg followed Lu meekly through the Plexiglas double doors. I went next, Gunther breathing down my neck behind me, probably contemplating how easy it would be to separate my head from my body.

A gangway connected our car to the next: a loud, lurching hallway with automatic double doors on either end, a closet-size restroom in one corner and exterior doors to port and starboard. I considered throwing myself out of one of these exits and hoping for the best, but I feared 'the best' would mean dying on impact with the ground. It was pitch-black outside. Judging from the rumble of the corrugated steel panels beneath my feet, I guessed the train was going well over a hundred miles an hour.

Through the far set of Plexiglas doors, I spied the café car: a grim concession counter, a row of booths and a half-dozen large men milling around – more Germani. Nothing good was going to happen in there. If Meg and I were going to make a break for it, this was our chance.

Before I could make any sort of desperate move, Luguselwa stopped abruptly just before the café-car doors. She turned to face us.

'Gunther,' she snapped, 'check the bathroom for infiltrators.'

This seemed to confuse Gunther as much as it did me, either because he didn't see the point, or he had no idea what an infiltrator was.

I wondered why Luguselwa was acting so paranoid. Did she worry we had a legion of demigods stashed in the restroom, waiting to spring out and rescue us? Or perhaps like me she'd once surprised a Cyclops on the porcelain throne and no longer trusted public toilets.

After a brief stare-down, Gunther muttered 'Hmph' and did as he was told.

As soon as he poked his head in the loo, Lu (the other Lu, not *loo*) fixed us with an intent stare. 'When we go through the tunnel to New York,' she said, 'you will both ask to use the toilet.'

I'd taken a lot of silly commands before, mostly from Meg, but this was a new low.

'Actually, I need to go now,' I said.

'Hold it,' she said.

I glanced at Meg to see if this made any sense to her, but she was staring morosely at the floor.

Gunther emerged from potty patrol. 'Nobody.'

Poor guy. If you had to check a train's toilet for infiltrators, the *least* you could hope for was a few infiltrators to kill.

'Right, then,' said Lu. 'Come on.'

She herded us into the café car. Six Germani turned and stared at us, their meaty fists full of Danishes and cups of coffee. Barbarians! Who else would eat breakfast pastries at night? The warriors were dressed like Gunther in hides and gold armour, cleverly disguised behind Amtrak name tags. One of the men, AEDELBEORT (the number-one most popular Germanic baby boy's name in 162 BCE), barked a question at Lu in a language I didn't recognize. Lu responded in the same tongue. Her answer seemed to satisfy the warriors, who went back to their coffee and Danishes. Gunther joined them, grumbling about how hard it was to find good enemies to decapitate.

'Sit there,' Lu told us, pointing to a window booth.

Meg slid in glumly. I settled in across from her, propping my longbow, quiver and backpack next to me. Lu stood within earshot, just in case we tried to discuss an escape plan. She needn't have worried. Meg still wouldn't meet my eyes.

I wondered again who Luguselwa was, and what she meant to Meg. Not once in our months of travel had Meg mentioned her. This fact disturbed me. Rather than indicating that Lu was unimportant, it made me suspect she was very important indeed.

And why a Gaul? Gauls had been unusual in Nero's Rome. By the time he became emperor, most of them had been conquered and forcibly 'civilized'. Those who still wore tattoos and torques and lived according to the old ways had been pushed to the fringes of Brittany or forced over to the British Isles. The name Luguselwa . . . My Gaulish had never been very good, but I thought it meant *beloved of the god Lugus*. I shuddered. Those Celtic deities were a strange, fierce bunch.

My thoughts were too unhinged to solve the puzzle of Lu. I kept thinking back to the poor amphisbaena she'd killed – a harmless monster commuter who would never make it home to his wife, all because a prophecy had made him its pawn.

His message had left me shaken – a verse in terza rima, like the one we'd received at Camp Jupiter:

> *O son of Zeus the final challenge face.*
> *The tow'r of Nero two alone ascend.*
> *Dislodge the beast that hast usurped thy place.*

Yes, I had memorized the cursed thing.

Now we had our second set of instructions, clearly linked to the previous set, because the first and third lines rhymed with *ascend*. Stupid Dante and his stupid idea for a never-ending poem structure:

> *The son of Hades, cavern-runners' friend,*
> *Must show the secret way unto the throne.*
> *On Nero's own your lives do now depend.*

I knew a son of Hades: Nico di Angelo. He was probably still at Camp Half-Blood on Long Island. If he had some secret way to Nero's throne, he'd never get the chance to show us unless we escaped this train. How Nico might be a 'cavern-runners' friend', I had no idea.

The last line of the new verse was just cruel. We were presently surrounded by 'Nero's own', so of course our lives depended on them. I wanted to believe there was more to that line, something positive . . . maybe tied to the fact that Lu had ordered us to go to the bathroom when we entered the tunnel to New York. But, given Lu's hostile expression, and the presence of her seven heavily caffeinated and sugar-fuelled Germanus friends, I didn't feel optimistic.

I squirmed in my seat. Oh, *why* had I thought about the bathroom? I *really* needed to go now.

Outside, the illuminated billboards of New Jersey zipped

by: ads for auto dealerships where you could buy an imprac-
tical race car; injury lawyers you could employ to blame the
other drivers once you crashed that race car; casinos where
you could gamble away the money you won from the injury
lawsuits. The great circle of life.

The station-stop for Newark Airport came and went.
Gods help me, I was so desperate I considered making a
break for it. In *Newark*.

Meg stayed put, so I did, too.

The tunnel to New York would be coming up soon. Perhaps, instead of asking to use the restroom, we could spring
into action against our captors . . .

Lu seemed to read my thoughts. 'It's a good thing you
surrendered. Nero has three other teams like mine on this
train alone. *Every* passage – every train, bus and flight into
Manhattan – has been covered. Nero's got the Oracle of
Delphi on his side, remember. He knew you were coming
tonight. You were never going to get into the city without
being caught.'

Way to crush my hopes, Luguselwa. Telling me that
Nero had his ally Python peering into the future for him,
using *my* sacred Oracle against me . . . Harsh.

Meg, however, suddenly perked up, as if something Lu
said gave her hope. 'So how is it *you're* the one who found
us, Lu? Just luck?'

Lu's tattoos rippled as she flexed her arms, the swirling
Celtic circles making me seasick.

'I *know* you, Sapling,' she said. 'I know how to track
you. There is no luck.'

I could think of several gods of luck who would disagree

with that statement, but I didn't argue. Being a captive had dampened my desire for small talk.

Lu turned to her companions. 'As soon as we get to Penn Station, we deliver our captives to the escort team. I want no mistakes. No one kills the girl or the god unless it's absolutely necessary.'

'Is it necessary now?' Gunther asked.

'No,' Lu said. 'The *princeps* has plans for them. He wants them alive.'

The princeps. My mouth tasted bitterer than the bitterest Amtrak coffee. Being marched through Nero's front door was *not* how I'd planned to confront him.

One moment we were rumbling across a wasteland of New Jersey warehouses and dockyards. The next, we plunged into darkness, entering the tunnel that would take us under the Hudson River. On the intercom, a garbled announcement informed us that our next stop would be Penn Station.

'I need to pee,' Meg announced.

I stared at her, dumbfounded. Was she *really* going to follow Lu's strange instructions? The Gaul had captured us and killed an innocent two-headed snake. Why would Meg trust her?

Meg pressed her heel hard on the top of my foot.

'Yes,' I squeaked. 'I also need to pee.' For me, at least, this was painfully true.

'Hold it,' Gunther grumbled.

'I *really* need to pee.' Meg bounced up and down.

Lu heaved a sigh. Her exasperation did not sound faked.

'Fine.' She turned to her squad. 'I'll take them. The rest of you stay here and prepare to disembark.'

None of the Germani objected. They'd probably heard enough of Gunther's complaints about potty patrol. They began shoving last-minute Danishes into their mouths and gathering up their equipment as Meg and I extracted ourselves from our booth.

'Your gear,' Lu reminded me.

I blinked. Right. Who went to the bathroom without their bow and quiver? That would be stupid. I grabbed my things.

Lu herded us back into the gangway. As soon as the double doors closed behind her, she murmured, '*Now.*'

Meg bolted for the quiet car.

'Hey!' Lu shoved me out of the way, pausing long enough to mutter, 'Block the door. Decouple the coaches,' then raced after Meg.

Do what *now?*

Two scimitars flashed into existence in Lu's hands. Wait – she had Meg's swords? No. Just before the end of the gangway, Meg turned to face her, summoning her own blades, and the two women fought like demons. They were *both dimachaeri*, the rarest form of gladiator? That must mean – I didn't have time to think about what that meant.

Behind me, the Germani were shouting and scrambling. They would be through the doors any second.

I didn't understand exactly what was happening, but it occurred to my stupid slow mortal brain that perhaps, just perhaps, Lu was trying to help us. If I didn't block the doors like she'd asked, we would be overrun by seven angry sticky-fingered barbarians.

I slammed my foot against the base of the double doors. There were no handles. I had to press my palms against the panels and push them together to keep them shut.

Gunther tackled the doors at full speed, the impact nearly dislocating my jaw. The other Germani piled in behind him. My only advantages were the narrow space they were in, which made it difficult for them to combine their strength, and the Germani's own lack of sense. Instead of working together to prise the doors apart, they simply pushed and shoved against one another, using Gunther's face as a battering ram.

Behind me, Lu and Meg jabbed and slashed, their blades furiously clanging against one another.

'Good, Sapling,' Lu said under her breath. 'You remember your training.' Then louder, for the sake of our audience: 'I'll kill you, foolish girl!'

I imagined how this must look to the Germani on the other side of the Plexiglas: their comrade Lu, trapped in combat with an escaped prisoner, while I attempted to hold them back. My hands were going numb. My arm and chest muscles ached. I glanced around desperately for an emergency door lock, but there was only an emergency OPEN button. What good was that?

The train roared on through the tunnel. I estimated we had only minutes before we pulled into Penn Station, where Nero's 'escort team' would be waiting. I did not wish to be escorted.

Decouple the coaches, Lu had told me.

How was I supposed to do that, especially while holding the gangway doors shut? I was no train engineer! Choo-choos were more Hephaestus's thing.

I looked over my shoulder, scanning the gangway. Shockingly, there was no clearly labelled switch that would allow a passenger to decouple the train. What was wrong with Amtrak?

There! On the floor, a series of hinged metal flaps over-lapped, creating a safe surface for passengers to walk across when the train twisted and turned. One of those flaps had been kicked open, perhaps by Lu, exposing the coupling underneath.

Even if I could reach it from where I stood, which I couldn't, I doubted I would have the strength and dexterity to stick my arm down there, cut the cables and prise open the clamp. The gap between the floor panels was too nar-row, the coupling too far down. Just to hit it from here, I would have to be the world's greatest archer!

Oh. Wait . . .

Against my chest, the doors were bowing under the weight of seven barbarians. An axe blade jutted through the rubber lining next to my ear. Turning around so I could shoot my bow would be madness.

Yes, I thought hysterically. Let's do that.

I bought myself a moment by pulling out an arrow and jabbing it through the gap between the doors. Gunther howled. The pressure eased as the clump of Germani readjusted. I flipped around so my back was to the Plexiglas, one heel wedged against the base of the doors. I fumbled with my bow and managed to nock an arrow.

My new bow was a god-level weapon from the vaults of Camp Jupiter. My archery skills had improved dramatically over the last six months. Still, this was a terrible idea. It was impossible to shoot properly with one's back against a hard surface. I simply couldn't draw the bowstring far enough.

Nevertheless, I fired. The arrow disappeared into the gap in the floor, completely missing the coupling.

'Penn Station in just a minute,' said a voice on the PA system. 'Doors will open on the left.'

'Running out of time!' Lu shouted. She slashed at Meg's head. Meg jabbed low, nearly impaling the Gaul's thigh.

I shot another arrow. This time the point sparked against the clasp, but the train cars remained stubbornly connected.

The Germani pounded against the doors. A Plexiglas panel popped out of its frame. A fist reached through and grabbed my shirt.

With a desperate shriek, I lurched away from the doors and shot one last time at a full draw. The arrow sliced through the cables and slammed into the clasp. With a shudder and a groan, the coupling broke.

Germani poured into the gangway as I leaped across the widening gap between the coaches. I almost skewered myself on Meg's and Lu's scimitars, but I somehow managed to regain my footing.

I turned as the rest of the train shot into the darkness at seventy miles an hour, seven Germani staring at us in disbelief and yelling insults I will not repeat.

For another fifty feet, our decoupled section of the train rolled forward of its own momentum, then slowed to a stop.

Meg and Lu lowered their weapons. A brave passenger from the quiet car dared to stick her head out and ask what was going on.

I shushed her.

Lu glared at me. 'Took you long enough, Lester. Now let's move before my men come back. You two just went from *capture alive* to *proof of death is acceptable.*'

3

Arrow of wisdom,

Hook me up with a hideout.

No, not that one. NO!

'I'M CONFUSED,' I SAID AS WE STUMBLED along in the dark tunnels. 'Are we still prisoners?'

Lu glanced at me, then at Meg. 'Dense for a god, isn't he?'

'You have no idea,' Meg grumbled.

'Do you work for Nero or not?' I demanded. 'And how exactly . . . ?'

I wagged my finger from Lu to Meg, silently asking, *How do you know each other?* Or perhaps, *Are you related since you're equally annoying?*

Then I caught the glint of their matching gold rings, one on each of their middle fingers. I remembered the way Lu and Meg had fought, their four blades slicing and stabbing in perfect synchronization. The obvious truth smacked me in the face.

'You trained Meg,' I realized. 'To be a dimachaerus.'

'And she's kept her skills sharp.' Lu elbowed Meg affectionately. 'I'm pleased, Sapling.'

I had never seen Meg look so proud about *anything*.

She tackled her old trainer in a hug. 'I knew you weren't bad.'

'Hmm.' Lu didn't seem to know what to do with the hug. She patted Meg on the shoulder. 'I'm plenty bad, Sapling. But I'm not going to let Nero torture you any more. Let's keep moving.'

Torture. Yes, that was the word.

I wondered how Meg could trust this woman. She'd killed the amphisbaena without batting an eye. I had no doubt she would do the same to me if she felt it necessary.

Worse: Nero paid her salary. Whether Lu had saved us from capture or not, she'd trained Meg, which meant she must have stood by for years while Nero tormented my young friend emotionally and mentally. Lu had been part of the problem – part of Meg's indoctrination into the emperor's twisted family. I worried that Meg was slipping into her old patterns. Perhaps Nero had figured out a way to manipulate her indirectly through this former teacher she admired.

On the other hand, I wasn't sure how to broach that subject. We were trekking through a maze of subway-maintenance tunnels with only Lu as our guide. She had a lot more weapons than I did. Also, Meg was my master. She'd told me we were going to follow Lu, so that's what we did.

We continued our march, Meg and Lu trudging side by side, me straggling behind. I'd like to tell you I was 'guarding their six', or performing some other important task, but I think Meg had just forgotten about me.

Overhead, steel-caged work lights cast prison-bar

shadows across the brick walls. Mud and slime coated the floor, exuding a smell like the old casks of 'wine' Dionysus insisted on keeping in his cellar, despite the fact that they had long ago turned to vinegar. At least Meg's sneakers would no longer smell like horse poop. They would now be coated with new and different toxic waste.

After stumbling along for another million miles, I ventured to ask, 'Miss Lu, where are we going?' I was startled by the volume of my own voice echoing through the dark.

'Away from the search grid,' she said, as if this were obvious. 'Nero has tapped most of the closed-circuit cameras in Manhattan. We need to get off his radar.'

It was a bit jarring to hear a Gaulish warrior talking about radar and cameras.

I wondered again how Lu had come into Nero's service.

As much as I hated to admit it, the emperors of the Triumvirate were basically minor gods. They were picky about which followers they allowed to spend eternity with them. The Germani made sense. Dense and cruel as they might be, the imperial bodyguards were fiercely loyal. But why a Gaul? Luguselwa must have been valuable to Nero for reasons beyond her sword skills. I didn't trust that such a warrior would turn on her master after two millennia.

My suspicions must have radiated from me like heat from an oven. Lu glanced back and noted my frown. 'Apollo, if I wanted you dead, you would already be dead.'

True, I thought, but Lu could have added, *If I wanted to trick you into following me so I could deliver you alive to Nero, this is exactly what I'd be doing.*

Lu quickened her pace. Meg scowled at me like, *Be nice to my Gaul*, then she hurried to catch up.

I lost track of time. The adrenalin spike from the train fight faded, leaving me weary and sore. Sure, I was still running for my life, but I'd spent most of the last six months running for my life. I couldn't maintain a productive state of panic indefinitely. Tunnel goo soaked into my socks. My shoes felt like squishy clay pots.

For a while, I was impressed by how well Lu knew the tunnels. She forged ahead, taking us down one turn after another. Then, when she hesitated at a junction a bit too long, I realized the truth.

'You don't know where we're going,' I said.

She scowled. 'I told you. Away from the –'

'Search grid. Cameras. Yes. But where are we *going?*'

'Somewhere. Anywhere safe.'

I laughed. I surprised myself by actually feeling *relieved*. If Lu was this clueless about our destination, then I felt safer trusting her. She had no grand plan. We were lost. What a relief!

Lu did not seem to appreciate my sense of humour.

'Excuse me if I had to improvise,' she grumbled. 'You're fortunate *I* found you on that train rather than one of the emperor's other search parties. Otherwise you'd be in Nero's holding cell right now.'

Meg gave me another scowl. 'Yeah, Lester. Besides, it's fine.'

She pointed to an old section of Greek-key-design tile along the left-hand corridor, perhaps left over from an abandoned subway line. 'I recognize that. There should be an exit up ahead.'

I wanted to ask how she could possibly know this. Then I remembered Meg had spent a great deal of her childhood roaming dark alleys, derelict buildings and other strange and unusual places in Manhattan with Nero's blessing – the evil imperial version of free-range parenting.

I could imagine a younger Meg exploring these tunnels, doing cartwheels in the muck and growing mushrooms in forgotten locations.

We followed her for . . . I don't know, six or seven miles? That's what it felt like, at least. Once, we stopped abruptly when a deep and distant BOOM echoed through the corridor.

'Train?' I asked nervously, though we'd left the tracks behind long ago.

Lu tilted her head. 'No. That was thunder.'

I didn't see how that could be. When we'd entered the tunnel in New Jersey, there'd been no sign of rain. I didn't like the idea of sudden thunderstorms so close to the Empire State Building – entrance to Mount Olympus, home of Zeus, aka Big Daddy Lightning Bolt.

Undeterred, Meg forged ahead.

Finally, our tunnel dead-ended at a metal ladder. Overhead was a loose manhole cover, light and water spilling from one edge like a weeping crescent moon.

'I remember this opens to an alleyway,' Meg announced. 'No cameras – at least there weren't any last time I was here.'

Lu grunted as if to say, *Good work*, or maybe just, *This is going to suck*.

The Gaul ascended first. Moments later, the three of us stood in a storm-lashed alley between two apartment buildings. Lightning forked overhead, lacing the dark clouds with gold. Rain needled my face and poked me in the eyes.

Where had this tempest come from? Was it a welcome-home present from my father, or a warning? Or maybe it was just a regular summer storm. Sadly, my time as Lester had taught me that not every meteorological event was about me.

Thunder rattled the windows on either side of us. Judging from the yellow-brick facades of the buildings, I guessed we were on the Upper East Side somewhere, though that seemed an impossibly long underground walk from Penn Station. At the end of the alley, taxis zipped down a busy street: Park Avenue? Lexington?

I hugged my arms. My teeth chattered. My quiver was starting to fill with water, the strap getting heavier across my shoulder. I turned to Lu and Meg. 'I don't suppose either of you has a magic item that stops rain?'

From her belt of infinite weapons, Lu pulled something that I'd assumed was a police baton. She clicked a button on the side and it blossomed into an umbrella. Naturally, it was just big enough for Lu and Meg.

I sighed. 'I walked right into that, didn't I?'

'Yep,' Meg agreed.

I pulled my backpack over my head, which effectively stopped 0.003 percent of the rain from hitting my face. My

clothes were plastered to my skin. My heart slowed and
sped up at random, as if it couldn't decide whether to be
exhausted or terrified.

'What now?' I asked.

'We find someplace to regroup,' said Lu.

I eyed the nearest dumpster. 'With all the real estate
Nero controls in Manhattan, you don't have *one* secret base
we could use?'

Lu's laugh was the only dry thing in that alley. 'I told
you, Nero monitors all public security cameras in New York.
How closely do you think he monitors his own properties?
You want to risk it?'

I hated that she had a point.

I wanted to trust Luguselwa, because Meg trusted her.
I recognized that Lu had saved us on the train. Also, the
amphisbaena's last line of prophecy tumbled around in my
head: *On Nero's own your lives do now depend.*

That could refer to Lu, which meant she might be
trustworthy.

On the other hand, Lu had killed the amphisbaena. For
all I knew, if he had lived a few more minutes, he might
have spouted another bit of iambic pentameter: *Not Lu.
Not Lu. Don't ever trust the Gaul.*

'So if you're on our side,' I said, 'why all the pretending
on the train? Why kill that amphisbaena? Why the charade
about escorting us to the bathroom?'

Lu grunted. 'First of all, I'm on Meg's side. Don't much
care about you.'

Meg smirked. 'That's a good point.'

'As for the monster . . .' Lu shrugged. 'It was a monster. It'll regenerate in Tartarus eventually. No great loss.'

I suspected Mr Snake's wife might disagree with that. Then again, not too long ago, I had regarded demigods in much the same way that Lu regarded the amphisbaena.

'As for the play-acting,' she said, 'if I'd turned on my comrades, I ran the risk of you two getting killed, me getting killed or one of my men escaping and reporting back to Nero. I would have been outed as a traitor.'

'But they *all* got away,' I protested. 'They'll *all* report back to Nero and . . . Oh. They'll tell Nero –'

'That the last time they saw me,' Lu said, 'I was fighting like crazy, trying to stop you from escaping.'

Meg detached herself from Lu's side, her eyes widening. 'But Nero will think you're dead! You can stay with us!'

Lu gave her a rueful smile. 'No, Sapling. I'll have to go back soon. If we're lucky, Nero will believe I'm still on his side.'

'But *why?*' Meg demanded. 'You can't go back!'

'It's the only way,' Lu said. 'I had to make sure you didn't get caught coming into the city. Now . . . I need time to explain to you what's going on . . . what Nero is planning.'

I didn't like the hesitation in her voice. Whatever Nero was planning, it had shaken Lu badly.

'Besides,' she continued, 'if you're going to stand any chance of beating him, you'll need someone on the inside. It's important that Nero think I tried to stop you, failed, then returned to him with my tail between my legs.'

'But . . .' My brain was too waterlogged to form any more questions. 'Never mind. You can explain when we get somewhere dry. Speaking of which –'

'I've got an idea,' Meg said.

She jogged to the corner of the alley. Lu and I sloshed along behind her. The signs on the nearest corner informed us that we were at Lexington and Seventy-Fifth.

Meg grinned. 'See?'

'See what?' I said. 'What are you . . . ?'

Her meaning hit me like an Amtrak quiet car. 'Oh, no,' I said. 'No, they've done enough for us. I *won't* put them in any more danger, especially if Nero is after us.'

'But last time you were totally fine with –'

'Meg, no!'

Lu looked back and forth between us. 'What are you talking about?'

I wanted to stick my head in my backpack and scream. Six months ago, I'd had no qualms about hitting up an old friend who lived a few blocks from here. But now . . . after all the trouble and heartbreak I'd brought to every place that had harboured me . . . No. I could *not* do that again.

'How about this?' I drew the Arrow of Dodona from my quiver. 'We'll ask my prophetic friend. Surely it has a better idea – perhaps access to last-minute hotel deals!'

I lifted the projectile in my trembling fingers. 'O great Arrow of Dodona –'

'Is he talking to that arrow?' Lu asked Meg.

'He talks to inanimate objects,' Meg told her. 'Humour him.'

'We need your advice!' I said, suppressing the urge to kick Meg in the shin. 'Where should we go for shelter?'

The arrow's voice buzzed in my brain: *DIDST THOU CALLEST ME THY FRIEND?* It sounded pleased.

'Uh, yes.' I gave my companions a thumbs-up. 'We need a place to hide out and regroup – somewhere nearby, but away from Nero's surveillance cameras and whatnot.'

THE EMPEROR'S WHATNOT IS FORMIDABLE INDEED, the arrow agreed. *BUT THOU ALREADY KNOWEST THE ANSWER TO THY QUESTION, O LESTER. SEEKEST THOU THE PLACE OF THE SEVEN-LAYER DIP.*

With that, the projectile fell silent.

I groaned in misery. The arrow's message was perfectly clear. Oh, for the yummy seven-layer dip of our hostess! Oh, for the comfort of that cosy apartment! But it wasn't right. I couldn't . . .

'What did it say?' Meg demanded.

I tried to think of an alternative, but I was so tired I couldn't even lie.

'Fine,' I said. 'We go to Percy Jackson's place.'

4

This child is too cute.

Please, no more adorable.

Whoops. My heart just broke.

'HELLO, MRS JACKSON! IS PERCY HOME?'

I shivered and dripped on her welcome mat, my two equally bedraggled companions behind me.

For a heartbeat, Sally Jackson remained frozen in her doorway, a smile on her face, as if she'd been expecting a delivery of flowers or cookies. We were not that.

Her driftwood-brown hair was tinselled with more grey than it was six months ago. She wore tattered jeans, a loose green blouse and a blob of apple sauce on the top of her bare left foot. She was not pregnant any more, which probably explained the sound of the giggling baby inside her apartment.

Her surprise passed quickly. Since she'd raised a demigod, she'd doubtless had lots of experience with the unexpected. 'Apollo! Meg! And –' She sized up our gigantic tattooed, mohawked train conductor. 'Hello! You poor things. Come in and dry off.'

The Jackson living room was as cosy as I remembered. The smell of baking mozzarella and tomatoes wafted from the kitchen. Jazz played on an old-fashioned turntable – ah, Wynton Marsalis! Several comfy sofas and chairs were available to plop upon. I scanned the room for Percy Jackson but found only a middle-aged man with salt-and-pepper hair, rumpled khakis, oven mitts and a pink dress shirt covered by a bright-yellow apron splattered with tomato sauce. He was bouncing a giggly baby on his hip. The child's yellow onesie pyjamas matched the man's apron so perfectly that I wondered if they'd come as a set.

I'm sure the chef and baby made for an adorable, heartwarming scene. Unfortunately, I'd grown up on stories about Titans and gods who cooked and/or ate their children, so I was perhaps not quite as charmed as I might have been.

'There is a man in your apartment,' I informed Mrs Jackson.

Sally laughed. 'This is my husband, Paul. Excuse me a sec. I'll be right back.' She dashed towards the bathroom.

'Hi!' Paul smiled at us. 'This is Estelle.'

Estelle giggled and drooled as if her own name was the funniest joke in the universe. She had Percy's sea-green eyes and clearly her mother's good nature. She also had wisps of black and silver hair like Paul, which I had never seen on a baby. She would be the world's first salt-and-pepper toddler. All in all, it seemed Estelle had inherited a good genetic package.

'Hello.' I wasn't sure whether to address Paul, Estelle or whatever was cooking in the kitchen, which smelled delicious. 'Er, not to be rude, but we were hoping to – Oh, thanks, Mrs Jackson.'

Sally had emerged from the bathroom and was now busily wrapping Meg, Lu and me in fluffy turquoise bath towels.

'We were hoping to see Percy,' I finished.

Estelle squealed with delight. She seemed to like the name *Percy*.

'I'd like to see him, too,' Sally said. 'But he's on his way to the West Coast. With Annabeth. They left a few days ago.'

She pointed to a framed picture on the nearest end table. In the photo, my old friends Percy and Annabeth sat side by side in the Jackson family's dented Prius, both of them smiling out of the driver's-side window. In the back seat was our mutual satyr friend Grover Underwood, mugging for the camera – eyes crossed, tongue stuck out sideways, hands flashing peace signs. Annabeth leaned into Percy, her arms wrapped around his neck like she was about to kiss him or possibly choke him. Behind the wheel, Percy gave the camera a big thumbs-up. He seemed to be telling me directly, *We're outta here! You have fun with your quests or whatever!*

'He graduated high school,' Meg said, as if she'd witnessed a miracle.

'I know,' Sally said. 'We even had cake.' She pointed to another picture of Percy and Sally, beaming as they held up a baby-blue cake with darker blue icing that read CONGRATULATIONS, PERCY THE GRADUTE! I did not ask why *graduate* was misspelled, dyslexia being so common in demigod families.

'Then –' I gulped – 'he's not here.'

It was a silly thing to say, but some stubborn part of me insisted that Percy Jackson *must* be here somewhere, waiting to do dangerous tasks for me. That was his *job*!

But, no. That was the *old* Apollo's way of thinking – the Apollo I'd been the last time I was in this apartment. Percy was entitled to his own life. He was trying to have one, and – oh, the bitter truth! – it had nothing to do with me.

'I'm happy for him,' I said. 'And Annabeth . . .'

Then it occurred to me that they'd probably been incommunicado since they left New York. Cell phones attracted too much monstrous attention for demigods to use, especially on a road trip. Magical means of communications were slowly coming back online since we'd released the god of silence, Harpocrates, but they were still spotty. Percy and Annabeth might have no idea about all the tragedies we'd faced on the West Coast – at Camp Jupiter, and before that in Santa Barbara . . .

'Oh, dear,' I muttered to myself. 'I suppose that means they haven't heard –'

Meg coughed loudly. She gave me a hard *shut-up* glare.

Right. It would be cruel to burden Sally and Paul with news of Jason Grace's death, especially when Percy and Annabeth were making their way to California and Sally must already be worried about them.

'Haven't heard what?' Sally asked.

I swallowed dryly. 'That we were coming back to New York. No matter. We'll just –'

'Enough small talk,' Lu interrupted. 'We are in grave danger. These mortals cannot help us. We must go.'

Lu's tone wasn't exactly disdainful – just irritated, and

maybe concerned for our hosts. If Nero tracked us to this apartment, he wouldn't spare Percy's family just because they weren't demigods.

On the other hand, the Arrow of Dodona had told us to come here. There had to be a reason. I hoped it had something to do with what Paul was cooking.

Sally studied our large tattooed friend. She didn't look offended, more like she was taking Lu's measure and pondering whether she had any clothes large enough to fit her. 'Well, you can't leave dripping wet. Let's get you some dry things to wear, at least, and some food if you're hungry.'

'Yes, please,' Meg said. 'I love you.'

Estelle burst into a fresh peal of giggles. She had apparently just discovered that her father's fingers could wiggle, and she considered this hilarious.

Sally smiled at her baby, then at Meg. 'I love you, too, dear. Percy's friends are always welcome.'

'I have no idea who this *Percy* is,' Lu protested.

'*Anyone* who needs help is always welcome,' Sally amended. 'Believe me, we've been in danger before, and we've come through it. Right, Paul?'

'Yep,' he agreed without hesitation. 'There's plenty of food. I think Percy has some clothes that will fit, uh, is it Apollo?'

I nodded morosely. I knew all too well that Percy's clothes would fit me, because I'd left here six months ago wearing his hand-me-downs. 'Thank you, Paul.'

Lu grunted. 'I suppose . . . Is that lasagne I smell?'

Paul grinned. 'The Blofis family recipe.'

'Hm. I suppose we could stay for a bit,' Lu decided.

The wonders never ceased. The Gaul and I actually agreed on something.

'Here, try this.' Paul tossed me a faded Percy T-shirt to go with my ratty Percy jeans.

I did not complain. The clothes were clean, warm and dry, and after trudging underground across half of Manhattan my old outfit smelled so bad it would have to be sealed in a hazardous waste pouch and incinerated.

I sat on Percy's bed next to Estelle, who lay on her back, staring in fascination at a blue plastic doughnut.

I ran my hand across the faded words on the T-shirt: AHS SWIM TEAM. 'What does AHS stand for?'

Paul wrinkled his nose. 'Alternative High School. It was the only place that would take Percy for just his senior year, after . . . You know.'

I remembered. Percy had disappeared for the entirety of his junior year thanks to the meddling of Hera, who zapped him across the country and gave him amnesia, all for the sake of making the Greek and Roman demigod camps unite for the war with Gaia. My stepmother just loved bringing people together.

'You didn't approve of the situation, or the school?' I asked.

Paul shrugged. He looked uncomfortable, as if saying anything negative would go against his nature.

Estelle gave me a drooling grin. 'Gah?' I took this to mean *Can you believe how lucky we are to be alive right now?*

Paul sat next to her and gently cupped his hand over her wispy hair.

'I'm an English teacher at another high school,' he said. 'AHS was . . . not the best. For kids who are struggling, at risk, you want a safe place with good accommodations and excellent support. You want to understand each student as an individual. Alt High was more like a holding pen for everybody who didn't fit into the system. Percy had been through so much . . . I was worried about him. But he made the best of the situation. He *really* wanted to get that diploma. I'm proud of him.'

Estelle cooed. Paul's eyes wrinkled around the edges. He tapped her nose. 'Boop.'

The baby was stunned for a millisecond. Then she laughed with such glee I worried she might choke on her own spit.

I found myself staring in amazement at Paul and Estelle, who struck me as even greater miracles than Percy's graduation. Paul seemed like a caring husband, a loving father, a kind stepfather. In my own experience, such a creature was harder to find than an albino unicorn or three-winged griffin.

As for baby Estelle, her good nature and sense of wonder rose to the level of superpowers. If this child grew up to be as perceptive and charismatic as she appeared to be now, she would rule the world. I decided not to tell Zeus about her.

'Paul . . .' I ventured. 'Aren't you worried about having us here? We might endanger your family.'

The corners of his mouth tightened. 'I was at the Battle of Manhattan. I've heard about some of the horrible things Sally went through – fighting the Minotaur, being imprisoned in the Underworld. And Percy's adventures?' He shook his head in respect. 'Percy has put himself on the line for us, for his friends, for the world, plenty of times. So, can I risk giving you a place to catch your breath, some fresh clothes and a hot meal? Yeah, how could I not?'

'You are a good man, Paul Blofis.'

He tilted his head, as if wondering what other kind of man anyone would possibly try to be. 'Well, I'll leave you to get cleaned up and dressed. We don't want dinner to get burned, do we, Estelle?'

The baby went into a fit of giggles as her father scooped her up and carried her out of the room.

I took my time in the shower. I needed a good scrubbing, yes. But mostly I needed to stand with my forehead against the tiles, shaking and weeping until I felt like I could face other people again.

What was it about kindness? In my time as Lester Papadopoulos, I had learned to stand up under horrendous verbal abuse and constant life-threatening violence, but the smallest act of generosity could ninja-kick me right in the heart and break me into a blubbering mess of emotions.

Darn you, Paul and Sally, and your cute baby, too!

How could I repay them for providing me this temporary refuge? I felt like I owed them the same thing I owed Camp Jupiter and Camp Half-Blood, the Waystation and the Cistern, Piper and Frank and Hazel and Leo and, yes, especially Jason Grace. I owed them *everything*.

How could I not?

Once I was dressed, I staggered out to the dining area. Everyone was seated around the table except Estelle, who

Paul informed me was down for the night. No doubt all that pure joy required a great amount of energy.

Meg wore a new pink smock dress and white leggings. If she cherished these as much as the last outfit Sally had given her, she would end up wearing them until they fell off her body in burned-and-shredded rags. Together with her red high-tops – which thankfully had been well cleaned – she sported a Valentine's Day colour theme that seemed quite out of character, unless you considered her sweetheart to be the mountain of garlic bread she was shovelling into her mouth.

Lu was dressed in an XXL men's work shirt with ELECTRONICS MEGA-MART stitched over the pocket. She wore a fluffy turquoise towel around her waist like a kilt, because, she informed me, the only other trousers in the apartment large enough to fit her were Sally's old maternity trousers and, no thank you, Lu would just wait for hers to get out of the dryer.

Sally and Paul provided us with heaping plates of salad, lasagne and garlic bread. It wasn't Sally's famous seven-layer dip, but it *was* a family-style feast like I hadn't experienced since the Waystation. That memory gave me a twinge of melancholy. I wondered how everyone there was doing: Leo, Calypso, Emmie, Jo, little Georgina . . . At the time, our trials in Indianapolis had felt like a nightmare, but in retrospect they seemed like happier, simpler days.

Sally Jackson sat down and smiled. 'Well, this is nice.' Shockingly, she sounded sincere. 'We don't have guests often. Now, let's eat, and you can tell us who or what is trying to kill you this time.'

5

No swearing at the
Table? Then don't talk about
That #@$%-@&* Nero.

I WISHED WE COULD HAVE HAD REGULAR
small talk around the dinner table: the weather, who liked
whom at school, which gods were casting plagues on which
cities and why. But *no*, it was always about who was trying
to kill me.

I didn't want to ruin anyone's appetite, especially since
Paul's savoury family-recipe lasagne was making me drool
like Estelle. Also, I wasn't sure I trusted Luguselwa enough
to share our whole story.

Meg had no such qualms. She opened up about everything we'd been through – with the exception of the tragic
deaths. I was sure she only skipped those to spare Sally and
Paul from worrying too much about Percy.

I don't think I'd ever heard Meg talk as much as she did
at Sally and Paul's dinner table, as if the presence of kindly
parental figures had uncorked something inside her.

Meg told them of our battles with Commodus and
Caligula. She explained how we had freed four ancient
Oracles and had now returned to New York to face the last
and most powerful emperor, Nero. Paul and Sally listened

intently, interrupting only to express concern or sympathy. When Sally looked at me and said, 'You poor dear,' I almost lost it again. I wanted to cry on her shoulder. I wanted Paul to dress me in a yellow onesie and rock me until I fell asleep.

'So, Nero is after you,' Paul said at last. '*The* Nero. A Roman emperor has set up his evil lair in a Midtown high-rise.'

He sat back and placed his hands on the table, as if trying to digest the news along with the meal. 'I guess that's not the craziest thing I've ever heard. And now you have to do what . . . defeat him in combat? Another Battle of Manhattan?'

I shuddered. 'I hope not. The battle with Commodus and Caligula was . . . hard for Camp Jupiter. If I asked Camp Half-Blood to attack Nero's base –'

'No.' Lu dipped her garlic bread in her salad dressing, proving her barbarian bona fides. 'A large-scale assault would be suicide. Nero is expecting one. He's *hoping* for one. He's prepared to cause massive collateral damage.'

Outside, rain lashed the windows. Lightning boomed as if Zeus were warning me not to get too comfortable with these kindly surrogate parents.

As much as I distrusted Luguselwa, I believed what she said. Nero would relish a fight, despite what had happened to his two compadres in the Bay Area, or maybe *because* of it. I was afraid to ask what Lu meant by *massive collateral damage*.

An all-out war with Nero would not be another Battle of Manhattan. When Kronos's army had stormed the

Empire State Building, entrance to Mount Olympus, the
Titan Morpheus had put all the mortals in the city to sleep.
The damage to the city itself, and its human population,
had been negligible.

Nero didn't work that way. He liked drama. He would
welcome chaos, screaming crowds, countless civilian deaths.
This was a man who burned people alive to illuminate his
garden parties.

'There has to be another way,' I decided. 'I won't let
any more innocents suffer on my account.'

Sally Jackson crossed her arms. In spite of the grim matters we were discussing, she smiled. 'You've grown up.'

I assumed she was talking about Meg. Over the last few
months, my young friend had indeed got taller and – Wait.
Was Sally referring to *me*?

My first thought: preposterous! I was four thousand
years old. I didn't *grow up*.

She reached across the table and squeezed my hand.
'The last time you were here, you were so lost. So . . . well,
if you don't mind me saying –'

'Pathetic,' I blurted out. 'Whiny, entitled, selfish. I felt
terribly sorry for myself.'

Meg nodded along with my words as if listening to her
favourite song. 'You *still* feel sorry for yourself.'

'But now,' Sally said, sitting back again, 'you're
more . . . human, I suppose.'

There was that word again: *human*, which not long ago
I would have considered a terrible insult. Now, every time I
heard it, I thought of Jason Grace's admonition: *Remember
what it's like to be human.*

He hadn't meant all the terrible things about being human, of which there were plenty. He'd meant the *best* things: standing up for a just cause, putting others first, having stubborn faith that you could make a difference, even if it meant you had to die to protect your friends and what you believed in. These were not the kind of feelings that gods had . . . well, ever.

Sally Jackson meant the term in the same way Jason had – as something worth aspiring to.

'Thank you,' I managed.

She nodded. 'So how can we help?'

Lu slurped the last of the lasagne from her plate. 'You've done more than enough, Jackson Mother and Blofis Father. We must go.'

Meg glanced out of the window at the thunderstorm, then at the remaining garlic bread in the basket. 'Maybe we could stay until the morning?'

'That's a good idea,' Paul agreed. 'We have plenty of space. If Nero's men are out there searching for you in the dark and the lashing rain . . . wouldn't you rather they be out there while you're in here, warm and comfortable?'

Lu seemed to consider this. She belched, long and deep, which in her culture was probably a sign of appreciation, or a sign that she had gas.

'Your words are sensible, Blofis Father. Your lasagne is good. Very well. I suppose the cameras will see us better in the morning anyway.'

'Cameras?' I sat up. 'As in Nero's surveillance cameras? I thought we don't want to be seen.'

Lu shrugged. 'I have a plan.'

'A plan like the one on the train? Because –'

'Listen here, small Lester –'

'Hold it,' Paul ordered. His voice was calm but firm, giving me an inkling as to how this kind, gentle man could control a classroom. 'Let's not argue. We'll wake Estelle. I guess I should have asked this before, but, uh . . .' He glanced between Meg, me and Lu. 'How exactly do you know each other?'

'Lu held us hostage on a train,' I said.

'I *saved* you from capture on a train,' she corrected.

'Lu's my guardian,' Meg said.

That got everyone's attention.

Sally raised her eyebrows. Lu's ears turned bright red.

Paul's face remained in teacher mode. I could imagine him asking Meg to elaborate on her statement, to provide three examples in a well-argued paragraph.

'Guardian in what sense, Meg?' he asked.

Lu glanced at the girl. The Gaul had a strange look of hurt in her eyes as she waited for Meg to describe their relationship.

Meg pushed her fork across her plate. 'Legally. Like, if I needed somebody to sign stuff. Or pick me up from the police station or . . . whatever.'

The more I thought about this, the less absurd it seemed. Nero wouldn't bother with the technicalities of parenthood. Signing a permission slip? Taking Meg to the doctor? No, thanks. He would delegate such things. And legal status? Nero didn't care about formal guardianship. In his mind, he *owned* Meg.

'Lu taught me swords.' Meg squirmed in her new pink

dress. 'She taught me . . . well, most stuff. When I lived in the palace, Nero's tower, Lu tried to help me. She was . . . She was the nice one.'

I studied the giant Gaul in her Electronics Mega-Mart shirt and her bath-towel kilt. I could think of many descriptions for her. *Nice* wasn't the first one that sprang to mind.

However, I *could* imagine her being nicer than Nero. That was a low bar. And I could imagine Nero using Lu as his proxy – giving Meg another authority figure to look up to, a woman warrior. After dealing with Nero and his terrifying alternate personality the Beast, Meg would have seen Lu as a welcome relief.

'You were the good cop,' I guessed.

Lu's neck veins bulged against her golden torque. 'Call me what you like. I didn't do enough for my Sapling, but I did what I could. She and I trained together for years.'

'Sapling?' Paul asked. 'Oh, right. Because Meg's a daughter of Demeter.' His expression remained serious, but his eyes twinkled, like he couldn't believe he was lucky enough to be having this conversation.

I didn't feel quite as fortunate. I was gripping my fork so tightly my fist trembled. The gesture might have looked threatening if the tines hadn't been topped with a cherry tomato.

'You were Meg's *legal* guardian.' I glared at Lu. 'You could have taken her out of that tower. You could have relocated. Run with her. But you stayed. For years.'

'Hey,' Meg warned.

'No, he's right.' Lu's eyes bored a hole in the casserole dish. 'I owed Nero my life. Back in the old times, he spared

me from . . . Well, it doesn't matter now, but I served him
for centuries. I've done many hard things for him. Then
the sapling came along. I did my best. Wasn't enough.
Then Meg ran away with you. I heard what Nero was planning, what would happen when you two came back to the
city . . .' She shook her head. 'It was too much. I couldn't
bring Meg back to that tower.'

'You followed your conscience,' Sally said.

I wished I could be as forgiving as our hostess. 'Nero
doesn't hire warriors for their consciences.'

The big woman scowled. 'That's true, little Lester.
Believe me, or don't. But if we can't work together, if you
don't listen to me, then Nero will win. He'll destroy all of
this.'

She gestured around the room. Whether she meant the
world, Manhattan or the Jackson/Blofis apartment, any of
those possibilities was unacceptable.

'I believe you,' Sally announced.

It seemed ridiculous that a huge warrior like Lu would
care about Sally Jackson's approval, but the Gaul looked
genuinely relieved. Her facial muscles relaxed. The elon-
gated Celtic tattoos on her arms settled back into concentric
circles. 'Thank you, Jackson Mother.'

'I believe you, too.' Meg frowned at me, her meaning
clear: *And so will you, or I'll order you to run into a wall.*

I set down my tomato-topped fork. It was the best gesture of peace I could offer.

I couldn't make myself trust Luguselwa completely. A
'good cop' was still a cop . . . still a part of the mind game.
And Nero was an expert at playing with people's heads.

I glanced at Paul, hoping for support, but he gave me an almost imperceptible shrug: *What else can you do?*

'Very well, Luguselwa,' I said. 'Tell us your plan.'

Paul and Sally leaned forward, ready for marching orders.

Lu shook her head. 'Not you, my good hosts. I have no doubt you are brave and strong, but I will not see any harm come to this family.'

I nodded. 'On that, at least, we agree. Once the morning comes, we're out of here. Possibly after a good breakfast, if it's not too much trouble.'

Sally smiled, though there was a tinge of disappointment in her eyes, as if she'd been looking forward to busting some evil Roman heads. 'I still want to hear the plan. What will you do?'

'Best to not share too many details,' Lu said. 'But there is a secret way into Nero's tower – from below. It is the way that Nero takes to visit . . . the reptile.'

Coils of lasagne seemed to tighten in my stomach. *The reptile.* Python. Interloper at Delphi, my archnemesis and winner of *Olympus Magazine*'s Least Popular Serpent award for four thousand years running.

'That sounds like a terrible way in,' I noted.

'It is not wonderful,' Lu agreed.

'But we can use it to sneak in,' Meg guessed. 'Surprise Nero?'

Lu snorted. 'Nothing so easy, Sapling. The way is secret, but it is still heavily guarded and under constant surveillance. If you tried to sneak in, you would be caught.'

'I'm sorry,' I said. 'I'm still not hearing anything resembling a plan.'

Lu took a moment to gather her patience. I was familiar with this look. I got it often from Meg, and my sister Artemis, and . . . well, everyone, actually.

'The way is not for you,' she said. 'But it *could* be used to sneak in a small squad of demigods, if any were brave enough and sufficiently skilled at navigating underground.'

Son of Hades, I thought, the amphisbaena's words echoing in my head, *cavern-runners' friend, / Must show the secret way unto the throne.*

The only thing more unsettling than not understanding a prophecy was beginning to understand it.

'Then *they* would just get captured,' I said.

'Not necessarily,' Lu said. 'Not if Nero were sufficiently distracted.'

I had a feeling I was not going to like the answer to my next question. 'Distracted by what?'

'Your surrender,' Lu said.

I waited. Lu did not seem the type for practical jokes, but this would have been a good moment for her to laugh and yell *NOT!*

'You can't be serious,' I said.

'I'm with Apollo,' Sally said. 'If Nero wants to kill him, why would he –?'

'It's the only way.' Lu took a deep breath. 'Listen, I know how Nero thinks. When I return to him and tell him you two got away, he will issue an ultimatum.'

Paul frowned. 'To whom?'

'Camp Half-Blood,' Lu said. 'Any demigods, any allies anywhere who are harbouring Apollo. Nero's terms will be simple: Apollo and Meg surrender themselves within a certain amount of time, or Nero destroys New York.'

I wanted to laugh. It seemed impossible, ridiculous. Then I remembered Caligula's yachts in San Francisco Bay, launching a barrage of Greek-fire projectiles that would have destroyed the entire East Bay if Lavinia Asimov hadn't sabotaged them. Nero would have at least as many resources at his disposal, and Manhattan was a much more densely populated target.

Would he burn his own city, with his own palatial tower in the middle of it?

Dumb question, Apollo. Nero had done it before. Just ask Ancient Rome.

'So you rescued us,' I said, 'just to tell us we should surrender to Nero. That's your plan.'

'Nero must believe he has already won,' Lu said. 'Once he has you two in his grasp, he will relax his guard. This may give your demigod team a chance to infiltrate the tower from below.'

'*May*,' I echoed.

'The timing will be tricky,' Lu admitted, 'but Nero will keep you alive for a while, Apollo. He and the reptile . . . They have plans for you.'

A distant thunderclap shook my chair. Either that, or I was trembling. I could imagine what sort of plans Nero and Python might have for me. None of them included a nice lasagne dinner.

'And, Sapling,' Lu continued, 'I know it will be hard

for you, going back to that place, but I will be there to protect you, as I've done many times before. I will be your inside woman. When your friends invade, I can free you both. Then, together, we can take down the emperor.'

Why did Meg look so pensive, as if she were actually considering this insane strategy?

'Just a minute,' I protested. 'Even if we trust you, why would *Nero*? You say you'll go back to him with your tail between your legs and report that we got away. Why would he believe that? Why won't he suspect you've turned on him?'

'I have a plan for that, too,' Lu said. 'It involves you pushing me off a building.'

6

Bye, Luguselwa.
Don't forget to write if you
Ever hit the ground.

I'D HEARD WORSE PLANS.

But while the idea of pushing Lu off a building had a certain appeal, I was sceptical that she really meant it, especially since she wouldn't explain further or offer us details.

'Tomorrow,' she insisted. 'Once we're on our way.'

The next morning, Sally made us breakfast. Estelle giggled at us hysterically. Paul apologized for not having a car to lend us, since the family Prius, which we usually crashed, was on its way to California with Percy, Grover and Annabeth. The best Paul could offer us was a subway pass, but I wasn't ready to ride any more trains.

Sally gave us all hugs and wished us well. Then she said she had to get back to baking cookies, which she did to relieve stress while she was working on the revisions for her second novel.

This raised many questions for me. Second novel? We hadn't discussed her writing at all the night before. Cookies? Could we wait until they were done?

But I suspected that good food was a never-ending temptation here at the Jackson/Blofis home. There would always be a next sweet or savoury snack that was more appealing than facing the harsh world.

Also, I respected the fact that Sally needed to work. As the god of poetry, I understood revisions. Facing monsters and imperial mercenaries was much easier.

At least the rain had stopped, leaving us a steamy June morning. Lu, Meg and I headed towards the East River on foot, ducking from alley to alley until Lu found a location that seemed to satisfy her.

Just off First Avenue, a ten-storey apartment building was in the process of a gut renovation. Its brick facade was a hollow shell, its windows empty frames. We sneaked through the alley behind the lot, climbed over a chain-link construction fence, and found the back entrance blocked only by a sheet of plywood. Lu broke through it with one sturdy kick.

'After you,' she said.

I eyed the dark doorway. 'We really have to go through with this?'

'I'm the one who has to fall off the roof,' she muttered. 'Stop complaining.'

The building's interior was reinforced with metal scaffolding – rung ladders leading from one level to the next. Oh, good. After climbing Sutro Tower, I just *loved* the idea of more ladders. Rays of sunlight sliced through the structure's hollow interior, swirling up dust clouds and miniature rainbows. Above us, the roof was still intact. From the topmost tier of scaffolding, a final ladder led up to a landing with a metal door.

Lu began to climb. She had changed back into her

Amtrak disguise so she wouldn't have to explain the Electronics Mega-Mart shirt to Nero. I followed in my Percy Jackson hand-me-downs. My funny valentine, Meg, brought up the rear. Just like old times at Sutro Tower, except with one hundred percent less Reyna Avila Ramírez-Arellano and one hundred percent more tattooed Gaul.

On each level, Meg stopped to sneeze and wipe her nose. Lu did her best to stay away from the windows, as if worried that Nero might burst through one and yell, *Boare!*

(I'm pretty sure that was Latin for *boo!* It's been a while since I attended one of Cicero's famous haunted-house parties. That man did love to put a toga over his head and scare his guests.)

Finally, we reached the metal door, which had been spray-painted with a red-stencilled warning, ROOF ACCESS RESTRICTED. I was sweaty and out of breath. Lu seemed unperturbed by the climb. Meg kicked absently at the nearest brick as if wondering whether she could collapse the building.

'Here's the plan,' Lu said. 'I know for a fact Nero has cameras in the office building across the street. It's one of his properties. When we burst out this door, his surveillance team should get some good footage of us on the roof.'

'Remind us why that's a good thing?' I asked.

Lu muttered something under her breath, perhaps a prayer for her Celtic gods to smack me upside the head. 'Because we're going to let Nero see what we *want* him to see. We're going to put on a show.'

Meg nodded. 'Like on the train.'

'Exactly,' Lu said. 'You two run out first. I'll follow

a few steps behind, like I've finally cornered you and am ready to kill you.'

'In a strictly play-acting way,' I hoped.

'It has to look real,' Lu said.

'We can do it.' Meg turned to me with a look of pride. 'You saw us on the train, Lester, and that was with no planning. When I lived at the tower? Lu would help me fake these incredible battles so Father – Nero, I mean – would think I killed my opponents.'

I stared at her. 'Kill. Your opponents.'

'Like servants, or prisoners, or just people he didn't like. Lu and I would work it out beforehand. I'd pretend to kill them. Fake blood and everything. Then, after, Lu would drag them out of the arena and let them go. The deaths looked so real that Nero never caught on.'

I couldn't decide what I found most horrifying: Meg's uncomfortable slip calling Nero *Father*, or the fact that Nero had expected his young stepdaughter to execute prisoners for his amusement, or the fact that Lu had conspired to make the show non-lethal to spare Meg's feelings rather than – oh, I don't know – refusing to do Nero's dirty work in the first place and getting Meg out of that house of horrors.

And are you any better? taunted a small voice in my brain. *How many times have you stood up to Zeus?*

Okay, small voice. Fair point. Tyrants are not easy to oppose or walk away from, especially when you depend on them for everything.

I swallowed the bitter taste in my mouth. 'What's my role?'

'Meg and I will do most of the fighting.' Lu hefted her crossbow. 'Apollo, you stumble around and cower in fear.'

'I can do that.'

'Then, when it looks like I'm about to kill Meg, you scream and charge me. You have bursts of godly strength from time to time, I've heard.'

'I can't summon one on command!'

'You don't have to. Pretend. Push me as hard as you can – right off the roof. I'll let you do it.'

I looked over the scaffold railing. 'We're ten stories up. I know this because . . . we're ten stories up.'

'Yes,' Lu agreed. 'Should be about right. I don't die easily, little Lester. I'll break some bones, no doubt, but with luck, I'll survive.'

'With luck?' Meg suddenly didn't sound so confident.

Lu summoned a scimitar into her free hand. 'We have to risk it, Sapling. Nero has to believe I did my very best to catch you. If he suspects something . . . Well, we can't have that.' She faced me. 'Ready?'

'No!' I said. 'You still haven't explained how Nero intends to burn down the city, or what we're supposed to do once we get captured.'

Lu's fiery look was quite convincing. I actually *believed* she wanted to kill me. 'He has Greek fire. More than Caligula did. More than anyone else has ever dared to stockpile. He has some delivery system in place. I don't know the details. But as soon as he suspects something is wrong, one push of a button and it's all over. That's why we have to go through this elaborate charade. We have to get you inside without him realizing it's a trick.'

I was trembling again. I stared down at the concrete floor and imagined it disintegrating, dropping into a sea of green flame. 'So what happens when we're captured?'

'The holding cells,' Lu said. 'They're very close to the vault where Nero keeps his *fasces*.'

My spirits rose at least a millimetre. This wasn't good news, exactly, but at least Lu's plan now seemed a little less insane. The emperor's fasces, the golden axe that symbolized his power, would be connected to Nero's life force. In San Francisco, we'd destroyed the *fasces* of Commodus and Caligula and weakened the emperors just enough to kill them. If we could do the same to Nero . . .

'So you break us out of our cells,' I guessed, 'and lead us to this vault.'

'That's the idea.' Lu's expression turned grim. 'Of course, the fasces is guarded by . . . well, something terrible.'

'What?' Meg asked.

Lu's hesitation scared me worse than any monster she might have named. 'Let's deal with that later. One impossible thing at a time.'

Yet again I found myself agreeing with the Gaul. This worried me.

'Okay, then,' she said. 'Lester, after you push me off the roof, you and Meg get to Camp Half-Blood as fast as you can, find a demigod team to infiltrate the tunnels. Nero's people won't be far behind you.'

'But we don't have a car.'

'Ah. Almost forgot.' Lu glanced down at her belt as if she wanted to grab something, then realized her hands were full of weapons. 'Sapling, reach into my pouch.'

Meg opened the small leather bag. She gasped at whatever she saw inside, then pulled it out tightly clutched in her hand, not letting me see.

'Really?' She bounced up and down with excitement. 'I get to?'

Lu chuckled. 'Why not? Special occasion.'

'Yay!' Meg slipped whatever it was into one of her gardening pouches.

I felt like I'd missed something important. 'Um, what –?'

'Enough chat,' Lu said. 'Ready? Run!'

I was not ready, but I'd got used to being told to run. My body reacted for me, and Meg and I burst through the door.

We scrambled over the silver tar surface, dodging air vents and stumbling on loose bricks. I got into my role with depressing ease. Running for my life, terrified and helpless? Over the last six months, I'd rehearsed that plenty.

Lu bellowed and charged after us. Twin crossbow bolts whistled past my ear. She was *really* selling the whole 'murderous Gaul' thing. My heart leaped into my throat as if I were actually in mortal danger.

Too quickly, I reached the edge of the roof. Nothing but a waist-high lip of brick separated me from a hundred-foot drop into the alley below. I turned and screamed as Lu's blade slashed towards my face.

I arched backwards – not fast enough. Her blade sliced a thin line across my forehead.

Meg materialized, screaming with rage. She blocked

the Gaul's next strike and forced her to turn. Lu dropped her crossbow and summoned her second blade, and the two dimachaeri went at it in a full-bore dramatic interpretation of kung-fu Cuisinarts.

I stumbled, too stunned to feel pain. I wondered why warm rain was trickling into my eyes. Then I wiped it away, looked at my fingers and realized, *Nope, that's not rain.* Rain wasn't usually bright red.

Meg's swords flashed, driving the big Gaul back. Lu kicked her in the gut and sent her reeling.

My thoughts were sluggish, pushing through a syrupy haze of shock, but I seemed to remember I had a role in this drama. What was I supposed to do after the running and the cowering?

Oh, yes. I was supposed to throw Lu off the roof.

A giggle bubbled up in my lungs. I couldn't see with the blood in my eyes. My hands and feet felt like water balloons – wobbly and warm and about to burst. But, sure, no problem. I would just throw a huge dual-sword-wielding warrior off the roof.

I staggered forward.

Lu thrust with her left blade, stabbing Meg in the thigh. Meg yelped and stumbled, crossing her swords just in time to catch Lu's next strike, which would have cleaved her head in two.

Wait a second. This fight *couldn't* be an act. Pure rage lit the Gaul's eyes.

Lu had deceived us, and Meg was in real danger.

Fury swelled inside me. A flood of heat burned away the haze and filled me with godly power. I bellowed like one of

Poseidon's sacred bulls at the altar. (And, let me tell you, those bulls did not go gently to the slaughter.) I barrelled towards Luguselwa, who turned, wide-eyed, but had no time to defend herself. I tackled her around the waist, lifted her over my head as easily as if she were a medicine ball and tossed her off the side of the building.

I overdid it. Rather than dropping into the alley, she sailed over the rooftops of the next block and disappeared. A half second later, a distant metallic *clunk* echoed from the canyon of First Avenue, followed by the angry *weep-weep-weep* of a car alarm.

My strength evaporated. I wobbled and fell to my knees, blood trickling down my face.

Meg stumbled over to me. Her new white leggings were soaked through from the wound on her thigh.

'Your head,' she murmured.

'I know. Your leg.'

She fumbled through her gardening pouches until she found two rolls of gauze. We did our best to mummify each other and stop the bleeding. Meg's fingers trembled. Tears welled in her eyes.

'I'm sorry,' I told her. 'I didn't mean to throw Lu so far. I just – I thought she was really trying to kill you.'

Meg peered in the direction of First Avenue. 'It's fine. She's tough. She's – she's probably fine.'

'But –'

'No time to talk. Come on.'

She grabbed my waist and pulled me up. We somehow made it back inside, then managed to navigate the scaffolds and ladders to get out of the hollow apartment building.

As we limped to the nearest intersection, my heartbeat flumped irregularly, like a trout on the floorboards of a boat. (Ugh. I had Poseidon on the brain now.)

I imagined a caravan of shiny black SUVs full of Germani roaring towards us, encircling our location to take us into custody. If Nero had indeed seen what had happened on that rooftop, it was only a matter of time. We'd given him quite a show. He would want our autographs, followed by our heads on a silver plate.

At the corner of Eighty-First and First, I scanned the traffic. No sign of Germani yet. No monsters. No police or civilians screaming that they'd just witnessed a Gaulish warrior fall from the sky.

'What now?' I asked, really hoping Meg had an answer.

From her belt pouches, Meg fished out the item Lu had given her: a shiny golden Roman coin. Despite everything we'd just been through, I detected a gleam of excitement in my young friend's eyes.

'Now I summon a ride,' she said.

With a cold flush of dread, I understood what she was talking about. I realized why Luguselwa had given her that coin, and part of me wished I had thrown the Gaul a few more blocks.

'Oh, no,' I pleaded. 'You can't mean them. Not them!'

'They're great,' Meg insisted.

'No, they are *not* great! They're awful!'

'Maybe don't tell them that,' Meg said, then she threw the coin into the street and yelled in Latin, '*Stop, O Chariot of Damnation!*'

7

Chariot of dam-
nation, why stoppest thou here?
I don't use your app.

CALL ME SUPERSTITIOUS. IF YOU'RE GOING
to hail a chariot, you should at least try for one that doesn't
have *damnation* right there in the name.

Meg's coin hit the road and disappeared in a flash.
Instantly, a car-size section of asphalt liquefied into a boiling pool of blood and tar. (At least that's what it looked
like. I did not test the ingredients.)

A taxi erupted from the goo like a submarine breaking
the surface. It was similar to a standard New York cab, but
grey instead of yellow: the colour of dust, or tombstones, or
probably my face at that moment. Painted across the door
were the words GREY SISTERS. Inside, sitting shoulder to
shoulder across the driver's bench, were the three old hags
(excuse me, the three *mature female siblings*) themselves.

The passenger-side window rolled down. The sister
riding shotgun stuck out her head and croaked, 'Passage?
Passage?'

She was just as lovely as I remembered: a face like a rubber Halloween mask, sunken craters where her eyes should

have been and a cobweb-and-linen shawl over her bristly white hair.

'Hello, Tempest.' I sighed. 'It's been a while.'

She tilted her head. 'Who's that? Don't recognize your voice. Passage or not? We have other fares!'

'It is I,' I said miserably. 'The god Apollo.'

Tempest sniffed the air. She smacked her lips, running her tongue over her single yellow tooth. 'Don't sound like Apollo. Don't smell like Apollo. Let me bite you.'

'Um, no,' I said. 'You'll have to take my word for it. We need –'

'Wait.' Meg looked at me in wonder. 'You *know* the Grey Sisters?'

She said this as if I'd been holding out on her – as if I knew all three founding members of Bananarama and had not yet got Meg their autographs. (My history with Bananarama – how I introduced them to the actual Venus and inspired their number-one hit cover of that song – is a story for another time.)

'Yes, Meg,' I said. 'I am a god. I know people.'

Tempest grunted. 'Don't smell like a god.' She yelled at the sister on her left: 'Wasp, take a gander. Who is this guy?'

The middle sister shoved her way to the window. She looked almost exactly like Tempest – to tell them apart, you'd have to have known them for a few millennia, which, unfortunately, I had – but today she had the trio's single communal eye: a slimy, milky orb that peered at me from the depths of her left socket.

As unhappy as I was to see her again, I was even more unhappy that, by process of elimination, the third sister, Anger, had to be driving the taxi. Having Anger behind the wheel was never a good thing.

'It's some mortal boy with a blood-soaked bandanna on his head,' Wasp pronounced after ogling me. 'Not interesting. Not a god.'

'That's just hurtful,' I said. 'It *is* me. Apollo.'

Meg threw her hands up. 'Does it matter? I paid a coin. Can we get in, please?'

You might think Meg had a point. Why did I want to reveal myself? The thing was, the Grey Sisters would not take regular mortals in their cab. Also, given my history with them, I thought it best to be up-front about my identity, rather than have the Grey Sisters find out halfway through the ride and chuck me out of a moving vehicle.

'Ladies,' I said, using the term loosely, 'I may not look like Apollo, but I assure you it's me, trapped in this mortal body. Otherwise, how could I know so much about you?'

'Like what?' demanded Tempest.

'Your favourite nectar flavour is caramel crème,' I said. 'Your favourite Beatle is Ringo. For centuries, all three of you had a massive crush on Ganymede, but now you like –'

'He's Apollo!' Wasp yelped.

'Definitely Apollo!' Tempest wailed. 'Annoying! Knows things!'

'Let me in,' I said, 'and I'll shut up.'

That wasn't an offer I usually made.

The back-door lock popped up. I held the door open for Meg.

She grinned. 'Who do they like now?'

I mouthed, *Tell you later.*

Inside, we strapped ourselves in with black chain seat belts. The bench was about as comfortable as a beanbag stuffed with silverware.

Behind the wheel, the third sister, Anger, grumbled, 'Where to?'

I said, 'Camp –'

Anger hit the gas. My head slammed into the backrest, and Manhattan blurred into a light-speed smear. I hoped Anger understood I meant Camp *Half-Blood,* or we might end up at Camp Jupiter, Camp David or Campobello, New Brunswick, though I suspected those were outside the Grey Sisters' regular service area.

The cab's TV monitor flickered to life. An orchestra and a studio audience laugh track blared from the speaker. 'Every night at eleven!' an announcer said. 'It's . . . *Late Night with Thalia!*'

I mashed the OFF button as fast as I could.

'I like the commercials,' Meg complained.

'They'll rot your brain,' I said.

In truth, *Late Night with Thalia!* had once been my favourite show. Thalia (the Muse of comedy, not my demigod comrade Thalia Grace) had invited me on dozens of times as the featured musical guest. I'd sat on her sofa, traded jokes with her, played her silly games like Smite that City! and Prank Call Prophecy. But now I didn't want any more reminders of my former divine life.

Not that I missed it. I was . . . Yes, I'm going to say it. I was *embarrassed* by the things I used to consider important.

Ratings. Worshippers. The rise and fall of civilizations that liked me best. What were these things compared to keeping my friends safe? New York could *not* burn. Little Estelle Blofis had to grow up free to giggle and dominate the planet. Nero had to pay. I could not have got my face nearly chopped off that morning and thrown Luguselwa into a parked car two blocks away for nothing.

Meg appeared unfazed by my dark mood and her own wounded leg.

Deprived of commercials, she sat back and watched the blur of landscape out of the window – the East River, then Queens, zipping by at a speed that mortal commuters could only dream of . . . which, to be fair, was anything above ten miles an hour. Anger steered, completely blind, as Wasp occasionally called out course corrections. 'Left. Brake. Left. No, the other left!'

'So cool,' Meg said. 'I love this cab.'

I frowned. 'Have you taken the Grey Sisters' cab often?'

My tone was the same as one might say *You enjoy homework?*

'It was a special treat,' Meg said. 'When Lu decided I'd trained really well, we'd go for rides.'

I tried to wrap my mind around the concept of this mode of transportation as a treat. Truly, the emperor's household was a twisted, evil place.

'The girl has taste!' Wasp cried. 'We *are* the best way around the New York area! Don't trust those ride-sharing services! Most of them are run by unlicensed harpies.'

'Harpies!' Tempest howled.

'Stealing our business!' Anger agreed.

I had a momentary vision of our friend Ella behind the wheel of a car. It made me almost glad to be in this taxi. Almost.

'We've upgraded our service, too!' Tempest boasted.

I forced myself to focus on her eye sockets. 'How?'

'You can use our app!' she said. 'You don't have to summon us with gold coins any more!'

She pointed to a sign on the Plexiglas partition. Apparently, I could now link my favourite magic weapon to their cab and pay via virtual drachma using something called GREY RYYD.

I shuddered to think what the Arrow of Dodona might do if I allowed it to make online purchases. If I ever got back to Olympus, I'd find my accounts frozen and my palace in foreclosure because the arrow had bought every known copy of Shakespeare's First Folio.

'Cash is fine,' I said.

Wasp grumbled to Anger, 'You and your predictions. I told you the app was a stupid idea.'

'Stopping for Apollo was stupider,' she muttered back. 'That was *your* prediction.'

'You're both stupid!' snapped Tempest. 'That's *my* prediction!'

The reasons for my long-standing dislike of the Grey Sisters were starting to come back to me. It wasn't just that they were ugly, rude, gross and smelled of grave rot. Or that the three of them shared one eye, one tooth and zero social skills.

It wasn't even the awful job they did hiding their celebrity crushes. In Ancient Greek days, they'd had a crush on me, which was uncomfortable, but at least understandable. Then – if you can believe it – they got over me. For the past few centuries they'd been in the Ganymede Fan Club. Their Instagod posts about how hot he was got so annoying, I finally had to leave a snarky comment. You know that meme with the honey bear and the caption *honey, he gay?* Yes, I created that. And in Ganymede's case, it was hardly news.

These days they'd decided to have a collective crush on Deimos, the god of fear, which just made no romantic sense to me. Sure, he's buff, and he has nice eyes, but . . .

Wait. What was I talking about again?

Oh, right. The biggest friction between the Grey Sisters and me was professional jealousy.

I was a god of prophecy. The Grey Sisters told the future, too, but they weren't under my corporate umbrella. They paid me no tribute, no royalties, nothing. They got their wisdom from . . . Actually, I didn't know. Rumour had it they were born of the primal sea gods, created from swirls of foam and scum, so they knew little bits of wisdom and prophecy that got swept up in the tides. Whatever the case, I didn't like them poaching my territory, and for some inexplicable reason, they didn't like me back.

Their predictions . . . Hold on. I did a mental rewind. 'Did you say something about *predicting* you would pick me up?'

'Ha!' Tempest said. 'Wouldn't you like to know!'

Anger cackled. 'As if we would share that bit of doggerel we have for you –'

'Shut up, Anger!' Wasp slapped her sister. 'He didn't ask yet!'

Meg perked up. 'You have a dog for Apollo?'

I cursed under my breath. I saw where this conversation was going. The Three Sisters loved to play coy with their auguries. They liked to make their passengers beg and plead to find out what they knew about the future. But, really, the old grey dingbats were dying to share.

In the past, every time I'd agreed to listen to their so-called prophetic poetry, it turned out to be a prediction of what I would have for lunch, or an expert opinion about which Olympian god I most resembled. (Hint: It was never Apollo.) Then they would pester me for a critique and ask if I would share their poetry with my literary agent. Ugh.

I wasn't sure what titbits they might have for me this time, but I was not going to give them the satisfaction of asking. I already had enough *actual* prophetic verse to worry about.

'Doggerel,' I explained for Meg's sake, 'means a few irregular lines of poetry. With these three, that's redundant, since everything they do is irregular.'

'We won't tell you, then!' Wasp threatened.

'We will never tell!' Anger agreed.

'I didn't ask,' I said blandly.

'I want to hear about the dog,' Meg said.

'No, you don't,' I assured her.

Outside, Queens blurred into the Long Island suburbs. In the front seat, the Grey Sisters practically quivered with eagerness to spill what they knew.

'Very important words!' Wasp said. 'But you'll never hear them!'

'Okay,' I agreed.

'You can't make us!' Tempest said. 'Even though your fate depends on it!'

A hint of doubt crept into my cranium. Was it possible –? No, surely not. If I fell for their tricks, I'd most likely get the Grey Sisters' hot take on which facial products were perfect for my skin undertones.

'Not buying it,' I said.

'Not selling!' Wasp shrieked. 'Too important, these lines! We would only tell you if you threatened us with terrible things!'

'I will not resort to threatening you –'

'He's threatening us!' Tempest flailed. She slammed Wasp on the back so hard the communal eyeball popped right out of her socket. Wasp snatched it – and with a terrible show of fumbling, intentionally chucked it over her shoulder, right into my lap.

I screamed.

The sisters screamed, too. Anger, now bereft of guidance, swerved all over the road, sending my stomach into my oesophagus.

'He's stolen our eye!' cried Tempest. 'We can't see!'

'I have not!' I yelped. 'It's disgusting!'

Meg whooped with pleasure. 'THIS. IS. SO. COOL!'

'Get it off!' I squirmed and tilted my hips, hoping the eye would roll away, but it stayed stubbornly in my lap, staring up at me with the accusatory glare of a dead catfish. Meg did not help. Clearly, she didn't want to do anything that might interfere with the coolness of us dying in a faster-than-light car crash.

'He will crush our eye,' Anger cried, 'if we don't recite our verses!'

'I will not!'

'We will all die!' Wasp said. 'He is crazy!'

'I AM NOT!'

'Fine, you win!' Tempest howled. She drew herself up and recited as if performing for the people in Connecticut ten miles away: 'A *dare reveals the path that was unknown!*'

Anger chimed in: 'And *bears destruction; lion, snake-entwined!*'

Wasp concluded: '*Or else the princeps never be o'erthrown!*'

Meg clapped.

I stared at the Grey Sisters in disbelief. 'That wasn't doggerel. That was terza rima! You just gave us the next stanza of our actual prophecy!'

'Well, that's all we've got for you!' Anger said. 'Now give me the eye, quick. We're almost at camp!'

Panic overcame my shock. If Anger couldn't stop at our destination, we'd accelerate past the point of no return and vaporize in a colourful streak of plasma across Long Island.

And yet that *still* sounded better than touching the eye-ball in my lap. 'Meg! Kleenex?'

She snorted. 'Wimp.' She scooped up the eye with her bare hand and tossed it to Anger.

Anger shoved the eye in her socket. She blinked at the road, yelled 'YIKES!' and slammed on the brakes so hard my chin hit my sternum.

Once the smoke cleared, I saw we had skidded to a

stop on the old farm road just outside of camp. To our left loomed Half-Blood Hill, a single great pine tree rising from its summit, the Golden Fleece glittering from the lowest branch. Coiled around the base of the tree was Peleus the dragon. And standing next to the dragon, casually scratching its ears, was an old frenemy of mine: Dionysus, the god of doing things to annoy Apollo.

8

I am Mr A.

I am here to fix toilets

And also pass out.

PERHAPS THAT LAST COMMENT WAS UNFAIR.

Dionysus was the god of other things, such as wine, madness, Oscar-night after-parties and certain types of vegetation. But, to me, he would always be the annoying little brother who followed me around, trying to get my attention by imitating everything I did.

You know the type. You're a god. Your little brother pesters Dad to make *him* a god, too, even though being a god is supposed to be *your* thing. You have a nice chariot pulled by fiery horses. Your little brother insists on getting his own chariot pulled by leopards. You lay waste to the Greek armies at Troy. Your little brother decides to invade India. Pretty typical stuff.

Dionysus stood at the top of the hill, as if he'd been expecting us. Being a god, maybe he had. His leopard-skin golf shirt matched the Golden Fleece in the branch above him quite well. His mauve golf slacks did not. In the old days, I might have teased him about his taste in clothes. Now, I couldn't risk it.

A lump formed in my throat. I was already carsick from

our taxi ride and our impromptu game of catch-the-eyeball. My wounded forehead throbbed. My brain swirled with the new lines of prophecy the Grey Sisters had given us. I didn't need any more things to worry about. But seeing Dionysus again . . . This would be complicated.

Meg slammed the taxi door behind her. 'Thanks, guys!' she told the Grey Sisters. 'Next time, tell me about the dog!'

Without so much as a goodbye or a plea to share their poetry with my literary agent, the Grey Sisters submerged in a pool of red-black tar.

Meg squinted up at the hill's summit. 'Who's that guy? We didn't meet him before.' She sounded suspicious, as if he were intruding on her territory.

'That,' I said, 'is the god Dionysus.'

Meg frowned. 'Why?'

She might have meant *Why is he a god? Why is he standing up there?* or *Why is this our life?* All three questions were equally valid.

'I don't know,' I said. 'Let's find out.'

Trekking up the hill, I fought the urge to burst into hysterical sobbing or laughter. Probably I was going into shock. It had been a rough day, and it wasn't even lunchtime yet. However, given the fact that we were approaching the god of madness, I had to consider the more serious possibility that I was having a psychotic or manic break.

I already felt disconnected from reality. I couldn't concentrate. I didn't know who I was, who I was supposed to be or even who I wanted to be. I was getting emotional whiplash from my exhilarating surges of godlike power, my depressing crashes back into mortal frailty and my adrenalin-charged bouts of terror. In such a condition, approaching Dionysus was asking for trouble. Just being near him could widen the cracks in anyone's psyche.

Meg and I reached the summit. Peleus welcomed us with a puff of steam from his nostrils. Meg gave the dragon a hug around the neck, which I'm not sure I would have recommended. Dragons are notoriously *not* huggers.

Dionysus eyed me with a mixture of shock and horror, much the same way I looked at myself in the mirror these days.

'So, it's true, what Father did to you,' he said. 'That cold-hearted *glámon*.'

In Ancient Greek, *glámon* meant something like *dirty old man*. Given Zeus's romantic track record, I doubted he would even consider it an insult.

Dionysus gripped my shoulders.

I didn't trust myself to speak.

He looked the same as he had for the past half century: a short middle-aged man with a potbelly, sagging jowls, a red nose and curly black hair. The violet tint of his irises was the only indicator that he might be more than human.

Other Olympians could never comprehend why Dionysus chose this form when he could look like anything he wanted. In ancient times, he'd been famous for his youthful beauty that defied gender.

But I understood. For the crime of chasing the wrong nymph (translation: one our father wanted instead), Dionysus had been sentenced to run this camp for a hundred years. He had been denied wine, his most noble creation, and forbidden access to Olympus except for special meeting days.

In retaliation, Dionysus had decided to look and act as ungodly as possible. He was like a child refusing to tuck in his shirt, comb his hair or brush his teeth, just to show his parents how little he cared.

'Poor, poor Apollo.' He hugged me. His hair smelled faintly of grape-flavoured bubblegum.

This unexpected show of sympathy brought me close to tears . . . until Dionysus pulled away, held me at arm's length and gave me a triumphant smirk.

'*Now* you understand how miserable I've been,' he said. 'Finally, someone got punished even more harshly than me!'

I nodded, swallowing back a sob. Here was the old, on-brand Dionysus I knew and didn't exactly love. 'Yes. Hello, Brother. This is Meg –'

'Don't care.' Dionysus's eyes remained fixed on me, his tone infused with joy.

'Hmph.' Meg crossed her arms. 'Where's Chiron? I liked him better.'

'Who?' Dionysus said. 'Oh, him. Long story. Let's get you into camp, Apollo. I can't wait to show you off to the demigods. You look *horrible!*'

We took the long way through camp. Dionysus seemed determined to make sure everyone saw me.

'This is Mr A,' he told all the newcomers we encountered. 'He's my assistant. If you have any complaints or problems – toilets backing up or whatnot – talk to him.'

'Could you not?' I muttered.

Dionysus smiled. 'If I am Mr D, you can be Mr A.'

'He's Lester,' Meg complained. 'And he's *my* assistant.'

Dionysus ignored her. 'Oh, look, another batch of first-year campers! Let's go introduce you.'

My legs were wobbly. My head ached. I needed lunch, rest, antibiotics and a new identity, not necessarily in that order. But we trudged on.

The camp was busier than it had been the winter when Meg and I first straggled in. Then, only a core group of year-rounders had been present. Now, waves of newly discovered demigods were arriving for the summer – dozens of dazed kids from all over the world, many still accompanied by the satyrs who had located them. Some demigods, who, evidently, had recently fought off monsters, were injured even worse than I was, which I suppose is why Meg and I didn't get more stares.

We made our way through the camp's central green. Around its edges, most of the twenty cabins buzzed with activity. Senior counsellors stood in the doorways, welcoming new members or providing directions. At the Hermes cabin, Julia Feingold looked especially overwhelmed, trying to find temporary spots for all the campers still unclaimed by their godly parents. At the Ares cabin, Sherman Yang barked at anyone who got too close to the building, warning them to look out for the land mines around the perimeter. Whether or not that was a joke, no one seemed anxious to find out. Young Harley from the Hephaestus cabin dashed around with a huge grin on his face, challenging the newbies to arm-wrestling contests.

Across the green, I spotted two of my own children –
Austin and Kayla – but, as much as I wanted to talk with
them, they were embroiled in some sort of conflict resolu-
tion between a group of security harpies and a new kid who
had apparently done something the harpies didn't like. I
caught Austin's words: 'No, you can't just eat a new camper.
They get two warnings first!'

Even Dionysus didn't want to get involved in that conversation. We kept walking.

The damage from our wintertime battle against Nero's
Colossus had been mostly repaired, though some of the dining hall's columns were still broken. Nestled between two
hills was a new pond in the shape of a giant's footprint. We
passed the volleyball court, the sword-fighting arena and
the strawberry fields until finally Dionysus took pity on me
and led us to camp headquarters.

Compared to the camp's Greek temples and amphi-
theatres, the four-storey sky-blue Victorian known as the
Big House looked quaint and homey. Its white trim gleamed
like cake frosting. Its bronze eagle weathervane drifted lazily
in the breeze. On its wraparound front porch, enjoying lemonade at the card table, sat Nico di Angelo and Will Solace.

'Dad!' Will shot to his feet. He ran down the steps and
tackled me in a hug.

That's when I lost it. I wept openly.

My beautiful son, with his kind eyes, his healer's hands,
his sun-warm demeanour. Somehow, he had inherited all my
best qualities and none of the worst. He guided me up the
steps and insisted I take his seat. He pressed a cold glass

of lemonade into my hands, then started fussing over my wounded head.

'I'm fine,' I murmured, though clearly I wasn't.

His boyfriend, Nico di Angelo, hovered at the edge of our reunion – observing, keeping to the shadows, as children of Hades tend to do. His dark hair had grown longer. He was barefoot, in tattered jeans and a black version of the camp's standard T-shirt, with a skeletal pegasus on the front above the words CABIN 13.

'Meg,' Nico said, 'take my chair. Your leg looks bad.' He scowled at Dionysus, as if the god should have arranged a golf cart for us.

'Yes, fine, sit.' Dionysus gestured listlessly at the card table. 'I was attempting to teach Will and Nico the rules of pinochle, but they're hopeless.'

'Ooh, pinochle,' Meg said. 'I like pinochle!'

Dionysus narrowed his eyes as if Meg were a small dog who had suddenly begun to spout Emily Dickinson. 'Is that so? Wonders never cease.'

Nico met my gaze, his eyes pools of ink. 'So, is it true? Is Jason . . . ?'

'Nico,' Will chided. 'Don't pressure him.'

The ice cubes shook in my glass. I couldn't make myself speak, but my expression must have told Nico everything he needed to know. Meg offered Nico her hand. He took it in both of his.

He didn't look angry, exactly. He looked as if he'd been hit in the gut not just once but so many times over the course of so many years that he was beginning to lose perspective on what it meant to be in pain. He swayed on his feet. He blinked. Then he flinched, jerking his hands away from Meg's as if he'd just remembered his own touch was poison.

'I . . .' he faltered. '*Scusatemi.*'

He hurried down the steps and across the lawn, his bare feet leaving a trail of dead grass.

Will shook his head. 'He only slips into Italian when he's *really* upset.'

'The boy has had too much bad news already,' Dionysus said with a tone of grudging sympathy.

I wanted to ask what he meant about bad news. I wanted to apologize for bringing more trouble. I wanted to explain all the tremendous and spectacular ways I had failed since the last time I had seen Camp Half-Blood.

Instead, the lemonade glass slipped from my fingers. It shattered on the floor. I tipped sideways in my chair as Will's voice receded down a long dark tunnel. 'Dad! Guys, help me!'

Then I spiralled into unconsciousness.

9

Breakfast is the meal
With pancakes and burnt yogurt
And insanity.

BAD DREAMS?

Sure, why not!

I suffered a series of Instagram-boomerang nightmares –
the same short scenes looped over and over: Luguselwa
hurtling over a rooftop. The amphisbaena staring at me in
bewilderment as two crossbow bolts pinned his necks to the
wall. The Grey Sisters' eyeball flying into my lap and sticking there like it was coated in glue.

I tried to channel my dreams in a more peaceful
direction – my favourite beach in Fiji, my old festival day in
Athens, the gig I played with Duke Ellington at the Cotton
Club in 1930. Nothing worked.

Instead, I found myself in Nero's throne room.

The loft space took up one whole floor of his tower. In
every direction, glass walls looked out over the spires of
Manhattan. In the centre of the room, on a marble dais, the
emperor sprawled across a gaudy velvet couch throne. His
purple satin pyjamas and tiger-striped bathrobe would've
made Dionysus jealous. His crown of golden laurels sat

askew on his head, which made me want to adjust the neck beard that wrapped around his chin like a strap.

To his left stood a line of young people; demigods, I assumed – adopted members of the imperial family like Meg had been. I counted eleven in all, arranged from tallest to shortest, their ages ranging from about eighteen to eight. They wore purple-trimmed togas over their motley assortment of street clothes, to indicate their royal status. Their expressions were a case study in the results of Nero's abusive parenting style. The youngest seemed struck with wonder, fear and hero worship. The slightly older ones looked broken and traumatized, their eyes hollow. The adolescents showed a range of anger, resentment and self-loathing, all bottled up and carefully *not* directed at Nero. The oldest teens looked like mini-Neros: cynical, hard, cruel junior sociopaths.

I could not imagine Meg McCaffrey in that assembly. And yet I couldn't stop wondering where she would fall in the line of horrific expressions.

Two Germani lumbered into the throne room carrying a stretcher. On it lay the large, battered form of Luguselwa. They set her down at Nero's feet, and she let out a miserable groan. At least she was still alive.

'The hunter returns empty-handed,' Nero sneered. 'Plan B it is, then. A forty-eight-hour ultimatum seems reasonable.' He turned to his adopted children. 'Lucius, double security at the storage vats. Aemillia, send out invitations. And order a cake. Something nice. It's not every day we get to destroy a city the size of New York.'

My dream-self plummeted through the tower into the depths of the earth.

I stood in a vast cavern. I knew I must be somewhere beneath Delphi, the seat of my most sacred Oracle, because the soup of volcanic fumes swirling around me smelled like nothing else in the world. I could hear my archnemesis, Python, somewhere in the darkness, dragging his immense body over the stone floor.

'You still do not see it.' His voice was a low rumble. 'Oh, Apollo, bless your tiny, inadequate brain. You charge around, knocking over pieces, but you never look at the whole board. A few hours, at most. That is all it will take once the last pawn falls. And you will do the hard work for me!'

His laughter was like an explosion sunk deep into stone, designed to bring down a hillside. Fear rolled over me until I could no longer breathe.

I woke feeling like I'd spent hours trying to squirm out of a stone cocoon. Every muscle in my body ached.

I wished I could just *once* wake up refreshed after a dream about getting seaweed wraps and pedicures with the Nine Muses. Oh, I missed our spa decades! But no. I got sneering emperors and giant laughing reptiles instead.

I sat up, woozy and blurry-eyed. I was lying in my old cot in the Me cabin. Sunlight streamed through the windows – *morning* light? Had I really slept that long? Snuggled up next to me, something warm and furry was growling and snuffling on my pillow. At first glance, I thought it might be a pit bull, though I was fairly sure I did not own a pit bull. Then it looked up, and I realized it was the disembodied head of a leopard.

One nanosecond later, I was standing at the opposite end of the cabin, screaming. It was the closest I'd come to teleporting since I'd lost my godly powers.

'Oh, you're awake!' My son Will emerged from the bathroom in a billow of steam, his blond hair dripping wet and a towel around his waist. On his left pectoral was a stylized sun tattoo, which seemed unnecessary to me – as if he could be mistaken for anything but a child of the sun god.

He froze when he registered the panic in my eyes. 'What's wrong?'

GRR! said the leopard.

'Seymour?' Will marched over to my cot and picked up the leopard head – which at some point in the distant past had been taxidermied and stuck on a plaque, then liberated from a garage sale by Dionysus and granted new life. Normally, as I recalled, Seymour resided over the fireplace mantel in the Big House, which did not explain why he had been chewing on my pillow.

'What are you doing here?' Will demanded of the leopard. Then, to me: 'I swear I did *not* put him in your bed.'

'I did.' Dionysus materialized right next to me.

My tortured lungs could not manage another scream, but I leaped back an additional few inches.

Dionysus gave me his patented smirk. 'I thought you might like some company. I always sleep better with a teddy leopard.'

'Very kind.' I tried my best to kill him with eye daggers. 'But I prefer to sleep alone.'

'As you wish. Seymour, back to the Big House.' Dionysus snapped his fingers and the leopard head vanished from Will's hands.

'Well, then . . .' Dionysus studied me. 'Feeling better after nineteen hours of sleep?'

I realized I was wearing nothing but my underwear. With my pale, lumpy mortal form covered in bruises and scars, I looked less than ever like a god and more like a grub that had been prised from the soil with a stick.

'Feeling great,' I grumbled.

'Excellent! Will, get him presentable. I'll see you both at breakfast.'

'Breakfast . . . ?' I said in a daze.

'Yes,' Dionysus said. 'It's the meal with pancakes. I do love pancakes.'

He disappeared in a grape-scented cloud of glitter.

'Such a show-off,' I muttered.

Will laughed. 'You really have changed.'

'I wish people would stop pointing that out.'

'It's a good thing.'

I looked down again at my battered body. 'If you say so. Do you have any clothing, or possibly a burlap sack I might borrow?'

Here's all you need to know about Will Solace: he had clothes waiting for me. On his last trip into town, he'd gone shopping specifically for things that might fit me.

'I figured you'd come back to camp eventually,' he said.

'I hoped you would, anyway. I wanted you to feel at home.'

It was enough to start me crying again. Gods, I was an emotional wreck. Will hadn't inherited his thoughtfulness from me. That was all his mother, Naomi, bless her kind heart.

I thought about giving Will a hug, but since we were clad in just underwear and a towel, respectively, that seemed awkward. He patted me on the shoulder instead.

'Go take a shower,' he advised. 'The others took an early-morning hike –' he gestured at the empty bunks – 'but they'll be back soon. I'll wait for you.'

Once I was showered and dressed – in a fresh pair of jeans and a V-necked olive tee, both of which fit perfectly – Will re-bandaged my forehead. He gave me some aspirin for my aching everything. I was starting to feel almost human again – in a good way – when a conch horn sounded in the distance, calling the camp to breakfast.

On our way out of the cabin, we collided with Kayla and Austin, just returning from their hike with three younger campers in tow. More tears and hugs were exchanged.

'You've grown up!' Kayla gripped my shoulders with her archery-strong hands. The June sunlight made her freckles more pronounced. The green-tinted tips of her orange hair made me think of Halloween-pumpkin candy. 'You're two inches taller at least! Isn't he, Austin?'

'Definitely,' Austin agreed.

As a jazz musician, Austin was usually smooth and cool, but he gave me a serene smile like I'd just nailed a solo worthy of Ornette Coleman. His sleeveless orange camp tee

showed off his dark arms. His cornrows were done in swirls
like alien crop circles.

'It's not just the height,' he decided. 'It's the way you
hold yourself . . .'

'Ahem,' said one of the kids behind him.

'Oh, right. Sorry, guys!' Austin stepped aside. 'We got
three new campers this year, Dad. I'm sure you remember
your children Gracie and Jerry and Yan . . . Guys, this is
Apollo!'

Austin introduced them casually, like *I know you don't
have a clue who these three kids are that you sired and forgot
about twelve or thirteen years ago, but don't worry, Dad, I
got you.*

Jerry was from London, Gracie from Idaho and Yan
from Hong Kong. (When had I been in Hong Kong?) All
three seemed stunned to meet me – but more in a *you-
have-to-be-kidding-me* way, not in a *wow-cool* sort of way. I
muttered some apologies about being a terrible father. The
newcomers exchanged glances and apparently decided, by
silent agreement, to put me out of my misery.

'I'm famished,' Jerry said.

'Yeah,' Gracie said. 'Dining hall!'

And off we trekked like one big super-awkward family.

Campers from other cabins were also streaming towards
the dining pavilion. I spotted Meg halfway up the hill, chatting excitedly with her siblings from the Demeter cabin. At
her side trotted Peaches, her fruit-tree spirit companion.
The little diapered fellow seemed quite happy, alternately
flapping his leafy wings and grabbing Meg's leg to get her

attention. We hadn't seen Peaches since Kentucky, as he tended to only show up in natural settings, or when Meg was in dire trouble, or when breakfast was about to be served.

Meg and I had been together so long, usually just the two of us, that I felt a pang in my heart watching her stroll along with a different set of friends. She looked so content without me. If I ever made it back to Mount Olympus, I wondered if she would decide to stay at Camp Half-Blood. I also wondered why the thought made me so sad.

After the horrors she'd suffered in Nero's Imperial Household, she deserved some peace.

That made me think about my dream of Luguselwa, battered and broken on a stretcher in front of Nero's throne. Perhaps I had more in common with the Gaul than I wanted to admit. Meg needed a better family, a better home than either Lu *or* I could give her. But that didn't make it any easier to contemplate letting her go.

Just ahead of us, a boy of about nine stumbled from the Ares cabin. His helmet had completely swallowed his head. He ran to catch up to his cabinmates, the point of his too-long sword tracing a serpentine line in the dirt behind him.

'The newbies all look so young,' Will murmured. 'Were we ever that young?'

Kayla and Austin nodded in agreement.

Yan grumbled. 'We newbies are right *here*.'

I wanted to tell them that they were *all* so young. Their lifespans were a blink of an eye compared to my four millennia. I should be wrapping them all in warm blankets and giving them cookies rather than expecting them to be heroes, slay monsters and buy me clothes.

On the other hand, Achilles hadn't even started shaving yet when he sailed off to the Trojan War. I'd watched so many young heroes march bravely to their deaths over the centuries . . . Just thinking about it made me feel older than Kronos's teething ring.

After the relatively ordered meals of the Twelfth Legion at Camp Jupiter, breakfast at the dining pavilion was quite a shock. Counsellors tried to explain the seating rules (such as they were) while returning campers jockeyed for spots next to their friends, and the newbies tried not to kill themselves or each other with their new weapons. Dryads wove through the crowd with platters of food, satyrs trotting behind them and stealing bites. Honeysuckle vines bloomed on the Greek columns, filling the air with perfume.

At the sacrificial fire, demigods took turns scraping parts of their meals into the flames as offerings to the gods – corn flakes, bacon, toast, yogurt. (Yogurt?) A steady plume of smoke rolled into the heavens. As a former god, I appreciated the sentiment, but I also wondered whether the smell of burning yogurt was worth the air pollution.

Will offered me a seat next to him, then passed me a goblet of orange juice.

'Thank you,' I managed. 'But where's, uh . . . ?'

I scanned the crowd for Nico di Angelo, remembering how he normally sat at Will's table, regardless of cabin rules.

'Up there,' Will said, apparently guessing my thoughts.

The son of Hades sat next to Dionysus at the head table. The god's plate was piled high with pancakes. Nico's was empty. They seemed an odd pair, sitting together, but they appeared to be in a deep and serious conversation.

Dionysus rarely tolerated demigods at his table. If he was giving Nico such undivided attention, something must be seriously wrong.

I remembered what Mr D had said yesterday, just before I passed out. '"That boy has had too much bad news already",' I repeated, then frowned at Will. 'What did that mean?'

Will picked at the wrapper of his bran muffin. 'It's complicated. Nico sensed Jason's death weeks ago. It sent him into a rage.'

'I'm so sorry . . .'

'It's not your fault,' Will assured me. 'When you got here, you just confirmed what Nico already knew. The thing is . . . Nico lost his sister Bianca a few years back. He spent a long time raging about that. He wanted to go into the Underworld to retrieve her, which . . . I guess, as a son of Hades, he's really *not* supposed to do. Anyway, he was finally starting to come to terms with her death. Then he learned about Jason, the first person he really considered a friend. It triggered a lot of stuff for him. Nico has travelled to the deepest parts of the Underworld, even down in Tartarus. The fact that he came through it in one piece is a miracle.'

'With his sanity intact,' I agreed. Then I looked again at Dionysus, god of madness, who seemed to be giving Nico advice. 'Oh . . .'

'Yeah,' Will agreed, his face drawn with worry. 'They've been eating most meals together, though Nico doesn't eat much these days. Nico has been having . . . I guess you'd call it post-traumatic stress disorder. He gets flashbacks. He has waking dreams. Dionysus is trying to help him make sense of it all. The worst part is the voices.'

A dryad slammed a plate of huevos rancheros in front of me, almost making me jump out of my jeans. She smirked and walked off, looking quite pleased with herself.

'Voices?' I asked Will.

Will turned up his palms. 'Nico won't tell me much. Just . . . someone in Tartarus keeps calling his name. Someone needs his help. It's been all I could do to stop him from storming down into the Underworld by himself. I told him: talk to Dionysus first. Figure out what's real and what's not. Then, if he has to go . . . we'll go together.'

A rivulet of cold sweat trickled between my shoulder blades. I couldn't imagine Will in the Underworld – a place with no sunshine, no healing, no kindness.

'I hope it doesn't come to that,' I said.

Will nodded. 'Maybe if we can take down Nero – maybe that will give Nico something else to focus on for a while, assuming we can help you.'

Kayla had been listening quietly, but now she leaned in. 'Yeah, Meg was telling us about this prophecy you got. The Tower of Nero and all that. If there's a battle, we want in.'

Austin wagged a breakfast sausage at me. 'Word.'

Their willingness to help made me feel grateful. If I had to go to war, I would want Kayla's bow at my side. Will's healing skill might keep me alive, despite my best efforts to get killed. Austin could terrify our enemies with diminished minor riffs on his saxophone.

On the other hand, I remembered Luguselwa's warning about Nero's readiness. He *wanted* us to attack. A full frontal assault would be suicide. I would not let my children come to harm, even if my only other option was to trust Lu's crazy plan and surrender myself to the emperor.

A *forty-eight-hour ultimatum*, Nero had said in my dream. Then he would burn down New York.

Gods, why wasn't there an option C on this multiple-choice test?

Clink, clink, clink.

Dionysus rose at the head table, a glass and spoon in his hands. The dining pavilion fell silent. Demigods turned and waited for morning announcements. I recalled Chiron having much more trouble getting everyone's attention. Then again, Chiron didn't have the power to turn the entire assembly into bunches of grapes.

'Mr A and Will Solace, report to the head table,' Dionysus said.

The campers waited for more.

'That's all,' Mr D said. 'Honestly, do I need to tell you how to eat breakfast? Carry on!'

The campers resumed their normal happy chaos. Will and I picked up our plates.

'Good luck,' Kayla said. 'I have a feeling you'll need it.'

We went to join Dionysus and Nico at the International Head-table of Pancakes.

10

Huevos rancheros
Do not go with prophecies,
Much like happiness.

DIONYSUS HAD NOT ASKED FOR MEG, BUT she joined us anyway.

She plopped down next to me with her plate of pancakes and snapped her fingers at Dionysus. 'Pass the syrup.'

I feared Mr D might turn her into a taxidermied back end for Seymour, but he simply did as she asked. I suppose he didn't want to polymorph the only other person at camp who liked pinochle.

Peaches stayed behind at the Demeter table, where he was getting fawned over by the campers. This was just as well, since grape gods and peach spirits don't mix.

Will sat next to Nico and put an apple on his empty plate. 'Eat something.'

'Hmph,' Nico said, though he leaned into Will ever so slightly.

'Right.' Dionysus held up a cream-coloured piece of stationery between his fingers, like a magician producing a card. 'This came for me last night via harpy courier.'

He slid it across the table so I could read the fancy print.

Nero Claudius Caesar Augustus Germanicus
Requests the pleasure of your company
At the burning of
The Greater New York Metropolitan Area
Forty-eight hours after receipt of this Invitation
UNLESS
The former god Apollo, now known as
Lester Papadopoulos,
Surrenders himself before that time to imperial justice
At the Tower of Nero
IN WHICH CASE
We will just have cake

GIFTS:
Only expensive ones, please

R.S.V.P.
Don't bother. If you don't show up, we'll know.

I pushed away my huevos rancheros. My appetite had vanished. It was one thing to hear about Nero's diabolical plans in my nightmares. It was another thing to see them spelled out in black-and-white calligraphy with a promise of cake.

'Forty-eight hours from last night,' I said.

'Yes,' Dionysus mused. 'I've always liked Nero. He has panache.'

Meg stabbed viciously at her pancakes. She filled her mouth with fluffy, syrupy goodness, probably to keep herself from muttering curse words.

Nico caught my gaze across the table. His dark eyes swam with anger and worry. On his plate, the apple started to wither.

Will squeezed his hand. 'Hey, stop.'

Nico's expression softened a bit. The apple stopped its premature slide into old age. 'Sorry. I just – I'm tired of talking about problems I can't fix. I want to help.'

He said *help* as if it meant *chop our enemies into small pieces*.

Nico di Angelo wasn't physically imposing like Sherman Yang. He didn't have Reyna Ramírez-Arellano's air of authority, or Hazel Levesque's commanding presence when she charged into battle on horseback. But Nico wasn't someone I would *ever* want as an enemy.

He was deceptively quiet. He appeared anaemic and frail. He kept himself on the periphery. But Will was right about how much Nico had been through. He had been born in Mussolini's Italy. He had survived decades in the time-warp reality of the Lotus Casino. He'd emerged in modern times disoriented and culture-shocked, arrived at Camp Half-Blood, and promptly lost his sister Bianca to a dangerous quest. He had wandered the Labyrinth in self-imposed exile, being tortured and brainwashed by a malevolent ghost. He'd overcome everyone's distrust and emerged from the Battle of Manhattan as a hero. He'd been captured by giants during the rise of Gaia. He'd wandered Tartarus alone and somehow managed to come out alive. And, through it all, he'd struggled with his upbringing as a conservative Catholic Italian male from the 1930s and finally learned to accept himself as a young gay man.

Anyone who could survive all that had more resilience than Stygian iron.

'We do need your help,' I promised. 'Meg told you about the prophetic verses?'

'Meg told Will,' Nico said. 'Will told me. Terza rima. Like in Dante. We had to study him in elementary school in Italy. Gotta say, I never thought it would come in handy.'

Will poked at his bran muffin. 'Just so I'm clear . . . You got the first stanza from a Cyclops's armpit, the second from a two-headed snake and the third from three old ladies who drive a taxi?'

'We didn't have much choice in the matter,' I said. 'But yes.'

'Does the poem ever end?' Will asked. 'If the rhyme scheme interlocks stanza to stanza, couldn't it keep going forever?'

I shuddered. 'I hope not. Usually the last stanza would include a closing couplet, but we haven't heard one yet.'

'Which means,' Nico said, 'that there are more stanzas to come.'

'Yippee.' Meg shoved more pancake in her mouth.

Dionysus matched her with a mouthful of his own, as if they were engaged in a competition to see who could devour the most and enjoy it the least.

'Well, then,' Will said with forced cheerfulness, 'let's discuss the stanzas we have. What was it – *The tow'r of Nero two alone ascend?* That part is obvious enough. It must mean Apollo and Meg, right?'

'We surrender,' Meg said. 'That's Luguselwa's plan.'

Dionysus snorted. 'Apollo, please tell me you're not going to trust a Gaul. You haven't got *that* addle-brained, have you?'

'Hey!' Meg said. 'We can trust Lu. She let Lester throw her off a roof.'

Dionysus narrowed his eyes. 'Did she survive?'

Meg looked flustered. 'I mean –'

'Yes,' I interrupted. 'She did.'

I told them what I had seen in my dreams: the broken Gaul brought before Nero's throne, the emperor's ultimatum, then my plunge into the caverns beneath Delphi, where Python blessed my tiny brain.

Dionysus nodded thoughtfully. 'Ah, yes, Python. If you survive Nero, you have *that* to look forward to.'

I didn't appreciate the reminder. Stopping a power-mad emperor from taking over the world and destroying a city . . . that was one thing. Python was a more nebulous threat, harder to quantify, but potentially a thousand times more dangerous.

Meg and I had freed four Oracles from the grasp of the Triumvirate, but Delphi still remained firmly under Python's control. That meant the world's main source of prophecy was being slowly choked off, poisoned, manipulated. In ancient times, Delphi had been called the *omphalos*, the navel of the world. Unless I managed to defeat Python and retake the Oracle, the entire fate of humanity was at risk. Delphic prophecies were not simply glimpses into the future. They *shaped* the future. And you did not want an enormous malevolent monster controlling a wellspring of power like that, calling the shots for all human civilization.

I frowned at Dionysus. 'You could always, oh, I don't know, decide to *help*.'

He scoffed. 'You know as well as I do, Apollo, that quests like this are demigod business. As for advising, guiding, helping . . . that's really more Chiron's job. He should be back from his meeting . . . oh, tomorrow night, I would think, but that will be too late for you.'

I wished he hadn't put it that way: *too late for you*.

'What meeting?' Meg asked.

Dionysus waved the question away. 'Some . . . joint task force, he called it? The world often has more than one crisis happening at a time. Perhaps you've noticed. He said he had an emergency meeting with a cat and a severed head, whatever that means.'

'So instead we get you,' Meg said.

'Believe me, child, I would rather not be here with you delightful rapscallions, either. After I was so helpful in the wars against Kronos and Gaia, I was hoping Zeus might grant me early parole from my servitude in this miserable place. But, as you can see, he sent me right back to complete my hundred years. Our father does love to punish his children.'

He gave me that smirk again – the one that meant *at least you got it worse*.

I wished Chiron were here, but there was no point in dwelling on that, or on whatever the old centaur might be up to at his emergency meeting. We had enough to worry about on our own.

Python's words kept slithering around in my brain: *You never look at the whole board*.

The evil reptile was playing a game inside a game. No great surprise that he would be using the Triumvirate for his own purposes, but Python seemed to relish the idea that I might kill his last ally, Nero. And after that? *A few hours, at most. That is all it will take once the last pawn falls.*

I had no idea what that meant. Python was right that I couldn't see the whole board. I didn't understand the rules. I just wanted to sweep the pieces away and shout, *I'm going home!*

'Whatever.' Meg poured more syrup onto her plate in an effort to create Lake Pancake. 'Point is – that other line says our lives depend on Nero's own. That means we can trust Lu. We'll surrender before the deadline, like she told us.'

Nico tilted his head. 'Even if you do surrender, what makes you think Nero will honour his word? If he's gone to all the trouble to rig enough Greek fire to burn down New York, why wouldn't he just do it anyway?'

'He would,' I said. 'Most definitely.'

Dionysus seemed to ponder this. 'But these fires wouldn't extend as far as, say, Camp Half-Blood.'

'Dude,' Will said.

'What?' the god asked. 'I am only in charge of the safety of this camp.'

'Lu has a plan,' Meg insisted. 'Once we're captured, Nero will relax his guard. Lu will free us. We'll destroy . . .' She hesitated. 'We'll destroy his fasces. Then he'll be weak. We can beat him before he burns the city.'

I wondered if anyone else had caught her change of direction – the way she'd felt too uncomfortable to say *We'll destroy Nero.*

At the other tables, campers continued eating breakfast, jostling each other good-naturedly, chatting about the day's scheduled activities.

None of them paid much attention to our conversation.

No one was glancing nervously at me and asking their cabinmates if I was really the god Apollo.

Why would they? This was a new generation of demi-gods, just starting their first summer at camp. For all they knew, I was a normal fixture of the landscape like Mr D, the satyrs and ritual yogurt-burnings. *Mr A? Oh, yeah. He used to be a god or something. Just ignore him.*

Many times over the centuries, I had felt out-of-date and forgotten. Never more so than at that moment.

'If Lu is telling the truth,' Will was saying, 'and *if* Nero still trusts her –'

'And *if* she can break you out,' Nico added, 'and *if* you can destroy the fasces before Nero burns down the city . . . That's a lot of ifs. I don't like scenarios with more than one *if.*'

'Like I might take you out for pizza this weekend,' Will offered, '*if* you're not too annoying.'

'Exactly.' Nico's smile was a bit of winter sun breaking between snow flurries. 'So, assuming you guys go through with this crazy plan, what are we supposed to do?'

Meg belched. 'It's right there in the prophecy. The son-of-Hades thing.'

Nico's face clouded over. 'What *son-of-Hades* thing?'

Will developed a sudden interest in his bran muffin's wrapper. Nico seemed to realize, at the same time I did, that Will hadn't shared all the lines of the prophecy with him.

'William Andrew Solace,' Nico said, 'do you have something to confess?'

'I was going to mention it.' Will looked at me plead-ingly, as if he couldn't make himself say the lines.

'*The son of Hades, cavern-runners' friend,*' I recited. '*Must show the secret way unto the throne.*'

Nico scowled with such intensity I feared he might make Will wither like the apple. 'You think that might have been good to mention sooner?'

'Hold on,' I said, partly to spare Will from Nico's wrath, and partly because I had been racking my brain, trying to think who these 'cavern-runners' might be, and I still had no clue. 'Nico, do you know what those lines mean?'

Nico nodded. 'The cavern-runners are . . . new friends of mine.'

'They're hardly friends,' Will muttered.

'They're experts on subterranean geography,' Nico said. 'I've been talking to them about . . . other business.'

'Which is not good for your mental health,' Dionysus added in a singsong voice.

Nico gave him a death-to-apples look. 'If there *is* a secret way into Nero's tower, they might know it.'

Will shook his head. 'Every time you visit them . . .' He let his statement die, but the concern in his voice was as jagged as broken glass.

'Then come with me this time,' Nico said. '*Help* me.'

Will's expression was miserable. I could tell he desperately wanted to protect Nico, to help him any way he could. He also desperately did not want to visit these cavern-runners.

'Who are they?' Meg said, between bites of pancake. 'Are they horrible?'

'Yes,' Will said.

'No,' Nico said.

'Well, that's settled, then,' Dionysus said. 'Since Mr di Angelo seems intent on ignoring my mental-health advice and going on this quest –'

'That's not fair,' Nico protested. 'You heard the prophecy. I *have* to.'

'The whole concept of "have to" is strange to me,' Dionysus said, 'but if your mind is made up, you'd best get going, eh? Apollo only has until tomorrow night to surrender, or fake-surrender, or whatever you wish to call it.'

'Anxious to get rid of us?' Meg asked.

Dionysus laughed. 'And people say there are no stupid questions. But if you trust your friend Lululemon –'

'Luguselwa,' Meg growled.

'Whatever. Shouldn't you hurry back to her?'

Nico folded his arms. 'I'll need some time before we leave. If I want to ask my new friends a favour, I can't show up empty-handed.'

'Oh, ick,' Will said. 'You're not going to . . .'

Nico raised an eyebrow at him, like, *Really, boyfriend? You're already in the doghouse.*

Will sighed. 'Fine. I'll go with you to . . . gather supplies.'

Nico nodded. 'That'll take us most of the day. Apollo, Meg, how about you stay at camp and rest up for now? The four of us can leave for the city first thing tomorrow morning. That should still give us enough time.'

'But . . .' My voice faltered.

I wanted to protest, but I wasn't sure on what grounds. Only a day at Camp Half-Blood before our final push towards destruction and death? That wasn't nearly enough time to

procrastinate! 'I, uh . . . I thought a quest had to be formally authorized.'

'I formally authorize it,' Dionysus said.

'But it can only be three people!' I said.

Dionysus looked at Will, Nico and me. 'I'm only counting three.'

'Hey!' Meg said. 'I'm coming, too!'

Dionysus pointedly ignored her.

'We don't even have a plan!' I said. 'Once we find this
secret path, what do we do with it? Where do we start?'

'We start with Rachel,' Will said, still picking glumly at
his muffin. 'A Dare *reveals the path that was unknown.*'

The truth pierced the base of my neck like an acupunc-
ture needle.

Of course, Will's interpretation made total sense. Our
old friend would probably be at home in Brooklyn, just
starting her summer break, not expecting me to crash her
place and demand help.

'Rachel Elizabeth Dare,' I said. 'My Delphic priestess.'

'Excellent,' Dionysus said. 'Now that you've got your
suicidal quest figured out, can we please finish breakfast?
And stop hogging the syrup, McCaffrey. Other people have
pancakes, too.'

11

I apologize
To my arrow, and undies,
And, well, everything.

WHAT WOULD YOU DO IF YOU ONLY HAD
one day at Camp Half-Blood?

Perhaps you'd partake in a game of capture the flag,
or ride a pegasus over the beach, or laze in the meadow
enjoying the sunshine and the sweet fragrance of ripening
strawberries.

All good choices. I did none of them.

I spent my day running around in a panic, trying to
prepare myself for imminent death.

After breakfast, Nico refused to share any more information about the mysterious cave-runners. 'You'll find out
tomorrow' was all he said.

When I asked Will, he clammed up and looked so sad I
didn't have the heart to press him.

Dionysus probably could have enlightened me, but he'd
already checked us off his to-do list.

'I told you, Apollo, the world has many crises. Just
this morning, scientists released another study tying soda
to hypertension. If they continue to disparage the name of

Diet Coke, I will have to smite someone!' He stormed off to plot his revenge on the health industry.

I thought Meg, at least, would stay at my side as we got ready for our quest. Instead, she chose to spend her morning planting squash with the Demeter cabin. That's correct, dear reader. She chose ornamental gourds over me.

My first stop was the Ares cabin, where I asked Sherman Yang if he had any helpful intel on Nero's tower.

'It's a fortress,' he said. 'A frontal attack would be –'

'Suicide,' I guessed. 'No secret entrances?'

'Not that I know of. If there were, they'd be heavily guarded and set with traps.' He got a faraway look on his face. 'Maybe motion-activated flamethrowers. That would be cool.'

I began to wonder if Sherman would be more helpful as an advisor to Nero.

'Is it possible,' I asked, 'that Nero could have a doomsday weapon in place? For instance, enough Greek fire to destroy New York at the push of a button?'

'Whoa . . .' Sherman developed the lovestruck expression of someone seeing Aphrodite for the first time. 'That would be amazing. I mean *bad*. That would be bad. But . . . yeah, it's possible. With his wealth and resources? The amount of time he's had to plan? Sure. He'd need a central storage facility and a delivery system for rapid dispersal. My guess? It would be underground – to take advantage of the city's pipes, sewers, tunnels and whatnot. You think he's really got something like that? When do we leave for battle?'

I realized I may have told Sherman Yang too much. 'I'll get back to you,' I muttered, and beat a hasty retreat.

Next stop: the Athena cabin.

I asked their current head counsellor, Malcolm, if he had any information about the Tower of Nero or creatures called 'cave-runners,' or any hypotheses about why a Gaul like Luguselwa might be working for Nero, and whether or not she could be trusted.

Malcolm paced the cabin, frowning at various wall maps and bookshelves. 'I could do some research,' he offered. 'We could come up with a solid intelligence dossier and a plan of attack.'

'That – that would be amazing!'

'It'll take us about four weeks. Maybe three, if we push it. When do you have to leave?'

I exited the cabin in tears.

Before lunchtime, I decided to consult my weapon of last resort: the Arrow of Dodona. I moved into the woods, thinking perhaps the arrow would be more prophetic if I brought it closer to its place of origin, the Grove of Dodona, where trees whispered the future and every branch dreamed of growing up to be a Shakespeare-spouting projectile. Also, I wanted to be far enough from the cabins that no one would see me talking to an inanimate object.

I updated the arrow on the latest developments and prophecy verses. Then, gods help me, I asked its advice.

I TOLDST THOU BEFORE, the arrow said. *I SEEST NO OTHER INTERPRETATION. THOU MUST TRUST THE EMPEROR'S OWN.*

'Meaning Luguselwa,' I said. 'Meaning I should surrender myself to Nero, because a Gaul I barely know tells me it's the only way to stop the emperor.'

VERILY, said the arrow.

'And seest thou – Can you see what will happen after we surrender?'

NAY.

'Maybe if I brought you back to the Grove of Dodona?'

NAY! It spoke so forcefully that it almost rattled out of my grasp.

I stared at the arrow, waiting for more, but I got the feeling its outburst had surprised even it.

'So . . . are you just making horse sounds now?'

A FIG! it cursed. At least, I assumed it was a swear and not a lunch order. *TAKEST ME NOT TO THE GROVE, PERNICIOUS LESTER! THINKEST THOU I SHOULDST BE WELCOMED THERE, MY QUEST INCOMPLETE?*

Its tone wasn't easy to understand, since its voice resonated straight into the plates of my skull, but I thought it sounded . . . hurt.

'I – I'm sorry,' I said. 'I didn't realize –'

OF COURSE THOU DIDST NOT. Its fletching rippled. *I LEFT NOT WILLINGLY FROM MY HOME, O LESTER. I WAS FORCED, CAST OUT! ONE SMALL BRANCH, EXPENDABLE, FORGETTABLE, EXILED FROM THE CHORUS OF TREES UNTIL I SHOULDST PROVE MYSELF! IF NOW I RETURNED, THE ENTIRE GROVE WOULD LAUGH. THE HUMILIATION . . .*

It became still in my hand.

FORGETTEST THOU WHAT I SAID, it hummed. *PRETENDEST THOU IT NEVER HAPPENED.*

I wasn't sure what to say. All my years as a god of archery had not prepared me for playing therapist to an arrow. And yet . . . I felt terrible for the poor projectile. I had hauled it across the country and back again. I had complained about its shortcomings. I had belittled its advice and made fun of its lofty language. I had never stopped to consider that it had feelings, hopes, dreams and perhaps even a family as dysfunctional and unsupportive as mine.

I wondered, bitterly, if there was *anyone* I hadn't neglected, hurt or overlooked during my time as a mortal – strike that – during my four thousand years of existence, period. I could only be grateful that my shoes were not sentient. Or my underwear. Gods, I would never be able to stop apologizing.

'I have used you poorly,' I told the arrow. 'I'm sorry. Once we've succeeded in our quest, I'll return you to the Grove of Dodona, and you'll be welcomed back as a hero.'

I could feel the pulse in my fingertips beating against the arrow's shaft. It remained quiet for six heartbeats.

AYE, it said at last. *DOUBTLESS YOU ARE RIGHT.*

As far as red flags went, the Arrow of Dodona telling me I was right was the reddest and flaggiest I could imagine.

'What is it?' I demanded. 'You've seen something in the future? Something bad?'

Its point shuddered. *WORRY NOT, THOU. I MUST NEEDS RETURN TO MY QUIVER. THOU SHOULDST SPEAK TO MEG.*

The arrow fell silent. I wanted to know more. I knew there *was* more. But the arrow had signalled that it was done talking, and, for once, I thought I should consider what it wanted.

I returned it to the quiver and began my hike back to the cabins.

Perhaps I was overreacting. Just because my life was doom and gloom did not necessarily mean the arrow was doomed, too.

Maybe it was just being evasive because, at the end of my journeys, whether I died or not, it was planning to pitch my life story to one of the Muses' new streaming services. I would be remembered only as a limited series on Calliope+.

Yes, that was probably it. What a relief . . .

I was almost to the edge of the forest when I heard laughter – the laughter of *dryads*, I deduced, based on my centuries of experience as a dryad stalker. I followed the sound to a nearby outcropping of rocks, where Meg McCaffrey and Peaches were hanging out with half a dozen tree spirits.

The dryads were fawning over the fruit spirit, who, being no fool, was doing his best to look adorable for the ladies – which meant not baring his fangs, growling or showing his claws. He was also wearing a clean loincloth, which was more than he'd ever done around me.

'Oh, he's precious!' said one of the dryads, ruffling Peaches' leafy green hair.

'These little toes!' said another, giving him a foot massage.

The *karpos* purred and fluttered his branchy wings. The dryads did not seem to mind that he looked like a killer baby grown from a chia kit.

Meg tickled his belly. 'Yeah, he's pretty awesome. I found him –'

That's when the dryads saw me.

'Gotta go,' said one, disappearing in a whirl of leaves.

'Yeah, I have this . . . thing,' said another, and poofed into pollen.

The other dryads followed suit, until it was only Meg, Peaches, me and the lingering scent of Dryadique™ bio-degradable shampoo.

Peaches growled at me. 'Peaches.'

Which no doubt meant *Dude, you scared off my groupies.*

'Sorry. I was just . . .' I waved my hand. 'Passing by? Wandering around, waiting to die? I'm not sure.'

'S'okay,' Meg said. 'Pull up a rock.'

Peaches snarled, perhaps doubting my willingness to massage his feet.

Meg pacified him by scratching behind his ear, which reduced him to a purring puddle of bliss.

It felt good to sit, even on a jagged chunk of quartz. The sunshine was pleasant without being too warm. (Yes, I used to be a sun god. Now I am a temperature wimp.)

Meg was dressed in her Sally Jackson Valentine's Day outfit. The pink dress had been washed since our arrival, thank goodness, but the knees of her white leggings were newly stained from her morning digging in the squash garden. Her glasses had been cleaned. The rhinestone-studded rims glittered, and I could actually see her eyes through the lenses. Her hair had been shampooed and corralled with red hair clips. I suspected somebody in the Demeter cabin had given her some loving care in the grooming department.

Not that I could criticize. I was wearing clothes Will Solace had bought for me.

'Good gardening?' I asked.

'Awesome.' She wiped her nose on her sleeve. 'This new kid, Steve? He made a potato erupt in Douglas's jeans.'

'That does sound awesome.'

'Wish we could stay.' She tossed a chip of quartz into the grass.

My heart felt like an open blister. Thinking about the horrible things that awaited us back in Manhattan, I wanted to grant Meg's wish more than anything. She should have been able to stay at camp, laughing and making friends and watching potatoes erupt from her cabinmates' jeans like any normal kid.

I marvelled at how calm and content she appeared. I'd heard that young people were especially resilient when it came to surviving trauma. They were much tougher than, say, your average immortal. And yet, just for once, I wished I could provide Meg with a safe place to be, without the pressure of having to leave immediately to stop an apocalypse.

'I could go alone,' I found myself saying. 'I could surrender to Nero. There's no reason you have to –'

'Stop,' she ordered.

My throat closed up.

I could do nothing but wait as Meg twirled a blade of grass between her fingers.

'You say that because you don't trust me?' she asked at last.

'*What?*' Her question allowed me to speak again. 'Meg, no, that's not –'

'I betrayed you once,' she said. 'Right here in these woods.'

She didn't sound sad or ashamed about it, the way she once might have. She spoke with a sort of dreamy disbelief, as if trying to recall the person she'd been six months ago. That was a problem I could relate to.

'Meg, we've both changed a lot since then,' I said. 'I trust you with my life. I'm just worried about Nero . . . how he'll try to hurt you, *use* you.'

She gave me a look that was almost teacherly, as if cautioning *Are you sure that's your final answer?*

I realized what she must be thinking: I claimed I wasn't worried about her betraying me, but I *was* worried about how Nero could manipulate her. Wasn't that the same thing?

'I have to go back,' Meg insisted. 'I have to see if I'm strong enough.'

Peaches cuddled up next to her as if he had no such concerns.

Meg patted his leafy wings. 'Maybe I've got stronger. But, when I go back to the palace, will it be enough? Can I remember to be who I am now and not . . . who I was then?'

I didn't think she expected an answer. But it occurred to me that perhaps I should be asking myself the same question.

Since Jason Grace's death, I'd spent sleepless nights wondering if I could keep my promise to him. Assuming I made it back to Mount Olympus, could I remember what it was like to be human, or would I slip back into being the self-centred god I used to be?

Change is a fragile thing. It requires time and distance. Survivors of abuse, like Meg, have to get away from their abusers. Going back to that toxic environment was the worst thing she could do. And former arrogant gods like me couldn't hang around other arrogant gods and expect to stay unsullied.

But I supposed Meg was right. Going back was the only way to see how strong we'd got, even if it meant risking everything.

'Okay, I'm worried,' I admitted. 'About you. And me. I don't know the answer to your question.'

Meg nodded. 'But we have to try.'

'Together, then,' I said. 'One more time, into the lair of the Beast.'

'Peaches,' Peaches murmured.

Meg smirked. 'He says he'll stay here at camp. He needs some *me* time.'

I hate it when fruit spirits have more sense than me.

That afternoon I filled two quivers with arrows. I polished and restrung my bow. From the cabin's store of musical instruments, I picked a new ukulele – not as nice or durable as the bronze combat ukulele I had lost, but still a fearsome stringed instrument. I made sure I had plenty of medical supplies in my backpack, along with food and drink and the usual change of clothes and clean underwear. (I apologize, underwear!)

I moved through the afternoon hours in a daze, feeling as if I were preparing for a funeral . . . specifically my own. Austin and Kayla hovered nearby, trying to be helpful when they could, but without invading my space.

'We talked with Sherman and Malcolm,' Kayla told me. 'We'll be on standby.'

'If there is *any* chance we can help,' Austin said, 'we'll be ready to roll at a moment's notice.'

Words were not sufficient to thank them, but I hope they saw the gratitude in my teary, bruised, acne-pocked face.

That night we had the usual singalong at the campfire. No one mentioned our quest. No one offered a going-away good-luck speech. The first-time campers were still so new to the demigod experience, so amazed by it all, I doubted they would even notice we were gone. Perhaps that was for the best.

They didn't need to know how much was at stake: not just the burning of New York, but whether the Oracle of Delphi would ever be able to give them prophecies and offer them quests, or whether the future would be controlled and predetermined by an evil emperor and a giant reptile.

If I failed, these young demigods would grow up in a world where Nero's tyranny was the norm and there were only eleven Olympians.

I tried to shove those thoughts to the back of my mind. Austin and I played a duet for saxophone and guitar. Then

Kayla joined us to lead the camp in a rousing version of 'The Wheels on the Chariot Go 'Round and 'Round'. We roasted marshmallows, and Meg and I tried to enjoy our final hours among our friends.

Small mercies: that night I had no dreams.

At dawn, Will shook me awake. He and Nico had returned from wherever they had been 'gathering supplies', but he didn't want to talk about it.

Together, he and I met Meg and Nico on the road along the far side of Half-Blood Hill, where the camp's shuttle bus waited to take us to Rachel Elizabeth Dare's house in Brooklyn, and – one way or another – the final few days of my mortal life.

12

Billionaire's warehouse.
Grab your chocolate drink quickly,
The cows are watching.

BROOKLYN.

Normally, the greatest dangers there are congested traf-fic, expensive poke bowls and not enough tables at the local coffee shops for all the aspiring screenwriters. That morning, however, I could tell that our shuttle driver, Argus the giant, was keeping his eyes open for trouble.

This was a big deal for Argus, since he had a hundred sets of eyes all over his body. (I had not actually counted them, nor had I asked if he ever got black eyes on his pos-terior from sitting too long.)

As we drove down Flushing Avenue, his blue peepers blinked and twitched along his arms, around his neck and on his cheeks and chin, trying to look in every direction at once.

Clearly, he sensed that something was wrong. I felt it, too. There was an electric heaviness in the air, like just before Zeus hurled a massive lightning bolt or Beyoncé dropped a new album. The world was holding its breath.

Argus pulled over a block from the Dare house as if he feared to get any closer.

The harbour-front area had once been working docklands for local fishermen, if I recalled correctly from the 1800s. Then it had been populated mostly by railyards and factories. You could still see the pilings of decayed piers jutting out of the water. Redbrick shells and concrete smokestacks of old workhouses sat dark and abandoned like temple ruins. One open stretch of railyard was still in operation, with a few heavily graffitied freight cars on the tracks.

But, like the rest of Brooklyn, the neighbourhood was rapidly becoming gentrified. Across the street, a building that looked like a one-time machine shop now housed a café promising avocado bagels and pineapple matcha. Two blocks down, cranes loomed from the pit of a construction site. Signs on the fences read HARD HAT AREA, KEEP OUT! and LUXURY RENTALS COMING SOON! I wondered if the construction workers were required to wear luxury hard hats.

The Dare compound itself was a former industrial warehouse transformed into an ultra-modern estate. It occupied an acre of waterfront, making it approximately five billion times larger than the average New York City home. The facade was concrete and steel – like a combination art museum and bombproof bunker.

I had never met Mr Dare, the real-estate mogul, but I felt I didn't need to. I understood gods and their palaces. Mr Dare was operating along the same principles: look at me, look at my massive pad, spread word of my greatness. You may leave your burnt offerings on the welcome mat.

As soon as we were out of the van, Argus floored the accelerator. He sped off in a cloud of exhaust and premium gravel.

Will and Nico exchanged looks.

'I guess he figured we won't need a ride back,' Will said.

'We won't,' Nico said darkly. 'Come on.'

He led us to the main gates – huge panels of corrugated steel without any obvious opening mechanism or even an intercom. I suppose if you had to ask, you couldn't afford to go in.

Nico stood there and waited.

Meg cleared her throat. 'Uh, so –?'

The gates rolled open of their own accord. Standing before us was Rachel Elizabeth Dare.

Like all great artists, she was barefoot. (Leonardo would simply *never* put his sandals on.) Her jeans were covered in marker doodles that had got more complex and colourful over the years. Her white tank top was splattered with paint. Across her face, competing for attention with her orange freckles, were streaks of what looked like acrylic ultramarine blue. Some of it dotted her red hair like confetti.

'Come in quickly,' she said, as if she'd been expecting us for hours. 'The cattle are watching.'

'Yes, I said *cattle*,' she told me, pre-empting my question as we walked through the house. 'And, no, I'm not crazy. Hi, Meg. Will, Nico. Follow me. We've got the place to ourselves.'

This was like saying we had Yankee Stadium to ourselves. Great, I guess, but I wasn't sure what to do with it.

The mansion was organized around a central atrium – Roman style, looking inwards, so peons outside the walls couldn't ruin your view. But at least the Romans had gardens. Mr Dare seemed to believe only in concrete, metal and gravel. His atrium featured a giant stack of iron and stone that was either a brilliant avant-garde sculpture or a pile of leftover building materials.

We followed Rachel down a wide hall of painted cement, then up a floating stairway into the second level, which I would've called the living quarters, except that nothing about the mansion felt very alive. Rachel herself seemed small and out of place here, a warm, colourful aberration padding in her bare feet through an architectural mausoleum.

At least her room had floor-to-ceiling windows that overlooked the neighbouring railyard and the river beyond. Sunlight flooded in, illuminating the oak floors, the speckled tarps that doubled as throw rugs, several beanbag chairs, some open cans of paint, and massive easels where Rachel had six different canvases going at once. Spread across the back part of the floor was another half-finished painting that Rachel seemed to be working on with drips and splashes à la Jackson Pollock. Shoved in one corner were a refrigerator and a simple futon, as if eating and sleeping were complete afterthoughts for her.

'Wow.' Will moved to the windows to soak up the view and the sunshine.

Meg made a beeline for the refrigerator.

Nico drifted to the easels. 'These are amazing.' He traced the air, following the swirls of Rachel's paint across the canvas.

'Eh, thanks,' Rachel said absently. 'Just warm-ups, really.'

They looked more like full aerobic workouts to me – huge, aggressive brushstrokes, thick wedges of colour applied with a mason's trowel, splashes so large she must have swung an entire can of paint to apply them. At first glance, the works appeared to be abstract. Then I stepped back, and the shapes resolved into scenes.

That maroon square was the Waystation in Indianapolis. Those swirls were griffins in flight. A second canvas showed flames engulfing the Burning Maze and, floating in the upper right quadrant, a string of hazy glowing ships – the fleet of Caligula. A third painting . . . I began to get misty-eyed all over again. It was a funeral pyre – the last rites of Jason Grace.

'You've started having visions again,' I said.

She looked at me with a kind of resentful yearning, as if she were on a sugar detox and I was waving around a chocolate bar. 'Only glimpses. Every time you free an Oracle, I get a few moments of clarity. Then the fog settles again.' She pressed her fingertips against her forehead. 'It's like Python is inside my brain, toying with me. Sometimes I think . . .' She faltered, as if the idea were too disturbing to say aloud. 'Just tell me you're going to take him down. *Soon.*'

I nodded, not trusting myself to speak. It was one thing for Python to squat in my sacred caverns of Delphi. It was another for him to invade the mind of my chosen Pythia, the priestess of my prophecies. I had accepted Rachel Elizabeth Dare as my most important Oracle. I was responsible for her. If I failed to defeat Python, he would continue to grow stronger. He would eventually control the very flow of the future. And since Rachel was inextricably linked to the Delphic . . . No. I couldn't bear to think what that might mean for her.

'Whoa.' Meg surfaced from Rachel's refrigerator like a diver with gold doubloons. In her hand was a Yoo-hoo chocolate drink. 'Can I have one?'

Rachel managed a smile. 'Help yourself, Meg. And, hey, di Angelo –' she pushed him playfully away from the canvas he'd been ogling – 'don't brush against the art! I don't care about the paintings, but if you get any colour on you, you'll ruin that whole black-and-white aesthetic you've got going.'

'Hmph,' said Nico.

'Now what were we talking about . . . ?' Rachel mused.

Over at the window, Will tapped his knuckles against the glass. 'Are those the cattle?'

'Oh, right!' Rachel steered us in that direction.

About a hundred yards away, between us and the river, a line of three cattle cars sat on the railway tracks. Each car was occupied, as evidenced by the bovine snouts that occasionally poked out between the bars.

'Seems wrong to just leave them parked there,' Will said. 'It's going to get hot today.'

Rachel nodded. 'They've been there since yesterday. The cars just kind of appeared overnight. I've called the freight company, and the animal cruelty hotline. It's like the cars don't exist. Nobody has any record of them. Nobody will come out to check on them. Nobody's brought the animals any food or water –'

'We should free them,' Meg said.

'That would be a very bad idea,' Nico said.

Meg frowned. 'Do you hate cows?'

'I don't hate –' Nico paused. 'Well, okay, I'm not super fond of cows. But that's not the point. Those can't be ordinary animals.' He glanced at Rachel. 'You said they just appeared. People don't recognize they exist. You said the cattle were *watching?*'

Rachel edged away from the window. 'Sometimes I can see their eyes between the bars. They'll be looking right at me. And just about the time you arrived, they went crazy, rocking the cars like they were trying to get out. That's when I checked the security cameras and saw you guys at the front gate. Normally, I am not paranoid about cattle. But these . . . I don't know. Something doesn't feel right. At first, I thought it might have something to do with our neighbours . . .'

She gestured north along the waterfront to an unremarkable cluster of old residential towers. 'They do strange things sometimes.'

'In the housing project?' I asked.

She arched her eyebrows. 'You don't see the big mansion?'

'What mansion?'

She glanced at Will, Nico, Meg, who all shook their heads.

'Well,' Rachel said, 'you'll have to take my word for it. There's a big mansion over there. Lots of weird goings-on.'

We didn't argue with her. Though fully mortal, Rachel had the rare gift of clear sight. She could see through the Mist and other magical barriers better than most demigods, and apparently better than most Lesters.

She muttered, 'Once I saw a penguin waddling around their back deck –'

'A what-now?' Nico asked.

'But leaving cows in boxes like that for days without food or water, that seems like something different,' she said. 'Crueller. Those cows must be bad news.'

Meg scowled. 'They seem peaceful enough now. I still say we free them.'

'And then what?' Nico asked. 'Even if they're not dangerous, we just let three carloads of cattle wander around Brooklyn? I'm with Rachel. Something about this . . .' He looked like he was trying to dredge something from his memory with no luck – another feeling I knew well. 'I say we leave them alone.'

'That's mean!' said Meg. 'We can't –'

'Friends, please.' I stepped between Nico and Meg before things escalated into the biggest Hades/Demeter smackdown since Persephone's wedding shower. 'Since the cattle seem to be calm at the moment, let's circle back to that subject after we've discussed what we came here to discuss, yes?'

'The Tower of Nero,' Rachel surmised.

Will's eyes widened. 'Have you seen the future?'

'No, William, I used simple logic. But I *do* have some information that might help you. Everybody grab a Yoo-hoo and a beanbag, and let's chat about our least-favourite emperor.'

13

There is no blueprint
For taking down emperors.
Wait. Rachel has one.

WE CIRCLED UP OUR BEANBAGS.

Rachel spread blueprints across the floor between us. 'You guys know about the emperor's fasces?'

Meg and I shared a look that meant *I wish we didn't.*

'We're familiar,' I said. 'In San Francisco, we destroyed the fasces of Commodus and Caligula, which made them vulnerable enough to kill. I assume you're suggesting we do the same with Nero?'

Rachel pouted. 'That killed my big reveal. It took me a long time to figure this out.'

'You did great,' Meg assured her. 'Apollo just likes to hear himself talk.'

'I beg your pardon –'

'Did you find the exact location of Nero's fasces?' Nico interrupted. 'Because that would be really useful.'

Rachel straightened a bit. 'I think so, yeah. These are the original designs for Nero's tower. They were *not* easy to get.'

Will whistled appreciatively. 'I bet many Bothans died to bring us this information.'

Rachel stared at him. 'What?'

Nico sighed. 'I'm guessing that was a Star Wars reference. My boyfriend is a Star Wars geek of the worst kind.'

'Okay, Signor Myth-o-magic. If you would just watch the original trilogy . . .' Will looked at the rest of us for support and found nothing but blank expressions. 'Nobody? Oh, my gods. You people are hopeless.'

'Anyway,' Rachel continued, 'my theory is that Nero would keep his fasces here.' She tapped a point about halfway up the tower's cross-section schematic. 'Right in the middle of the building. It's the only level with no exterior windows. Special-elevator access only. All doors are Celestial-bronze-reinforced. I mean, the whole building is a fortress, but this level would be *impossible* to break into.'

Meg nodded. 'I know the floor you mean. We were never allowed in there. *Ever.*'

A chill settled over our little group. Goose bumps dotted Will's arms. The idea of Meg, *our* Meg, stuck in that fortress of evil was more disturbing than any number of mysterious cows or penguins.

Rachel flipped to another blueprint – a floor plan of the ultra-secure level. 'Here. This vault has to be it. You could never get close, unless . . .' She pointed to a nearby room. 'If I'm reading these designs correctly, this would be a holding cell for prisoners.' Her eyes were bright with excitement. 'If you could get yourself captured, then convince someone on the inside to help you escape –'

'Lu was right.' Meg looked at me triumphantly. 'I *told* you.'

Rachel frowned, bringing the blue paint spots on her forehead into a tighter cluster. 'Who is Lu?'

We told her about Luguselwa, and the special bonding time we'd shared before I threw her off a building.

Rachel shook her head. 'Okay . . . so if you've already thought of all my ideas, why am I even talking?'

'No, no,' Will said. 'You're *confirming*. And we trust you more than . . . er, other sources.'

I hoped he meant Lu and not me.

'Besides,' Nico said, 'you have actual blueprints.' He studied the floor plan. 'Why would Nero keep his prisoners on the same level as his most valuable possession, though?'

'Keep your fasces close,' I speculated, 'and your enemies closer.'

'Maybe,' Rachel said. 'But the fasces is heavily protected, and not just by security features or regular guards. There's something *in* that vault, something alive . . .'

It was my turn to get goosebumps. 'How do you know this?'

'A vision. Just a glimpse, almost like . . . like Python *wanted* me to see it. The figure looked like a man, but his head –'

'A lion's head,' I guessed.

Rachel flinched. 'Exactly. And slithering around his body –'

'Snakes.'

'So you know what it is?'

I grasped for the memory. As usual, it was just out of reach. You may wonder why I didn't have a better handle on my godly knowledge, but my mortal brain was an imperfect storage facility. I can only compare my frustration to how you might feel when taking a picky reading-comprehension quiz. You are assigned fifty pages. You actually *read* them. Then the teacher decides to test you by asking, *Quick! What was the first word on page thirty-seven?*

'I'm not sure,' I admitted. 'Some sort of powerful guardian, obviously. Our most recent prophecy stanza mentioned a *lion, snake-entwined.*' I filled Rachel in on our literally eye-popping ride with the Grey Sisters.

Nico scowled at the blueprints, as if he might intimidate them into giving up their secrets. 'So, whatever the guardian is, Nero trusts it with his life. Meg, I thought you said Luguselwa was this huge, mighty warrior?'

'She is.'

'So why can't she take out this guardian and destroy the fasces herself?' he asked. 'Why does she need . . . you know, you guys to get yourself captured?'

Nico phrased the question diplomatically, but I heard what he meant. If Lu couldn't take out this guardian, how could I, Lester Papadopoulos, the Not So Huge or Mighty?

'Dunno,' Meg said. 'But there must be a reason.'

Like Lu would rather see us get killed, I thought, but I knew better than to say that.

'Let's assume Lu is right,' Nico said. 'You get captured and put in this cell. She lets you out. You kill the guardian, destroy the fasces, weaken Nero, hooray. Even then, and I'm sorry to be a Debbie Downer –'

'I am calling you Debbie Downer from now on,' Will said gleefully.

'Shut up, Solace. Even *then*, you've got half a tower and

Nero's whole army of security guards between you and his throne room, right?'

'We've dealt with whole armies before,' Meg said.

Nico laughed, which I didn't know he was capable of. 'Okay. I like the confidence. But wasn't there that little detail about Nero's panic switch? If he feels threatened, he can blow up New York at the push of a button. How do you stop *that?*'

'Oh . . .' Rachel muttered a curse not appropriate for priestesses. 'That must be what *these* are for.'

Her hands trembling, she flipped to another page of the blueprints.

'I asked my dad's senior architect about them,' she said. 'He couldn't figure them out. Said there's no way the blue-prints could be right. Sixty feet underground, surrounded by triple retaining walls. Giant vats, like the building has its own reservoir or water-treatment facility. It's connected to the city's sewer mains, but the separate electrical grid, the generators, these pumps . . . It's like the whole system is designed to blast water *outwards* and flood the city.'

'Except not with water,' Will said. 'With Greek fire.'

'Debbie Downer,' Nico muttered.

I stared at the schematics, trying to imagine how such a system could have been built. During our last battle in the Bay Area, Meg and I had seen more Greek fire than had existed in the whole history of the Byzantine Empire. Nero had more. Exponentially more. It seemed impossible, but the emperor had had hundreds of years to plan, and almost infinite resources. Leave it to Nero to spend most of his money on a self-destruct system.

'He'll burn up, too,' I marvelled. 'All his family and guards, and his precious tower.'

'Maybe not,' Rachel said. 'The building is designed for self-containment. Thermal insulation, closed air circulation, reinforced heat-resistant materials. Even the windows are special blast-proof panes. Nero could burn the city down around him, and his tower would be the only thing left standing.'

Meg crumpled her empty Yoo-hoo box. 'Sounds like him.'

Will studied the plans. 'I'm not an expert on reading these things, but where are the access points to the vats?'

'There's only one,' Rachel said. 'Sealed off, automated, heavily guarded and under constant surveillance. Even if you could break or sneak through, you wouldn't have enough time to disable the generators before Nero pushed his panic button.'

'Unless,' Nico said, 'you tunnelled your way into those reservoirs from underneath. You could sabotage his whole delivery system without Nero ever knowing.'

'Aaand we're back to *that* terrible idea,' Will said.

'They're the best tunnellers in the world,' Nico insisted. 'They could get through all that concrete and steel and Celestial bronze with no one even noticing. This is *our* part of the plan, Will. While Apollo and Meg are getting themselves captured, keeping Nero distracted, *we* go underground and take out his doomsday weapon.'

'Hold on, Nico,' I said. 'It's high time you explained who these cave-runners are.'

The son of Hades fixed his dark eyes on me as if I were

another layer of concrete to dig through. 'A few months ago, I made contact with the troglodytes.'

I choked on a laugh. Nico's claim was the most ridiculous thing I'd heard since Mars swore to me that Elvis Presley was alive on, well, Mars.

'Troglodytes are a myth,' I said.

Nico frowned. 'A god is telling a demigod that something is a myth?'

'Oh, you know what I mean! They aren't *real*. That trashy author Aelian made them up to sell more copies of his books back in Ancient Rome. A race of subterranean humanoids who eat lizards and fight bulls? Please. I've never seen them. Not once in my millennia of life.'

'Did it ever occur to you,' Nico said, 'that troglodytes might go out of their way to hide from a sun god? They hate the light.'

'Well, I –'

'Did you ever actually look for them?' Nico persisted.

'Well, no, but –'

'They're real,' Will confirmed. 'Unfortunately, Nico found them.'

I tried to process this information. I'd never taken Aelian's stories about the troglodytes seriously. To be fair, though, I hadn't believed in rocs, either, until the day one flew over my sun chariot and bowel-bombed me. That was a bad day for me, the roc and several countries that my swerving chariot set on fire.

'If you say so. But do you know how to find the troglodytes again?' I asked. 'Do you think they would help us?'

'Those are two different questions,' Nico said. 'But I

think I can convince them to help. Maybe. If they like the gift I got them. And if they don't kill us on sight.'

'I love this plan,' Will grumbled.

'Guys,' Rachel said, 'you forgot about *me*.'

I stared at her. 'What do you mean?'

'I'm coming, too.'

'Certainly not!' I protested. 'You're mortal!'

'And essential,' Rachel said. 'Your prophecy told you so. A Dare *reveals the path that was unknown*. All I've done so far is show you blueprints, but I can do more. I can see things you can't. Besides, I've got a personal stake in this. If you don't survive the Tower of Nero, you can't fight Python. And if you can't defeat him . . .'

Her voice faltered. She swallowed and doubled over, choking.

At first, I thought some of her Yoo-hoo might have gone down the wrong way. I patted her on the back unhelpfully. Then she sat up again, her back rigid, her eyes glowing. Smoke billowed from her mouth, which is not something normally caused by chocolate drinks.

Will, Nico and Meg scooted away in their beanbags.

I would have done the same, but for half a second I thought I understood what was happening: a prophecy! Her Delphic powers had broken through!

Then, with sickening dread, I realized this smoke was the wrong colour: pallid yellow instead of dark green. And the stench . . . sour and decayed, like it was wafting straight from Python's armpits.

When Rachel spoke, it was with Python's voice – a gravelly rumble, charged with malice.

'Apollo's flesh and blood shall soon be mine.
Alone he must descend into the dark,
This sibyl never again to see his sign,
Lest grappling with me till his final spark
The god dissolves, leaving not a mark.'

The smoke dissipated. Rachel slumped against me, her body limp.

CRASH! A sound like shattering metal shook my bones. I was so terrified that I wasn't sure if the noise was from somewhere outside, or if it was just my nervous system shutting down.

Nico got up and ran to the windows. Meg scrambled over to help me with Rachel. Will checked her pulse and started to say, 'We need to get her –'

'Hey!' Nico turned from the window, his face pale with shock. 'We have to get out of here *now*. The cows are attacking.'

14

I fall in a hole
And choke on my own anger.
I am a cow. Moo.

IN NO CONTEXT CAN *THE COWS ARE ATTACK-*
ing be considered good news.

Will picked up Rachel in a firefighter's lift – for a gentle
healer, he was deceptively strong – and together we jogged
over to join Nico at the window.

In the railyard below, the cows were staging a revolu-
tion. They'd busted through the sides of their cattle cars
like an avalanche through a picket fence and were now
stampeding towards the Dare residence. I suspected the
cattle hadn't been *trapped* in those cars at all. They'd simply
been waiting for the right moment to break out and kill us.

They were beautiful in a nightmarish way. Each was
twice the size of a normal bovine, with bright blue eyes and
shaggy red hair that rippled in dizzying whorls like a living
Van Gogh painting. Both cows and bulls – yes, I could tell
the difference; I was a cow expert – possessed huge curved
horns that would have made excellent drinking cups for the
largest and thirstiest of Lu's Celtic kinfolk.

A line of freight cars stood between us and the cows, but

that didn't deter the herd. They barrelled straight through, toppling and flattening the cars like origami boxes.

'Do we fight?' Meg asked, her voice full of doubt.

The name of these creatures suddenly came back to me – too late, as usual. Earlier, I'd mentioned that troglodytes were known for fighting bulls, but I hadn't put the facts together. Perhaps Nero had parked the cattle cars here as a trap, knowing we might seek out Rachel's help. Or perhaps their presence was simply the Fates' cruel way of laughing at me. *Oh, you want to play the troglodyte card? We counter with cows!*

'Fighting would be no use,' I said miserably. 'Those are *tauri silvestres* – *forest bulls*, the Romans called them. Their hides cannot be pierced. According to legend, the tauri are ancestral enemies of Nico's friends, the troglodytes.'

'So *now* you believe the trogs exist?' Nico asked.

'I am learning to believe in all sorts of things that can kill me!'

The first wave of cattle reached the Dares' retaining wall. They ploughed through it and charged the house.

'We need to run!' I said, exercising my noble duty as Lord Obvious of Duh.

Nico led the way. Will followed close behind with Rachel still draped over his shoulder, Meg and me at his back.

We were halfway down the hall when the house began to shake. Cracks zigzagged up the walls. At the top of the floating staircase, we discovered (fun fact) a floating staircase will cease to float if a forest bull tries to climb it. The lower steps had been stripped from the wall. Bulls rampaged through the corridor below like a crowd of Black Friday bargain hunters, stomping on broken steps and crashing through the atrium's glass walls, renovating the Dares' house with extreme prejudice.

'At least they can't get up here,' Will said.

The floor shook again as the tauri took out another wall.

'We'll be down *there* soon enough,' Meg said. 'Is there another way out?'

Rachel groaned. 'Me. Down.'

Will eased her to her feet. She swayed and blinked, trying to process the scene below us.

'Cows,' Rachel said.

'Yeah,' Nico agreed.

Rachel pointed weakly down the hall we'd come from. 'This way.'

Using Meg as a crutch, Rachel led us back towards her bedroom. She took a sharp right, then clambered down another set of stairs into the garage. On the polished concrete floor sat two Ferraris, both bright red – because why have one midlife crisis when you can have two? In the house behind us, I could hear the cows bellowing angrily, crashing and smashing as they remodelled the Dare compound for that hot *apocalyptic barnyard* look.

'Keys,' Rachel said. 'Look for car keys!'

Will, Nico and I scrambled into action. We found no keys in the cars – that would have been too convenient. No keys on the wall hooks, in the storage bins or on the shelves. Either Mr Dare kept the keys with him at all times, or the Ferraris were meant to be purely decorative.

'Nothing!' I said.

Rachel muttered something about her father that I won't repeat. 'Never mind.' She hit a button on the wall. The garage door began to rumble open. 'I'm feeling better. We'll go on foot.'

We spilled into the street and headed north as fast as Rachel could hobble. We were half a block away when the Dare residence shuddered, groaned and imploded, exhaling a mushroom cloud of dust and debris.

'Rachel, I'm so sorry,' Will said.

'Don't care. I hated that place anyway. Dad will just move us to one of his *other* mansions.'

'But your art!' Meg said.

Rachel's expression tightened. 'Art can be made again. People can't. Keep moving!'

I knew we wouldn't have long before the tauri silvestres found us. Along this part of the Brooklyn waterfront, the blocks were long, the roads wide and the sight lines clear – perfect for a supernatural stampede. We had almost made it to the pineapple matcha café when Meg yelled, 'The Sylvesters are coming!'

'Meg,' I wheezed, 'the cows are not all named Sylvester.'

She was right about the threat, though. The demon cattle, apparently unfazed by a building falling on them, emerged from the wreckage of Chez Dare. The herd began to regroup in the middle of the street, shaking rubble from their red hides like dogs fresh from a bath.

'Get out of sight?' Nico asked, pointing to the café.

'Too late,' Will said.

The cows had spotted us. A dozen sets of blue eyes fixed on our position. The tauri raised their heads, mooed their battle moos and charged. I suppose we could still have ducked into the café, just so the cows would destroy it and save the neighbourhood from the threat of avocado bagels. Instead, we ran.

I realized this would only delay the inevitable. Even if Rachel hadn't been groggy from her snake-induced trance, we couldn't outrun the cows.

'They're gaining!' Meg yelled. 'You sure we can't fight them?'

'You want to try?' I asked. 'After what they did to the house?'

'So what's their weakness?' Rachel asked. 'They have to have an Achilles' heel!'

Why did people always assume this? Why did they obsess about an Achilles' heel? Just because *one* Greek hero had a vulnerable spot behind his foot, that didn't mean every monster, demigod and villain from Ancient Greek times also had a podiatric problem. Most monsters, in fact, did *not* have a secret weakness. They were annoying that way.

Nevertheless, I racked my brain for any factoids I might have gleaned from Aelian's trashy bestseller *On the Nature of Animals*. (Not that I normally read such things, of course.)

'Pits?' I speculated. 'I think farmers in Ethiopia used pits against the tauri.'

'Like peach pits?' Meg asked.

'No, like pits in the ground!'

'Fresh out of pits!' Rachel said.

The tauri had halved the distance between us. Another hundred yards and they would smash us into road jelly.

'There!' Nico yelled. 'Follow me!'

He sprinted into the lead.

I had to give him credit. When Nico chose a pit, he went for broke. He ran to the luxury-apartment construction site, summoned his black Stygian sword from thin air and slashed through the chain-link fence. We followed him inside, where a narrow rim of trailers and portable potties surrounded a fifty-foot-deep square crater. A giant crane rose from the centre of the chasm, its jib extending towards us at just about knee-level. The site seemed abandoned. Perhaps it was lunch hour? Perhaps all the workers were at the pineapple matcha café? Whatever the case, I was glad not to have mortals in the way of danger.

(Look at me, caring about innocent bystanders. The other Olympians would have teased me mercilessly.)

'Nico,' Rachel said, 'this is more of a canyon.'

'It's all we've got!' Nico ran to the edge of the pit . . . and jumped.

My heart felt like it jumped with him. I may have screamed.

Nico sailed over the abyss and landed on the crane's arm without even stumbling. He turned and extended his arm. 'Come on! It's only like eight feet. We practise bigger jumps at camp over lava!'

'Maybe *you* do,' I said.

The ground shook. The herd was right behind us.

Will backed up, took a running leap and landed next to Nico. He looked back at us with a reassuring nod. 'See? It's not that bad! We'll grab you!'

Rachel went next – no problem. Then Meg, the flying valentine. When her feet hit the crane, the whole arm creaked and shifted to the right, forcing my friends into a surfer's stance to catch their balance.

'Apollo,' Rachel said, 'hurry!'

She wasn't looking at me. She was looking *behind* me. The rumble of the herd was now a jackhammer in my spine.

I leaped, landing on the crane arm with the greatest belly flop since Icarus crashed into the Aegean.

My friends grabbed my arms to keep me from rolling into the abyss. I sat up, wheezing and groaning, just as the tauri reached the edge of the pit.

I hoped they would charge over and fall to their deaths like lemmings. Though, of course, lemmings don't actually do that. Bless their tiny hearts, lemmings are too smart to commit mass suicide. Unfortunately, so were the devil cows.

The first few tauri did indeed topple into the pit, unable to stop their momentum, but the rest of the herd successfully applied the brakes. There was a great deal of shoving and jostling and angry mooing from the back ranks, but it appeared that the one thing a forest bull could not smash through was another forest bull.

I muttered some bad words I hadn't used since #MinoansFirst was trending on social media. Across the narrow gap, the tauri stared at us with their murderous baby-blue eyes. The sour stench of their breath and the funk of their hides made my nostrils want to curl inwards and die. The animals fanned out around the lip of the chasm, but none tried to jump to the crane arm. Perhaps they'd learned their lesson from the Dares' floating staircase. Or perhaps they were smart enough to realize that hooves wouldn't do them much good on narrow steel girders.

Far below, the half-dozen fallen cattle were starting to get up, apparently unhurt by the fifty-foot drop. They paced around, mooing in outrage. Around the rim of the pit, the rest of the herd stood in a silent vigil as their fallen comrades grew more and more distressed. The six didn't seem physically injured, but their voices were clogged with rage. Their neck muscles bulged. Their eyes swelled. They stamped the ground, foamed at the mouth and then, one by one, fell over and lay motionless. Their bodies began to wither, their flesh dissolving until only their empty red hides remained.

Meg sobbed.

I couldn't blame her. Devilish or not, the cows' deaths were horrible to watch.

'What just happened?' Rachel's voice trembled.

'They choked on their own anger,' I said. 'I – I didn't think it was possible, but apparently Aelian got it right. Silvestres hate being stuck in pits so much they just . . . gag and die. It's the only way to kill them.'

Meg shuddered. 'That's awful.'

The herd stared at us in apparent agreement. Their blue eyes were like laser beams burning into my face. I got the feeling they'd been after us before just because it was in their nature to kill. Now, it was personal.

'So what do we do about the rest of them?' Will asked. 'Dad, you sure you can't . . .' He gestured at our bovine audience. 'I mean, you've got a god-level bow and two quivers of arrows at basically point-blank range.'

'Will!' Meg protested. Watching the bulls choke in the pit seemed to have sapped all her willingness to fight.

'I'm sorry, Meg,' Will said. 'But we're kind of stuck here.'

'It won't do any good,' I promised. 'Watch.'

I drew my bow. I nocked an arrow and aimed at the nearest cow. The cow simply stared back at me like, *Really, dude?*

I let the arrow fly – a perfect shot, right between the eyes with enough force to penetrate stone. The shaft splintered against the cow's forehead.

'Wow,' Nico said. 'Hard head.'

'It's the entire hide,' I told him. 'Look.'

I shot a second arrow at the cow's neck. The creature's shaggy red hair rippled, deflecting the arrowhead and turning the shaft downward so it skittered between the cow's legs.

'I could shoot at them all day,' I said. 'It won't help.'

'We can just wait them out,' Meg suggested. 'They'll get tired eventually and leave, right?'

Rachel shook her head. 'You forgot they waited outside my house in hot cattle cars for two days with no food or water until you showed up. I'm pretty sure these things can outlast us.'

I shivered. 'And we have a deadline. If we don't surrender to Nero by tonight . . .' I made the *explode-y hands* gesture.

Will frowned. 'You might not get the *chance* to surrender. If Nero sent these cows, he might already know you're here. His men could be on the way.'

My mouth tasted like cow breath. I remembered what

Luguselwa had told us about Nero having eyes every-where. For all I knew, this construction site was one of the Triumvirate's projects. Surveillance drones might be hover-ing overhead right now . . .

'We have to get out of here,' I decided.

'We could climb down the crane,' Will said. 'The cows couldn't follow us.'

'But then what?' Rachel asked. 'We'd be trapped in the pit.'

'Maybe not.' Nico stared into the chasm like he was calculating how many bodies could be buried in it. 'I see some good shadows down there. If we can reach the bottom safely . . . How do you all feel about shadow-travel?'

15

It's raining red cows,
But I don't care. I'm singing,
Singing in the cows!

I LOVED THE IDEA. I WAS IN FAVOUR OF ANY kind of travel that would get us away from the tauri. I would have even summoned the Grey Sisters again, except I doubted their taxi would appear on a crane jib, and, if it *did*, I suspected the sisters would instantly fall in love with Nico and Will because they were so cute together. I wouldn't wish that kind of attention on anyone.

Single file, we crawled towards the centre of the crane like a line of bedraggled ants. I tried not to look at the carcasses of the dead bulls below, but I could feel the malevolent gaze of the other silvestres as they tracked our progress. I had a sneaking suspicion they were placing bets on which of us would fall first.

Halfway to the main tower, Rachel spoke up behind me. 'Hey, are you going to tell me what happened back there?'

I glanced over my shoulder. The wind whipped Rachel's red hair around her face, making it swirl like the bulls' fur.

I tried to process her question. Had she missed the killer cows destroying her house? Had she been sleepwalking when she jumped onto the crane?

Then I realized she meant her prophetic trance. We'd been so busy running for our lives that I hadn't had time to think about it. Judging from my past experience with Delphic Oracles, I imagined Rachel had no recollection of what she'd said.

'You completed our prophecy,' I said. 'The last stanza of terza rima, plus a closing couplet. Except . . .'

'Except?'

'I'm afraid you were channelling Python.'

I crawled ahead, my eyes fixed on the tread of Meg's shoes, as I explained to Rachel what had happened: the yellow smoke boiling from her mouth, the glow of her eyes, the horribly deep voice of the serpent. I repeated the lines that she'd spoken.

She was silent for a count of five. 'That sounds bad.'

'My expert interpretation as well.'

My fingers felt numb against the girders. The prophecy's line about me dissolving, leaving no mark – those words seemed to work their way into my circulatory system, erasing my veins and arteries.

'We'll figure it out,' Rachel promised. 'Maybe Python was twisting my words. Maybe those lines aren't part of the real prophecy.'

I didn't look back, but I could hear the determination in her voice. Rachel had been dealing with Python's slithery presence in her head, possibly for months. She'd been struggling with it alone, trying to keep her sanity by working through her visions in her artwork. Today, she had been possessed by Python's voice and encircled by his poisonous fumes. Still, her first instinct was to reassure *me* that everything would be okay.

'I wish you were right,' I said. 'But the longer Python controls Delphi, the more he can poison the future. Whether he twisted your words or not, they are now part of the prophecy. What you predicted *will* happen.'

Apollo's flesh and blood shall soon be mine. The serpent's voice seemed to coil inside my head. *Alone he must descend into the dark.*

Shut up, I told the voice. But I was not Meg, and Python was not my Lester.

'Well, then,' Rachel said behind me, 'we'll just have to make sure the prophecy happens in a way that *doesn't* get you dissolved.'

She made it sound so doable . . . so *possible*.

'I don't deserve a priestess like you,' I said.

'No, you don't,' Rachel agreed. 'You can repay me by killing Python and getting the snake fumes out of my head.'

'Deal,' I said, trying to believe I could hold up my side of the bargain.

At last we reached the crane's central mast. Nico led us down the rungs of the ladder. My limbs shook with exhaustion. I was tempted to ask Meg if she could create another latticework of plants to carry us to the bottom like she'd done at Sutro Tower. I decided against it, because 1) I didn't want her to pass out from the effort, and 2) I really hated being tossed around by plants.

By the time we reached the ground, I felt wobbly and nauseated.

Nico didn't look much better. How he planned to summon enough energy to shadow-zap us to safety, I couldn't imagine. Above us, around the rim of the pit, the tauri watched in silence, their blue eyes gleaming like a string of angry Hanukkah lights.

Meg studied them warily. 'Nico, how soon can you shadow us out?'

'Catch . . . my . . . breath . . . first,' he said between gulps of air.

'Please,' Will agreed. 'If he's too tired, he might teleport us into a vat of Cheez Whiz in Venezuela.'

'Okay . . .' said Nico. 'We didn't end up *in* the vat.'

'Pretty close,' Will said. 'Definitely in the middle of Venezuela's biggest Cheez Whiz processing plant.'

'That was *one* time,' Nico grumbled.

'Uh, guys?' Rachel pointed to the rim of the pit, where the cows were becoming agitated. They jostled and pushed each other forward until one – either by choice or with pressure from the herd – toppled off the edge.

Watching it fall, kicking its legs and torquing its body, I remembered the time Ares dropped a cat from Mount Olympus to prove it would land on its feet in Manhattan. Athena had teleported the cat to safety, then beat Ares with the butt of her spear for putting the animal in danger, but the fall had been terrifying to witness, nonetheless.

The bull was not as lucky as the cat. It landed sideways in the dirt with a throaty grunt. The impact would have killed most creatures, but the bull just flailed its legs, righted itself and shook its horns. It glared at us as if to say, *Oh, you're gonna get it now.*

'Um . . .' Will edged backwards. 'It's in the pit. So why isn't it choking on its rage?'

'I – I think it's because *we're* here?' My voice sounded like I'd been sucking helium. 'It wants to kill us more than it wants to choke to death?'

'Great,' Meg said. 'Nico, shadow-travel. Now.'

Nico winced. 'I can't take all of you at once! Two plus me is pushing it. Last summer, with the Athena Parthenos . . . That almost killed me, and I had Reyna's help.'

The bull charged.

'Take Will and Rachel,' I said, hardly believing the words were coming out of my mouth. 'Return for Meg and me when you can.'

Nico started to protest.

'Apollo's right!' Meg said. 'Go!'

We didn't wait for a response. I drew my bow. Meg summoned her scimitars, and together we raced into battle.

There's an old saying: the definition of insanity is shooting an invulnerable cow in the face over and over and expecting a different result.

I went insane. I shot arrow after arrow at the bull – aiming at its mouth, its eyes, its nostrils, hoping to find a soft spot. Meanwhile, Meg slashed and stabbed with gusto, weaving like a boxer to keep away from the creature's horns. Her blades were useless. The bull's shaggy red hide swirled and rippled, deflecting each hit.

We only stayed alive because the bull couldn't decide which of us to kill first. It kept changing its mind and reversing course as we took turns annoying it.

Perhaps if we kept up the pressure, we could tire out the bull. Sadly, we were also tiring out ourselves, and dozens more bulls waited above, curious to see how their friend fared before they risked the fall themselves.

'Pretty cow!' Meg yelled, stabbing it in the face and then dancing out of horn range. 'Please go away!'

'It's having too much fun!' I said.

My next shot was the dreaded Triple P – the perfect posterior perforator. It didn't seem to hurt the bull, but I definitely got its attention. The animal bellowed and whirled to face me, its blue eyes blazing with fury.

While it studied me, probably deciding which of my limbs it wanted to pull off and beat me over the head with, Meg glanced at the rim of the pit.

'Um, hey, Apollo?'

I risked a look. A second bull tumbled into the pit. It landed on top of a portable toilet, crushing the box into a fibreglass pancake, then extracted itself from the wreckage and cried, 'Moooo!' (Which I suspected was Tauri for *I totally meant to do that!*)

'I'll take Potty Cow,' I told Meg. 'You distract our friend here.'

A completely random division of duties – in no way related to the fact that I did not want to face the bull I'd just poked in the nether region.

Meg began dancing with Cow the First as I charged towards Potty Cow. I was feeling good, feeling heroic, until I reached for my quivers and found myself out of arrows . . . except for Ye Olde Standby, the Arrow of Dodona, which would not appreciate being used against an invulnerable bovine butt.

I was already committed, though, so I ran at Potty Cow with great bravado and zero clue how to fight it.

'Hey!' I yelled, waving my arms in the dubious hope that I might look scary. 'Blah, blah, blah! Go away!'

The cow attacked.

This would have been an excellent time for my godly strength to kick in, so of course that didn't happen. Just before the bull could run me down, I screamed and leaped aside.

At that point, the bull should have executed a slow course correction, running around the entire perimeter of the pit to give me time to recover. I'd dated a matador in Madrid once who assured me bulls did this because they were courteous animals and also terrible at sharp turns.

Either my matador was a liar, or he'd never fought tauri. The bull pivoted in a perfect about-face and charged me again. I rolled to one side, desperately grabbing for anything that might help me. I came up holding the edge of a blue polyurethane tarp. Worst shield ever.

The bull promptly jabbed its horn through the material. I jumped back as it stepped on the tarp and got pulled down by its own weight like a person stumbling over their own toga. (Not that I had ever done this, but I'd heard stories.)

The bull roared, shaking its head to dislodge the tarp, which only got it more tangled up in the fabric. I retreated, trying to catch my breath.

About fifty feet to my left, Meg was playing death-tag

with Cow the First. She looked unharmed, but I could tell she was tiring, her reaction times slowing.

More cows began to fall into the pit like large, unco-ordinated Acapulco cliff-divers. I recalled something Dionysus had once told me about his twin sons, Castor and Pollux – back when he was living with his mortal wife dur-ing a short phase of 'domestic bliss'. He'd claimed that two was the best number for children, because after two your children outnumbered you.

The same was true for killer cows. Meg and I could not hope to fend off more than a pair of them. Our only hope was . . . My eyes fixed on the mast of the crane.

'Meg!' I yelled. 'Back to the ladder!'

She tried to comply, but Cow the First stood between her and the crane. I whipped out my ukulele and ran in their direction.

'Cowie, cowie, cow!' I strummed desperately. 'Hey, cow! Bad, cow! Run away, cowie, cowie, cow!'

I doubted the tune would win any Grammys, but I was hoping it might at least distract Cow the First long enough for Meg to get around it. The cow stayed stubbornly put. So did Meg.

I reached her side. I glanced back in time to see Potty Cow throw off the tarp and charge towards us. The newly fallen cows were also getting to their hooves.

I estimated we had about ten seconds to live.

'Go,' I told Meg. 'J-jump the cow and climb the ladder. I'll –'

I didn't know how to finish that statement. *I'll stay here and die? I'll compose another verse of 'Cowie, Cowie, Cow'?*

Just as Cow the First lowered its horns and charged, a hand grabbed my shoulder.

Nico di Angelo's voice said, 'Gotcha.'

And the world turned cold and dark.

16

Will Solace, healer,
The hero we don't deserve,
He has Kit Kat bars.

'JUMP THE COW?' MEG DEMANDED. 'THAT
was your plan?'

The five of us sat in a sewer, which was something I'd
grown accustomed to. Meg seemed to be bouncing back
quickly from her shadow-travel sickness, thanks to Will's
timely administration of nectar and Kit Kat bars. I, however, still felt like I was coming down with the flu: chills,
body aches, disorientation. I was not ready to be assaulted
for my choices in combat.

'I was improvising,' I said. 'I didn't want to see you die.'

Meg threw her hands up. 'And I didn't want to see *you*
die, dummy. Did you think of that?'

'Guys,' Rachel interrupted, a cold pack pressed against
her head. 'How about none of us lets any of us die? Okay?'

Will checked her bruised temple. 'Feeling any better?'

'I'll be fine,' Rachel said, then explained for my benefit:
'I managed to stumble into the wall when we teleported
here.'

Nico looked sheepish. 'Sorry about that.'

'Hey, I'm not complaining,' Rachel said. 'Better than being trampled.'

'Guess so,' he said. 'Once we . . .'

Nico's eyelids fluttered. His pupils rolled up in his head and he slumped against Will's shoulder. It might have been a clever ploy to fall into his boyfriend's arms – I had used the *catch me, handsome* fainting trick a few times myself – but since Nico immediately began to snore, I decided he was not faking.

'That's night-night for Nico.' Will pulled a travel pillow from his supply bag, which I suspected he carried just for these occasions. He eased the son of Hades into a comfortable sleeping position, then gave us a weary smile. 'He'll need about half an hour to recover. Until then, we might as well make ourselves comfortable.'

On the bright side, I'd had plenty of experience getting comfortable in sewers, and Nico had shadow-travelled us to the New York drainage system's equivalent of the presidential suite.

The vaulted ceiling was adorned with a redbrick herringbone pattern. Along either wall, terracotta pipes dripped only the finest goo into a canal running down the middle of the floor. The concrete ledge upon which we sat was comfortably upholstered with lichen and scum. In the dim golden glow of Meg's swords – our only illumination – the tunnel looked almost romantic.

Given New York rental prices, I imagined a place like this could go for quite a bit. Running water. Privacy. Lots of space. Great bones – mouse bones, chicken bones and some others I couldn't identify. And did I mention the stench? The stench was included at no extra cost.

Will tended to our various cuts and scrapes, which were surprisingly light given our morning's adventures. He insisted we partake liberally of his medicinal stockpile of Kit Kat bars.

'The best thing for recovering from shadow-travel,' he assured us.

Who was I to argue with the healing powers of chocolate and wafers?

We ate in silence for a while. Rachel held the cold pack against her head and stared glumly at the sewer water as if waiting for pieces of her family home to float by. Meg sprinkled seeds into the scum patches next to her, causing luminous mushrooms to pop into existence like tiny umbrellas. When life gives you scum, make mushrooms, I suppose.

'Those forest bulls were amazing,' Meg said after a while. 'If you could train them to carry . . .'

I groaned. 'It was bad enough when you weaponized unicorns.'

'Yeah. That was great.' She looked down the tunnel in both directions. 'Does anyone know how we can get out of here?'

'Nico does.' Will's eye twitched. 'Although he's not going to take us *out* so much as *down*.'

'To the troglodytes,' Rachel guessed. 'What are they like?'

Will moved his hands as if trying to shape something out of clay or indicate the size of a fish he'd caught. 'I – I can't describe them,' he decided.

That wasn't reassuring. As my child, Will was bound to have some of my poetic ability. If the troglodytes defied description in your average sonnet or limerick, I didn't want to meet them.

'I hope they can help.' Rachel held up her palm to ward off Will, who was coming to check on her bruised head again. 'I'm okay now, thanks.'

She smiled, but her voice was strained. I knew she liked Will. I also knew she had issues with personal space. Becoming the Pythia tended to do that to you. Having the power of Delphi possess your body and soul at random intervals could make you tetchy about people getting too close without your consent. Having Python whispering inside your head probably didn't help, either.

'I get it.' Will sat back. 'You've had a rough morning. I'm sorry we brought that kind of trouble to your door.'

Rachel shrugged. 'Like I said, I think I'm *supposed* to be in this trouble. It's not your fault. A Dare *reveals the path that was unknown*. For once, I'm part of the prophecy.'

She sounded strangely proud of this fact. Perhaps, after issuing perilous quests for so many other people, Rachel found it nice to be included in our communal death-wish adventure. People like to be seen – even if it's by the cold, cruel eyes of fate.

'Is it safe for you to come along, though?' Meg asked. 'Like . . . if you've got Python in your head or whatever? Won't he see what we're doing?'

Rachel pulled her ankles into a tighter crisscross. 'I don't think he's seeing *through* me. At least . . . not yet.' She let that idea settle around us like a layer of swamp gas.

'Anyway, you're not getting rid of me. Python has made this personal.'

She glanced at me, and I couldn't escape the feeling that Python wasn't the one she really blamed. This had been personal for her ever since I'd accepted Rachel as my priestess. Ever since . . . well, ever since I'd been Apollo. If my trials as a mortal had done anything, they had shown me how many times I'd abandoned, forgotten and failed my Oracles over the centuries. I could not abandon Rachel in the same way. I'd neglected the basic truth that they did not serve me; I was supposed to serve *them*.

'We're lucky to have you,' I said. 'I only wish we had more time to figure out a plan.'

Rachel checked her watch – a basic wind-up model, which she'd probably chosen after seeing how easily technology went haywire around demigods, monsters and the other sorts of magical people she hung out with. 'It's past lunchtime. You're supposed to surrender to Nero by nightfall. That doesn't give us much leeway.'

'Oh, lunchtime,' Meg said, staying reliably on-brand. 'Will, have you got anything besides Kit Kats? I'm starv–'

She jerked her hand away from Will's supply kit as if it had shocked her. 'Why is there a tail sticking out of your bag?'

Will furrowed his brow. 'Oh. Uh, yeah.' He pulled out what appeared to be a foot-long desiccated lizard wrapped in a handkerchief.

'Gross!' Meg said with enthusiasm. 'Is that for medicine or something?'

'Er, no,' Will said. 'You remember how Nico and I went hunting for a gift for the trogs? Well –'

'Ick.' Rachel scooted away. 'Why would they want *that*?'

Will glanced at me like *Please don't make me say it.*

I shuddered. 'The troglodytes . . . If the legends are true . . . they consider lizards a great, you know . . .' I mimed putting something in my mouth. 'Delicacy.'

Rachel hugged her stomach. 'Sorry I asked.'

'Cool,' said Meg. 'So, if we find the trogs, we give them the lizard and they'll help us?'

'I doubt it will be that simple,' I said. 'Meg, has anyone ever agreed to help you simply because you gave them a dead lizard?'

She pondered the question so long it made me wonder about her past gift-giving practices. 'I guess not?'

Will slipped the desiccated animal back in his bag. 'Well, this one is apparently rare and special. You don't want to know how difficult it was to find. Hopefully –'

Nico snorted and began to stir. 'Wh-what –?'

'It's okay,' Will reassured him. 'You're with friends.'

'Friends?' Nico sat up, bleary-eyed.

'Friends.' Will gave us a warning look, as if suggesting we shouldn't startle Nico with any sudden moves.

I gathered Nico was a grumpy napper like his father, Hades. Wake up Hades prematurely and you were likely to end up as a nuclear-blast shadow on his bedroom wall.

Nico rubbed his eyes and frowned at me. I tried to look harmless.

'Apollo,' he said. 'Right. I remember.'

'Good,' Will said. 'But you're still groggy. Have a Kit Kat.'

'Yes, doctor,' Nico muttered.

We waited while Nico refreshed himself with chocolate and a swig of nectar.

'Better.' He rose, still looking wobbly. 'Okay, everybody. I'm going to lead you into the troglodyte caverns. Keep your hands away from your weapons at all times. Let me go first and do the talking. The troglodytes can be a little . . . jumpy.'

'By *jumpy*,' Will said, 'Nico means *likely to murder us with no provocation*.'

'That's what I said.' Nico popped the last of his Kit Kat in his mouth. 'Ready? Let's do this.'

Want directions to the troglodyte caverns? No problem!

First you go down. Then you go down some more. Then you take the next three downward turns. You'll see a path going slightly up. Ignore that. Keep going down until your eardrums implode. Then go down even more.

We crawled through pipes. We waded through slime pits. We navigated brick tunnels, stone tunnels and dirt tunnels that looked like they had been excavated by the earthworm chew-and-poop method. At one point, we crawled through a copper pipe so narrow I feared we'd end up popping out of Nero's personal toilet like a bunch of beauty queens emerging from a giant birthday cake.

I imagined myself singing 'Happy Birthday, Mr

Emperor', then quickly tamped down the thought. The sewer gas must have been making me delirious.

After what seemed like hours of sewage-themed fun, we emerged in a circular room fashioned from panels of rough-hewn rock. In the centre, a massive stalagmite erupted from the floor and pierced the ceiling like the centre pole of a merry-go-round. (After surviving Tarquin's Tilden Park–carousel tomb, this was not a comparison I was pleased to make.)

'This is it,' Nico said.

He led us to the base of the stalagmite. An opening had been chipped away in the floor just big enough for someone to crawl through. Handholds had been carved into the side of the stalagmite, extending down into the darkness.

'Is this part of the Labyrinth?' I asked.

The place had a similar feel. The air coming from below was warm and somehow alive, like the breath of a sleeping leviathan. I had the sense that something was monitoring our progress – something intelligent and not necessarily friendly.

Nico shook his head. 'Please don't mention the Labyrinth. The trogs *detest* Daedalus's maze. They call it *shallow*. From here on down is all trog-built. We're deeper than the Labyrinth has ever gone.'

'Awesome,' Meg said.

'You can go ahead of me, then,' I said.

We followed Nico down the side of the stalagmite into a massive natural cavern. I couldn't see the edges, or even the bottom, but from the echoes I could tell it was bigger than my old temple at Didyma. (Not to brag about temple size, but that place was HUGE.)

The handholds were shallow and slippery, illuminated only by faintly glowing patches of lichen on the rock. It took all my concentration not to fall. I suspected the trogs had designed the entrance to their realm this way on purpose, so anyone foolish enough to invade would be forced to come down in single file – and might not make it to the bottom at all. The sounds of our breathing and our clinking supplies reverberated through the cave. Any number of hostiles could have been watching us as we descended, taking aim with all sorts of delightful missile weapons.

Finally, we reached the floor. My legs ached. My fingers curled into arthritic claws.

Rachel squinted into the gloom. 'What do we do now?'

'You guys stay behind me,' Nico said. 'Will, can you do your thing? The barest minimum, please.'

'Wait,' I said. 'What is Will's "thing"?'

Will kept his focus on Nico. 'Do I have to?'

'We can't use our weapons for light,' Nico reminded him. 'And we'll need a little bit more, because the trogs don't need any. I'd rather be able to see them.'

Will wrinkled his nose. 'Fine.' He set down his pack and stripped off his linen overshirt, leaving just his tank top.

I still had no idea what he was doing, though the girls didn't seem to mind letting him do his *thing*. Did Will keep a concealed flashlight in his undershirt? Was he going to provide light by rubbing lichen on himself and smiling brilliantly?

Whatever the case, I wasn't sure I *wanted* to see the trogs. I vaguely recalled a British Invasion band from the 1960s called the Troggs. I couldn't shake the feeling that this subterranean race might all have mop-top hairdos and black turtlenecks and would use the word *groovy* a lot. I did not need that level of horror in my life.

Will took a deep breath. When he exhaled . . .

I thought my eyes were playing tricks on me. We'd been in near-total darkness so long, I wasn't sure why Will's outline suddenly seemed clearer. I could see the texture of his jeans, the individual tufts of his hair, the blue of his eyes. His skin was glowing with a soft, warm golden light as if he'd ingested sunshine.

'Whoa,' Meg said.

Rachel's eyebrows floated towards her hairline.

Nico smirked. 'Friends, meet my glow-in-the-dark boyfriend.'

'Could you not make a big deal about it?' Will asked.

I was speechless. How could anyone *not* make a big deal about this? As far as demigod powers went, glowing in the dark was perhaps not as showy as skeleton-summoning or tomato-vine mastery, but it was still impressive. And, like Will's skill at healing, it was gentle, useful and exactly what we needed in a pinch.

'I'm so proud,' I said.

Will's face turned the colour of sunlight shining through a glass of cranberry juice. 'Dad, I'm just *glowing*. I'm not graduating at the top of my class.'

'I'll be proud when you do that, too,' I assured him.

'Anyway.' Nico's lips quivered like he was trying not to giggle. 'I'll call the cavern-runners now. Everybody stay calm, okay?'

'Why *are* they called cavern-runners?' Rachel asked.

Nico held up his hand, indicating *Wait* or *You're about to find out.*

He faced the darkness and shouted, 'Troglodytes! I am Nico di Angelo, son of Hades! I have returned with four companions!'

Shuffling and clicking filled the cavern, as if Nico's voice had dislodged a million bats. One moment, we were alone. The next moment, an army of troglodytes stood before us as if they'd materialized out of hyperspace. With unsettling certainty, I realized they had *run* here from wherever they'd been – yards away? miles away? – with speed that rivalled that of Hermes himself.

Nico's warnings suddenly made sense to me. These creatures were so fast they could have killed us before we had time to draw a breath. If I'd had a weapon in hand, and if I'd raised it instinctively, accidentally . . . I would now be the grease spot formerly known as Lester formerly known as Apollo.

The troglodytes looked even stranger than the 1960s band that had appropriated their name. They were small humanoids, the tallest barely Meg's height, with vaguely froglike features: wide thin mouths, recessed noses and giant, brown, heavily lidded orbs for eyes. Their skin came in every shade from obsidian to chalk. Bits of stone and moss decorated their dark plaited hair. They wore a riot of clothing styles from modern jeans and T-shirts to 1920s business suits to Colonial-era frilly shirts and silk waistcoats.

The real showstopper, however, was their selection of hats, some piled three or four high on their heads: tricorns, bowlers, racing caps, top hats, hard hats, ski caps and base-ball caps.

The trogs looked like a group of rowdy schoolchildren who'd been set loose in a costume store, told to try on what-ever they wanted, and then allowed to crawl through the mud in their new outfits.

'We see you, Nico di Angelo!' said a trog in a miniature George Washington costume. His speech was interspersed with clicks, screeches and growls, so it actually sounded like 'CLICK. We – *grr* – see you – *SCREEE* – Nico – CLICK – di Angelo – *grr*.'

George Washingtrog gave us a pointy-toothed grin. 'Are these the sacrifices you promised? The trogs are hungry!'

17

Speak to me of soup.
Let it be savoury broth
With a hint of skink.

MY LIFE DIDN'T FLASH BEFORE MY EYES,
but I did find myself reviewing the past for anything I might
have done to offend Nico di Angelo.

I imagined him saying *Yes, these are the sacrifices!*, then
taking Will's hand and skipping away into the darkness
while Rachel, Meg and I were devoured by an army of cos-
tumed, muddy miniature frogmen.

'These are not the sacrifices,' Nico said, allowing me to
breathe again. 'But I have brought you a better offering! I
see you, O great *Screech*-Bling!'

Nico did not say *screech*, mind you. He screeched in a
way that told me he'd been practising Troglodytish. He had
a lovely, ear-piercing accent.

The trogs leaned in, sniffing and waiting, while Nico
held out his hand to Will, like *gimme*.

Will reached into his bag. He pulled out the desiccated
lizard and handed it to Nico, who unwrapped it like a holy
relic and held it aloft.

The crowd let out a collective gasp. 'Oooh!'

Screech-Bling's nostrils quivered. I thought his tricorn hat might pop off his head from excitement. 'Is that a – GRR – five-lined skink – CLICK?'

'It is – GRR,' Nico said. 'This was difficult to find, O Screech-Bling, Wearer of the Finest Hats.'

Screech-Bling licked his lips. He was drooling all over his cravat. 'A rare gift indeed. We often find Italian wall lizards in our domain. Turtles. Wood frogs. Rat snakes. Occasionally, if we are very lucky, a pit viper.'

'Tasty!' shrieked a trog in the back. 'Tasty pit vipers!'

Several other trogs screeched and growled in agreement.

'But a five-lined skink,' Screech-Bling said, 'is a delicacy we seldom see.'

'My gift to you,' Nico said. 'A peace offering in hope of friendship.'

Screech-Bling took the skink in his long-fingered, pointy-clawed hands. I assumed he would shove the reptile in his mouth and be done with it. That's what any king or god would do, presented with his favourite delicacy.

Instead, he turned to his people and made a short speech in their own language. The trogs cheered and waved their chapeaus. A trog in a mud-splattered chef's hat pushed his way to the front of the crowd. He knelt before Screech-Bling and accepted the skink.

The chieftain turned to us with a grin. 'We will share this bounty! I, Screech-Bling, chief executive – CLICK – officer of the troglodytes, have decreed that a great soup shall be made, so that all shareholders may taste of the wondrous skink!'

More cheering from the troglodytes. *Of course*, I realized. If Screech-Bling modelled himself after George Washington, he would not be a king – he would be a chief executive.

'For this great gift,' he continued, 'we will not kill and eat you, Nico di Angelo, even though you are Italian, and we wonder if you might taste as good as an Italian wall lizard!'

Nico bowed his head. 'That is very kind.'

'We will also generously refrain from eating your companions –' a few of Screech-Bling's shareholders muttered, 'Aww, what?' – 'though it is true that, like you, they do not wear hats, and no hatless species can be considered civilized.'

Rachel and Meg looked alarmed, probably because Screech-Bling was still drooling profusely as he talked about not eating us. Or perhaps they were thinking about all the great hats they *could* have worn if they'd only known.

Glow-in-the-dark Will gave us a reassuring nod and mouthed, *It's cool.* Apparently, the giving of a gift, followed by the promise of not killing and eating your guests, was standard troglodyte diplomatic protocol.

'We see your generosity, O *Screech*-Bling!' Nico said. 'I would propose a pact between us – an agreement that would produce many hats for us all, as well as reptiles, fine clothing and rocks.'

An excited murmur rippled through the crowd. It seemed Nico had hit upon all four things on the troglodytes' Christmas wish list.

Screech-Bling summoned forward a few senior trogs, who I guessed were his board of directors. One was the chef.

The others wore the hats of a police officer, a firefighter and a cowboy. After a short consultation, Screech-Bling faced us with another pointy-toothed grin.

'Very well!' he said. 'We will take you to our corporate headquarters, where we will feast upon skink soup and – CLICK, GRR – talk more about these matters!'

We were surrounded by a throng of cheering, growling shareholders. With a total lack of regard for personal space, as one might expect from a tunnel-dwelling species, they picked us up and ran with us on their shoulders, sweeping us out of the cavern and into a maze of tunnels at a speed that would've put the tauri silvestres to shame.

'These guys are awesome,' Meg decided. 'They eat snakes.'

I knew several snakes, including Hermes's companions, George and Martha, who would have been uncomfortable with Meg's definition of awesomeness. Since we were now in the midst of the trogs' encampment, I decided not to bring that up.

At first glance, the troglodytes' corporate headquarters resembled an abandoned subway station. The wide platform was lined with columns holding up a barrelled ceiling of black tiles that drank in the dim light from pots of bioluminescent mushrooms scattered around the cavern. Along the left side of the platform, instead of a rail bed, was the sunken, packed-earth roadway that the trogs had used to bring us here. And at the speeds they ran, who needed a train?

Along the right side of the platform flowed a swift subterranean river. The trogs filled their gourds and cauldrons from this source, and also emptied their chamber pots into it – though being a civilized, hat-wearing people, they dumped the chamber pots downstream from where they drew their drinking water.

Unlike in a subway station, there were no obvious stairways leading up, no clearly marked exits. Just the river and the road we'd arrived on.

The platform buzzed with activity. Dozens of trogs rushed here and there, miraculously managing their daily chores without losing the stacks of hats on their heads. Some tended cooking pots on tripods over fire pits. Others – possibly merchants? – haggled over bins of rocks. Trog children, no bigger than human babies, frolicked around, playing catch with spheres of solid crystal.

Their dwellings were tents. Most had been appropriated from the human world, which gave me unpleasant flashbacks of the camping display at Macro's Military Madness in Palm Springs. Others appeared to be of trog design, carefully stitched from the shaggy red hides of the tauri silvestres. I had no idea how the trogs had managed to skin and stitch the impervious hides, but clearly, as the ancestral enemies of the forest bulls, they had found a way.

I wondered about that rivalry, too. How had a subterranean frog people in love with hats and lizards become mortal enemies to a breed of bright-red devil bulls? Perhaps at the beginning of time, the elder gods had told the first trogs, *You may now pick your nemesis!* And the first trogs had pointed across the newly made fields of creation and yelled, *We hate those cows!*

Whatever the case, I was comforted to know that even

if the trogs were not yet our friends, at least we had a mutual enemy.

Screech-Bling had given us a guest tent and a cold fire pit and told us to make ourselves at home while he saw to dinner preparations. Or, rather, he'd told *Nico* to make himself at home. The CEO kept eyeing Rachel, Meg and me like we were sides of beef hanging in a shop window. As for Will, the troglodytes seemed to ignore him. My best guess: because Will glowed, they considered him simply a movable light source, as if Nico had brought along his own pot of luminous mushrooms. Judging from Will's scowl, he did not appreciate this.

It would've been easier to relax if Rachel hadn't kept checking her watch – reminding us that it was now four in the afternoon, then four thirty, and that Meg and I were supposed to surrender by sundown. I could only hope the troglodytes were like senior citizens and ate supper early.

Meg busied herself collecting spores from the nearby mushroom pots, which she seemed to consider the coolest thing since snake-eating. Will and Nico sat on the other side of the fire pit having a tense discussion. I couldn't hear the words, but from their facial expressions and hand gestures, I got the gist:

Will: *Worry, worry, worry.*

Nico: *Calm down, probably won't die.*

Will: *Worry. Trogs. Dangerous. Yikes.*

Nico: *Trogs good. Nice hats.*

Or something along those lines.

After a while, the trog with the chef's hat materialized at our campsite. In his hand was a steaming ladle.

'*Screech*-Bling will talk to you now,' he said in heavily Troglodytish-laced English.

We all began to rise, but the chef stopped us with a sweep of his ladle. 'Only Nico, the Italian wall lizard – um, *SQUEAK* – I mean the Italian son of Hades. The rest of you will wait here until dinner.'

His gleaming eyes seemed to add, *When you may or may not be on the menu!*

Nico squeezed Will's hand. 'It'll be fine. Back soon.'

Then he and the chef were gone. In exasperation, Will threw himself down on his fireside mat and put his back-pack over his face, reducing our Will-glow illumination by about fifty percent.

Rachel scanned the encampment, her eyes glittering in the gloom.

I wondered what she saw with her ultra-clear vision. Perhaps the troglodytes looked even scarier than I realized. Perhaps their hats were even more magnificent. Whatever the case, her shoulders curved as tense as a drawn bow. Her fingers traced the soot-stained floor as if she were itching for her paintbrushes.

'When you surrender to Nero,' she told me, 'the first thing you'll need to do is buy us time.'

Her tone disturbed me almost as much as her words: *when* I surrendered, not *if*. Rachel had accepted that it was the only way. The reality of my predicament curled up and nestled in my throat like a five-lined skink.

I nodded. 'B-buy time. Yes.'

'Nero will want to burn down New York as soon as he

has you,' she said. 'Why would he wait? Unless you give him a reason . . .'

I had a feeling I would not like Rachel's next suggestion. I didn't have a clear understanding of what Nero intended to do to me once I surrendered – other than the obvious torture and death. Luguselwa seemed to believe the emperor would keep Meg and me alive at least for a while, though she had been vague about what she knew of Nero's plans.

Commodus had wanted to make a public spectacle out of my death. Caligula had wanted to extract what remained of my godhood and add it to his own power with the help of Medea's sorcery. Nero might have similar ideas. Or – and I feared this was most likely – once he finished torturing me, he might surrender me to Python to seal their alliance. No doubt my old reptilian enemy would enjoy swallowing me whole, letting me die in his belly over the course of many excruciating days of digestion. So, there was *that* to look forward to.

'Wh-what reason would make Nero wait?' I asked.

Apparently, I was picking up Troglodytish, because my voice was punctuated by clicks and squeaks.

Rachel traced curlicues in the soot – waves, perhaps, or a line of people's heads. 'You said Camp Half-Blood was standing by to help?'

'Yes . . . Kayla and Austin told me they would remain on alert. Chiron should be back at camp soon as well. But an attack on Nero's tower would be doomed. The whole point of our surrender –'

'Is to distract the emperor from what Nico, Will and

I will be doing, hopefully, with the trogs' help: disabling the Greek-fire vats. But you'll need to give Nero another incentive to keep him from pushing that button the minute you surrender. Otherwise we'll never have time to sabotage his doomsday weapon, no matter *how* fast the trogs can run or dig.'

I understood what she was suggesting. The five-lined skink of reality began its slow, painful slide down my oesophagus.

'You want to alert Camp Half-Blood,' I said. 'Have them initiate an attack anyway. Despite the risks.'

'I don't *want* any of this,' she said. 'But it's the only way. It'll have to be carefully timed. You and Meg surrender. We get to work with the troglodytes. Camp Half-Blood musters for an attack. But if Nero thinks the entire camp is coming to him –'

'That would be worth waiting for. To take out the entire population of Camp Half-Blood while he destroys the city, all in one terrible firestorm.' I swallowed. 'I could just bluff. I could *claim* reinforcements are coming.'

'No,' Rachel said. 'It has to be real. Nero has Python on his side. Python would *know*.'

I didn't bother asking her how. The monster might not have been able to see through Rachel's eyes yet, but I remembered all too well how his voice had sounded speaking through her mouth. They were connected. And that connection was getting stronger.

I was reluctant to consider the details of such an insane plan, but I found myself asking, 'How would you alert the camp?'

Rachel gave me a thin smile. '*I* can use cell phones. I don't normally carry one, but I'm not a demigod. Assuming I make it back to the surface, where cell phones actually, you know, *work*, I can buy a cheap one. Chiron has a crappy old computer in the Big House. He hardly ever uses it, but he knows to look for messages or emails in emergency situations. I'm pretty sure I can get his attention. Assuming he's there.'

She sounded so calm, which just made me feel more agitated.

'Rachel, I'm scared,' I admitted. 'It was one thing thinking about putting myself in danger. But the entire camp? Everyone?'

Strangely, this comment seemed to please her.

She took my hand. 'I know, Apollo. And the fact that you're worried about other people? That's beautiful. But you'll have to trust me. That secret path to the throne . . . the thing I am supposed to show you? I'm pretty sure this is it. This is how we make things right.'

Make things right.

What would such an ending even *look* like?

Six months ago, when I first plummeted to Manhattan, the answer had seemed obvious. I would return to Mount Olympus, my immortality restored, and everything would be great. After being Lester for a few more months, I might have added that destroying the Triumvirate and freeing the ancient Oracles would also be good . . . but mostly because that was the path back to my godhood. Now, after all the sacrifices I had seen, the pain suffered by so many . . . what could possibly make things right?

No amount of success would bring back Jason, or Dakota, or Don, or Crest, or Money Maker, or Heloise, or the many other heroes who had fallen. We could not undo those tragedies.

Mortals and gods had one thing in common: we were notoriously nostalgic for 'the good old days'. We were always looking back to some magical golden time before everything went bad. I remembered sitting with Socrates, back around 425 BCE, and us griping to each other about how the younger generations were ruining civilization.

As an immortal, of course, I should have known that there never were any 'good old days'. The problems humans face never really change, because mortals bring their own baggage with them. The same is true of gods.

I wanted to go back to a time before all the sacrifices had been made. Before I had experienced so much pain. But making things right could *not* mean rewinding the clock. Even Kronos hadn't had *that* much power over time.

I suspected that wasn't what Jason Grace would want, either.

When he'd told me to remember being human, he'd meant *building* on pain and tragedy, overcoming it, learning from it. That was something gods never did. We just complained.

To be human is to move forward, to adapt, to believe in your ability to make things better. That is the only way to make the pain and sacrifice mean something.

I met Rachel's gaze. 'I trust you. I'll make things right. Or I will die trying.'

The strange thing was, I meant it. A world in which

the future was controlled by a giant reptile, where hope was suffocated, where heroes sacrificed their lives for nothing, and pain and hardship could not yield a better life . . . that seemed much worse than a world without Apollo.

Rachel kissed my cheek – a sisterly gesture, except it was hard to imagine my actual sister Artemis doing that.

'I'm proud of you,' Rachel said. 'Whatever happens. Remember that.'

I was tongue-tied.

Meg turned towards us, her hands full of lichen and mushrooms. 'Rachel, did you just kiss him? Ew. Why?'

Before Rachel could answer, the chef reappeared at our campsite, his apron and hat splattered with steaming broth. He still had that hungry glint in his eyes. 'VISITORS – SQUEAK – come with me! We are ready for the feast!'

18

Our special tonight:
A lovely braised Apollo
Under a Mets hat

MY ADVICE: IF YOU'RE EVER GIVEN A CHOICE
between drinking skink soup or serving yourself up as the
troglodytes' main course, just flip a coin. Neither option is
survivable.

We sat on cushions around a communal mushroom pit
with a hundred or so troglodytes. As barbarian guests, we
were each given headwear, so as not to offend our hosts'
sensibilities. Meg wore a beekeeper's hat. Rachel got a pith
helmet. I was given a New York Mets cap because, I was
told, no one else wanted it. I found this insulting both to
me and the franchise.

Nico and Will sat on Screech-Bling's right. Nico sported
a top hat, which worked well with his black-and-white aesthetic. Will, my poor boy, had been given a lampshade. No
respect for the light-bringers of the world.

Sitting to my left was the chef, who introduced himself
as Click-Wrong (pronounce the W). His name made me
wonder if he'd been an impulse buy for his parents on Cyber
Monday, but I thought it would be rude to enquire.

The trog children had the job of serving. A tiny boy

in a propeller beanie offered me a black stone cup filled to the brim, then ran away giggling. The soup bubbled a rich golden brown.

'The secret is lots of turmeric,' Click-Wrong confided.

'Ah.' I raised my cup, as everyone else was doing. The trogs began slurping with blissful expressions and many *clicks*, *grrs* and yummy sounds.

The smell was not bad: like tangy chicken broth. Then I spotted a lizard foot floating in the foam, and I just couldn't.

I pressed my lips to the rim and pretended to sip. I waited for what I thought was a credible amount of time, allowing most of the trogs to finish their portions.

'Mmm!' I said. '*Click*-Wrong, your culinary skills astound me! Partaking in this soup is a great honour. In fact, having any more of it would be *too* much of an honour. May I give the rest to someone who can better appreciate the succulent flavours?'

'Me!' shouted a nearby trog.

'Me!' shouted another.

I passed the cup down the circle, where it was soon drained by happy troglodytes.

Click-Wrong did not appear insulted. He patted my shoulder sympathetically. 'I remember my first skink. It is a potent soup! You will be able to handle more next time.'

I was glad to hear he thought there would *be* a next time. It implied we would not be killed *this* time. Rachel, looking relieved, announced that she, too, was overwhelmed with honour and would be happy to share her portion.

I looked at Meg's bowl, which was already empty. 'Did you actually –?'

'What?' Her expression was unreadable behind the netting of her beekeeper's hat.

'Nothing.'

My stomach convulsed with a combination of nausea and hunger. I wondered if we would be honoured with a second course. Perhaps some breadsticks. Or really anything that wasn't garnished with skink feet.

Screech-Bling raised his hands and *click-click-click*ed for attention. 'Friends! Shareholders! I see you all!'

The troglodytes tapped their spoons against their stone cups, making a sound like a thousand clattering bones.

'Out of courtesy for our uncivilized guests,' Screech-Bling continued, 'I shall speak in the barbaric language of the crust-dwellers.'

Nico tipped his fine top hat. 'I see the honour you give us. Thank you, CEO *Screech*-Bling, for not eating us, and also speaking in our tongue.'

Screech-Bling nodded with a smug expression that said, *No problem, kid. We're just awesome that way.* 'The Italian wall lizard has told us many things!'

A board member standing behind him, the one with the cowboy hat, whispered in his ear.

'I mean the Italian son of Hades!' Screech-Bling corrected. 'He has explained the evil plans of Emperor Nero!'

The trogs muttered and hissed. Apparently, Nero's infamy had spread even to the deepest-dwelling corporations of hat-wearers. Screech-Bling pronounced the name *Nee-ACK-row*, with a sound in the middle like a cat being strangled, which seemed appropriate.

'The son of Hades wishes our help!' said Screech-Bling.

'The emperor has vats of fire-liquid. Many of you know the ones I speak of. Loud and clumsy was the digging when they installed those vats. Shoddy the workmanship!'

'Shoddy!' agreed many of the trogs.

'Soon,' said the CEO, 'Nee-ACK-row will unleash burning death across the Crusty Crust. The son of Hades has asked our help to dig to these vats and eat them!'

'You mean disable them?' Nico suggested.

'Yes, that!' Screech-Bling agreed. 'Your language is crude and difficult!'

On the opposite side of the circle, the board member with the police hat made a small *notice-me* sort of growl. 'O *Screech*-Bling, these fires will not reach us. We are too deep! Should we not let the Crusty Crust burn?'

'Hey!' Will spoke for the first time, looking about as serious as someone can while wearing a lampshade. 'We're talking about millions of innocent lives.'

Police Hat snarled. 'We trogs are only hundreds. We do not breed and breed and choke the world with our waste. Our lives are rare and precious. You crust-dwellers? No. Besides, you are blind to our existence. You would not help us.'

'*Grr*-Fred speaks the truth,' said Cowboy Hat. 'No offence to our guests.'

The child with the propeller beanie chose this moment to appear at my side, grinning and offering me a wicker basket covered by a napkin. 'Breadsticks?'

I was so upset I declined.

'– assure our guests,' Screech-Bling was saying. 'We have welcomed you to our table. We see you as intelligent beings. You must not think we are against your kind. We bear you no ill will! We simply do not care whether you live or die.'

There was a general muttering of agreement. Click-Wrong gave me a kindly glance that implied, *You can't argue with that logic!*

The scary thing was, back when I was a god, I might have agreed with the trogs. I'd destroyed a few cities myself in the old days. Humans always popped up again like weeds. Why fret about one little fiery apocalypse in New York?

Now, though, one of those 'not-so-rare' lives was Estelle Blofis's, giggler and future ruler of the Crusty Crust. And her parents, Sally and Paul . . . In fact, there wasn't a single mortal I considered expendable. Not *one* deserved to be snuffed out by Nero's cruelty. The revelation stunned me. I had become a human-life hoarder!

'It's not just crust-dwellers,' Nico was saying, his tone remarkably calm. 'Lizards, skinks, frogs, snakes . . . Your food supply will burn.'

This caused some uneasy mumbling, but I sensed that the trogs were still not swayed. They might have to range as far as New Jersey or Long Island to gather their reptiles. They might have to live on breadsticks for a while. But so what? The threat wasn't critical to their lives or their stock prices.

'What about hats?' Will asked. 'How many haberdasheries will burn if we don't stop Nero? Dead haberdashers cannot make trog haberdashery.'

More grumbling, but clearly this argument wasn't enough, either.

With a growing sense of helplessness, I realized that we

wouldn't be able to convince the troglodytes by appealing to their self-interest. If only a few hundred of them existed, why should they gamble their own lives by tunnelling into Nero's doomsday reservoir? No god or corporation would accept that level of risk.

Before I realized what I was doing, I had risen to my feet. 'Stop! Hear me, troglodytes!'

The crowd grew dangerously still. Hundreds of large brown eyes fixed on me.

One trog whispered, 'Who is that?'

His companion whispered back, 'Don't know, but he can't be important. He's wearing a Mets hat.'

Nico gave me an urgent *sit-down-before-you-get-us-killed* look.

'Friends,' I said, 'this is not about reptiles and hats.'

The trogs gasped. I had just implied that two of their favourite things were no more important than crust-dweller lives.

I forged ahead. 'The trogs are civilized! But what makes a people civilized?'

'Hats!' yelled one.

'Language!' yelled another.

'Soup?' enquired a third.

'You can *see*,' I said. 'That is how you greeted us. You *saw* the son of Hades. And I don't mean just seeing with your eyes. You see value, and honour, and worthiness. You see things as they are. Is this not true?'

The trogs nodded reluctantly, confirming that, yes, in terms of importance, seeing was probably up there with reptiles and hats.

'You're right about the crust-dwellers being blind,' I admitted. 'In many ways, they are. So was I, for centuries.'

'Centuries?' Click-Wrong leaned away as if realizing I was well past my expiration date. 'Who are you?'

'I was Apollo,' I said. 'God of the sun. Now I am a mortal named Lester.'

No one seemed awed or incredulous – just confused. Someone whispered to a friend, 'What's a sun?' Another asked, 'What's a Lester?'

'I thought I knew all the races of the world,' I continued, 'but I didn't believe troglodytes existed until Nico brought me here. I see your importance now! Like you, I once thought crust-dwellers' lives were common and unimportant. I have learned otherwise. I would like to help you see them as I have. Their value has nothing to do with hats.'

Screech-Bling narrowed his large brown eyes. 'Nothing to do with hats?'

'If I may?' As nonthreateningly as I could, I brought out my ukulele.

Nico's expression changed from urgency to despair, like I had signed our death warrants. I was used to such silent criticism from his father. Hades has *zero* appreciation for the fine arts.

I strummed a C major chord. The sound reverberated through the cavern like tonal thunder. Trogs covered their ears. Their jaws dropped. They stared in wonder as I began to sing.

As I had at Camp Jupiter, I made up the words as I went along. I sang of my trials, my travels with Meg and all the heroes who had helped us along the way. I sang of sacrifices and triumphs. I sang of Jason, our fallen shareholder, with honesty and heartache, though I may have embellished the number of fine hats he wore. I sang of the challenges we now faced – Nero's ultimatum for my surrender, the fiery death he had in mind for New York, and the even greater menace of Python, waiting in the caverns of Delphi, hoping to strangle the future itself.

The trogs listened with rapt attention. No one so much as crunched a breadstick. If our hosts had any inkling that I was recycling the melody from Hall and Oates's 'Kiss on My List', they gave no indication. (What can I tell you? Under pressure, I sometimes default to Hall and Oates.)

When the last chord ceased echoing through the cavern, no one moved.

Finally, Screech-Bling wiped tears from his eyes. 'That sound . . . was the most – *GRR* – horrible thing I have ever heard. Were the words true?'

'They were.' I decided perhaps the CEO had confused *horrible* with *wonderful*, the same way he'd confused *eat* with *disable*. 'I know this because my friend here, Rachel Elizabeth Dare, *sees* it. She is a prophetess and has the gift of clear sight.'

Rachel waved, her expression hidden under the shadow of her pith helmet. 'If Nero isn't stopped,' she said, 'he won't just take over the wor– the Crusty Crust. Eventually he will come for the trogs, too, and every other hat-wearing people. Python will do worse. He will take away the future from all of us. *Nothing* will happen unless he decrees it. Imagine your destiny controlled by a giant reptile.'

This last comment hit the crowd like a blast of Arctic air. Mothers hugged their children. Children hugged their breadstick baskets. Stacks of hats trembled on every trog-lodyte head. I supposed the trogs, being eaters of reptiles, could well imagine what a giant reptile might do to them.

'But that is not why you should help us,' I added. 'Not just because it is good for trogs, but because we must all help one another. That is the only way to be civilized. We . . . We must see the right way, and we must take it.'

Nico closed his eyes, as if saying his final prayers. Will glowed quietly under his lampshade. Meg gave me a stealthy thumbs-up, which I did not find encouraging.

The trogs waited for Screech-Bling to make his deci-sion as to whether or not we would be added to the dinner menu.

I felt strangely calm. I was convinced we'd made our best case. I had appealed to their altruism. Rachel had appealed to their fear of a giant reptile eating the future. Who could say which argument was stronger?

Screech-Bling studied me and my New York Mets hat. 'What would you have me do, Lester-Apollo?'

He used *Lester* the same way he used screeches or clicks before other names, almost like a title – as if showing me respect.

'Could you dig under the emperor's tower undetected?' I asked. 'Allowing my friends to disable the vats of Greek fire?'

He nodded curtly. 'It could be done.'

'Then I would ask you to take Will and Nico –'

Rachel coughed.

'And Rachel,' I added, hoping I was not sentencing my favourite priestess to die in a pith helmet. 'Meanwhile, Meg and I must go to the emperor's front door so we can surrender.'

The trogs shifted uneasily. Either they did not like what I said, or the skink soup had started to reach their intestines.

Grr-Fred glared at me from under his police hat. 'I still do not trust you. Why would you surrender to Nero?'

'I see you, O Grr-Fred,' Nico said, 'Mighty of Hats, Corporate Security Chief! You are right to be wary, but Apollo's surrender is a distraction, a trick. He will keep the emperor's eyes away from us while we tunnel. If we can fool the emperor into letting down his guard . . .'

His voice trailed off. He looked at the ceiling as if he'd heard something far above.

A heartbeat later, the trogs stirred. They shot to their feet, overturning soup bowls and breadbaskets. Many grabbed obsidian knives and spears.

Screech-Bling snarled at Nico. 'Tauri silvestres approach! What have you done, son of Hades?'

Nico looked dumbfounded. 'Nothing! W-we fought a herd on the surface. But we shadow-travelled away. There's no chance they could've –'

'Foolish crust-dwellers!' howled Grr-Fred. 'Tauri silvestres can track their prey anywhere! You have brought our enemies to our headquarters. Creak-Morris, take charge of the tunnel-lings! Get them to safety!'

Creak-Morris began gathering up the children. Other adults started pulling down tents, collecting their best rocks, hats and other supplies.

'It is well for you we are the fastest runners in existence,' snarled Click-Wrong, his chef's hat quivering with rage. 'You have endangered us all!' He hefted his empty soup cauldron, jumped onto the roadway and vanished in a skink-scented *whoosh*.

'What of the crust-dwellers?' Grr-Fred asked his CEO. 'Do we kill them or leave them for the bulls?'

Screech-Bling glowered at me. '*Grr*-Fred, take Lester-Apollo and Meg-Girl to the Tower of Nero. If they wish to surrender, we will not stop them. As for these other three, I will –'

The platform shook, the ceiling cracked, and cows rained down on the encampment.

19

Flow on, River Ouch!

Take me – ouch! – away from – ouch!

Blessed River – ouch!

THE NEXT FIVE MINUTES WEREN'T JUST chaotic. They were what Chaos is like when Chaos wants to let her hair down and go nuts. And, believe me, you *never* want to see a primordial goddess go nuts.

Tauri silvestres dropped from cracks in the ceiling – crashing into tents, flattening troglodytes, scattering hats and soup bowls and pots of mushrooms. Almost immediately, I lost track of Will, Rachel and Nico in the pandemonium. I could only hope Screech-Bling and his lieutenants had whisked them to safety.

A bull landed in a heap right in front of me, separating me from Meg and Grr-Fred. As the beast scrambled to gain its footing (hoofing?), I parkoured over it, desperate not to lose my young master.

I spotted her – now ten feet away, Grr-Fred rapidly dragging her towards the river for reasons unknown. The close quarters and obstacles on the platform seemed to hamper the trogs' natural running skills, but Grr-Fred was still moving at a fast clip. If Meg hadn't kept tripping as they wove through the destruction, I would've stood no chance of catching up.

I leaped over a second bull. (Hey, if the cow could jump over the moon, I didn't see why the sun couldn't jump over two cows.) Another barrelled blindly past me, lowing in panic as it tried to shake a bull-hide tent off its horns. To be fair, I would've panicked too if I'd had the skin of one of my own kind wrapped around my head.

I'd almost reached Meg when I spotted a crisis unfolding across the platform. The little trog with the propeller beanie, my server during dinner, had got separated from the other children. Oblivious to danger, he was now stumbling after his ball of crystal as it rolled across the platform, straight into the path of a charging bull.

I reached for my bow, then remembered my quivers were exhausted. With a curse, I snatched up the nearest thing I could find – an obsidian dagger – and spun it towards the bull's head.

'HEY!' I shouted.

This accomplished two things: it stopped the trog in his tracks, and it caused the bull to face me just in time to get a dagger in its nostril.

'Moo!' said the bull.

'My ball!' shouted Beanie Boy as his crystal sphere rolled between the bull's legs, heading in my direction.

'I'll get it back to you!' I said, which seemed like a silly thing to promise, given the circumstances. 'Run! Get to safety!'

With one last forlorn glance at his crystal ball, Beanie Boy leaped off the platform and disappeared down the road.

The bull blew the dagger out of its nose. It glared at me, its blue eyes as bright and hot as butane flames in the gloom of the cavern. Then it charged.

Like the heroes of old, I stepped back, stumbled on a cooking pot and fell hard on my butt. Just before the bull could trample me into Apollo-flavoured marmalade, glowing mushrooms erupted all over its head. The bull, blinded, screamed and veered off into the bedlam.

'Come on!' Meg stood a few feet away, having somehow convinced Grr-Fred to double back. 'Lester, we've got to go!' She said this as if the idea might not have occurred to me.

I snatched up Beanie Boy's crystal ball, struggled to my feet and followed Grr-Fred and Meg to the edge of the river.

'Jump in!' ordered Grr-Fred.

'But there's a perfectly good road!' I fumbled to secure the crystal ball in my pack. 'And you dump your chamber pots in that water!'

'Tauri can follow us on the road,' shouted Grr-Fred. 'You don't run fast enough.'

'Can they swim?' I asked.

'Yes, but not as quickly as they run! Now, jump or die!'

I liked a good simple choice. I grabbed Meg's hand. Together we jumped.

Ah, subterranean rivers. So cold. So fast. So very full of rocks.

You'd think all those jagged, spearlike stones in the water would have been eroded over time by the swift current, but no. They clubbed and clawed and stabbed me relentlessly as I sped by. We hurtled through darkness, spinning and somersaulting at the mercy of the river, my head going under and coming back out at random intervals. Somehow, I always picked the wrong moment to try breathing. Despite it all, I kept my grip on Meg's hand.

I have no idea how long this water torture lasted. It seemed longer than most centuries I'd lived through – except perhaps the fourteenth CE, a horrible time to be alive. I was starting to wonder whether I would die of hypothermia, drowning or blunt-force trauma when Meg's grip tightened on mine. My arm was nearly wrenched out of its socket when we lurched to a stop. Some superhuman force hauled me out of the river like a dugong in a fishing net.

I landed on a slick stone ledge. I curled up, spluttering, shivering, miserable. I was dimly aware of Meg coughing and retching next to me. Someone's pointy-toed shoe kicked me between the shoulder blades.

'Get up, get up!' Grr-Fred said. 'No time to nap!'

I groaned. 'Is this what naps look like on your planet?'

He loomed over me, his police hat miraculously intact, his fists planted on his hips. It occurred to me that *he* must have pulled us out of the river when he spotted this ledge, but that seemed impossible. Grr-Fred must have had to have enough body strength to bench-press a washing machine.

'The forest bulls can swim!' he reminded me. 'We must be gone before they can sniff out this ledge. Here.'

He handed me a piece of jerky. At least it smelled like it *had* been jerky before our dip in the River Ouch. Now it looked more like deli-sliced sea sponge.

'Eat it,' he ordered.

He handed a piece to Meg as well. Her beekeeper's hat had been swept away in the flood, leaving her with a hairdo that looked like a dead wet badger. Her glasses were cockeyed. She had a few scrapes on her arms. Some of her seed packages had exploded in her gardening belt, giving her a bumper crop of acorn squash around her waist. But otherwise she looked well enough. She shoved the jerky in her mouth and chewed.

'Good,' she pronounced, which didn't surprise me from a girl who drank skink soup.

Grr-Fred glared at me until I relented and tried a bite of jerky, too. It was not good. It was, however, bland and edible. As the first bite went down my throat, warmth coursed through my limbs. My blood hummed. My ears popped. I swore I could feel the acne clearing up on my cheeks.

'Wow,' I said. 'Do you sell this stuff?'

'Let me work,' growled our guide. 'Wasted too much time already.'

He turned and examined the wall of the tunnel.

As my vision cleared and my teeth stopped chattering quite so violently, I took stock of our sanctuary. At our feet, the river continued to roar, fierce and loud. Downstream, the channel shrank until there was no headroom at all – meaning Grr-Fred had pulled us to safety just in time if we wanted to keep breathing. Our ledge was wide enough for us all to sit on, barely, but the ceiling was so low even Grr-Fred had to stoop a little.

Other than the river, I saw no way out – just the blank rock wall Grr-Fred was staring at.

'Is there a secret passage?' I asked him.

He scowled like I was not worth the strip of sponge jerky he'd given me. 'No passage *yet*, crust-dweller.'

He cracked his knuckles, wriggled his fingers and began to dig. Under his bare hands, the rock crumbled into light-weight chunks like meringue, which Grr-Fred scooped away and tossed in the river. Within minutes, he had cleared twenty cubic feet of stone as easily as a mortal might pull clothes from a closet. And he kept digging.

I picked up a piece of debris, wondering if it was still brittle. I squeezed it and promptly cut my finger.

Meg pointed to my half-eaten jerky. 'You going to finish that?'

I'd been planning to save the jerky for later – in case I got hungry, required extra strength or got a bad attack of pimples – but Meg looked so ravenous I handed it over.

I spent the next few minutes emptying the water from my ukulele, my quivers and my shoes as Grr-Fred continued to dig.

At last, a cloud of dust billowed from his excavation hole. The trog grunted with satisfaction. He stepped out, revealing a passage now five feet deep, opening into a different cavern.

'Hurry,' he said. 'I will seal the tunnel behind us. If we are lucky, that will be enough to throw the tauri off our scent for a while.'

Our luck held. Enjoy that sentence, dear reader, because I don't get to use it often. As we picked our way through the next cavern, I kept glancing back at the wall Grr-Fred had sealed, waiting for a herd of wet evil red cows to bust through, but none did.

Grr-Fred led us upward through a winding maze of tunnels until at last we emerged in a brickwork corridor where the air smelled much worse, like city sewage.

Grr-Fred sniffed in disapproval. 'Human territory.'

I was so relieved I could have hugged a sewer rat. 'Which way to daylight?'

Grr-Fred bared his teeth. 'Do not use that language with me.'

'What language? Day–?'

He hissed. 'If you were a tunnel-ling, I would wash your mouth out with basalt!'

Meg smirked. 'I'd kinda like to see that.'

'Hmph,' said Grr-Fred. 'This way.'

He led us onward into the dark.

I had lost track of time, but I could imagine Rachel Elizabeth Dare tapping her watch, reminding me I was late, late, late. I could only hope we would reach Nero's tower before sundown.

Just as fervently, I hoped Nico, Will and Rachel had survived the bulls' attack. Our friends were resourceful and brave, yes. Hopefully, they still had the assistance of the troglodytes. But, too often, survival depended on sheer luck. This was something we gods didn't like to advertise, as it cut down on donations at our temples.

'Grr-Fred –?' I started to ask.

'It's Grr-Fred,' he corrected.

'GRR-Fred?'

'Grr-Fred.'

'gRR-Fred?'

'Grr-Fred!'

You would think, with my musical skills, I would be better at picking up the nuances of languages, but apparently I did not have Nico's panache for Troglodytish.

'Honoured guide,' I said, 'what of our friends? Do you believe Screech-Bling will keep his promise and help them dig to the emperor's fire vats?'

Grr-Fred sneered. 'Did the CEO make such a promise? I did not hear that.'

'But –'

'We have arrived.' He stopped at the end of the corridor, where a narrow brick stairwell led upward. 'This is as far as I can go. These steps will take you into one of the humans' subway stations. From there, you can find your way to the Crusty Crust. You will surface within fifty feet of Nero's tower.'

I blinked. 'How can you be sure?'

'I am a trog,' he said, as if explaining something to a particularly slow tunnel-ling.

Meg bowed, making her acorn squash knock together. 'Thank you, Grr-Fred.'

He nodded gruffly. I noticed he didn't correct *her* pronunciation.

'I have done my duty,' he said. 'What happens to your friends is up to Screech-Bling, assuming the CEO is even alive after the destruction you hatless barbarians brought to our headquarters. If it were up to me . . .'

He didn't bother finishing the thought. I gathered

Grr-Fred would *not* be voting in favour of offering us stock options at the next troglodyte shareholders' meeting.

From my soggy backpack, I fished out Beanie Boy's crystal ball and offered it to Grr-Fred. 'Please, would you take this back to its owner? And thank you for guiding us. For what it is worth, I meant what I said. We have to help one another. That's the only future worth fighting for.'

Grr-Fred turned the crystal sphere in his fingers. His brown eyes were inscrutable as cavern walls. They might have been hard and unmovable, or about to turn to meringue, or on the verge of being broken through by angry cows.

'Good digging,' he said at last. Then he was gone.

Meg peered up the stairwell. Her hands trembled, and I didn't think it was from the cold.

'Are you sure about this?' I asked.

She started, as if she'd forgotten I was there. 'Like you said, either we help each other, or we let a snake eat the future.'

'That's not exactly what I –'

'Come on, Lester.' She took a deep breath. 'Let's get going.'

Phrased as an order, it wasn't something I could have refused, but I got the feeling Meg was saying it to steel her own resolve as much as mine.

Together we climbed back towards the Crusty Crust.

20

Have you had your lunch?
This part is not good to read
If you've just eaten.

I EXPECTED A MOAT FILLED WITH ALLI-
gators. A wrought-iron portcullis. Possibly some vats of
boiling oil.

In my mind, I'd built up the Tower of Nero as a fortress
of darkness with all the evil trimmings. Instead, it was a
glass-and-steel monstrosity of the ordinary Midtown variety.

Meg and I had surfaced from the subway about an hour
before sunset. Luxuriously early, by our standards. Now we
stood across Seventh Avenue from the tower, observing and
gathering our nerve.

The scene on the sidewalk out front could've been anywhere in Manhattan. Annoyed New Yorkers jostled past
groups of gawping tourists. Kebab-scented steam wafted
from a halal food cart. Funk music blared from a Mister
Softee ice-cream truck. A street artist hawked airbrushed
celebrity paintings. No one paid any special attention to
the corporate-looking building that housed Triumvirate
Holdings Ltd and the doomsday button that would destroy
the city in approximately fifty-eight minutes.

From across the street, I spotted no armed guards, no

monsters or Germani on patrol – just black marble pillars flanking a plate-glass entrance, and, inside, a typical oversize lobby with abstract art on the walls, a manned security desk and glass turnstiles protecting access to the elevator banks.

It was after 7:00 p.m., but employees were still leaving the building in small clusters. Folks in business suits clutched briefcases and phones as they hurried to catch their trains. Some exchanged pleasantries with the security guy on their way out. I tried to imagine those conversations. *Bye, Caleb. Say hi to the family. See you tomorrow for another day of evil business transactions!*

Suddenly, I felt as if we'd come all this way to surrender to a brokerage firm.

Meg and I crossed at the pedestrian crossing. Gods forbid we jaywalk and get hit by a car on our way to a painful death. We attracted some strange looks from other pedestrians, which was fair since we were still dripping wet and smelled like a troglodyte's armpit. Nevertheless, this being New York, most people ignored us.

Meg and I didn't speak as we climbed the front steps. By silent agreement, we gripped each other's hands as if another river might sweep us away.

No alarms went off. No guards jumped out of hiding. No bear traps were triggered. We pushed open the heavy glass doors and walked into the lobby.

Light classical music wafted through the chilly air. Above the security desk hung a metal sculpture with slowly swirling primary-coloured shapes. The guard bent forward in his chair, reading a paperback, his face pale blue in the light of his desktop monitors.

'Help you?' he said without looking up.

I glanced at Meg, silently double-checking that we were in the right building. She nodded.

'We're here to surrender,' I told the guard.

Surely this would make him look up. But no.

He could *not* have acted less interested in us. I was reminded of the guest entrance to Mount Olympus, through the lobby of the Empire State Building. Normally, I never went that way, but I knew Zeus hired the most unimpressible, disinterested beings he could find to guard the desk as a way to discourage visitors. I wondered if Nero had intentionally done the same thing here.

'I'm Apollo,' I continued. 'And this is Meg. I believe we're expected? As in . . . hard deadline at sunset or the city burns?'

The guard took a deep breath, as if it pained him to move. Keeping one finger in his novel, he picked up a pen and slapped it on the counter next to the sign-in book. 'Names. IDs.'

'You need our IDs to take us prisoner?' I asked.

The guard turned the page in his book and kept reading.

With a sigh, I pulled out my New York State junior driver's licence. I suppose I shouldn't have been surprised that I'd have to show it one last time, just to complete my humiliation. I slid it across the counter. Then I signed the logbook for both of us. *Name(s): Lester (Apollo) and Meg. Here to see: Nero. Business: Surrender. Time in: 7:16 p.m. Time out: Probably never.*

Since Meg was a minor, I didn't expect her to have an ID, but she removed her gold scimitar rings and placed them next to my licence. I stifled the urge to shout, *Are you insane?* But Meg gave them up as if she'd done this a million times before. The guard took the rings and examined them without comment. He held up my licence and compared it to my face. His eyes were the colour of decade-old ice cubes.

He seemed to decide that, tragically, I looked as bad in real life as I did in my licence photo. He handed it back, along with Meg's rings.

'Elevator nine to your right,' he announced.

I almost thanked him. Then I thought better of it.

Meg grabbed my sleeve. 'Come on, Lester.'

She led the way through the turnstile to elevator nine. Inside, the stainless-steel box had no buttons. It simply rose on its own as soon as the doors slid closed. One small mercy: no elevator music, just the smooth hum of machinery, as bright and efficient as an industrial-grade meat slicer.

'What should I expect when we get to the top?' I asked Meg.

I imagined the elevator was under surveillance, but I couldn't help asking. I wanted to hear Meg's voice. I also wanted to keep her from sinking completely into her own dark thoughts. She was getting that shuttered expression she often had when she thought about her horrible stepfather, as if her brain were shutting down all non-essential services and boarding itself up in preparation for a hurricane.

She pushed her rings back on her middle fingers. 'Take whatever you think might happen,' she advised, 'and turn it upside down and inside out.'

That was not exactly the reassurance I'd been hoping for. My chest already felt like it was being turned upside down and inside out. I was unnerved to be entering Nero's lair with two empty quivers and a waterlogged ukulele. I was unnerved that no one had arrested us on sight, and that the security guard had given Meg back her rings, as if a couple of magical scimitars would make absolutely no difference to our fate.

Nevertheless, I straightened my back and squeezed Meg's hand one more time. 'We'll do what we have to.'

The elevator doors slid open, and we stepped into the imperial antechamber.

'Welcome!'

The young lady who greeted us wore a black business suit, high heels and an earpiece in her left ear. Her luxurious green hair was tied back in a ponytail. Her face was made up to give her a rosier, more human complexion, but the green tint in her eyes and the points of her ears gave her away as a dryad. 'I'm Areca. Before you meet the emperor, can I get you a beverage? Water? Coffee? Tea?'

She spoke with forced cheerfulness. Her eyes said, *Help, I'm a hostage!*

'Um, I'm good,' I said, a feeble lie. Meg shook her head.

'Great!' Areca lied in return. 'Follow me!'

I translated this to mean *Run while you can!* She hesitated, giving us time to reconsider our life choices. When we did not scream and dive back into the elevator, she guided us towards a set of double golden doors at the end of the hallway.

These opened from within, revealing the loft space/throne room I'd seen in my nightmare.

Floor-to-ceiling windows provided a 360-degree view

of Manhattan at sunset. To the west, the sky was blood-red over New Jersey, the Hudson River a glowing purple artery. To the east, the urban canyons filled with shadow. Several varieties of potted trees lined the windows, which struck me as strange. Nero's decorating taste usually tended more towards gold filigree and severed heads.

Rich Persian rugs made an asymmetrical chequerboard across the hardwood floor. Rows of black marble pillars supported the ceiling, reminding me a bit too much of Kronos's palace. (He and his Titans had been all about black marble. That was one reason Zeus insisted on Mount Olympus's strict building codes that kept everything blinding white.)

The room was full of people, carefully positioned, frozen in place, all staring at us as if they'd been practising on their marks for days and Nero had shrieked only seconds ago, *Places, everyone! They're here!* If they started in on a choreographed dance number, I was going to dive through the nearest window.

Lined up on Nero's left were the eleven young demigods of the Imperial Household, aka the Evil von Trapp children, all wearing their best purple-trimmed togas over fashionably tattered jeans and collared shirts, perhaps because T-shirts were against the dress code when the family welcomed important prisoners to be executed. Many of the older demigods glared at Meg.

On the emperor's right stood a dozen servants: young ladies with serving trays and drink pitchers; buff young men with palm-frond fans, though the room's AC was set to *Antarctic winter*. One young man, who had obviously lost a bet, was massaging the emperor's feet.

Half a dozen Germani flanked the throne – including Gunther, our buddy from the Acela ride into New York. He studied me, as if imagining all the interesting and painful ways he could remove my head from my shoulders. Next to him, at the emperor's right hand, stood Luguselwa.

I had to force myself not to sigh with relief. Of course, she looked terrible. Steel braces encased her legs. She had a crutch under each arm. She wore a neck brace as well, and the skin around her eyes was a raccoon mask of bruises. Her mohawk was the only part of her that didn't appear damaged. But, considering that I'd thrown her off a building only three days before, it was remarkable to see her on her feet at all. We needed her for our plan to succeed. Also, if Lu had ended up dying from her injuries, Meg probably would have killed me before Nero got the chance.

The emperor himself lounged on his gaudy purple sofa. He had exchanged his bathrobe for a tunic and traditional Roman toga, which I supposed wasn't much different from his bed-wear. His golden laurels had been recently polished. His neck beard glistened with oil. If his expression had been any smugger, the entire species of domestic cats would have sued him for plagiarism.

'Your Imperial Majesty!' Our guide, Areca, tried for a cheerful tone, but her voice cracked with fear. 'Your guests have arrived!'

Nero shooed her away. Areca hurried to the side of the room and stood by one of the potted plants, which was . . . Oh, of course. My heart thumped with sympathetic pain. Areca was standing by an areca palm, her life force. The emperor had decorated his throne room with the enslaved: potted dryads.

Next to me, I could actually *hear* Meg's teeth grinding. I presumed the dryads were a new addition, maybe put here just to remind Meg who held all the power.

'Well, well!' Nero kicked away the young man who had been giving him a foot massage. 'Apollo. I am amazed.'

Luguselwa shifted on her crutches. On her shaved scalp, veins stood out as stiff as tree roots. 'You see, my lord? I told you they would come.'

'Yes. Yes, you did.' Nero's voice was heavy and cold. He leaned forward and laced his fingers, his belly bulging against his tunic. I thought of Dionysus staying in a schlubby dad bod as a form of protest against Zeus. I wondered what Nero's excuse was.

'So, *Lester*, after all the trouble you've caused me, why would you roll over and surrender now?'

I blinked. 'You threatened to burn down the city.'

'Oh, come now.' He gave me a conspiratorial smile. 'You and I have both stood by and watched cities burn before. Now, my precious Meg here . . .' He regarded her with such tender warmth I wanted to vomit on his Persian rug. 'I can believe *she* might want to save a city. She is a fine hero.'

The other demigods of the Imperial Household exchanged disgusted glances. Clearly, Meg was a favourite of Nero's, which made her an enemy of everyone else in her loving adopted family of sociopaths.

'But, you, Lester,' Nero continued. 'No . . . I can't

believe you've turned so noble. We can't change thousands of years of our nature so quickly, can we? You wouldn't be here if you didn't think it would serve . . . *you.*'

He pointed at my sternum. I could almost feel the pressure of his fingertip.

I tried to look agitated, which wasn't hard. 'Do you want me to surrender or not?'

Nero smiled at Luguselwa, then at Meg.

'You know, Apollo,' he said lazily, 'it's fascinating how bad acts can be good, and vice versa. You remember my mother, Agrippina? Terrible woman. Always trying to rule for me, telling me what to do. I had to kill her in the end. Well, not me personally, of course. I had my man Anicetus do it.' He gave me a little shrug, like, *Mothers, am I right?* 'Anyway, matricide was one of the worst crimes for a Roman. Yet, after I killed her, the people loved me even more! I'd stood up for myself, shown my independence. I became a hero to the common man! Then there were all those stories about me burning Christians alive . . .'

I wasn't sure where Nero was going with all this. We'd been talking about my surrender. Now he was telling me about his mother and his Christian-burning parties. I just wanted to get thrown in a cell with Meg, preferably un-tortured, so Lu could come by later and release us and help us destroy the whole tower. Was that too much to ask? But when an emperor starts talking about himself, you just have to roll with it. You could be there for a while.

'You're claiming those Christian-burning stories weren't true?' I asked.

He laughed. 'Of course they were true. The

Christians were terrorists, out to undermine traditional Roman values. Oh, they *claimed* to be a religion of peace, but they fooled no one. The point is, *real* Romans loved me for taking a hard line. After I died . . . Did you know this? After I died, the commoners rioted. They refused to believe I was dead. There was a wave of rebellions, and every rebel leader claimed to be me reborn.' He got a dreamy look in his eyes. 'I was beloved. My so-called bad acts made me wildly popular, while my *good* acts, like pardoning my enemies, bringing the empire peace and stability . . . those things just made me look soft and got me killed. This time, I will do things differently. I will bring back traditional Roman values. I will stop worrying about good and evil. The people who survive the transition . . . they will love me like a father.'

He gestured to his line of adopted children, all of whom knew enough to keep their expressions carefully neutral.

That old metaphorical skink was trying to claw its way back up my throat. The fact that Nero – a man who had killed his own mother – was talking about defending traditional Roman values . . . that was just about the most Roman thing I could imagine. And the idea that he wanted to play Daddy to the entire world made my guts churn. I pictured my friends from Camp Half-Blood forced to stand in rows behind the emperor's servants. I thought of Meg falling back into line with the rest of the Imperial Household.

She would be the twelfth, I realized. Twelve foster children to Nero, like the twelve Olympians. That couldn't be a coincidence. Nero was raising them as young gods-in-training to take over his nightmarish new world. That made Nero the new Kronos, the all-powerful father who could either shower his children with blessings or devour them as he wished. I had *badly* underestimated Nero's megalomania.

'Where was I?' Nero mused, coming back from his pleasant thoughts of massacre.

'The villain monologue,' I said.

'Ah, now I remember! Good and bad acts. You, Apollo, are here to surrender, sacrificing yourself to save the city. Seems like a good act! That's exactly why I suspect it's bad. Luguselwa!'

The Gaul didn't strike me as someone who flinched easily, but when Nero yelled her name her leg braces squeaked. 'My lord?'

'What was the plan?' Nero asked.

Frost formed in my lungs.

Lu did her best to look confused. 'My lord?'

'The plan,' he snapped. 'You let these two go on purpose. They turn themselves in just before my ultimatum deadline. What were you hoping to gain when you betrayed me?'

'My lord, no. I –'

'Seize them!'

The throne-room choreography suddenly became clear. Everyone played their parts beautifully. The servants backed away. The demigods of the Imperial Household stepped forward and drew swords. I didn't notice the Germani sneaking up behind us until two burly giants gripped my arms. Two more took hold of Meg. Gunther and a friend grabbed hold of Luguselwa with such gusto her crutches clattered to the floor. Fully healed, Luguselwa doubtless would have given them a good fight, but in her current condition there was no contest. They pushed her down, prostrate, in front of the emperor, ignoring her screams and the creaking of her leg braces.

'Stop it!' Meg thrashed, but her captors outweighed her by several hundred pounds. I kicked my Germani in the shins to no avail. I might as well have been kicking a forest bull.

Nero's eyes gleamed with amusement. 'You see, children,' he told his adopted eleven, 'if you ever decide to depose me, you'll have to do *much* better than this. Honestly, I'm disappointed.'

He twirled some whiskers in his chin beard, probably because he didn't have a proper villain's moustache. 'Let's see if I have this right, Apollo. You surrender yourself to get inside my tower, hoping this convinces me not to burn the city, while also making me lower my guard. Meanwhile, your little army of demigods musters at Camp Half-Blood . . .' He smiled cruelly. 'Yes, I have it on good authority they are preparing to march. So exciting! Then, when they attack, Luguselwa frees you from your cell, and, together, in all the confusion, you somehow manage to kill me. Is that about it?'

My heart clawed at my chest like a troglodyte at a rock wall. If Camp Half-Blood was truly on the march, that meant Rachel might have got to the surface and contacted them. Which meant Will and Nico might also still be alive, and still with the troglodytes. Or Nero could be lying. Or he could know more than he was letting on. In any case, Luguselwa was exposed, which meant she couldn't free us or help us destroy the emperor's fasces. Whether or not Nico and the trogs managed their sabotage, our friends from camp would be charging to their own slaughter. Oh, and, also, I would die.

Nero laughed with delight. 'There it is!' He pointed to my face. 'The expression someone makes when they realize their life is over. You can't fake that. So beautifully honest! And you're right, of course.'

'Nero, don't!' Meg yelled. 'F-Father!'

The word seemed to hurt her, like she was coughing up a chunk of glass.

Nero pouted and spread his arms, as if he would welcome Meg into his loving embrace if it weren't for the two large goons holding her in place. 'Oh, my dear sweet daughter. I am so sorry you decided to be part of this. I wish I could spare you from the pain that is to come. But you know very well . . . you should never anger the Beast.'

Meg wailed and tried to bite one of her guards. I wished I had her ferocity. Absolute terror had turned my limbs to putty.

'Cassius,' Nero called, 'come forward, Son.'

The youngest demigod hurried to the dais. He couldn't have been more than eight years old.

Nero patted his cheek. 'There's a good boy. Go and collect your sister's gold rings, will you? I hope you will put them to better use than she did.'

After a moment's hesitation, as if translating these instructions from Neroese, Cassius jogged over to Meg. He carefully avoided her eyes as he worked the rings from her middle fingers.

'Cass.' Meg was weeping now. 'Don't. Don't listen to him.'

The little boy blushed, but he kept working silently at the rings. He had pink stains around his lips from something he'd been drinking – juice, soda. His fluffy blond hair reminded me . . . No. No, I refused to think it. Argh. Too late! Curse my imagination! He reminded me of a young Jason Grace.

When he had tugged both rings free, Cassius hurried back to his stepfather.

'Good, good,' Nero said, with a hint of impatience. 'Put them on. You've trained with scimitars, have you not?'

Cassius nodded, fumbling to comply.

Nero smiled at me, rather like the emcee of a show. *Thank you for your patience. We're experiencing technical difficulties.*

'You know, Apollo,' he said, 'there is one saying I like from the Christians. How does it go? *If your hands offend you, cut them off* . . . Something like that.' He looked down at Lu. 'Oh, Lu, I'm afraid your hands have offended me. Cassius, do the honours.'

Luguselwa struggled and screamed as the guards stretched her arms in front of her, but she was weak and already in pain. Cassius swallowed, his face a mixture of horror and hunger.

Nero's hard eyes, the eyes of the Beast, bored into him. 'Now, boy,' he said with chilling calm.

Cassius summoned the golden blades. As he brought them down on Lu's wrists, the whole room seemed to tilt and blur. I could no longer tell who was screaming – Lu, or Meg, or me.

Through a fog of pain and nausea, I heard Nero snap, 'Bind her wounds! She won't get to die so easily!' Then he turned the eyes of the Beast on me. 'Now, Apollo, let me tell you the *new* plan. You will be thrown into a cell with this traitor, Luguselwa. And Meg, dear Meg, we will begin your rehabilitation. Welcome home.'

21

Fear the comfy couch.
Fear the jailer's fruit platter
And shiny toilet.

NERO'S CELL WAS THE NICEST PLACE I'D
ever been imprisoned in. I would have rated it five stars.
Absolute luxury! Would die here again!

From the high ceiling hung a chandelier . . . a *chandelier*, much too far out of reach for a prisoner to grab. Crystal
pendants danced in the LED lights, casting diamond-shaped
reflections across the eggshell-white walls. In the back of
the room sat a sink with gold fixtures and an automated toilet with a bidet, all shielded behind a privacy screen – what
pampering! One of Nero's Persian carpets covered the floor.
Two plush Roman-style sofas were arranged in a V on either
side of a coffee table overflowing with cheese, crackers and
fruit, plus a silver pitcher of water and two goblets, in case
we prisoners wanted to toast our good luck. Only the front
wall had a jailhouse look, since it was nothing but a row
of thick metal bars, but even these were coated with – or
perhaps made from – Imperial gold.

I spent the first twenty or thirty minutes alone in the
cell. It was hard to measure time. I paced, I screamed, I
demanded to see Meg. I banged a silver platter against the

bars and howled into the empty corridor outside. Finally, as my fear and queasiness got the best of me, I discovered the joys of vomiting into a high-end toilet with a heated seat and multiple self-cleaning options.

I was beginning to think Luguselwa must have died. Why else was she not in the cell with me, as Nero had promised? How could she have survived the shock of double amputation when she was already so badly injured?

Just as I was convincing myself I would die alone in this cell, with no one to help me eat the cheese and crackers, a door banged open somewhere down the hall, followed by heavy footsteps and lots of grunting. Gunther and another Germanus came into view, dragging Luguselwa between them. The middle three bars of the cell entrance fell away, retracting into the floor as fast as sheathed blades. The guards pushed Lu inside, and the bars snapped closed again.

I rushed to Lu's side. She curled on the Persian carpet, her body shivering and splattered with blood. Her leg braces had been removed. Her face was paler than the walls. Her wrists had been bandaged, but the wrappings were already soaked through. Her brow burned with fever.

'She needs a doctor!' I yelled.

Gunther leered at me. 'Ain't you a healing god?'

His friend snorted, then the two of them lumbered back down the hall.

'Erggh,' Lu muttered.

'Hold on,' I said. Then I winced, realizing that probably wasn't a sensitive thing to say, given her condition. I scrambled back to my comfy sofa and rummaged through my pack. The guards had taken my bow and quivers, including the Arrow of Dodona, but they'd left me everything that wasn't obviously a weapon – my waterlogged ukulele and my backpack, including some med supplies Will had given me: bandages, ointments, pills, nectar, ambrosia. Could Gauls take ambrosia? Could they take aspirin? I had no time to worry about that.

I soaked some linen napkins in the ice-water pitcher and wrapped them across Lu's head and neck to lower her temperature. I crushed some painkillers together with ambrosia and nectar and fed her some of the mush, though she could barely swallow. Her eyes were unfocused. Her shivering was getting worse.

She croaked, 'Meg –?'

'Hush,' I said, trying not to cry. 'We'll save her, I swear. But first you have to heal.'

She whimpered, then made a high-pitched noise like a scream with no energy behind it. She had to be in unbelievable pain. She should have been dead already, but the Gaul was tough.

'You need to be asleep for what comes next,' I warned. 'I – I'm sorry. But I have to check your wrists. I have to clean the wounds and re-bandage them or you'll die from sepsis.'

I had no idea how I was going to accomplish this without her dying from blood loss or shock, but I had to try. The guards had tied off her wrists sloppily. I doubted they'd bothered with sterilization. They had slowed the bleeding, but Lu would still die unless I intervened.

I grabbed another napkin and a vial of chloroform – one of Will's more dangerous med-kit components. Using it was a huge risk, but the desperate circumstances left me little choice, unless I wanted to knock Lu over the head with a cheese platter.

I moved the soaked napkin over her face.

'No,' she said feebly. 'Can't . . .'

'It's either this or pass out from the pain as soon as I touch those wrists.'

She grimaced, then nodded.

I pressed the cloth against her nose and mouth. Two breaths, and her body went limp. For her own sake, I prayed she would stay unconscious.

I worked as fast as I could. My hands were surprisingly steady. The medical knowledge came back out of instinct. I didn't think about the grave injuries I was looking at, nor the amount of blood . . . I just did the work. Tourniquet. Sterilize. I would've tried to reattach her hands, despite the hopeless odds, but they hadn't bothered to bring them. Sure, give me a chandelier and a selection of fruit, but no hands.

'Cauterize,' I mumbled to myself. 'I need –'

My right hand burst into flame.

At the time, I didn't find this strange. A little spark of my old sun-god power? Sure, why not? I sealed the stumps of Lu's poor wrists, slathered them with healing ointment, then re-bandaged them properly, leaving her with two stubby Q-tips instead of hands.

'I'm so sorry,' I said.

Guilt weighed me down like a suit of armour. I had been so suspicious of Lu, when all the time she'd been risking her life trying to help. Her only crime was underestimating Nero, just as we all had. And the price she'd paid . . .

You have to understand, to a musician like me, no punishment could be as bad as losing one's hands – to no longer be able to play the keyboard or the fretboard, to never again summon music with one's fingers. Making music was its own sort of divinity. I imagined Lu felt the same way about her fighting skills. She would never again hold a weapon.

Nero's cruelty was beyond measure. I wanted to cauterize the smirk off his smug face.

Attend to your patient, I chided myself.

I grabbed pillows from the sofa and positioned them around Lu, trying to make her as comfortable on the carpet as I could. Even if I'd wanted to risk moving her to the sofa, I doubted I would have had the strength. I dabbed her forehead with more cold cloths. I dribbled water and nectar into her mouth. Then I put my hand against her carotid artery and concentrated with all my might. *Heal, heal, heal.*

Perhaps it was my imagination, but I thought some of my old power stirred. My fingers warmed against her skin. Her pulse began to stabilize. Her breathing came easier. Her fever lessened.

I had done what I could. I crawled across the floor and climbed onto my sofa, my head swimming with exhaustion.

How much time had passed? I didn't know if Nero had decided to destroy New York or wait until the forces of Camp Half-Blood came within range. The city could be burning around me right now and I'd see no sign of it in this windowless cell within Nero's self-contained tower.

The AC would keep blowing. The chandelier would keep glittering. The toilet would keep flushing.

And Meg . . . Oh, gods, what would Nero be doing to 'rehabilitate' her?

I couldn't bear it. I had to get up. I had to save my friend. But my exhausted body had other ideas.

My vision turned watery. I keeled over sideways, and my thoughts sank into a pool of shadow.

'Hey, man.'

The familiar voice seemed to come from half a world away over a weak satellite connection.

As the scene resolved, I found myself sitting at a picnic table on the beach in Santa Monica. Nearby stood the fish-taco shack where Jason, Piper, Meg and I had eaten our last meal before infiltrating Caligula's fleet of mega-yachts. Across the table sat Jason Grace, glowing and insubstantial, like a video projected against a cloud.

'Jason.' My voice was a ruined sob. 'You're here.'

His smile flickered. His eyes were nothing but smudges of turquoise dye. Still, I could feel the quiet strength of his presence, and I heard the kindness in his voice. 'Not really, Apollo. I'm dead. You're dreaming. But it's good to see you.'

I looked down, not trusting myself to speak. Before me sat a plate of fish tacos that had been turned into gold, like the work of King Midas. I didn't know what that meant. I didn't like it.

'I'm so sorry,' I managed at last.

'No, no,' Jason said. 'I made my choice. You're not to

blame. You don't owe me anything except to remember what I said. Remember what's important.'

'*You're* important,' I said. 'Your life!'

Jason tilted his head. 'I mean . . . sure. But if a hero isn't ready to lose everything for a greater cause, is that person really a hero?'

He weighted the word *person* subtly, as if to stress it could mean a human, a faun, a dryad, a griffin, a *pandos* . . . even a god.

'But . . .' I struggled to find a counter-argument. I wanted so badly to reach across the table, grip Jason's wrists and pull him back into the world of the living. But, even if I could, I realized I wouldn't have been doing it for Jason. He was at peace with his choices. I would have been bringing him back for my own selfish reasons, because I didn't want to deal with the sorrow and grief of having lost him.

'All right,' I relented. A fist of pain that had been clenching in my chest for weeks began to loosen. 'All right, Jason. We miss you, though.'

His face rippled into coloured smoke. 'I miss you, too. All of you. Apollo, do me a favour. Beware Mithras's servant – the lion, snake-entwined. You know what it is, and what it can do.'

'I – what? No, I don't! Tell me, please!'

Jason managed one last faint smile. 'I'm just a dream in your head, man. You've already got the info. I'm just say-ing . . . there's a price for bargaining with the guardian of the stars. Sometimes you have to pay that price. Sometimes, you have to let someone else do it.'

This cleared up absolutely nothing, but the dream allowed me no more time for questions.

Jason dissolved. My golden fish tacos turned to dust. The Santa Barbara coastline melted, and I woke with a start on my comfy sofa.

'You alive?' asked a hoarse voice.

Lu lay on the opposite couch. How she'd got herself there from the floor, I couldn't imagine. Her cheeks and eyes were sunken. Her bandaged stumps were speckled with brown polka dots where new blood had seeped through. But she looked a bit less pale, and her eyes were remarkably clear. I could only conclude that my godly healing powers – wherever they had come from – must have done some good.

I was so surprised that I needed a moment to find my voice. 'I – I should be asking *you* that question. How is the pain?'

She lifted her stumps gingerly. 'What, these? I've had worse.'

'My gods,' I marvelled. 'A sense of humour? You really are indestructible.'

Her facial muscles tensed – maybe an attempt to smile, or just a reaction to her constant searing agony. 'Meg. What happened to her? How do we find her?'

I couldn't help but admire her singlemindedness. Despite her pain and her unfair punishment, Lu was still focused on helping our young friend.

'I'm not sure,' I said. 'We'll find her, but first you have to get your strength back. When we break out of here, you'll have to be able to move under your own power. I don't think I can carry you.'

'No?' Lu asked. 'I was looking forward to a piggyback ride.'

Wow, I guess Gauls get punchy when they suffer life-threatening injuries.

Of course, the whole idea of us busting out of our cell was absurd. Even if we managed it, we were in no shape to rescue Meg or fight the emperor's forces. But I couldn't lose hope, especially when my no-handed companion was still able to crack jokes.

Also, my dream of Jason had reminded me that the emperor's fasces was hidden somewhere on this floor of the tower, guarded by the snake-entwined lion. The guardian of the stars, Mithras's servant, whatever that meant – it had to be close. And if it required a price for letting us stomp-kick Nero's rod of immortality into splinters, I was willing to pay it.

'I've got some ambrosia left.' I turned and groped for my med pack. 'You need to eat –'

The door at the end of the corridor slammed open. Gunther appeared outside our cell, holding a silver tray laden with sandwiches and assorted canned sodas.

He grinned, showing off all three of his teeth. 'Lunch.'

The cell's middle bars dropped with the speed of a guillotine. Gunther slid the tray through, and the bars snapped shut again before I could even think of making a move for our captor.

I needed food badly, but just looking at the sandwiches made my stomach roil. Someone had trimmed the crusts off the bread. They were cut into squares rather than triangles.

This is how you can tell when your lunch has been prepared by barbarians.

'Get your strength back!' Gunther said cheerfully. 'Don't die before the party!'

'Party?' I asked, feeling the tiniest spark of hope.

Not because parties were fun, or because I liked cake (both were true), but because if Nero had postponed his big celebration, then perhaps he hadn't yet pressed his dooms-day button.

'Oh, yes!' Gunther said. 'Tonight! Torture for you both. And then we burn down the city!'

With that happy thought, Gunther strolled back down the hall, chuckling to himself, leaving us with our tray of barbarian sandwiches.

22

I will go to sleep
To save everyone I love.
Don't thank me. It's cool.

GODS AREN'T GREAT WITH DEADLINES.

The concept of having a limited time to do something just doesn't make much sense to an immortal. Since turning into Lester Papadopoulos, I'd got used to the idea: go here by this date or the world ends. Get this item by next week or everyone you know will die.

Still, I was shocked to realize that Nero was planning to burn down New York that very evening – with cake, festivities and a good deal of torture – and there was nothing I could do about it.

I stared through the bars after Gunther left. I waited for him to skip back into view and yell, *Just kidding!*, but the hallway remained empty. I could see very little of it except for blank white walls and a single security camera mounted on the ceiling, staring at me with its glossy black eye.

I turned to Lu. 'I have determined that our situation sucks.'

'Thanks.' She crossed her stumps over her chest like a pharaoh. 'I needed that perspective.'

'There's a security camera out there.'

'Sure.'

'Then how were you planning on breaking us out? You would've been seen.'

Lu grunted. 'That's only *one* camera. Easy to evade. The residential areas? They're completely covered with surveillance from every angle, miked for sound, with motion detectors on all the entrances –'

'I get the idea.'

It infuriated me, but did not surprise me, that Nero's family would be under heavier surveillance than his prisoners. After all, this was a man who'd killed his own mother. Now he was raising his own brood of junior despots. I *had* to get to Meg.

I shook the bars, just to say I'd tried. They didn't budge. I needed a burst of godly strength to Apollo-smash my way out, but I couldn't rely on my powers to pay heed to what I wanted.

Trudging back to my sofa, I glared at the offensive sandwiches and sodas.

I tried to imagine what Meg was going through right now.

I pictured her in an opulent room much like this one – minus the bars, perhaps, but a cell nonetheless. Her every move would be recorded, her every conversation overheard. No wonder, back in the old days, she preferred to roam the alleys of Hell's Kitchen, accosting thugs with bags of rotten vegetables and adopting former gods to be her servants. She wouldn't have that outlet now. She wouldn't have me or Luguselwa by her side. She would be utterly surrounded and utterly alone.

I had a sense of how Nero's mind games worked. As

a god of healing, I knew something about psychology and mental health, though I'll admit I did not always apply best practices to myself.

Having unleashed the Beast, Nero would now feign kindness. He would try to convince Meg that she was home. If she just let him 'help' her, she would be forgiven. Nero was his own good cop/bad cop – the consummate manipulator.

The thought of him trying to comfort a young girl he had just traumatized made me sick to my core.

Meg had got away from Nero once before. Defying his will must have taken more strength and courage than most gods I knew would ever possess. But now . . . thrust back into her old abusive environment, which Nero had passed off as normal for most of her childhood, she would need to be even stronger not to crumble. It would be so easy for her to forget how far she'd gone.

Remember what's important. Jason's voice echoed in my head, but Nero's words were knocking around in there, too. *We can't change thousands of years of our nature so quickly, can we?*

I knew my anxiety about my own weakness was getting mixed up with my anxiety about Meg. Even if I somehow made my way back to Mount Olympus, I didn't trust myself to hold on to the important things I'd learned as a mortal. That made me doubt Meg's ability to stay strong in her old toxic home.

The similarities between Nero's household and my family on Mount Olympus made me increasingly uneasy. The idea that we gods were just as manipulative, just as abusive as the worst Roman emperor . . . Surely that couldn't be true.

Oh, wait. Yes, it could. Ugh. I hated clarity. I preferred a softer Instagram filter on my life – Amaro, maybe, or Perpetua.

'We will get out of here.' Lu's voice shook me from my miserable thoughts. 'Then we'll help Meg.'

Given her condition, this was a bold statement. I realized she was trying to lift my spirits. It felt unfair that she had to . . . and even more unfair that I needed it so much.

The only response I could think of was 'Do you want a sandwich?'

She glanced down at the platter. 'Yeah. Cucumber and cream cheese, if there is one. The chef does a good cucumber and cream cheese.'

I found the appropriate flavour. I wondered if, back in ancient times, roving bands of Celtic warriors had ridden into battle with their packs full of cucumber-and-cream-cheese sandwiches. Perhaps that had been the secret to their success.

I fed her a few bites, but she became impatient. 'Just set it on my chest. I'll figure it out. I have to start sometime.'

She used her stumps to manoeuvre the food towards her mouth. How she could do this without passing out from pain, I didn't know, but I respected her wishes. My son Asclepius, god of medicine, used to chide me about helping those with disabilities. *You can help them if they ask. But wait for them to ask. It's their choice to make, not yours.*

For a god, this was a hard thing to understand, much like deadlines, but I left Lu to her meal. I picked out a couple of sandwiches for myself: ham and cheese, egg salad. It had been a long time since I'd eaten. I had no appetite, but I would need energy if we were going to get out of here.

Energy . . . and information.

I looked at Lu. 'You mentioned microphones.'

Her sandwich slipped from between her stumps and landed in her lap. With the slightest of frowns, she began the slow process of corralling it again. 'Surveillance mikes, you mean. What about them?'

'Are there any in this cell?'

Lu looked confused. 'You want to know if the guards are listening to us? I don't think so. Unless they've installed mikes in the last twenty-four hours. Nero doesn't care what prisoners chat about. He doesn't like it when people whine and complain. He's the only one allowed to do that.'

That made perfect Nero-ish sense.

I wanted to discuss plans with Lu – if for no other reason than to raise her spirits, to let her know that my terrific troglodyte tunnelling team might be on their way to scuttle Nero's Greek-fire Sewer Super Soakers, which would mean that Lu's sacrifice had not been completely in vain. Still, I would have to be careful what I said. I didn't want to assume we had privacy. We'd underestimated Nero too many times already.

'The emperor didn't seem to know about . . . the *other* thing,' I said.

Lu's sandwich toppled into her lap again. 'You mean the other thing is *happening*? You were able to arrange it?'

I could only hope we were talking about the same *other thing*. Lu had instructed us to arrange an underground sabotage of some sort, but for obvious reasons I hadn't had a chance to tell her specifics about Nico, Will, Rachel and the troglodytes. (Which, by the way, would make the worst band name of all time.)

'I hope so,' I said. 'Assuming everything went according to plan.' I did not add *And the troglodytes didn't eat my friends because we brought evil red cattle into their encampment.* 'But, let's be honest, so far things have not gone according to plan.'

Lu picked up her sandwich again – this time with more dexterity. 'I don't know about you, but I've got Nero exactly where I want him.'

I had to smile. My gods, this Gaul . . . I had gone from disliking and distrusting her to being ready to take a bullet for her. I wanted her at my side, hands or no, as we took down the emperor and saved Meg. And we *would* do it, if I could muster even a little bit of Lu's toughness.

'Nero should fear you,' I agreed. 'Let's assume *the other thing* is happening. Let's also assume we can get out of here and take care of the . . . um, *other* other thing.'

Lu rolled her eyes. 'You mean the emperor's fasces.'

I winced. 'Yes, fine. That. It would be helpful if I had more information about its protector. Jason called it a guardian of the stars, a creature of Mithras, but –'

'Wait. Who is Jason?'

I didn't want to revisit that painful subject, but I gave her the basics, then explained what I had discussed with the son of Jupiter in my dream.

Lu tried to sit up. Her face turned the colour of putty, making her tattoos darken to purple.

'Oof.' She reclined again. 'Mithras, eh? Haven't heard that name in a while. Lots of Roman officers worshipped him, back in the day, but I never took to those Persian gods. You had to join his cult to find out all the secret handshakes and whatnot. Elite, members-only society, blah, blah. The emperor was an automatic member, of course, which makes sense . . .'

'Because?'

She chewed her cucumber sandwich. 'Explains how Nero would have found this guardian. I – I don't know what it is. I saw it only once, when Nero . . . installed it, I guess you'd say. Years ago.' She shuddered. 'Never want to see it again. That lion's face, those eyes . . . like it could see everything about me, like it was challenging me to . . .' She shook her head. 'You're right. We need more information if we're going to beat it. And we need to know how Meg is doing.'

Why was she looking at me so expectantly?

'That would be great,' I agreed. 'But since we're stuck in a cell –'

'You just told me you had a dream vision. Do you have those often?'

'Well, yes. But I don't control them. At least, not well.'

Lu snorted. 'Typical Roman.'

'Greek.'

'Whatever. Dreams are a vehicle, like a chariot. You have to drive them. You can't let them drive you.'

'You want me to, what . . . go back to sleep? Gather more information in my dreams?'

Her eyelids started to droop. Perhaps the word *sleep* had

reminded her body that this was a great idea. In her condition, just being awake a few hours and eating a sandwich
would have been equivalent to running a marathon.

'Sounds like a plan,' Lu agreed. 'If it's lunchtime now,
that gives us what – seven, eight hours before sunset? Nero
will have his party at sunset, I'm sure. Best time of day to
watch a city burn. Wake me up when you know more.'

'But what if I can't get to sleep? And, if I do, who's going
to wake me up?'

Lu started to snore.

A tiny piece of cucumber was stuck to her chin, but I
decided to leave it there. She might want it later.

I sat back on my sofa and stared at the chandelier twink-
ling cheerfully above.

A party tonight for the burning of Manhattan. Nero
would torture us. Then, I imagined, he would sacrifice me
in one way or another to appease Python and seal their
alliance.

I had to think fast and move faster.

I needed my powers – strength to bend bars or break
through walls, fire to melt Gunther's face the next time he
brought us crustless sandwiches.

I did not need a nap.

And yet . . . Lu wasn't wrong. Dreams could be vehicles.

As the god of prophecy, I'd often sent visions to those
who needed them – warnings, glimpses of the future, sug-
gestions for what sort of temple incense I liked best. I'd
driven dreams right into people's heads. But, since I'd been
mortal, I'd lost that confidence. I had let my dreams drive
me, rather than taking the reins like when I drove the sun

chariot. My team of fiery horses could always feel when their driver was weak or uncertain. (Poor Phaethon had found that out the hard way.) Dreams were no less ornery.

I needed to see what was happening with Meg. I needed to see this guardian that watched the emperor's fasces, so I could figure out how to destroy it. I needed to know whether Nico, Will and Rachel were safe.

If I took the reins of my dreams and yelled, *Giddyap!*, what would happen? At the very least, I would have unsettling nightmares. At worst, I might drive my mind over the Cliffs of Insanity and never wake up.

But my friends were counting on me.

So I did the heroic thing. I closed my eyes and went to sleep.

23

Dream chariot, go!
Out of my way, I'm a god!
Honk, honk. Beep, beep. Zoom.

DRIVING THE DREAM CHARIOT DID NOT
go well. If the dream police had been on patrol, they would
have pulled me over and given me a ticket.

Immediately, a psychic crosswind caught my consciousness. I tumbled through the floor, falling past stairwells and
offices and broom closets, swirling into the bowels of the
tower like I'd been flushed down the cosmic toilet. (Which
is a disgusting plumbing fixture, by the way. No one ever
cleans it.)

GO UP, GO UP! I willed my dream, but I couldn't seem
to find the reins.

I plummeted straight through a vat of Greek fire. That
was different. I hit the tunnels below Manhattan, glancing
around desperately for any sign of my friends and the troglodytes, but I was travelling too fast, spinning like a pinwheel.
I broke through into the Labyrinth and hurtled sideways,
swept along by a current of superheated ether.

I can do this, I told myself. *It's just like driving a chariot.*
Except with no horses. Or chariot. Or body.

I ordered my dream to take me to Meg – the person

I most wanted to see. I imagined my hands reaching out, grasping reins. Just when I thought I had them, my dream-scape stabilized. I found myself back in the caverns of Delphi, volcanic gases layering the air, the dark shape of Python moving heavily in the shadows.

'So, I have you again,' he gloated. 'You shall perish –'

'I don't have time for you right now.' My voice surprised me almost as much as it did the reptile.

'What?'

'Gotta go.' I lashed the reins of my dream.

'How dare you! You cannot –'

I rocketed into reverse like I was tied to a rubber band.

Why backwards? I hated sitting backwards in a moving vehicle, but I suppose the dream was still trying to show me who was boss. I did a roller-coaster rewind through the Labyrinth, the mortal tunnels, the stairwells of the tower. Finally, I lurched to a stop. My stomach clenched, and I retched up . . . well, whatever ethereal spirit-stuff one can retch in the dream world.

My head and stomach orbited each other like wobbly lava planets. I found myself on my knees in an extravagant bedroom. Floor-to-ceiling windows overlooked Midtown all the way to the Hudson River. The cityscape was still merci-fully un-torched.

Meg McCaffrey was busy trashing the bedroom. Even without her blades, she was doing an A+ demolition job with a broken chair leg, which she swung wildly into just about everything. Meanwhile, a Germanus stood blocking the only exit, his arms folded, his expression unimpressed. A woman in an old-fashioned black-and-white maid's uniform

wrung her hands and winced every time something went
CRASH. She held a stack of what looked like party dresses
draped over one arm.

'Miss,' said the maid, 'if you could just choose an outfit
for tonight. Perhaps if you didn't . . . Oh. Oh, that was an
antique. No, that's fine. I'll get another – OH! Very well,
Miss, if you don't like those bed linens I can – There's no
need to shred them, Miss!'

Meg's tantrum raised my spirits considerably. *That's it,
my friend!* I thought. *Give them Tartarus!* Meg threw her
broken chair leg into a lamp, then picked up another whole
chair and raised it over her head, ready to hurl it at the
window.

A faint knock on the bedroom door made her freeze.
The Germanus stepped aside, opened the door and bowed
as Nero swept into the room.

'Oh, my dear, I'm so sorry.' The emperor's voice oozed
sympathy. 'Come. Sit with me.'

He moved smoothly to the bed and sat at the edge, patting the ripped comforter next to him.

I silently rooted for Meg to brain him with the chair. He
was right there, in easy reach. But I realized that was Nero's
intention . . . to make himself seem to be at Meg's mercy. To
make *her* responsible for choosing violence. And, if she did,
he would be free to punish her.

She put down the chair, but she didn't go to Nero. She
turned her back and crossed her arms. Her lips trembled.
I wanted so badly to go to her, to shield her. I wanted to
drive my dream chariot into Nero's face, but I could only
watch.

'I know you feel terrible,' Nero said, 'after what you did to your friend.'

She wheeled around. 'After what I DID?!'

She picked up the chair again and threw it across the room – but not at Nero. It whanged off the window, leaving a smudge but no cracks. I caught the flicker of a smile on Nero's face – a smile of satisfaction – before his expression fixed back into a mask of sympathy. 'Yes, dear. This anger comes from guilt. You led Apollo here. You understood what that meant, what would happen. But you did it anyway. That must be so painful . . . knowing you brought him to his end.'

Her arms trembled. 'I – no. You cut off –' She gagged, clearly unable to say the words. She stared down at her own fists, clenched as if they might fly off her wrists if left unattended.

'You can't blame yourself,' Nero said in a tone that somehow implied, *This is all your fault.*

'Luguselwa made the wrong choice. You know that. You must have understood what would happen. You are too smart to be blind. We've talked about consequences so often.' He sighed with regret. 'Perhaps Cassius *was* too harsh, taking her hands.' He tilted his head. 'If you like, I can punish him for that.'

'What?' Meg was shaking, as if no longer sure where to direct the giant cannon of her anger. 'No! It wasn't him. It was –'

She choked on the obvious answer: YOU.

With Nero sitting right in front of her, talking in gentle tones, giving her his full attention, she faltered.

Meg! I shouted, but no sound came forth. *Meg, keep smashing things!*

'You have a kind heart,' Nero said with another sigh. 'You care about Apollo. About Lu. I understand that. And when you unleash the Beast . . .' He spread his hands. 'I know that is unsettling. But it isn't over, Meg. Will you sit with me? I'm not asking for a hug, or for you to stop being angry. But I have some news that may make you feel better.'

He patted the mattress again. The maid wrung her hands. The Germanus picked his teeth.

Meg wavered. I could imagine the thoughts racing through her head: *Is the news about Apollo? Will you offer to let him go if I cooperate? Is Lu still alive? Will she be released? And, if I don't play along with your wishes, will I be endangering them?*

Nero's unspoken message seemed to hang in the air: *This is all your fault, but you can still make it right.*

Slowly, Meg moved to the bed. She sat, her posture stiff and guarded. I wanted to lunge between her and Nero, to insert myself in the gap and make sure he could not get any closer, but I feared his influence was worse than physical . . . He was worming his way into her mind.

'Here is the good news, Meg,' he said. 'We will always have each other. I will never abandon you. You can never make a mistake so great I will not take you back. Lu betrayed you when she betrayed me. Apollo was unreliable, selfish and – dare I say – a narcissist. But I know you. I have raised you. This is your home.'

Oh, gods, I thought. Nero was so good at being evil, and so evil at being good, he made the words lose their meaning. He could tell you the floor was the ceiling with such conviction you might start believing it, especially since any disagreement would unleash the Beast.

I marvelled how such a man could rise to be emperor of Rome. Then I marvelled how such a man could ever lose *control* of Rome. It was easy to see how he'd got the mobs on his side.

Meg shivered, but whether from rage or despair, I couldn't be sure.

'There, there.' Nero put an arm around her shoulders. 'You can cry. It's all right. I'm here.'

A cold knot formed in my gut. I suspected that as soon as Meg's tears fell, the game would be over. All the independence she'd built and fought so hard to maintain would crumble. She would fold herself against Nero's chest, just as she'd done as a little girl, after Nero killed her real father. The Meg I knew would disappear under the twisted, tortured mess Nero had spent years cultivating.

The scene lost cohesion – perhaps because I was too upset to control my dream. Or perhaps I simply couldn't bear to watch what happened next. I tumbled down through the tower, floor after floor, trying to regain the reins.

I'm not done, I insisted. *I need more information!*

Unfortunately, I got it.

I stopped in front of a golden door – never a good sign, golden doors. The dream swept me inside a small vault. I felt as if I'd entered a reactor core. Intense heat threatened to burn my dream-self into a cloud of dream-ashes. The air smelled heavy and toxic. Before me, floating above a pedestal of Stygian iron, was the fasces of Nero – a five-foot-tall golden axe, bundled with wooden rods and lashed together by gold cords. The ceremonial weapon pulsed with power – exponentially more than the two fasces Meg and I had destroyed at Sutro Tower.

The meaning of this dawned on me . . . whispered into my brain like a line of Python's poisoned prophecy. The three emperors of the Triumvirate hadn't just linked themselves through a corporation. Their life forces, their ambitions, their greed and malice, had entwined over the centuries. By killing Commodus and Caligula, I had consolidated all the power of the Triumvirate into the fasces of Nero. I had made the surviving emperor three times as powerful and harder to kill. Even if the fasces were unguarded, destroying it would be difficult.

And the fasces was *not* unguarded.

Behind the glowing axe, his hands spread as if in benediction, the guardian stood. His body was humanoid, seven feet tall. Patches of gold fur covered his muscular chest, arms and legs. His feathery white wings reminded me of one of Zeus's wind spirits, or the angels that Christians liked to paint.

His face, however, was not angelic. He had the shaggy-maned visage of a lion, ears rimmed with black fur, mouth open to reveal fangs and a panting red tongue. His huge golden eyes radiated a sort of sleepy, self-confident strength.

But the strangest thing about the guardian was the serpent that encircled his body from ankles to neck – a slithering spiral of green flesh that corkscrewed around him like an endless escalator – a snake with no head or tail.

The lion man saw me. My dream state was nothing to

him. Those gold eyes locked onto me and would not let me go. They turned me and examined me as if I were a trog boy's crystal sphere.

He communicated wordlessly. He told me he was the *leontocephaline*, a creation of Mithras, a Persian god so secretive even we Olympians had never really understood him. In Mithras's name, the leontocephaline had overseen the movement of the stars and the phases of the zodiac. He had also been the keeper of Mithras's great sceptre of immortality, but that had been lost aeons ago. Now the leontocephaline had been given a new job, a new symbol of power to guard.

Just looking at him threatened to tear my mind apart. I tried to ask him questions. I understood that fighting him was impossible. He was eternal. He could no more be killed than one could kill time. He guarded the immortality of Nero, but wasn't there any way . . . ?

Oh, yes. He could be bargained with. I saw what he wanted. The realization made my soul curl up like a squashed spider.

Nero was clever. Horribly, evilly clever. He had set a trap with his own symbol of power. He was cynically betting that I would never pay the price.

At last, his point made, the leontocephaline released me. My dream-self snapped back into my body.

I sat up in bed, gasping and soaked in sweat.

'About time,' Lu said.

Incredibly, she was on her feet, pacing the cell. My healing power must have done more than just soothe her amputation wounds. She wobbled a bit, but she did not look like someone who'd been using crutches and leg braces just a day ago. Even the bruises on her face had faded.

'You . . . You look better,' I noted. 'How long was I out?'

'Too long. Gunther brought dinner an hour ago.' She nodded to a new platter of food on the floor. 'He said he'd be back soon to get us for the party. But the fool was care-less. He left us silverware!'

She brandished her stumps.

Oh, gods. What had she done? Somehow, she had man-aged to attach a fork to one stump and a knife to the other. She had inserted the handles into the folds of her bandages, then fastened them in place with . . . Wait. Was that my surgical tape?

I looked at the foot of my bed. Sure enough, my pack was open, the contents scattered about.

I tried to ask *how* and *why* at the same time, so it came out as 'Hawhy?'

'If you have enough time, some tape and a set of work-ing teeth, you can do a lot,' Lu said proudly. 'I couldn't wait for you to wake up. Didn't know when Gunther would be back. Sorry about the mess.'

'I –'

'You can help.' She tested her silverware attachments with a few kung fu jabs. 'I tied these babies on as tight as I could, but you can wrap them one more time. I have to be able to use them in combat.'

'Er –'

She plopped down on the sofa next to me. 'While you work, you can tell me what you learned.'

I was not about to argue with someone who could poke me in the eye with a fork. I was dubious about the effectiveness of her new combat attachments, but I didn't say anything. I understood that this was about Luguselwa taking charge of her situation, not giving up, doing what she could with what she had. When you've gone through a life-changing shock, positive thinking is the most effective weapon you can wield.

I wrapped her utensils more tightly in place while explaining what I'd seen in my dream drive: Meg trying not to crumble under the influence of Nero, the emperor's fasces floating in its radioactive room, and the leontocephaline, waiting for us to try and take it.

'We'd best hurry, then.' Lu grimaced. 'Tighter with that tape.'

My efforts obviously hurt her, judging from the crinkles around her eyes, but I did as she asked.

'Right,' she said, swiping the air with her utensils. 'That'll have to do.'

I tried for a supportive smile. I wasn't sure Captain Fork and Knife would have much luck against Gunther or the leontocephaline, but if we met a hostile rib-eye steak, Lu would be queen of the combat.

'And no sign of the *other thing*?' she asked.

I wished I could've told her yes. I had wanted so badly to see visions of the entire troglodyte corporation digging into Nero's basement and disabling his fire vats. I would have settled for a dream of Nico, Will and Rachel charging to our rescue, yelling loudly and waving noisemakers.

'Nothing,' I said. 'But we still have time.'

'Yeah,' Lu agreed. 'Minutes and minutes. Then the party starts and the city burns. But, okay. Let's concentrate on what we can do. I have a plan to get us out of here.'

A cold shiver ran down my neck as I thought about my silent conversation with the guardian of the fasces. 'And I have a plan for what to do when we get out.'

Then we both said together, 'You're not going to like it.'

'Oh, joy.' I sighed. 'Let's hear yours first.'

24

Fie upon Nero,
Who wants not my arrow's speech!
(I can relate, though.)

LU WAS RIGHT.

I hated her plan, but since time was short and Gunther might show up any minute with our party hats and various torture devices, I agreed to do my part.

Full disclosure: I also hated *my* plan. I explained to Lu what the leontocephaline would demand in exchange for the fasces.

Lu glowered like an angry water buffalo. 'You're sure?'

'I'm afraid so. He guards immortality, so –'

'He expects a sacrifice of immortality.'

The words hung in the air like cigar smoke – cloying and suffocating. This was what all my trials had led to – this choice. This was why Python had been laughing at me for months in my dreams. Nero had made the cost of his destruction giving up the one thing I wanted most. To destroy him, I'd have to forfeit my own godhood forever.

Lu scratched her chin with her fork hand. 'We must help Meg, whatever the cost.'

'Agreed.'

She nodded grimly. 'Okay, then that's what we'll do.'

I swallowed the coppery taste in my mouth. I was ready to pay the price. If it meant freeing Meg from the Beast, freeing the world, freeing Delphi . . . then I would. But it would've been nice if Lu had protested just a little on my behalf. *Oh, no, Apollo! You can't!*

I suppose our relationship was past the point of sugar-coating, though. Lu was too practical for that. She was the sort of woman who didn't whine about getting her hands cut off. She just taped silverware to her stumps and got on with business. She wasn't going to give me a pat on the back for doing the right thing, however painful it was.

Still . . . I wondered if I was missing something. I wondered if we were *really* on the same page. Lu had a far-away look in her eyes, like she was calculating losses on a battlefield.

Maybe what I sensed was her worry about Meg.

We both knew that, under most circumstances, Meg was fully capable of rescuing herself. But with Nero . . . I suspected Lu, like me, *wanted* Meg to be strong enough to save herself. We couldn't make the hard choices for her. Yet it was excruciating to stand by while Meg's sense of independence was tested. Lu and I were like nervous parents leaving our child at school for the first day of kindergarten . . . except in this case the kindergarten teacher was a homicidal megalo-maniac emperor. Call us crazy, but we didn't trust what Meg might learn in that classroom.

Lu met my eyes one last time. I imagined her packing away her doubts and fears in her mental saddlebags for later, when she had time for them, along with her cucumber-and-cream-cheese sandwiches.

'Let's get to work,' she told me.

It wasn't long before we heard the hallway door bang open and heavy footsteps approaching the cell.

'Look casual,' Lu ordered, reclining on her couch.

I leaned against the wall and whistled the tune to 'Maneater'. Gunther appeared, a batch of neon-yellow zip-tie restraints in his hand.

I pointed a finger gun at him. 'Hey, what's up?'

He scowled. Then he looked at Lu with her new silverware attachments, and his face split into a grin. 'What are *you* supposed to be? HA-HA-HA-HA-HA!'

Lu raised her fork and knife. 'Thought I'd carve you up like the turkey you are.'

Gunther started to giggle, which was disturbing in a man of his size. 'Stupid Lu. You have fork-and-knife hands . . . HA-HA-HA-HA-HA!' He tossed the zip-ties through the cell's bars. 'You, ugly boy, tie her arms behind her back. Then I tie you.'

'No,' I said. 'I don't think so.'

His mirth dissipated like foam on skink soup. 'What you say?'

'You want to tie us up,' I said very slowly, 'you'll have to do it yourself.'

He frowned, trying to make sense of the fact that a teenaged boy was telling him what to do. Clearly, he'd never had children.

'I will call other guards.'

Lu snorted. 'You do that. Can't handle us yourself. I'm too dangerous.' She held up her knife hand in what could have been taken as a rude gesture.

Gunther's face turned a mottled red. 'You're not the boss of me no more, Luguselwa.'

'*Not the boss of me*,' Lu mimicked. 'Go on, get help. Tell them you couldn't tie up a weakling boy and a no-handed woman by yourself. Or come in here, and I will tie *you* up.'

Her plan depended on Gunther taking the bait. He needed to come inside. With his barbarian manhood in question, and his honour insulted by a rude piece of silverware, he did not disappoint. The middle bars of the cell retracted into the floor. Gunther strode through. He didn't notice the salve I'd slathered across the threshold – and let me assure you, Will Solace's burn ointment is slippery stuff.

I'd been wondering which direction Gunther might fall. Turns out, backwards. His heel shot out from under him, his legs crumpled, and his head slammed hard against the marble floor, leaving him flat on his back and groaning halfway inside the cell.

'Now!' Lu yelled.

I charged the door.

Lu had told me that the cell bars were motion sensitive. They snapped upward, determined to stop my escape, but they had not been designed to compensate for the weight of a Germanus lying across the threshold.

The bars smashed Gunther against the ceiling like a hyperactive forklift, then lowered him again, their hidden mechanisms whirring and creaking in protest. Gunther gurgled in pain. His eyes crossed. His armor was thoroughly crushed. His ribs probably weren't in much better shape, but at least the bars hadn't gone straight through him. I did not want to witness that kind of mess, nor step through it.

'Get his sword,' Lu ordered.

I did. Then, using Gunther's body as a bridge across the slippery salve, we escaped into the hall, the eye of the security camera watching as we fled.

'Here.' Lu gestured to what appeared to be a closet door.

I kicked it in, realizing only afterwards that 1) I had no idea why, and 2) I trusted Lu enough not to ask.

Inside were shelves stacked with personal possessions – packs, clothes, weapons, shields. I wondered what unfortunate prisoners they had once belonged to. Leaning against a back corner were my bow and quivers.

'Aha!' I grabbed them. With amazement, I drew the Arrow of Dodona from my otherwise empty quivers. 'Thank the gods. How are you still here?'

THOU ART PLEASED TO SEE ME, the arrow noted.

'Well, I thought the emperor would have taken you. Or turned you into kindling!'

NERO IS NOT WORTH A FIG, said the arrow. HE SEES NOT MY BRILLIANCE.

Somewhere down the hall, an alarm began to blare. The overhead lighting changed from white to red.

'Could you talk with your projectile later?' Lu suggested. 'We have to move!'

'Right,' I said. 'Which way to the fasces?'

'Left,' Lu said. 'So you go right.'

'Wait, what? You said it's left.'

'Right.'

'Right?'

ODS BODKINS! The arrow vibrated in my hand. JUST
LISTEN TO THE GAUL!

'I'm going after the fasces,' Lu explained. 'You're going
to find Meg.'

'But . . .' My head spun. Was this a trick? Hadn't we
agreed? I was ready for my close-up, my big heroic sacrifice.
'The leontocephaline demands immortality for immortality.
I have to –'

'I've got it covered,' Lu said. 'Don't worry. Besides, we
Celts lost most of our gods long ago. I'm not going to stand
by while another deity dies.'

'But you're not –'

I stopped myself. I was about to say immortal. Then I
considered how many centuries Lu had been alive. Would
the leontocephaline accept her life as payment?

My eyes filled with tears. 'No,' I said. 'Meg can't lose
you.'

Lu snorted. 'I won't get myself killed if I can help it. I
have a plan, but you need to move. Meg is in danger. Her
room is six floors up. Southeast corner. Follow the stairs at
the end of the hall.'

I started to protest, but the Arrow of Dodona buzzed in
warning. I needed to trust Lu. I needed to cede the battle to
the better warrior.

'Fine,' I relented. 'Can I at least tape a sword to your
arm?'

'No time,' she said. 'Too unwieldy. Wait, actually. That
dagger over there. Unsheathe it and put the blade between
my teeth.'

'How will that help?'

'Probably won't,' she admitted. 'But it'll look cool.'

I did as she asked.

Now she stood before me as LuBeard the Pirate, cutlery-wielding terror of the Seven Seas.

'Ood ruhk,' she mumbled around the blade. Then she turned and raced away.

'What just happened?' I asked.

THOU HAST MADE A FRIEND, the arrow said. NOW REFILLEST THY QUIVERS SO THOU SHALT NOT SHOOT WITH ME.

'Right.' With shaky hands, I scavenged as many intact arrows as I could find in the prisoners' storeroom and added them to my arsenal. Alarms kept blaring. The blood-red light was not helping my anxiety level.

I started down the hall. I'd barely made it halfway when the Arrow of Dodona buzzed, LOOK OUT!

A mortal security guard in tactical riot gear rounded the corner, barrelling towards me with his handgun raised. Not being well prepared, I screamed and threw Gunther's sword at him. By some miracle, the hilt hit him in the face and knocked him down.

THAT IS NOT NORMALLY HOW ONE USETH A SWORD, the arrow said.

'Always a critic,' I grumbled.

MEG IS IN PERIL, he said.

'Meg is in peril,' I agreed. I stepped over the mortal guard, now curled on the floor and groaning. 'Terribly sorry.' I kicked him in the face. He stopped moving and began to snore. I ran on.

I burst into the stairwell and took the concrete steps two at a time. The Arrow of Dodona remained clutched in my hand. I probably should have put it away and readied my bow with normal missiles, but to my surprise I found that its running Shakespearean commentary boosted my shaky morale.

From the floor above me, two Germani rushed into the stairwell and charged me with spears levelled.

Now lacking even Gunther's sword, I thrust out my free hand, shut my eyes and screamed as if this would make them go away, or at least make my death less painful.

My fingers burned. Flames roared. The two Germani yelled in terror, then were silent.

When I opened my eyes, my hand was smoking but unharmed. Flames licked at the peeling paint on the walls. On the steps above me were two piles of ash where the Germani had been.

THOU SHOULDST DO THAT MORE OFTEN, the arrow advised.

The idea made me sick to my stomach. Once, I would have been delighted to summon the power to blowtorch my enemies. But now, after knowing Lu, I wondered how many of these Germani really wanted to serve Nero, and how many had been conscripted into his service with no choice. Enough people had died. My grudge was with only one person, Nero, and one reptile, Python.

HURRY, the arrow said with new urgency. *I SENSE . . . YES. NERO HAS SENT GUARDS TO FETCH MEG.*

I wasn't sure how it had gleaned this information – if it was monitoring the building's security system or eavesdropping on Nero's personal psychic hotline – but the news made me clench my teeth.

'There will be no Meg-fetching on my watch,' I growled.

I slid the Arrow of Dodona into one of my quivers and drew a missile of the non-Shakespearean variety.

I bounded up the stairs.

I worried about Luguselwa, who must have been facing the leontocephaline by now. I worried about Nico, Will and Rachel, whom I hadn't seen any sign of in my dreams. I worried about the forces of Camp Half-Blood, who might be charging into a suicidal rescue mission at this very moment. Most of all, I worried about Meg.

To find her, I would fight the entire tower by myself if I had to.

I reached the next landing. Had Lu said five floors up? Six? How many had I already climbed? Argh, I hated numbers!

I shouldered my way into another bland white corridor and ran in the direction I thought might be southeast.

I kicked open a door and discovered (try not to be too shocked) that I was in the entirely wrong place. A large control room glowed with dozens of monitors. Many showed live feeds of huge metal reservoirs – the emperor's Greek-fire vats. Mortal technicians turned and gawked at me. Germani looked up and frowned. A Germanus who must have been the commander, judging from the quality of his armour and the number of shiny beads in his beard, scowled at me with disdain.

'You heard the emperor's order,' he snarled at the technicians. 'Light those fires NOW. And, guards, kill this fool.'

25

Beware, tech support!
Don't press the naughty button!
Welp. Now you did it.

HOW MANY TIMES HAD I SAID THOSE words? *Kill this fool.*

We gods bandied about statements like that all the time, but we never gave thought to the cost. Like, actual fools may *die*. And in this situation, that fool was me.

A millisecond's scan of the room showed me ten enemies in various states of readiness. In the far corner, four Germani were scrunched together on a broken-down sofa, eating Chinese food from takeaway boxes. Three technicians sat in swivel chairs, manning control consoles. They were human security, each with a sidearm, but they were too focused on their work to be an immediate threat. A mortal guard stood right next to me, looking surprised that I'd just pushed through the door he was monitoring. Oh, hello! A second guard stood across the room, blocking the other exit. That left just the Germanus leader, who was now rising from his chair, drawing his sword.

So many questions flashed through my mind.

What did the mortal technicians see through the Mist?

How would I get out of here alive?

How did Leader Guy sit comfortably in that swivel chair while wearing a sword?

Was that lemon chicken I smelled, and was there enough for me?

I was tempted to say, *Wrong room*, close the door and beat it down the hall. But since the technicians had just been ordered to burn down the city, that wasn't an option.

'STOP!' I sang out of instinct. 'IN THE NAME OF LOVE!'

Everyone froze – maybe because my voice had magic powers, or maybe because I was horribly off-key. I bow-punched the guy next to me in the face. If you have never been punched by a fist holding a bow, I do not recommend it. The experience is like being hit with brass knuckles, except it hurts the archer's fingers much more. Door Guy #1 went down.

Across the room, Door Guy #2 raised his gun and fired. The bullet sparked off the door next to my head.

Fun fact from a former god who knows acoustics: if you fire a gun in an enclosed space, you have just deafened everyone in that room. The technicians flinched and covered their ears. The Germani's Chinese-takeaway boxes went flying. Even Leader Guy stumbled half out of his chair.

My ears ringing, I drew my bow and shot two arrows at once – the first knocking the gun out of Door Guy #2's hand, the second pinning his sleeve to the wall. Yes, this ex-archery god still had some moves!

The technicians returned their attention to their

controls. The Chinese-food contingent tried to extract themselves from their sofa. Leader Guy charged me, his sword in both hands, pointed directly at my soft underbelly.

'Ha-ha!' I initiated a home-plate slide. In my mind, the manoeuvre had seemed so simple: I would glide effortlessly across the floor, avoiding Leader Guy's thrust, veering between his legs as I fired at multiple targets from a supine position. If Orlando Bloom could do it in *Lord of the Rings*, why couldn't I?

I neglected to consider that this floor was carpeted. I fell flat on my back and Leader Guy tripped over me, barrelling headfirst into the wall.

I did get off one shot – an arrow that skimmed across the nearest technician's control panel and knocked him out of his chair in surprise. I rolled aside as Leader Guy turned and hacked at me. Having no time to nock another arrow, I pulled one out and jabbed it into his shin.

Leader Guy howled. I scrambled to my feet and jumped onto the bank of control consoles.

'Back off!' I yelled at the technicians, doing my best to aim one arrow at all three of them.

Meanwhile, the Chinese Food Four were fumbling with their swords. Door Guy #2 had tugged his sleeve free of the wall and was hunting around for his pistol.

One of the technicians reached for his gun.

'NOPE!' I fired a warning arrow, impaling the seat of his chair a millimetre from his crotch. I was loath to harm hapless mortals (wow, I really wrote that sentence), but I had to keep these guys away from the naughty buttons that would destroy New York.

I nocked three more arrows at once and did my best to look threatening. 'Get out of here! Go!'

The technicians looked tempted – it was, after all, a very fair offer – but their fear of me was apparently not as great as their fear of the Germani.

Still growling in pain from the arrow in his leg, Leader Guy yelled, 'Do your job!'

The technicians lunged towards their naughty buttons. The four Germani charged me.

'Sorry, guys.' I split my arrows, shooting each technician in the foot, which I hoped would keep them distracted long enough for me to deal with the Germani.

I blasted the closest barbarian into dust with an arrow to the chest, but the other three kept coming. I leaped into their midst: bow-punching, elbow-jabbing, arrow-poking like a maniac. With another lucky shot, I took down a second Chinese-food eater, then wrestled free long enough to throw a chair at Door Guy #2, who had just located his gun. One of the metal legs knocked him out cold.

Two lemon-chicken-splattered Germani remained. As they charged, I ran between them with my bow horizontal, at face level, smacking them each in the nose. They staggered back as I fired two more shots, point-blank. It wasn't very sporting, but it *was* effective. The Germani collapsed into piles of dust and sticky rice.

I was feeling pretty smug . . . until someone hit me in the back of the head. The room went red and purple. I crumpled to my hands and knees, rolled over to defend myself and found Leader Guy standing over me, the tip of his sword in my face.

'Enough,' he snarled. His leg was soaked in blood, my arrow still stuck through his shin like a Halloween gag. He barked at the technicians, 'START THOSE PUMPS!'

In a last desperate attempt to intervene, I sang, 'DON'T DO ME LIKE THAT!' in a voice that would have made Tom Petty cringe.

Leader Guy dug his sword point into my Adam's apple. 'Sing one more word and I will cut out your vocal cords.'

I frantically tried to think of more tricks I could pull. I'd been doing so well. I couldn't give up now. But lying on the floor, exhausted and battered and buzzing from adrenalin burnout, my head started to spin. My vision doubled. Two Leader Guys floated above me. Six blurry technicians with arrows in their shoes limped back to their control panels.

'What's the hold-up?' yelled Leader Guy.

'W-we're trying, sir,' said one of the techs. 'The controls aren't . . . I can't get any readings.'

Both of Leader Guy's blurry faces glared down at me. 'I'm glad you're not dead yet. Because I'm going to kill you *slowly*.'

Strangely, I felt elated. I may even have grinned. Had I somehow short-circuited the control panels when I stomped across them? Cool! I might die, but I had saved New York!

'Try unplugging it,' said the second tech. 'Then plug it back in.'

Clearly, he was the senior troubleshooter for 1-555-ASK-EVIL.

Tech #3 crawled under the table and rummaged with cords.

'It won't work!' I croaked. 'Your diabolical plan has been foiled!'

'No, we're good now,' announced Tech #1. 'Readings are nominal.' He turned to Leader Guy. 'Shall I –?'

'WHY ARE YOU EVEN ASKING?' Leader Guy bellowed. 'DO IT!'

'No!' I wailed.

Leader Guy dug his sword point a little deeper into my throat, but not enough to kill. Apparently, he was serious about wanting a slow death for me.

The technicians punched their naughty buttons. They stared at the video monitors expectantly. I said a silent prayer, hoping the New York metropolitan area would forgive me my latest, most horrible failure.

The techs fiddled with buttons some more.

'Everything looks normal,' said Tech #1, in a puzzled tone that indicated everything did *not* look normal.

'I don't see anything happening,' said Leader Guy, scanning the monitors. 'Why aren't there flames? Explosions?'

'I – I don't understand.' Tech #2 banged his monitor. 'The fuel isn't . . . It's not going anywhere.'

I couldn't help it. I began to giggle.

Leader Guy kicked me in the face. It hurt so much I had to giggle even harder.

'What did you do to my fire vats?' he demanded. '*What did you do?*'

'Me?' I cackled. My nose felt broken. I was bubbling mucus and blood in a way that must have been extremely attractive. 'Nothing!'

I laughed at him. It was just so perfect. The thought of dying here, surrounded by Chinese food and barbarians, seemed absolutely perfect. Either Nero's doomsday machines had malfunctioned all by themselves, I had done more damage to the controls than I'd realized, or somewhere deep beneath the building, something had gone right for a change, and I owed every troglodyte a new hat.

The idea made me laugh hysterically, which hurt a great deal.

Leader Guy spat. 'Now, I kill you.'

He raised his sword . . . and froze. His face turned pale. His skin began to shrivel. His beard fell out whisker by whisker like dead pine needles. Finally, his skin crumbled away, along with his clothes and flesh, until Leader Guy was nothing but a bleached-white skeleton, holding a sword in his bony hands.

Standing behind him, his hand on the skeleton's shoulder, was Nico di Angelo.

'That's better,' Nico said. 'Now stand down.'

The skeleton obeyed, lowering its sword and stepping away from me.

The technicians whimpered in terror. They were mortals, so I wasn't sure what they *thought* they'd just seen, but it was nothing good.

Nico looked at them. 'Run away.'

They fell all over each other to comply. They couldn't run very well with arrows in their feet, but they were out of the door faster than you could say, *Holy Hades, that dude just turned Leader Guy into a skeleton.*

Nico frowned down at me. 'You look awful.'

I laughed weakly, bubbling snot. 'I know, right?'

My sense of humour didn't seem to reassure him.

'Let's get you out of here,' Nico said. 'This whole building is a combat zone, and our job isn't done.'

26

Tower of fun times.
Giggle with me as we climb.
For Meg! Glory! Hats!

AS NICO HELPED ME TO MY FEET, LEADER Guy collapsed into a pile of bones.

I guess controlling an animated skeleton while hauling my sorry butt off the floor was too much effort even for Nico.

He was surprisingly strong. I had to lean against him with most of my weight since the room was still spinning, my face was throbbing, and I was still suffering from a bout of near-death giggles.

'Where – where's Will?' I asked.

'Not sure.' Nico pulled my arm tighter around his shoulders. 'He suddenly said, "I am needed," and darted off in another direction. We'll find him.' Nico sounded worried nonetheless. 'What about you? How exactly did you . . . uh, do all this?'

I suppose he was talking about the piles of ash and rice, the broken chairs and control panels, and the blood of my enemies decorating the walls and the carpet. I tried not to laugh like a lunatic. 'Just lucky?'

'Nobody's that lucky. I think your godly powers are starting to come back more. Like, a *lot* more.'

'Yay!' My knees buckled. 'Where's Rachel?'

Nico grunted, trying to keep me on my feet. 'She was fine last I saw her. She's the one who sent me here to get you – she's been having visions like crazy for the last day now. She's with the trogs.'

'We have trogs! Whee!' I leaned my head against Nico's and sighed contentedly. His hair smelled like rain against stone . . . a pleasant scent.

'Are you smelling my head?' he asked.

'Um –'

'Could you not? You're getting nose blood all over me.'

'Sorry.' Then I laughed again.

Wow, I thought distantly. That kick to the face must have rattled my brain loose.

Nico half dragged me down the corridor as he briefed me on their adventures since the trog encampment. I couldn't concentrate, and I kept giggling at inappropriate moments, but I gleaned that, yes, the trogs had helped them disable the Greek-fire vats; Rachel had managed to summon help from Camp Half-Blood; and Nero's tower was now the world's largest urban-warfare play structure.

In return, I told him that Lu now had silverware for hands . . .

'Huh?'

She had gone to get Nero's fasces from a leontocepha-line . . .

'A *what*-now?'

And I had to get to the southeast corner of the residence wing to find Meg.

That, at least, Nico understood. 'You're three floors too low.'

'I *knew* something was wrong!'

'It'll be tough getting you through all the fighting. Every level is, well . . .'

We'd reached the end of the hallway. He kicked open a door and we stepped into the Conference Room of Calamity.

A half-dozen troglodytes bounced around the room fighting an equal number of mortal security guards. Along with their fine clothing and hats, the trogs all wore thick dark goggles to protect their eyes from the light, so they looked like miniature aviators at a costume party. Some guards were trying to shoot them, but the trogs were small and fast. Even when a bullet hit one of them, it simply glanced off their rock-like skin, making them hiss with annoyance. Other guards had resorted to riot batons, which weren't any more effective. The trogs leaped around the mortals, whacking them with clubs, stealing their helmets and basically having a grand old time.

My old friend Grr-Fred, Mighty of Hats, Corporate Security Chief, leaped from a light fixture, brained a guard, then landed on the conference table and grinned at me. He'd topped his police hat with a new baseball cap that read TRIUMVIRATE HOLDINGS.

'GOOD COMBAT, Lester-Apollo!' He beat his tiny fists against his chest, then ripped a speakerphone from the table and threw it in the face of an oncoming guard.

Nico guided me through the chaos. We ducked through

another doorway and ran straight into a Germanus, whom Nico impaled with his Stygian iron blade without even breaking stride.

'The Camp Half-Blood landing zone is just ahead,' he told me as if nothing had happened.

'Landing zone?'

'Yeah. Pretty much everybody came to help.'

'Even Dionysus?' I would've paid real drachma to watch him turn our enemies into grapes and stomp on them. That was *always* good for a laugh.

'Well, no, not Mr D,' Nico said. 'You know how it is. Gods don't fight demigod battles. Present company excepted.'

'I'm an exception!' I kissed the top of Nico's head in delight.

'Please don't do that.'

'Okay! Who else is here? Tell me! Tell me!' I felt like he was guiding me towards my own birthday party, and I was dying to know the guest list. Also, I felt like I was dying!

'Um, well . . .'

We'd arrived at a set of heavy mahogany sliding doors.

Nico dragged one open and the setting sun nearly blinded me. 'Here we are now.'

A wide terrace ran along the entire side of the building, providing multimillion-dollar views of the Hudson River and New Jersey cliffs beyond, tinged burgundy in the sunset.

The scene on the terrace was even more chaotic than the one in the conference room. Pegasi swooped through the air like giant seagulls, occasionally landing on the deck to unload new demigod reinforcements in orange Camp

Half-Blood shirts. Nasty-looking Celestial bronze harpoon turrets lined the rails, but most of them had been blown up or crushed. Lounge chairs were on fire. Our friends from camp were engaged in close-quarters fighting with dozens of Nero's forces: a few of the older demigod kids from Nero's Imperial Household, a squad of Germani, mortal security guards and even a few cynocephali – wolf-headed warriors with nasty claws and rabid, slavering mouths.

Against the wall stood a line of potted trees, similar to in the throne room. Their dryads had risen up to fight alongside Camp Half-Blood against Nero's oppression.

'Come, sisters!' cried a ficus spirit, brandishing a pointy stick. 'We have nothing to lose but our potting soil!'

In the centre of the chaos, Chiron himself clopped back and forth, his white stallion lower half draped with extra quivers, weapons, shields and water bottles, like a combination demigod soccer mom and minivan. He wielded his bow as well as I ever could have (though that comment should be considered strictly off the record) while shouting encouragement and directions to his young charges. 'Dennis, try not to kill enemy demigods or mortals! Okay, well, from now on, then! Evette, watch your left flank! Ben – whoa, watch out there, Ben!'

This last comment was directed at a young man in a hand-powered wheelchair, his muscular upper body clad in a racing shirt, his driving gloves studded with spikes. His wild black hair flew in every direction, and as he turned blades jutted from the rims of his wheels, mowing down anyone who dared to get close. His last one-eighty had almost caught Chiron's back legs, but fortunately the old centaur was nimble.

'Sorry!' Ben grinned, seeming not sorry at all, then he wheeled himself straight into a pack of cynocephali.

'Dad!' Kayla came racing towards me. 'Oh, gods, what happened to you? Nico, where's Will?'

'That's a great question,' Nico said. 'Kayla, can you take Apollo while I go look?'

'Yeah, go!'

Nico raced off while Kayla dragged me to the safest corner she could find. She propped me in the only intact chaise longue and began rummaging through her med pack.

I had a lovely view of the sunset and the carnage in progress. I wondered if I could get one of Nero's servants to bring me a fancy drink decorated with a tiny umbrella. I started to giggle again, though what was left of my common sense whispered, *Stop it. Stop it. This is not funny.*

Kayla frowned, clearly worried by my mirth. She dabbed some menthol-scented healing ointment on my busted nose. 'Oh, Dad. I'm afraid you're going to have a scar.'

'I know.' I giggled. 'I'm so glad to see you.'

Kayla managed a weak smile. 'You, too. Been a crazy afternoon. Nico and those trogs infiltrated the building from below. The rest of us hit the tower on several levels at once, overwhelmed their security. The Hermes cabin disarmed a lot of the traps and turrets and whatnot, but we've still got fierce fighting pretty much everywhere.'

'Are we winning?' I asked.

A Germanus screamed as Sherman Yang, head counsellor of Ares cabin, threw him off the side of the building.

'Hard to tell,' Kayla said. 'Chiron told the newbies this
was a field trip. Like a training exercise. They gotta learn
sooner or later.'

I scanned the terrace. Many of those first-time campers,
some no older than eleven or twelve, were fighting wide-
eyed alongside their cabinmates, trying to imitate whatever
their counsellors were doing. They seemed so very young,
but, then again, they were demigods. They'd probably
already survived numerous terrifying events in their short
lives. And Kayla was right – adventures would not wait for
them to be ready. They had to jump in, sooner better than
later.

'Rosamie!' Chiron called. 'Sword higher, dear!'

The young girl grinned and lifted her blade, intercepting the strike of a security guard's baton. She smacked her
foe across the face with the flat of her blade. 'Do we have
field trips every week? This is cool!'

Chiron gave her a pained smile, then continued shooting down enemies.

Kayla bandaged my face as best she could – wrapping
white gauze around my nose and making me go cross-eyed.
I imagined I looked like the Partially Invisible Man, which
made me giggle again.

Kayla grimaced. 'Okay, we gotta clear your head. Drink
this.' She lifted a vial to my lips.

'Nectar?'

'Definitely *not* nectar.'

The taste exploded in my mouth. Immediately, I realized what she was giving me and why: Mountain Dew, the glowing-lime-green elixir of perfect sobriety. I don't know what effect it has on mortals, but ask any supernatural entity and they will tell you that Mountain Dew's combination of sweetness, caffeine and otherworldly *je-ne-sais-quoi-peut-être-radioactif* taste is enough to bring complete focus and seriousness to any god. My eyesight cleared. My giddiness evaporated. I had zero desire to giggle. A grim sense of danger and impending death gripped my heart. Mountain Dew is the equivalent of the enslaved servant who would ride behind the emperor during his triumphal parades, whispering, *Remember, you are mortal, and you will die* to keep him from getting a big head.

'Meg,' I said, recalling what was most important. 'I need to find Meg.'

Kayla nodded grimly. 'Then that's what we'll do. I brought you some extra arrows. Thought you might need them.'

'You are the most thoughtful daughter ever.'

She blushed right down to the red roots of her hair. 'Can you walk? Let's get moving.'

We ran inside and turned down a corridor that Kayla thought might lead to the stairwell. We pushed through another set of doors and found ourselves in the Dining Room of Disaster.

Under different circumstances, it might have been a lovely place for a dinner party: a table big enough for twenty guests, a Tiffany chandelier, a huge marble fireplace

and wood-panelled walls with niches for marble busts –
each depicting the face of the same Roman emperor. (If
you guessed Nero, you win a Mountain Dew.)

Not part of the dinner plans: a red forest bull had somehow found its way into the room and was now chasing a
group of young demigods around the table while they yelled
insults and pelted it with Nero's golden plates, cups and
cutlery. The bull didn't seem to realize it could simply smash
through the dining table and trample the demigods, but I
suspected it would eventually figure that out.

'Ugh, these things,' said Kayla when she saw the bull.

I thought this would make an excellent description in
the camp's encyclopedia of monsters. *Ugh, these things* was
really all you needed to know about tauri silvestres.

'They can't be killed,' I warned as we joined the other
demigods in their game of ring-around-the-dining-table.

'Yeah, I know.' Kayla's tone told me she'd already had
a crash course in forest bulls during her field-trip fun. 'Hey,
guys,' she said to her young comrades. 'We need to lure this
thing outside. If we can trick it off the edge of the terrace –'

At the opposite end of the room, the doors burst open.
My son Austin appeared, his tenor sax at the ready. Finding
himself right next to the bull's head, he yelped, 'Whoa!'
then let loose a dissonant *squeak-blatt* on the sax that would
have made Coltrane proud. The bull lurched away, shaking
its head in dismay, as Austin vaulted over the dining table
and slid to our side.

'Hey, guys,' he said. 'We having fun yet?'

'Austin,' Kayla said with relief. 'I need to lure this bull
outside. Can you –?' She pointed at me.

'We playing pass-the-Apollo?' Austin grinned. 'Sure. C'mon, Dad. I got you.'

As Kayla mustered the younger demigods and began shooting arrows to goad the bull into following her, Austin hustled me through a side door.

'Where to, Dad?' He politely did not ask why my nose was bandaged or why my breath smelled of Mountain Dew.

'I have to find Meg,' I said. 'Three stories up? South-east corner?'

Austin kept jogging with me down the corridor, but his mouth tightened in a thoughtful frown. 'I don't think anybody's managed to fight their way up to that level yet, but let's do it.'

We found a grand circular stairwell that took us up one more floor. We navigated a maze of corridors, then shouldered through a narrow door into the Hat Room of Horrors.

Troglodytes had found the mother lode of haberdashery. The oversize walk-in closet must have served as Nero's seasonal coat-check area, because fall and winter jackets lined the walls. Shelves overflowed with scarves, gloves and, yes, every conceivable manner of hat and cap. The trogs rifled through the collection with glee, stacking hats six or seven high on their heads, trying on scarves and galoshes to augment their incredibly civilized fashion sense.

One trog looked up at me through his dark goggles, cords of drool hanging from his lips. 'Haaats!'

I could only smile and nod and creep carefully around the edge of the closet, hoping none of the trogs mistook us for chapeau poachers.

Thankfully, the trogs paid us no mind. We emerged

from the other side of the closet into a marble foyer with a bank of elevators.

My hopes rose. Assuming this was the main entrance to Nero's residential levels, where his most favoured guests would be received, we were getting closer to Meg.

Austin stopped in front of a keypad with a golden inlaid SPQR symbol. 'Looks like this elevator gives you direct access to the imperial apartments. But we'd need a key card.'

'Stairs?' I asked.

'I don't know,' he said. 'This close to the emperor's quarters, I bet any passage up will be locked and booby-trapped. The Hermes cabin swept the lower stairwells, but I doubt they've made it this far. We're the first.' He fingered the pads of his saxophone. 'Maybe I could open the elevator with the right sequence of tones . . . ?'

His voice trailed off as the elevator doors opened by themselves.

Inside stood a young demigod with dishevelled blond hair and rumpled street clothes. Two golden rings gleamed on his middle fingers.

Cassius's eyes widened when he saw me. Clearly, he hadn't been expecting to run into me ever again. He looked like his last twenty-four hours had been almost as bad as mine. His face was grey, his eyes swollen and red from crying. He seemed to have developed a nervous twitch that travelled randomly around his body.

'I –' His voice cracked. 'I didn't want . . .' His hands trembling, he pulled off Meg's rings and offered them to me. 'Please . . .'

He looked past me. Clearly, he just wanted to leave, to get out of this tower.

I'll admit I felt a surge of anger. This child had cut off Luguselwa's hands with Meg's own blades. But he was so small and so terrified. He looked like he expected me to turn into the Beast, as Nero would have done, and punish him for what Nero had made him do.

My anger dissolved. I let him drop Meg's rings into my palm. 'Go.'

Austin cleared his throat. 'Yeah, but first . . . how about that key card?' He pointed to a laminated square hanging from a lanyard around Cassius's neck. It looked so much like a school ID that any kid might wear that I hadn't even registered it.

Cassius fumbled to remove it. He handed it to Austin. Then he ran.

Austin tried to read my expression. 'I take it you've met that kid before?'

'Long, bad story,' I said. 'Will it be safe for us to use his elevator pass?'

'Maybe, maybe not,' Austin said. 'Let's find out.'

27

Can't fight in person?
We can videoconference.
I'll kill you online.

THE WONDERS NEVER CEASED.

The key card worked. The elevator did not incinerate us or drop us to our deaths. Unlike the previous elevator I'd taken, however, this one *did* have background music. We rose smoothly and slowly, as if Nero wanted to give us plenty of time to enjoy it.

I've always thought you can judge the quality of a villain by his elevator music. Easy listening? Pedestrian villainy with no imagination. Smooth jazz? Devious villainy with an inferiority complex. Pop hits? Ageing villainy trying desperately to be hip.

Nero had chosen soft classical, as in the lobby. Oh, well played. This was self-assured villainy. Villainy that said *I already own everything and have all the power. Relax. You're going to die in a minute, so you might as well enjoy this soothing string quartet.*

Next to me, Austin fingered the keys of his saxophone. I could tell he, too, was worried about the soundtrack.

'Wish it was Miles Davis,' he said.

'That would be nice.'

'Hey, if we don't get out of this –'

'None of that talk,' I chided.

'Yeah, but I wanted to tell you, I'm glad we had some time together. Like . . . *time* time.'

His words warmed me even more than Paul Blofis's lasagne.

I knew what he meant. While I'd been Lester Papadopoulos, I hadn't spent much time with Austin, or any of the people I'd stayed with, really, but it had been more than we'd *ever* spent together when I was a god. Austin and I had got to know each other – not just as god and mortal, or father and son, but as two people working side by side, helping each other get through our often messed-up lives. That had been a precious gift.

I was tempted to promise we'd do this more often if we survived, but I'd learned that promises are precious. If you're not absolutely sure you can keep them, you should never make them, much like chocolate chip cookies.

Instead, I smiled and squeezed his shoulder, not trusting myself to speak.

Also, I couldn't help thinking about Meg. If so little time with Austin had been this meaningful, how could I possibly quantify what my adventures with Meg had meant to me? I'd shared almost my entire journey with that silly, brave, infuriating, wonderful girl. I *had* to find her.

The elevator doors slid open. We stepped into a hall-way with a floor mosaic depicting a triumphal procession through a burning New York cityscape. Clearly, Nero had been planning for months, perhaps years, to unleash his inferno no matter what I did. I found this so appalling and so in-character for him, I couldn't even get angry.

We stopped just before the end of the hall, where it split into a T. From the corridor to the right came the sounds of many voices in conversation, glasses clinking, even some laughter. From the corridor on the left, I heard nothing.

Austin motioned for me to wait. He carefully removed a long brass rod from the body of his sax. He had all sorts of nonstandard attachments on his instrument, including a bag of exploding reeds, tone-hole cleaners that doubled as zip-ties and a stiletto knife for stabbing monsters and unappreciative music critics. The rod he chose now was fitted with a small curved mirror on one end. He edged this into the hallway like a periscope, studied the reflections, then pulled it back.

'Party room on the right,' he whispered in my ear. 'Full of guards, bunch of folks that look like guests. Library on the left, looks empty. If you need to get to the southeast corner to find Meg, you'll have to go straight through that crowd.'

I clenched my fists, ready to do whatever was necessary.

From the party room came the voice of a young woman making an announcement. I thought I recognized the polite and terrified tone of the dryad Areca.

'Thank you all for your patience!' she told the crowd. 'The emperor is just finishing up a few matters in the throne room. And the, ah, minor disruptions on the lower floors will be taken care of very soon. In the meantime, please enjoy cake and beverages while we wait for –' her voice cracked – 'the burning to start.'

The guests gave her a polite smattering of applause.

I readied my bow. I wanted to charge into that crowd, free Areca, shoot everybody else and stomp on their cake. Instead, Austin grabbed my arm and pulled me back a few steps towards the elevator.

'There's too many of them,' he said. 'Let me cause a distraction. I'll draw as many as I can into the library and lead them on a chase. Hopefully that'll clear a path for you to get to Meg.'

I shook my head. 'It's too dangerous. I can't let you –'

'Hey.' Austin smirked. For a moment, I glimpsed my own old godly self-confidence in him – that look that said, *I'm a musician. Trust me.* 'Dangerous is part of the job description. Let me do this. You hang back until I draw them out. Then go find our girl. I'll see you on the other side.'

Before I could protest, Austin ran to the junction of the corridor and yelled, 'Hey, idiots! You're all gonna *die!*' Then he put his mouthpiece to his lips and blasted out 'Pop Goes the Weasel'.

Even without the insults, that particular song, when played by a child of Apollo, will cause a stampede one hundred percent of the time. I pressed myself against the wall by the elevator as Austin dashed towards the library, pursued by fifty or sixty angry screaming party guests and Germani. I could only hope Austin found a second exit from the library, or else this would be a very short chase.

I forced myself to move. *Find our girl*, Austin had said.

Yes. That was the plan.

I sprinted to the right and into the party room.

Austin had cleared out the place completely. Even Areca seemed to have followed the rampaging 'Pop Goes the Weasel' mob.

Left behind were dozens of high cocktail tables covered in linen, sprinkled with glitter and rose petals, and topped with balsa-wood centrepiece sculptures of Manhattan going up in painted flames. Even for Nero, I found this over the top. The sideboard was loaded with every conceivable party appetizer, plus a multilayered red-and-yellow flame-motif cake. A banner across the back wall read HAPPY INFERNO!

Along the other wall, plate-glass windows (no doubt heavily insulated) looked over the city, allowing for a beautiful view of the promised firestorm, which now – bless the trogs and their magnificent hats – would not be happening.

In one corner, a small stage had been set up with a single microphone and a stand of instruments: a guitar, a lyre and a violin. Oh, Nero. As a sick joke, he had intended to fiddle while New York burned. No doubt his guests would have laughed and clapped politely as the city exploded and millions perished to the tune of 'This Land Is Your Land'. And who were these guests? The emperor's billionaire golf buddies? Adult demigods who had been recruited for his postapocalyptic empire? Whoever they were, I hoped Austin stampeded them straight into a mob of angry troglodyte shareholders.

It was fortunate no one was left in the room. They would have faced my wrath. As it was, I shot an arrow into the cake, which wasn't a very satisfying experience.

I marched through the room, and then, impatient with the sheer size of the place, began to jog. At the far end, I kicked through a doorway, my bow drawn and ready, but found only another empty hallway.

I recognized this area from my dreams, though. Finally, I had reached the imperial family's living area. Where were the guards? The servants? I decided I didn't care. Just up ahead would be Meg's door. I ran.

'Meg!' I barrelled into her bedroom.

No one was there.

The bed had been perfectly made up with a new comforter. The broken chairs had been replaced. The room smelled of Pine Sol, so even Meg's scent had been erased along with any sign of her rebellion. I'd never felt so depressed and alone.

'Hello!' said a small, tinny voice to my left.

I shot an arrow at the nightstand, cracking the screen of a laptop computer showing Nero's face on a live video call.

'Oh, no,' he said dryly, his image now fractured and pixelated. 'You got me.'

His image jiggled, too large and off-centre, as if he were holding the camera phone himself and not used to using it. I wondered if the emperor had to worry about cell phones malfunctioning, the way demigods did, or if the phone would broadcast his location to monsters. Then I realized there was no monster within five hundred miles worse than Nero.

I lowered my bow. I had to unclench my jaw in order to speak. 'Where is Meg?'

'Oh, she's quite well. She's here with me in the throne room. I imagined you'd stumble in front of that monitor sooner or later, so we could chat about your situation.'

'My situation? You're under siege. We've ruined your inferno party. Your forces are being routed. I'm coming for you now, and, if you so much as touch a rhinestone on Meg's glasses, I'll kill you.'

Nero laughed gently, as if he had no concerns in the world. I didn't catch the first part of his response, because my attention was drawn to a flash of movement in the hallway. Screech-Bling, CEO of the troglodytes, materialized in Meg's bedroom doorway, grinning with delight, his colonial outfit covered with monster dust and tufts of red bull fur, his tricorn hat topped with several new headwear acquisitions.

Before Screech-Bling could say anything that would announce his presence, I gave him a subtle shake of the head, warning him to stay put, out of range of the laptop camera. I didn't want to give Nero any more information about our allies than necessary.

It was impossible to read Screech-Bling's eyes behind his dark goggles, but, being a smart trog, he seemed to understand.

Nero was saying '– quite a different situation. Have you heard of Sassanid gas, Apollo?'

I had no idea what that was, but Screech-Bling almost leaped out of his buckle shoes. His lips curled in a distasteful sneer.

'Ingenious, really,' Nero continued. 'The Persians used

it against our troops in Syria. Sulphur, bitumen, a few other secret ingredients. Horribly poisonous, causes excruciating death, especially effective in enclosed spaces like tunnels . . . or buildings.'

My neck hairs stood on end. 'Nero. No.'

'Oh, I think yes,' he countered, his voice still pleasant. 'You've robbed me of my chance to burn down the city, but surely you didn't think that was my *only* plan. The backup system is quite intact. You've done me the favour of gathering the entire Greek camp in one place! Now, with just a push of a button, everything below the throne room level –'

'Your own people are down here!' I yelled, shaking with fury.

Nero's distorted face looked pained. 'It's unfortunate, yes. But you've forced my hand. At least my darling Meg is here, and some of my other favourites. We will survive. What you don't seem to realize, Apollo, is that you can't destroy bank accounts with a bow and arrows. All my assets, all the power I've built up for centuries – it's all safe. And Python is still waiting for your corpse to be delivered to him. So let's make a deal. I will delay releasing my Sassanid surprise for . . . say, fifteen minutes. That should be enough time for you to reach the throne room. I'll let in you, and *only* you.'

'And Meg?'

Nero looked baffled. 'As I said, Meg is fine. I would never hurt her.'

'You –' I choked on my rage. 'You do nothing *but* hurt her.'

He rolled his eyes. 'Come on up and we'll have a chat.

I'll even . . .' He paused, then laughed as if he'd had a sudden inspiration. 'I'll even let Meg decide what to do with you! Surely that's more than fair. Your other option is that I release the gas now, then come down and collect your corpse at my leisure, along with those of your friends –'

'No!' I tried to curb the desperation in my voice. 'No, I'm coming up.'

'Excellent.' Nero gave me a smug smile. 'Ta-ta.'

The screen went dark.

I faced Screech-Bling. He stared back, his expression grim.

'Sassanid gas is very – GRR – bad,' he said. 'I see why Red Priestess sent me here.'

'Red – you mean Rachel? She told you to find me?'

Screech-Bling nodded. 'She sees things, as you said. The future. The worst enemies. The best hats. She told me to come to this place.'

His voice conveyed a level of reverence that suggested Rachel Elizabeth Dare would be getting free skink soup for the rest of her life. I missed my Pythia. I wished she had sought me out herself, rather than sending Screech-Bling, but since the trog could run at supersonic speed and tear through solid rock, I guessed it made sense.

The CEO scowled at the laptop's dark cracked monitor. 'Is it possible Ne-ACK-ro is bluffing about the gas?'

'No,' I said bitterly. 'Nero doesn't bluff. He likes to boast, then follow through. He'll release that gas as soon as he has me in the throne room.'

'Fifteen minutes,' Screech-Bling mused. 'Not much

time. Try to stall him. I will gather the trogs. We will dis-able this gas, or I will see you in Underheaven!'

'But –'

Screech-Bling vanished in a cloud of dust and bull hair.

I tried to steady my breathing. The troglodytes had come through for us once before when I didn't believe they would. Still, we weren't underground now. Nero would not have told me about his poison-gas delivery system if it was easy to find or disarm. If he could fumigate an entire sky-scraper at the touch of a button, I didn't see how the trogs would have time to stop him, or even get our forces safely out of the building. And, when I faced the emperor, I had no chance of beating him . . . unless Lu had succeeded in get-ting his fasces from the leontocephaline, and that mission also seemed impossible.

On the other hand, I didn't have much choice but to hope. I had a part to play. Stall Nero. Find Meg.

I marched out of the bedroom.

Fifteen minutes. Then I would end Nero, or he would end me.

28

Signs of the end times:
Torches, rolling grapes, neck beards.
Meg gets cleaned up nice.

THE BLAST DOORS WERE A NICE TOUCH.

I'd found my way back to the throne room level with no problem. The elevators cooperated. The halls were eerily quiet. This time, no one greeted me in the antechamber.

Where the ornamental golden doors had stood before, the entrance to Nero's inner sanctum was now sealed by massive panels of titanium and Imperial gold. Hephaestus would have salivated at the sight – so much beautiful metalwork, inscribed with sorcerous charms of protection worthy of Hecate. All to keep one slimy emperor safe in his panic room.

Finding no doorbell, I rapped my knuckles on the titanium: *Shave and a haircut . . .*

No one gave the proper response, because barbarians. Instead, at the upper left-hand corner of the wall, a security camera light blinked from red to green.

'Good.' Nero's voice crackled from a speaker in the ceiling. 'You're alone. Smart boy.'

I could have got offended by his *boy* comment, but

there was so much else to feel offended by that I figured I'd better pace myself. The doors rumbled, parting just enough for me to squeeze through. They closed behind me.

I scanned the room for Meg. She was nowhere in sight, which made me want to smack a Nero.

The room was mostly unchanged. At the foot of Nero's dais, the Persian rugs had been replaced to get rid of those annoying bloodstains from Luguselwa's double amputation. The servants had been cleared out. Forming a semicircle behind Nero's throne were a dozen Germani, some looking like they'd served as target practice for Camp Half-Blood's 'field trip'. Where Lu and Gunther had stood before, at the emperor's right hand, a new Germanus had taken their place. He had a stark white beard, a deep vertical scar on the side of his face and armour stitched from shaggy pelts that would have won him no friends in the animal-rights community.

Rows of Imperial-gold bars had been lowered over all the windows, making the entire throne room feel appropriately like a cage. Enslaved dryads hovered nervously near their potted plants. The children of the Imperial Household – only seven of them, now – stood next to each plant with burning torches in their hands. Since Nero had raised them to be despicable, I supposed they would burn the dryads if I didn't cooperate.

My hand rested against my jeans pocket, where I'd tucked Meg's golden rings. I was relieved that at least she wasn't standing with her siblings. I was glad young Cassius had run away from this place. I wondered where the other three missing adoptees had gone – if they'd been captured or had fallen in battle to Camp Half-Blood. I tried not to feel any satisfaction at the thought, but it was difficult.

'Hello!' Nero sounded genuinely happy to see me. He reclined on his couch, popping grapes in his mouth from a silver platter at his side. 'Weapons on the floor, please.'

'Where is Meg?' I demanded.

'Meg . . . ?' Nero feigned confusion. He scanned the line of his torch-bearing children. 'Meg. Let's see . . . where did I leave her? Which one is Meg?'

The other demigods gave him forced smiles, perhaps not sure if Dear Old Dad was joking.

'She's close,' Nero assured me, his expression hardening. 'But, first, weapons on the floor. I am taking no chances that you will harm my daughter.'

'You –' I was so angry I couldn't finish the sentence.

How could someone twist the truth with such brazenness, telling you the exact opposite of what was clear and obvious, and *still* sound like they believed what they were saying? How could you defend against lies that were so blatant and brash they should have required no challenge?

I put down my bow and quivers. I doubted they would matter. Nero wouldn't have let me into his presence if he thought they were a threat.

'And the ukulele,' he said. 'And the backpack.'

Oh, he was good.

I set these next to my quivers.

I realized that even if I tried something – even if I could throw flames at Nero or shoot him in the face or Apollo-smash his horrible purple love seat – it wouldn't matter if his fasces was still intact. He looked completely at ease, as if he knew he was invulnerable.

All my bad behaviour would do is hurt others. The dryads would burn. If the demigods refused to burn them, then Nero would have the Germani punish the demigods. And if the Germani hesitated to carry out his orders . . . Well, after what had happened to Luguselwa, I doubted any of the guards would dare challenge Nero. The emperor held everyone in this room in a web of fear and threats. But what about Meg? She was the only wild card I could hope to play.

As if reading my thoughts, Nero gave me a thin smile.

'Meg, my dear,' he called, 'it's safe to come forward.'

She appeared from behind one of the columns in the back of the room. Two cynocephali flanked her. The wolf-headed men did not touch her, but they walked beside her in such a tight orbit they reminded me of sheepdogs herding a wayward lamb.

Meg looked physically unhurt, though she'd been bathed to within an inch of her life. All the hard-earned grime, ash and dirt she'd accumulated on her way to the tower had been scrubbed away. Her pageboy haircut had been reshaped in a layered pixie style, parted in the middle, making Meg resemble the dryads a little too closely. And her clothes: gone was Sally Jackson's valentine dress. In its place, Meg wore a sleeveless purple gown, gathered at the waist by a golden cord. Her red high-tops had been exchanged for gold-corded sandals. The only thing that remained of her old look was her glasses, without which she couldn't see, but I was surprised Nero had let her keep even those.

My heart broke. Meg looked elegant, older and quite

beautiful. She also looked utterly, completely no longer her-self. Nero had tried to strip away everything she had been, every choice she'd made, and replace her with someone else – a proper young lady of the Imperial Household.

Her foster siblings watched her approach with undis-guised loathing and jealousy.

'There you are!' Nero said with delight. 'Come join me, dear.'

Meg met my eyes. I tried to transmit how concerned and anguished I felt for her, but her expression remained carefully neutral. She made her way towards Nero, each step cautious, as if the slightest false step or betrayal of emotion might cause invisible mines to explode around her.

Nero patted the cushions next to him, but Meg stopped at the base of the dais. I chose to take this as a hopeful sign. Nero's face tightened with displeasure, but he masked it quickly, no doubt deciding, like the professional abusive villain he was, not to exert more pressure than was neces-sary, to keep the line taut without breaking it.

'And so here we are!' He spread his arms to take in this special occasion. 'Lester, it's a shame you ruined our fire-works display. We could have been down in the parlour right now with our guests, watching a lovely sunset as the city burned. We could've had canapés and cake. But no matter. We still have so much to celebrate! Meg is home!'

He turned to the white-bearded Germanus. 'Vercorix, bring me the remote control, would you?' He gestured vaguely to the coffee table, where a black lacquered tray was piled with tech gadgets.

Vercorix lumbered over and picked one.

'No, that's for the television,' said Nero. 'No, that's the DVR. Yes, that's the one, I think.'

Panic swelled in my throat as I realized what Nero wanted: the control for releasing his Sassanid gas. Naturally, he would keep it with his TV remotes.

'Stop!' I yelled. 'You said Meg would decide.'

Meg's eyes widened. Apparently, she hadn't heard Nero's plan. She looked back and forth between us, as if worried which of us might attack her first. Watching her inner turmoil made me want to weep.

Nero smirked. 'Well, of course she will! Meg, my dear, you know the situation. Apollo has failed you yet again. His plans are in ruins. He has sacrificed his allies' lives to make it this far –'

'That's not true!' I said.

Nero raised an eyebrow. 'No? When I warned you that this tower was a death trap for your demigod friends, did you rush down to save them? Did you hurry them out of the building? I gave you ample time. No. You *used* them. You let them keep fighting to distract my guards, so you could sneak up here and try to reclaim your precious immortality.'

'I – What? I didn't –'

Nero swept his fruit platter off the sofa. It clattered across the floor. Grapes rolled everywhere. Everyone in the throne room flinched, including me . . . and this was obviously Nero's intention. He was a master at theatrics. He knew how to work a crowd, keep us on our toes.

He invested his voice with so much righteous indignation, even *I* wondered if I should believe him. 'You are a user, Apollo! You always have been. You leave a wake of ruined lives wherever you go. Hyacinthus. Daphne. Marsyas. Koronis. And your own Oracles: Trophonius, Herophile, the Cumaean Sibyl.' He turned to Meg. 'You've *seen* this with your own eyes, my dear. You know what I mean. Oh, Lester, I've been living among mortals for thousands of years. You know how many lives I've destroyed? None! I've raised a family of orphans.' He gestured at his adopted children, some of whom winced as if he might throw a platter of grapes at them. 'I've given them luxury, security, love! I've employed thousands. I've improved the world! But you, Apollo, you've been on Earth barely six months. How many lives have you wrecked in that time? How many have died trying to defend you? That poor griffin, Heloise. The dryad, Money Maker. Crest the pandos. And, of course, Jason Grace.'

'Don't you *dare*,' I snarled.

Nero spread his hands. 'Should I go on? The deaths at Camp Jupiter: Don, Dakota. The parents of that poor little girl Julia. All for what? Because *you* want to be a god again. You've whined and complained across this country and back again. So I ask you: are you *worthy* of being a god?'

He had done his homework. It wasn't like Nero to remember the names of so many people he didn't care about. But this was an important scene. He was putting on a performance for all of us, especially Meg.

'You're twisting everything into lies!' I said. 'Just like you always have for Meg and your other poor children.'

I shouldn't have called them *poor*. The seven torch-bearers glared at me with disdain. Clearly, they didn't want my pity. Meg's expression remained blank, but her eyes slid away from me and fixed on the patterns in the carpet. That probably wasn't a good sign.

Nero chuckled. 'Oh, Apollo, Apollo . . . You want to lecture *me* about my *poor children*? How have you treated yours?'

He began rattling off a list of my parenting failures, which were many, but I only half listened.

I wondered how much time had passed since I'd seen Screech-Bling. How long could I keep Nero talking, and would it be enough for the trogs to disable the poison gas, or at least clear the building?

Whatever the case, with those blast doors sealed and the windows barred, Meg and I were on our own. We would have to save each other, because no one else would. I had to believe we were still a team.

'And even now,' Nero continued, 'your children are fighting and dying below, while you are here.' He shook his head in disgust. 'I tell you what. Let's set aside the issue of fumigating my tower for the moment.' He placed the remote control next to him on the sofa, somehow making it seem like an incredibly generous concession that he would wait a few more minutes before gassing all my friends to death.

He turned to Meg. 'My dear, you can choose, as I promised. Which of our nature spirits should have the honour of killing this pathetic former god? We will make him fight his own battle for once.'

Meg stared at Nero as if he'd just spoken backwards. 'I . . . I can't . . .'

She wrung her fingers where her gold rings used to be.

I wanted to give them back to her so badly, but I was afraid even to breathe. Meg seemed to be teetering on the edge of an abyss. I feared any change in the room – the slightest vibration in the floor, a shift in the light, a cough or a sigh – might push her over.

'You can't choose?' Nero asked, his voice dripping with sympathy. 'I understand. We have so many dryads here, and they all deserve vengeance. After all, their species has only one natural predator: the Olympian gods.' He scowled at me. 'Meg is right! We will not choose. Apollo, in the name of Daphne, and all the other dryads whom you have tormented over the centuries . . . I decree that *all* our dryad friends will be allowed to tear you apart. Let's see how you defend yourself when you don't have any demigods to hide behind!'

He snapped his fingers. The dryads didn't seem too excited about tearing me apart, but the children of the Imperial Household held their torches closer to their potted trees, and something in the dryads seemed to break, flooding them with desperation, horror and rage.

They may have preferred to attack Nero, but since they couldn't, they did what he asked. They attacked me.

29

When you're burning trees
And it's allergy season,
Expect some sniffles.

IF THEIR HEARTS HAD BEEN IN IT, I WOULD have died.

I've seen actual mobs of bloodthirsty dryads attack. It's not something any mortal could live through. These tree spirits seemed more interested in just playing the part. They staggered towards me, yelling *RAWR*, while occasionally glancing over their shoulders to make sure the torch-bearing demigods hadn't set fire to their life sources.

I dodged the first two palm-tree spirits who lunged at me.

'I won't fight you!' I yelled. A sturdy ficus jumped on me from behind, forcing me to throw her off. 'We're not enemies!'

A fiddle-leaf fig was hanging back, perhaps waiting for her turn to get me, or just hoping she wouldn't get noticed. Her demigod keeper noticed, though. He lowered his torch and the fig tree went up in flames as if it had been doused in oil. The dryad screamed and combusted, collapsing in a heap of ash.

'Stop it!' Meg said, but her voice was so fragile it barely registered.

The other dryads attacked me in earnest. Their finger-nails stretched into talons. A lemon tree sprouted thorns all over her body and tackled me in a painful hug.

'Stop it!' Meg said, louder this time.

'Oh, let them try, my dear,' Nero said, as the trees piled onto my back. 'They deserve their revenge.'

The ficus got me in a chokehold. My knees buckled under the weight of six dryads. Thorns and talons raked every bit of exposed skin. I croaked, 'Meg!'

My eyes bulged. My vision blurred.

'STOP!' Meg ordered.

The dryads stopped. The ficus sobbed with relief and released her hold around my neck. The others backed off, leaving me on my hands and knees, gasping, bruised and bleeding.

Meg ran to me. She knelt and put her hand on my shoulder, studying my scrapes and cuts and my ruined, bandaged nose with an agonized expression. I would have been overjoyed to get this attention from her if we hadn't been in the middle of Nero's throne room, or if I could just, you know, breathe.

Her first whispered question was not the one I'd been expecting: 'Is Lu alive?'

I nodded, blinking away tears of pain. 'Last I saw,' I whispered back. 'Still fighting.'

Meg's brow furrowed. For the moment, her old spirit seemed rekindled, but it was difficult to visualize her the way she used to be. I had to concentrate on her eyes, framed by her wonderfully horrible cat-eye glasses, and ignore the new wispy haircut, the smell of lilac perfume, the purple gown and gold sandals and – OH, GODS! – someone had given her a pedicure.

I tried to contain my horror. 'Meg,' I said. 'There's only one person here you need to listen to: yourself. Trust yourself.'

I meant it, despite all my doubts and fears, despite all my complaints over the months about Meg being my master. She had chosen me, but I had also chosen her. I *did* trust her – not in spite of her past with Nero, but because of it. I had seen her struggle. I'd admired her hard-won progress. I had to believe in her for my own sake. She was – gods help me – my role model.

I pulled her gold rings from my pocket. She recoiled when she saw them, but I pressed them into her hands. 'You are stronger than he is.'

If I could have just kept her looking nowhere but at me, perhaps we could've survived in a small bubble of our old friendship, even surrounded by Nero's toxic environment.

But Nero couldn't allow that.

'Oh, my dear.' He sighed. 'I appreciate your kind heart. I do! But we can't interfere with justice.'

Meg stood and faced him. 'This isn't justice.'

His smile thinned. He glanced at me with a mixture of humour and pity, as if saying, *Now look what you've done.*

'Perhaps you're right, Meg,' he conceded. 'These dryads don't have the courage or the spirit to do what's necessary.'

Meg stiffened, apparently realizing what Nero intended to do. 'No.'

'We will have to try something else.' He gestured to the demigods, who lowered their torches into the plants.

'NO!' Meg screamed.

The room turned green. A storm of allergens exploded from Meg's body, as if she'd released an entire season of oak pollen in a single blast. Verdant dust coated the throne room – Nero, his couch, his guards, his rugs, his windows, his children. The demigods' torch flames spluttered and died.

The dryads' trees began to grow, roots breaking through their pots and anchoring to the floor, new leaves unfurling to replace the singed ones, branches thickening and stretching out, threatening to entangle their demigod minders. Not being complete fools, Nero's children scrambled away from their newly aggressive houseplants.

Meg turned to the dryads. They were huddled together trembling, burn marks steaming on their arms. 'Go heal,' she told them. 'I'll keep you safe.'

With a grateful collective sob, they vanished.

Nero calmly brushed the pollen from his face and clothes. His Germani seemed unperturbed, as if this sort of thing happened a lot. One of the cynocephali sneezed. His wolf-headed comrade offered him a Kleenex.

'My dear Meg,' Nero said, his voice even, 'we've talked about this before. You must control yourself.'

Meg clenched her fists. 'You didn't have the right. It wasn't fair –'

'Now, Meg.' His voice hardened, letting her know that his patience was strained. 'Apollo might still be allowed to live, if that's really what you want. We don't *have* to surrender him to Python. But, if we're going to take that kind of risk, I'll need you at my side with your wonderful powers. *Be* my daughter again. Let me save him for you.'

She said nothing. Her stance radiated stubbornness. I imagined her putting down her own roots, mooring herself in place.

Nero sighed. 'Everything becomes much, much harder when you wake the Beast. You don't want to make the wrong choice again, do you? And lose someone else like you lost your father?' He gestured to his dozen pollen-covered Germani, his pair of cynocephali, his seven demigod foster children – all of whom glared at us as if they, unlike the dryads, would be quite happy to tear us to pieces.

I wondered how quickly I could retrieve my bow, though I was in no shape for combat. I wondered how many opponents Meg could handle with her scimitars. Good as she was, I doubted she could fend off twenty-one. Then there was Nero himself, who had the constitution of a minor god. Despite her anger, Meg couldn't seem to make herself look him in the face.

I imagined Meg making these same calculations, perhaps deciding that there was no hope, that the only possibility of sparing my life was to give in to Nero.

'I didn't kill my father,' she said, her voice small and hard. 'I didn't cut off Lu's hands or enslave those dryads or twist us all up inside.' She swept a hand towards the other demigods of the household. '*You* did that, Nero. I hate you.'

The emperor's expression turned sad and weary. 'I see. Well . . . if you feel that way –'

'It's not about *feelings*,' Meg snapped. 'It's about the

truth. I'm not listening to you. And I'm not using *your* weapons to fight my fights any more.'

She tossed her rings away.

A small desperate yelp escaped my throat.

Nero chuckled. 'That, my dear, was foolish.'

For once, I was tempted to agree with the emperor. No matter how good my young friend was with gourds and pollen, no matter how glad I was to have her at my side, I couldn't imagine us getting out of this room alive unarmed.

The Germani hefted their spears. The imperial demigods drew their swords. The wolf-headed warriors snarled.

Nero raised his hand, ready to give the kill command, when behind me a mighty *BOOM!* shook the chamber. Half our enemies were thrown off their feet. Cracks sprouted in the windows and the marble columns. Ceiling tiles broke, raining dust like split bags of flour.

I turned to see the impenetrable blast doors lying twisted and broken, a strangely emaciated red bull standing in the breach. Behind it stood Nico di Angelo.

Safe to say, I had not been expecting this kind of partycrasher.

Clearly, Nero and his followers hadn't, either. They stared in amazement as the taurus silvestris lumbered across the threshold. Where the bull's blue eyes should have been, there were only dark holes. Its shaggy red hide hung loosely over its reanimated skeleton like a blanket. It was an undead thing with no flesh or soul – just the will of its master.

Nico scanned the room. He looked worse than the last

time I'd seen him. His face was covered in soot, his left eye
swollen shut. His shirt was ripped to shreds, and his black
sword dripped with some sort of monster blood. Worst of
all, someone (I'm guessing a trog) had forced him to wear a
white cowboy hat. I half expected him to say *yee-haw* in the
most unenthusiastic voice ever.

For the benefit of his skeleton bull, he pointed at Nero
and said, 'Kill that one.'

The bull charged. The followers of Nero went crazy.
Germani rushed the creature like linebackers going after
a wide receiver, desperate to stop it before it reached the
dais. The cynocephali howled and bounded in our direction. The imperial demigods faltered, looking at each other
for direction like, *Who do we attack? The bull? The emo kid?*
Dad? Each other? (This is the problem when you raise your
children to be paranoid murderers.)

'Vercorix!' Nero shrieked, his voice a half-octave higher
than usual. He leaped onto his couch, madly punching buttons on his Sassanid gas remote control and apparently
deciding that it was *not*, in fact, his Sassanid gas remote
control. 'Bring me the other controls! Hurry!'

Halfway to the bull, Vercorix stumbled and reversed
course for the coffee table, perhaps wondering why he'd
taken this promotion and why Nero couldn't fetch his own
stupid remotes.

Meg tugged at my arm, shaking me from my stupor.
'Get up!'

She dragged me out of the path of a cynocephalus, who
landed next to us on all fours, snarling and slavering. Before

I could decide whether to fight him with my bare hands or my bad breath, Nico leaped between us, his sword already in motion. He slashed the wolf-man into dust and dog fur.

'Hey, guys.' Nico's swollen eye made him look even fiercer than usual. 'You should probably find some weapons.'

I tried to remember how to speak. 'How did you –? Wait, let me guess. Rachel sent you.'

'Yup.'

Our reunion was interrupted by the second wolf-headed warrior, who loped towards us more cautiously than his fallen comrade, edging sideways and looking for an opening. Nico fended him off with his sword and his scary cowboy hat, but I had a feeling we'd be getting more company soon.

Nero himself was still screaming on his sofa while Vercorix fumbled with the tray of remote controls. A few feet away from us, the Germani were piling on top of the skeleton bull. Some of the imperial demigods ran to help them, but three of the more devious members of the family were hanging back, eyeing us, no doubt pondering the best way to kill us so they could get a gold star from Daddy on their weekly chore chart.

'What about the Sassanid gas?' I asked Nico.

'Trogs still working on that.'

I muttered a curse that would not have been appropriate for the ears of a youngster like Meg, except that Meg had taught me this particular curse.

'Has Camp Half-Blood evacuated?' Meg asked. I was relieved to hear her join the conversation. It made me feel like she was still one of us.

Nico shook his head. 'No. They're fighting against

Nero's forces on every floor. We warned everyone about the gas, but they won't leave until you guys leave.'

I felt a surge of gratitude and exasperation. Those stupid, beautiful Greek demigods, those brave, wonderful fools. I wanted to punch them all and then give them a big hug.

The cynocephalus lunged.

'Go!' Nico told us.

I sprinted towards the entrance where I'd dropped my supplies, Meg right beside me.

A Germanus flew overhead, kicked into oblivion by the bull. The zombie monster was about twenty feet from the emperor's dais now, struggling to make it to the goal line, but it was losing momentum under the weight of a dozen bodies. The three devious demigods were now prowling in our direction, paralleling our course towards the front of the room.

By the time I reached my possessions, I was gasping and sweating like I'd just run a marathon. I scooped up my ukulele, nocked an arrow in my bow and aimed at the approaching demigods, but two of them had disappeared. Perhaps they'd taken cover behind the columns? I fired at the only demigod still visible – Aemillia, was it? – but either I was weak and slow, or she was exceptionally well trained. She dodged my shot and kept coming.

'What about weapons for you?' I asked Meg, nocking another arrow.

She chin-pointed towards her foster sibling. 'I'll take hers. You concentrate on Nero.'

Off she ran in her silk dress and sandals like she was about to lay waste to a black-tie event.

Nico was still duelling with the wolf-dude. The zombie bull finally collapsed under the weight of Team Nero, meaning it wouldn't be long before the Germani came looking for new targets to tackle.

Vercorix tripped and fell as he reached the emperor's sofa, spilling the entire tray of remote controls across the cushions.

'That one! That one!' Nero yelled unhelpfully, pointing to all of them.

I took aim at Nero's chest. I was thinking how good it would feel to make this shot when someone leaped out of nowhere and stabbed me in the ribs.

Clever Apollo! I had found one of the missing demigods.

It was one of Nero's older boys – Lucius, perhaps? I would have apologized for not remembering his name, but since he had just driven a dagger into my side and now had me locked in a death embrace, I decided we could dispense with formalities. My vision swam. My lungs refused to fill with air.

Across the room, Meg fought bare-handed against Aemillia and the third missing demigod, who had apparently also been waiting in ambush.

Lucius drove his knife in deeper. I struggled, sensing with detached medical interest that my ribs had done their job. They'd deflected the blade from my vital organs, which was great except for the excruciating pain of having a knife embedded between my skin and ribcage, and the massive amount of blood now soaking through my shirt.

I couldn't shake Lucius. He was too strong, too close.

In desperation, I yanked back my fist and gave him a big thumbs-up right in the eye.

He screamed and staggered away. Eye injuries – the absolute worst. I'm a medical god and they even make *me* squeamish.

I didn't have the strength to nock another arrow. I stumbled, trying to stay conscious as I slipped in my own blood. It's always a fun time when Apollo goes to war.

Through the haze of agony, I saw Nero smiling triumphantly, holding aloft a remote control. 'Finally!'

No, I prayed. *Zeus, Artemis, Leto, anybody. NO!*

I couldn't stop the emperor. Meg was too far away, barely holding her own against her two siblings. The bull had been battered into a pile of bones. Nico had dispatched the wolf-man but now faced a line of angry Germani between him and the throne.

'It's over!' Nero gloated. 'Death to my enemies!'

And he pushed the button.

30

Stayin' alive is
Really hard when you're always
Trying to kill me.

DEATH TO MY ENEMIES WAS AN EXCELLENT
battle cry. A true classic, delivered with conviction!

Some of the drama was lost, however, when Nero pushed
the button and the shades on the windows began to lower.

The emperor uttered a curse – perhaps one Meg had
taught him – and dived into his sofa cushions, looking for
the *correct* correct remote.

Meg had disarmed Aemillia, as she'd promised, and was
now swinging her borrowed sword while more and more of
her foster siblings encircled her, anxious to have a part in
taking her down.

Nico waded through the Germani. They outnumbered
him more than ten to one, but they quickly developed a
healthy respect for his Stygian iron blade. Even barbarians
can master a steep learning curve if it is sharp and painful
enough. Nico couldn't last forever against so many, though,
especially since their spears had a longer reach and Nico
could only see through his right eye. Vercorix barked at his
men, ordering them to surround di Angelo. Unfortunately,

the grizzled lieutenant seemed much better at mustering his forces than he was at delivering remote controls.

As for me, how can I explain the difficulties of using a bow after being stabbed in the side? I was not dead yet, which confirmed that the blade had missed all my important arteries and organs, but raising my arm made me want to scream in pain. Actually aiming and drawing my bow was torture worse than anything in the Fields of Punishment, and Hades can quote me on that.

I'd lost blood. I was sweating and shivering. Nevertheless, my friends needed me. I had to do what I could.

'Mountain Dew, Mountain Dew,' I muttered, trying to clear my head.

First, I kicked Lucius in the face and knocked him out, because the sneaky little so-and-so deserved it. Then I fired an arrow at one of the other imperial demigods, who was about to stab Meg in the back. I was reluctant to kill, remembering Cassius's terrified face in the elevator, but I hit my target in the ankle, causing him to scream and do the chicken walk around the throne room. That was satisfying.

My real problem was Nero. With Meg and Nico overwhelmed, the emperor had plenty of time to fish through his sofa cushions for remotes. The fact that his blast doors were destroyed did not seem to dampen his enthusiasm for flooding the tower with poison gas. Perhaps, being a minor god, he would be immune. Perhaps he gargled with Sassanid gas every morning.

I fired at the emperor's centre mass – a shot that should have split his sternum. Instead, the arrow shattered on his toga. The garment had some form of protective magic, perhaps. Either that, or it was made by a really good tailor. With a great deal of pain, I nocked another arrow. This time I targeted Nero's head. I was reloading much too slowly. Every shot was an ordeal for my tortured body, but my aim was true. The arrow hit him right between the eyes. And shattered uselessly.

He scowled at me from across the room. 'Stop that!' Then he went back to searching for his remote.

My spirits fell even further. Clearly, Nero was still invulnerable. Luguselwa had failed to destroy his fasces. That meant we faced an emperor who had three times the power of Caligula or Commodus, and they hadn't exactly been pushovers. If Nero ever stopped obsessing about his poison-gas gadget and actually attacked us, we would be dead.

New strategy. I aimed at the remote controls. As he picked up the next one, I shot it out of his hand.

Nero snarled and grabbed another. I couldn't fire fast enough.

He pointed the gadget at me and mashed the buttons like this might erase me from existence. Instead, three giant TV screens lowered from the ceiling and flickered to life. The first showed local news: a live feed from a helicopter circling this very tower. Apparently, we were on fire. So much for the tower being indestructible. The second screen showed a PGA tournament. The third was split between Fox News and MSNBC, which side by side should have been enough to cause an antimatter explosion. I suppose it was a sign of Nero's apolitical bent, or perhaps his multiple personalities, that he watched them both.

Nero growled in frustration and tossed the remote away. 'Apollo, stop fighting me! You will *die* anyway. Don't you *understand* that? It's me or the reptile!'

The statement rattled me, making my next shot go wide. It hit the groin of the long-suffering Vercorix, who went cross-legged in pain as the arrow corroded his body to ash.

'Dude,' I muttered. 'I am *so* sorry.'

At the far end of the room, behind Nero's dais, more barbarians appeared, marching to the emperor's defence with their spears ready. Did Nero have a broom closet packed with reinforcements back there? That was totally unfair.

Meg was still encircled by her foster siblings. She'd managed to get a shield, but she was hopelessly outnumbered. I understood her desire to abandon the dual scimitars Nero had given her, but I was starting to question the timing of that decision. Also, she seemed determined not to kill her attackers, but her foster siblings had no such reservations. The other demigods closed in around her, their confident smirks indicating that they sensed imminent victory.

Nico was losing steam against the Germani. His sword seemed to become ten pounds heavier every time he swung it.

I reached for my quivers and realized I had only one arrow left to shoot, not including my Shakespearean life coach from Dodona.

Nero pulled out yet another remote. Before I could take aim, he pressed a button. A mirrored ball lowered from the middle of the ceiling. Lights flashed. The Bee Gees' 'Stayin' Alive' began to play, which everyone knows is one of the

Top Ten Omens of Impending Doom in the *Prophecy for Morons* handbook.

Nero threw away the remote and picked up . . . oh, gods. The *last* controller. The last one is *always* the right one.

'Nico!' I yelled.

I had no chance of bringing Nero down. Instead, I fired at the Germanus who stood directly between the son of Hades and the throne, blasting the barbarian to nothingness.

Bless his fancy cowboy hat, Nico understood. He charged, breaking out of the ring of Germani and leaping straight for the emperor with all his remaining strength.

Nico's downward slash should have cleaved Nero from head to devil tail, but, with his free hand, the emperor grabbed the blade and stopped it cold. The Stygian iron hissed and smoked in his grip. Golden blood trickled from between his fingers. He yanked the blade away from Nico and tossed it across the room. Nico lunged at Nero's throat, ready to choke him or make him into a Halloween skeleton. The emperor backhanded him with such force the son of Hades flew twenty feet and slammed into the nearest pillar.

'You fools cannot kill me!' Nero roared to the beat of the Bee Gees. 'I am immortal!'

He clicked his remote. Nothing obvious happened, but the emperor screeched with delight. 'That's it! That's the one! All your friends are dead now. HA-HA-HA-HA-HA!'

Meg screamed in outrage. She tried to break out of her circle of attackers, as Nico had done, but one of the demigods tripped her. She crashed face-first onto the carpet. Her borrowed sword clattered from her grip.

I wanted to run to her aid, but I knew I was too far away. Even if I shot the Arrow of Dodona, I couldn't take down an entire group of demigods.

We had failed. In the tower below, our friends would now be choking to death – the entire camp wiped out with a single click of Nero's remote.

The Germani hauled Nico to his feet and dragged him before the throne. The imperial demigods pointed their weapons at Meg, now prone and helpless.

'Excellent!' Nero beamed. 'But first things first. Guards, kill Apollo!'

The Germani reinforcements barrelled towards me.

I fumbled for my ukulele, desperately reviewing my repertoire for a song that would produce a stunning reversal of fortunes. 'I Believe in Miracles'? 'Make It Right'?

Behind me, a familiar voice roared, 'STOP!'

The tone was so commanding even Nero's guards and family members turned towards the broken blast doors.

On the threshold stood Will Solace, radiating brilliant light. At his left was Luguselwa, alive and well, her stumps now outfitted with daggers instead of silverware. At Will's right was Rachel Elizabeth Dare, holding a large axe wrapped in a golden bundle of rods: the fasces of Nero.

'*No one* hits my boyfriend,' Will thundered. 'And no one kills my dad!'

Nero's guards made ready to attack, but the emperor cried, 'EVERYONE FREEZE!'

His voice was so shrill that several of the Germani looked back to be sure he was the one who'd spoken.

The demigods of the imperial family did not look pleased. They'd been about to give Meg the Julius-Caesar-in-the-Senate treatment, but at Nero's command they stayed their weapons.

Rachel Dare scanned the room: the pollen-covered furniture and barbarians, the overgrown dryad trees, the pile of bull bones, the cracked windows and columns, the shades still going up and down on their own, the TVs blaring, the Bee Gees playing, the disco ball swirling.

'What have you guys been *doing* in here?' she muttered.

Will Solace strode confidently across the room, barking 'Out of my way!' to the Germani. He marched straight to Nico and helped the son of Hades to his feet. Then he dragged Nico back to the entrance. No one tried to stop them.

The emperor inched backwards on his dais. He put one hand behind him, as if to reassure himself that his sofa was still there in case he needed to faint dramatically. He ignored Will and Nico. His eyes were fixed on Rachel and the fasces.

'You.' Nero wagged his finger at my red-headed friend. 'You're the Pythia.'

Rachel hefted the fasces in her arms like a baby – a very heavy, pointy golden baby. 'Rachel Elizabeth Dare,' she said. 'And right now I'm the girl holding your life in her hands.'

Nero licked his lips. He frowned, then grimaced, as if exercising his facial muscles for an onstage soliloquy. 'You, ah, you all should be dead.'

He sounded both polite and vexed, as if chiding our comrades for not calling first before dropping by for dinner.

From behind Luguselwa, a smaller figure emerged: Screech-Bling, CEO of Troglodyte Inc., festooned with six new hats atop his tricorn. His grin was almost as bright as Will Solace.

'Gas traps are – CLICK – finicky!' he said. 'Have to be sure the detonators are working.' He opened his hand and let four nine-volt batteries tumble to the floor.

Nero glared at his foster children as if to say, *You had one job*.

'And how exactly . . . ?' Nero blinked and squinted. The glow of his own fasces seemed to hurt his eyes. 'The leontocephaline . . . You couldn't have defeated him.'

'I didn't.' Lu stepped forward, allowing me a closer look at her new attachments. Someone – I guessed Will – had fixed her up with fresh bandages, more surgical tape and better blades, giving her a low-budget Wolverine look. 'I traded what the guardian required: my immortality.'

'But you don't *have* . . .' Nero's throat seemed to close up. A look of dread came over his face, which was like watching someone press on wet sand and expel water from the centre.

I had to laugh. It was totally inappropriate, but it felt good.

'Lu has immortality,' I said, 'because *you're* immortal. The two of you have been connected for centuries.'

Nero's eye twitched. 'But that's *my* eternal life! You can't trade my life for my life!'

Lu shrugged. 'It's a little shady, I agree. But the leonto-cephaline seemed to find it . . . amusing.'

Nero stared at her in disbelief. 'You would kill yourself just to kill me?'

'In a heartbeat,' Lu said. 'But it won't come to that. I'm just a regular mortal now. Destroying the fasces will do the same to you.' She gestured to her Germanic former com-rades. 'And all your other guards, too. They'll be free of your bondage. Then . . . we'll see how long you last.'

Nero laughed as abruptly as I had. 'You can't! Don't *any* of you understand? All the power of the Triumvirate is mine now. My fasces . . .' His eyes lit with sudden hope. 'You haven't destroyed it yet, because you *can't*. Even if you could, you'd release so much power it would burn you to cinders. And, even if you didn't mind dying, the power . . . *all* the power I've been accumulating for centuries would just sink into Delphi . . . to – to *him*. You don't want that, believe me!'

The terror in his voice was absolutely genuine. I finally realized just how much fear he'd been living with. Python had always been the real power behind the throne – a big-ger puppet master than Nero's mother had ever been. Like most bullies, Nero had been shaped and manipulated by an even stronger abuser.

'You – Pythia,' he said. 'Raquel –'

'Rachel.'

'That's what I said! I can *influence* the reptile. I can con-vince him to give you your powers back. But kill me, and all is lost. He – he doesn't think like a human. He has no mercy, no compassion. He'll destroy the future of our kind!'

Rachel shrugged. 'Seems to me that you've chosen your kind, Nero. And it isn't humanity.'

Nero cast his eyes desperately around the room. He fixed his gaze on Meg, who was now on her feet, swaying wearily in the circle of her imperial siblings. 'Meg, dear. Tell them! I said I would let you choose. I trust your sweet nature, your good senses!'

Meg regarded him as if he were a distasteful wall painting.

She addressed her foster siblings: 'What you guys have done up till now . . . it isn't your fault. It's Nero's fault. But now you've got to make a choice. Stand up to him, like I did. Drop your weapons.'

Nero hissed. 'Ungrateful child. The Beast –'

'The Beast is dead.' Meg tapped the side of her head. 'I killed it. Surrender, Nero. My friends will let you live in a nice prison somewhere. It's more than you deserve.'

'That,' Lu said, 'is the best deal you're going to get, Emperor. Tell your followers to stand down.'

Nero looked on the verge of tears. He seemed like he was ready to set aside centuries of tyranny and power struggles and to betray his reptile overlord. Villainy, after all, was a thankless, exhausting job.

He took a deep breath.

Then he screamed, 'KILL THEM ALL!' And a dozen Germani charged me.

31

Godly tug-of-war
Not recommended for kids.
Or Lesters, either.

WE ALL MAKE OUR CHOICES.

Mine was to turn and run.

Not that I was terrified of a dozen Germani trying to kill me. Okay, yes, I was terrified of a dozen Germani trying to kill me. But also I had no arrows and no strength left. I badly wanted to hide behind – I mean, stand next to – Rachel, Screech-Bling and my old friend the low-budget Celtic Wolverine.

And . . . *and*. Nero's words rang in my ears. Destroying the fasces would be deadly. I could not allow anyone else to take that risk. Perhaps the leontocephaline had been amused for reasons Lu hadn't understood. Perhaps my sacrifice couldn't be avoided as easily as she believed.

I stumbled into Luguselwa, who managed to catch me without stabbing me to death. Will, still glowing like an overachieving night light, had propped Nico against the wall and was now tending to his wounds. Screech-Bling let out a high-pitched whistle, and more troglodytes poured into the room, charging the emperor's forces in a flurry of shrieks, mining picks and stylish headwear.

I gasped for breath, making a grabby-hand gesture at Rachel. 'Give me the fasces.'

'Please?' she prompted. 'And, *Gee, sorry, I underestimated you, Rachel, you're actually kind of a warrior queen?*'

'Yes, please, and thank you, and all of that!'

Lu scowled. 'Apollo, are you sure you can destroy it? I mean, without killing yourself?'

'No and no,' I said.

Rachel stared into the air, as if reading a prophecy written in the dancing lights of the disco ball. 'I can't see the outcome,' she said. 'But he has to try.'

I took the fasces, struggling not to collapse under its weight. The ceremonial weapon hummed and shuddered like an overheating race-car engine. Its aura made my pores pop and my ears ring. My side started to bleed again, if it had ever really stopped. I wasn't thrilled about the blood trickling down my chest and into my underwear while I had an important job to do. Sorry again, underwear.

'Cover me,' I told the ladies.

Lu leaped into battle, stabbing, slashing and kicking any Germani who got past the troglodytes. Rachel pulled out a blue plastic hairbrush and threw it at the nearest barbarian, beaning him in the eye and making him howl.

Sorry I underestimated you, Rachel, I thought distantly. *You're actually kind of a hairbrush ninja.*

I cast a worried glance across the room. Meg was all right. *More* than all right. She had convinced all her remaining foster siblings to throw down their weapons. Now she stood in front of them like a general trying to shore up her demoralized troops. Or – a less flattering comparison – she reminded me of one of Hades's dog trainers working with a pack of new hellhounds. At the moment, the demigods were obeying her commands and staying put, but any sign of weakness from her, any change in the temperature of the battle, and they might break ranks and slaughter everyone in sight.

It didn't help that Nero was stomping up and down on his couch, screeching, 'Kill Apollo! Kill Apollo!' as if I were a cockroach he'd just spotted scurrying across the floor.

For Meg's sake, I had to hurry.

I gripped the fasces with both hands and tried to prise it apart. The golden bundle of rods glowed brighter and warmer, illuminating the bones and red flesh of my fingers, but it didn't budge.

'Come on,' I muttered, trying again, hoping for a burst of godly strength. 'If you need another immortal life as a sacrifice, I'm right here!'

Maybe I should have felt foolish negotiating with a Roman ceremonial axe, but after my conversations with the Arrow of Dodona it seemed like a reasonable thing to try.

The troglodytes made the Germani look like the bumbling team the Harlem Globetrotters always played. (Sorry, Washington Generals.) Lu sliced and poked and parried with her knife hands. Rachel stood protectively in front of me and occasionally muttered, 'Apollo, now would be good,' which I did not find helpful.

Meg still had her foster siblings under control for the time being, but that could change. She was talking to them encouragingly, gesturing to me with a look that said *Apollo has this. He'll destroy Dad any minute. Just watch.*

I wished I shared her certainty.

I took a shaky breath. 'I can do this. I just need to concentrate. How hard can it be to destroy myself?'

I tried to break the fasces over my knee, which nearly broke my knee.

At last Nero lost his cool. I supposed there was only so much satisfaction he could get from stomping on his sofa and screaming at his minions.

'Do I have to do everything myself?' he yelled. 'Do I have to kill you *all*? You forget I AM A GOD!'

He jumped off his couch and marched straight towards me, his whole body starting to glow, because Will Solace couldn't have his own thing. Oh, no, Nero had to glow, too.

Trogs swarmed the emperor. He tossed them aside. Germani who didn't get out of his way fast enough were also thrown into the next time zone. Meg looked like she wanted to challenge Nero herself, but any move away from her foster siblings would have shattered their delicate stand-off. Nico was still only half-conscious. Will was busy trying to revive him.

That left Lu and Rachel as my last line of defence. I couldn't have that. They'd been in harm's way for my sake enough already.

Nero might've been the most minor of minor gods, but he still had divine strength. His glow was getting brighter as he approached the fasces – like Will, like me in my own godly moments of rage . . .

A thought came to me – or maybe something deeper than a thought, a sort of instinctive recognition. Like Caligula, Nero had always wanted to be the new sun god.

He'd designed his giant golden Colossus to look like my body with his head on it. This fasces wasn't just his symbol of power and immortality – it was his claim to godhood.

What had he asked me earlier . . . ? *Are you worthy of being a god?*

That was the central question. He believed he made a better deity than I did. Perhaps he was right, or perhaps neither of us was worthy. There was one way to find out. If I couldn't destroy the fasces myself, maybe with a little godly help . . .

'Get out of the way!' I told Lu and Rachel.

They glanced back at me like I was crazy.

'RUN!' I told them.

They broke to either side just before Nero would have ploughed through them.

The emperor stopped in front of me, his eyes flickering with power.

'You lose,' he said. 'Give it to me.'

'Take it if you can.' I began to glow myself. Radiance intensified around me, as it had months ago in Indianapolis, but slower this time, building to a crescendo. The fasces pulsed in sympathy, beginning to superheat. Nero snarled and grabbed the handle of the axe.

To our mutual surprise, the strength of my grip was equal to his. We played tug-of-war, swinging the blade back and forth, trying to kill each other, but neither of us could win. The glow around us increased like a feedback loop – bleaching the carpet under our feet, whitening the black marble columns. Germani had to stop fighting just to shield their eyes. Trogs screamed and retreated, their dark goggles insufficient protection.

'You – cannot – take – it, Lester!' Nero said through clenched teeth, pulling with all his might.

'I am Apollo,' I said, tugging the other direction. 'God of the sun. And I – revoke – your – divinity!'

The fasces cracked in two – the shaft shattering, the rods and golden blade exploding like a firebomb. A tsunami of flames washed over me, along with thousands of years of Nero's pent-up rage, fear and insatiable hunger – the twisted sources of his power. I stood my ground, but Nero hurtled backwards and landed on the carpet, his clothes smouldering, his skin mottled with burns.

My glow started to fade. I was unharmed . . . or at least no more harmed than I'd been before.

The fasces was broken, but Nero remained alive and intact. Had all this been for nothing, then?

At least he wasn't gloating any more. Instead, the emperor sobbed in despair. 'What have you done? Don't you see?'

Only then did he begin to crumble. His fingers disintegrated. His toga frayed into smoke. A glittery cloud plumed from his mouth and nose, as if he were exhaling his life force along with his final breaths. Worst of all – this glitter didn't simply vanish. It poured downward, seeping into the Persian rug, worming into cracks between the floor tiles, almost as if Nero were being pulled – *clawed and dragged* – into the depths, piece by piece.

'You've given him victory,' he whimpered. 'You've –'

The last of his mortal form dissolved and soaked through the floor.

Everyone in the room stared at me. The Germani dropped their weapons.

Nero was finally gone.

I wanted to feel joy and relief, but all I felt was exhaustion.

'Is it over?' Lu asked.

Rachel stood next to me, but her voice seemed to come from very far away: 'Not yet. Not even close.'

My consciousness was dimming, but I knew she was right. I understood the real threat now. I had to get going. There was no time to waste.

Instead, I toppled into Rachel's arms and passed out.

I found myself hovering over a different throne room – the Council of the Gods on Mount Olympus. Thrones curved around Hestia's great hearth, forming a U. My family, such as they were, sat watching a holographic image that floated above the flames. It was me, lying passed out in Rachel's arms in Nero's tower.

So . . . I was watching them watch me watch them . . . Nope. Too meta.

'This is the most critical time,' Athena said. She was dressed in her usual armour and oversize helmet, which I'm pretty sure she stole from Marvin the Martian in Looney Tunes. 'He is perilously close to failure.'

'Hmph.' Ares sat back and crossed his arms. 'I wish he'd get on with it, then. I have twenty golden drachma riding on this.'

'That is *so* callous,' Hermes chided. 'Besides, it's *thirty* drachmas, and I gave you very good odds.' He pulled out a leather-bound notepad and a pencil. 'Any final bets, people?'

'Stop,' Zeus rumbled. He was dressed in a sombre black three-piece suit, as if on his way to my funeral. His shaggy black beard was freshly combed and oiled. His eyes flickered with subdued lightning. He almost looked concerned for my situation.

Then again, he was as good an actor as Nero.

'We must wait for the final battle,' he announced. 'The worst is yet to come.'

'Hasn't he proved himself already?' Artemis demanded. My heart ached, seeing my sister again. 'He's suffered more in these last few months than even *you* could have expected! Whatever lesson you were trying to teach him, dear Father, he's learned it!'

Zeus glowered. 'You do not understand all the forces at work here, Daughter. Apollo *must* face the final challenge, for all our sakes.'

Hephaestus sat forward in his mechanical recliner, adjusting his leg braces. 'And, if he fails, what then? Eleven Olympian gods? That's a terribly unbalanced number.'

'It could work,' Aphrodite said.

'Don't you start!' Artemis snapped.

Aphrodite batted her eyelashes, feigning innocence. 'What? I'm just saying some pantheons have *way* less than twelve. Or we could elect a new twelfth.'

'A god of climate disasters!' Ares suggested. 'That would be awesome. He and I could work well together!'

'Stop it, all of you.' Queen Hera had been sitting back with a dark veil over her face. Now she lifted it. To my surprise, her eyes were red and swollen. She had been cry-ing. 'This has gone on long enough. Too much loss. Too much pain. But, if my *husband* insists on seeing it through, the least you all can do is not talk about Apollo as if he's already dead!'

Wow, I thought. *Who is this woman and what has she done with my stepmother?*

'Nonexistent,' Athena amended. 'If he fails, his fate will be much worse than death. But, whatever happens, it begins now.'

They all leaned forward, staring at the vision in the flames as my body began to stir.

Then I was back in my mortal form, looking up not at the Olympians, but at the faces of my friends.

32

The final push, fam.

Not throwing away my shot.

Wait. Where is my shot?

'I WAS DREAMING . . .' I POINTED WEAKLY at Meg. 'And you weren't there. Neither were you, Lu. Or Nico and Will . . .'

Will and Nico exchanged worried looks, no doubt wondering if I had suffered brain damage.

'We need to get you to camp,' Will said. 'I'll get one of the pegasi –'

'No.' I struggled to sit up. 'I – I have to leave.'

Lu snorted. 'Look at yourself, buddy. You're in worse shape than I am.'

She was right, of course. At the moment, I doubted my hands were working as well as Lu's dagger attachments. My whole body shook with exhaustion. My muscles felt like worn-out tension cords. I had more cuts and bruises than the average rugby team. Nevertheless . . .

'I have no choice,' I said. 'Nectar, please? And supplies. More arrows. My bow.'

'He's right, unfortunately,' Rachel said. 'Python . . .' She clenched her jaw as if forcing down a belch of serpent prophecy gas. 'Python is getting stronger by the second.'

Everyone looked grim, but no one argued. After all we'd been through, why would they? My confrontation with Python was just another impossible task in a day of impossible tasks.

'I'll gather some supplies.' Rachel kissed my forehead, then dashed off.

'Bow and quiver coming up,' Nico said.

'And ukulele,' Will added.

Nico winced. 'Do we really hate Python that much?'

Will raised an eyebrow.

'Fine.' Nico dashed off without kissing me on the forehead, which was just as well. He couldn't have reached my forehead with the massive brim of his cowboy hat.

Lu glowered at me. 'You did good, cellmate.'

Was I crying? Had there been any point in the last twenty-four hours when I hadn't been crying? 'Lu . . . You're good people. I'm sorry I mistrusted you.'

'Eh.' She waved one of her daggers. 'That's okay. I thought you were pretty useless, too.'

'I – I didn't say useless . . .'

'I should go check on the former imperial family,' she said. 'They're looking a little lost without General Sapling.' She winked at Meg, then lumbered off.

Will pressed a vial of nectar into my hands. 'Drink this. And this.' He passed me a Mountain Dew. 'And here's some salve for those wounds.' He handed the jar to Meg. 'Could you do the honours? I have to find more bandages. I used up my supply outfitting Luguselwa Dagger-Hands.'

He hurried away, leaving me alone with Meg.

She sat next to me, cross-legged, and started finger-painting my ouchies with healing ointment. She had plenty of ouchies to choose from. I alternated drinking my nectar and Mountain Dew, which was sort of like alternating between premium gasoline and regular gasoline.

Meg had thrown away her sandals, braving bare feet despite the arrows, rubble, bones and discarded blades that littered the floor. Someone had given her an orange Camp Half-Blood shirt, which she'd put on over her dress, making her allegiance clear. She still looked older and more sophisticated, but she also looked like my Meg.

'I'm so proud of you,' I said. I definitely was not weeping like a baby. 'You were so strong. So brilliant. So – OW!'

She poked the dagger wound in my side, effectively silencing my compliments. 'Yeah, I know. I had to be. For them.'

She chin-pointed to her wayward foster siblings, who had broken down in the wake of Nero's death. A couple of them stormed around the room, throwing things and screaming hateful comments while Luguselwa and some of our demigods stood by, giving them space, watching to make sure the imperials didn't hurt themselves or anyone else. Another child of Nero was curled up and sobbing between two Aphrodite campers who'd been pressed into service as grief counsellors. Nearby, one of the youngest imperials appeared catatonic in the arms of a Hypnos camper, who rocked the child back and forth while singing lullabies.

In the space of an evening, the imperial children had

gone from enemies to victims who needed help, and Camp Half-Blood was stepping up to the challenge.

'They'll need time,' Meg said. 'And a lot of good support, like I got.'

'They'll need *you*,' I added. 'You showed them the way out.'

She gave me a one-shoulder shrug. 'You really got a lot of wounds.'

I let her work, but as I sipped my high-octane beverages, I considered that perhaps courage was a self-perpetuating cycle, like abuse. Nero had hoped to create miniature, tortured versions of himself because that made him feel stronger. Meg had found the strength to oppose him because she saw how much her foster siblings needed her to succeed, to show them another way.

There were no guarantees. The imperial demigods had dealt with so much for so long, some of them might never be able to come back from the darkness. Then again, there had been no guarantees for Meg, either. There were still no guarantees that *I* would come back from what awaited me in the caverns of Delphi. All any of us could do was try, and hope that, in the end, the virtuous cycle would break the vicious one.

I scanned the rest of the throne room, wondering how long I had been unconscious. Outside it was full dark. Emergency lights pulsed against the side of the neighbouring building from the street far below. The *thwump-thwump-thwump* of a helicopter told me we were still making local news.

Most of the troglodytes had vanished, though Screech-Bling and a few of his lieutenants were here, having what looked like a serious conversation with Sherman Yang. Perhaps they were negotiating a division of the spoils of war. I imagined Camp Half-Blood was about to be flush with Greek fire and Imperial gold weapons, while the trogs would have a fabulous new selection of haberdashery and whatever lizards and rocks they could find.

Demigod children of Demeter were tending the overgrown dryads, discussing how best to transport them back to camp. Over by the emperor's dais, some of the Apollo kids (*my* kids) conducted triage operations. Jerry, Yan and Gracie – the newbies from camp – now all looked like seasoned pros, shouting orders to the stretcher-bearers, examining the wounded, treating campers and Germani alike.

The barbarians looked glum and dejected. None seemed to have the slightest interest in fighting. A few sported injuries that should have made them crumble to ash, but they were no longer creatures of Nero, bound to the living world by his power. They were just humans again, like Luguselwa. They would have to find a new purpose for their remaining years, and I supposed none of them loved the idea of staying loyal to the cause of a dead emperor.

'You were right,' I told Meg. 'About trusting Luguselwa. I was wrong.'

Meg patted my knuckles. 'Just keep saying that. I'm right. You're wrong. Been waiting months for you to realize it.'

She gave me a little smirk. Again, I could only marvel at how much she'd changed. She still looked ready to do a cartwheel for no reason, or wipe her nose on her sleeve with zero shame, or eat an entire birthday cake just because yum, but she was no longer the half-wild alley-dwelling urchin I'd met in January. She'd grown taller and more confident. She carried herself like someone who owned this tower. And for all I knew she might, now that Nero was dead, assuming the whole place didn't burn down.

'I . . .' My voice failed me. 'Meg, I have to –'

'I know.' She looked away long enough to wipe her cheek, knocking her glasses cockeyed in the process. 'You have to do this next part on your own, huh?'

I thought about the last time I'd physically stood in the depths of Delphi, when Meg and I had inadvertently wandered there through the Labyrinth during a three-legged race. (Ah, those were simpler times.) The situation now was different. Python had grown too powerful. Having seen his lair in my dreams, I knew that no demigod could survive that place. The poisonous air alone would burn away flesh and melt lungs. I did not expect to survive there long myself, but in my heart I had always known this would be a one-way trip.

'I must do this alone,' I agreed.

'How?'

Leave it to Meg to distil the most important crisis of my four-thousand-year-plus life into a single unanswerable question.

I shook my head, wishing I had an unquestionable answer. 'I guess I have to trust that . . . that I won't screw up.'

'Hmm.'

'Oh, shut it, McCaffrey.'

She forced a smile. After a few more moments of putting salve on my wounds, she said, 'So . . . this is goodbye?' She swallowed that last word.

I tried to find my voice. I seemed to have lost it somewhere down in my intestines. 'I – I will find you, Meg. Afterwards. Assuming . . .'

'No screw-ups.'

I made a sound between a laugh and a sob. 'Yes. But either way . . .'

She nodded. Even if I survived, I would not be the same. The best I could hope for was to emerge from Delphi with my godhood restored, which was what I had wanted and dreamed about for the past half a year. So why did I feel so reluctant about leaving behind the broken, battered form of Lester Papadopoulos?

'Just come back to me, dummy. That's an order.' Meg gave me a gentle hug, conscious of my injuries. Then she got to her feet and ran off to check on the imperial demigods – her former family, and possibly her family yet to be.

My other friends all seemed to understand, too.

Will did some last-minute bandaging. Nico handed me my weapons. Rachel gave me a new pack stuffed with supplies. But none of them offered any lingering goodbyes. They knew every minute counted now. They wished me luck and let me go.

As I passed, Screech-Bling and the troglodyte lieutenants stood at attention and removed their headwear – all six hundred and twenty hats. I recognized the honour. I nodded my thanks and forged on across the broken threshold before I could melt into another fit of ugly sobbing.

I passed Austin and Kayla in the antechamber, tending to more wounded and directing younger demigods in clean-up efforts. They both gave me weary smiles, acknowledging the million things we didn't have time to say. I pushed onward.

I ran into Chiron by the elevators, on his way to deliver more medical supplies.

'You came to our rescue,' I said. 'Thank you.'

He looked down at me benevolently, his head nearly scraping the ceiling, which had not been designed to accommodate centaurs. 'We all have a duty to rescue each other, wouldn't you say?'

I nodded, wondering how the centaur had become so wise over the centuries, and why that same wisdom had escaped me until I had been Lesterized. 'And did your . . . joint task force meeting go well?' I asked, trying to remember what Dionysus had told us about why Chiron had been away. It seemed like so long ago. 'Something about a severed cat's head?'

Chiron chuckled. 'A severed head. And a cat. Two different . . . uh, people. Acquaintances of mine from other pantheons. We were discussing a mutual problem.'

He just threw that information out there as if it wasn't a brain-exploding grenade. Chiron had acquaintances from other pantheons? Of course he did. And a mutual problem . . . ?

'Do I want to know?' I asked.

'No,' he said gravely. 'You really don't.' He offered his hand. 'Good luck, Apollo.'

We shook, and off I went.

I found the stairs and took them. I didn't trust the elevators. During my dream in the cell, I'd seen myself sweeping down the stairwells of the tower when I fell to Delphi. I was determined to take the same path in real life. Maybe it wouldn't matter, but I would've felt silly if I took a wrong turn on my way to confront Python and ended up getting arrested by the NYPD in the Triumvirate Holdings lobby.

My bow and quiver jostled against my back, clanging against my ukulele strings. My new supply pack felt cold and heavy. I held on to the railing so my wobbly legs wouldn't collapse under me. My ribs felt like they'd been newly tattooed with lava, but considering everything I'd been through, I felt remarkably whole. Maybe my mortal body was giving me one last push. Maybe my godly constitution was kicking in to help. Maybe it was the nectar-and-Mountain-Dew cocktail coursing through my bloodstream. Whatever it was, I would take all the help I could get.

Ten floors. Twenty floors. I lost track. Stairwells are horrible, disorienting places. I was alone with the sound of my breathing and the pounding of my feet against the steps.

A few more floors, and I began to smell smoke. The hazy air stung my eyes.

Apparently, part of the building was still on fire. Awesome.

The smoke got thicker as I continued to descend. I began to cough and gag. I pressed my forearm over my nose and mouth and found that this did not make a very good filter.

My consciousness swam. I considered opening a side door and trying to find fresh air, but I couldn't see any exits. Weren't stairwells supposed to have those? My lungs screamed. My oxygen-deprived brain felt like it was about to pop out of my skull, sprout wings and fly away.

I realized I might be starting to hallucinate. Brains with wings. Cool!

I trudged forward. Wait . . . What happened to the stairs? When had I reached a level surface? I could see nothing through the smoke. The ceiling got lower and lower. I stretched out my hands, searching for any kind of support. On either side of me, my fingers brushed against warm, solid rock.

The passageway continued to shrink. Ultimately I was forced to crawl, sandwiched between two horizontal sheets of stone with barely enough room to raise my head. My ukulele wedged itself in my armpit. My quiver scraped against the ceiling.

I began to squirm and hyperventilate from claustrophobia, but I forced myself to calm down. I was not stuck. I could breathe, strangely enough. The smoke had changed to volcanic gas, which tasted terrible and smelled worse, but my burning lungs somehow continued to process it. My respiratory system might melt later, but right now, I was still sucking in the sulphur.

I knew this smell. I was somewhere in the tunnels beneath Delphi. Thanks to the magic of the Labyrinth and/ or some strange sorcerous high-speed link that connected Nero's tower to the reptile's lair, I had climbed, walked, stumbled and crawled halfway across the world in a few minutes. My aching legs felt every mile.

I wriggled onward towards a dim light in the distance.

Rumbling noises echoed through a much larger space ahead. Something huge and heavy was breathing.

The crawl space ended abruptly. I found myself peering down from the lip of a small crevice, like an air vent. Below me spread an enormous cavern – the lair of Python.

When I had fought Python before, thousands of years ago, I hadn't needed to seek out this place. I had lured him into the upper world and fought him in the fresh air and sunlight, which had been much better.

Now, looking down from my crawl space, I wished I could be anywhere else. The floor stretched for several football fields, punctuated by stalagmites and split by a web of glowing volcanic fissures that spewed plumes of gas. The uneven rock surface was covered with a shag carpet of horror: centuries of discarded snakeskins, bones and the desiccated carcasses of . . . I didn't want to know. Python had all those volcanic crevices right there, and he couldn't be bothered to incinerate his trash?

The monster himself, roughly the size of a dozen jack-knifed cargo trucks, took up the back quarter of the cavern. His body was a mountain of reptilian coils, rippling with muscle, but he was more than simply a big snake. Python shifted and changed as it suited him – sprouting clawed feet, or vestigial bat wings, or extra hissing heads along the side of his body, all of which withered and dropped off as rapidly as they formed. He was the reptilian conglomeration of everything that mammals feared in their deepest, most primal nightmares.

I'd suppressed the memory of just how hideous he was. I preferred him when he'd been obscured in poisonous fumes. His cab-size head rested on one of his coils. His eyes were closed, but that did not fool me. The monster never really slept. He only waited . . . for his hunger to swell, for his chance at world domination, for small, foolish Lesters to jump into his cave.

At the moment, a shimmering haze seemed to be settling over him, like the embers of a spectacular fireworks show. With nauseating certainty, I realized I was watching Python absorb the last remnants of the fallen Triumvirate's power. The reptile looked blissful, soaking in all that warm, Nero-y goodness.

I had to hurry. I had one shot at defeating my old enemy.

I was not ready. I was not rested. I was definitely not bringing my A-game. In fact, I had been so far below my A-game for so long that I could barely remember any letters north of *LMNOP*.

Yet somehow I'd got this far. I felt a tingly sensation of power building just under my skin – perhaps my divine self, trying to reassert itself in the proximity of my old arch-enemy. I hoped it was that and not just my mortal body combusting.

I managed to manoeuvre my bow into my hands, draw an arrow and nock it – no easy task while lying flat on your belly in a crawl space. I even managed to avoid whanging my ukulele against the rocks and giving away my position with a rousing open chord.

So far, so good.

Deep breath. This was for Meg. This was for Jason. This was for everyone who had fought and sacrificed to drag my sorry mortal butt from quest to quest for the last six months, just to get me this chance at redemption.

I kicked forward, spilling head first out of the crack in the ceiling. I flipped in mid-air, aimed . . . and fired my arrow at Python's head.

33

Seriously, guys,
I know my shot was right here.
Help me look for it.

I MISSED.

Don't even pretend you're surprised.

Rather than piercing the monster's skull as I'd hoped, my arrow shattered on the rocks a few feet from his head. Splinters skittered harmlessly across the cavern floor. Python's lamp-like eyes snapped open.

I landed in the centre of the room, ankle-deep in a bed of old snakeskin. At least I didn't break my legs on impact. I could save that disaster for my big finale.

Python studied me, his gaze cutting like headlights through the volcanic fumes. The shimmering haze that surrounded him was snuffed out. Whether he had finished digesting its power, or whether I had interrupted him, I couldn't be sure.

I hoped he might roar in frustration. Instead, he laughed – a deep rumble that liquefied my courage. It's unnerving to watch a reptile laugh. Their faces are simply not designed for showing humour. Python didn't smile, per se, but he bared his fangs, pulled back his Tootsie-roll-segmented lips and let his forked tongue lash the air, probably savouring the scent of my fear.

'And here we are.' His voice came from all around me, each word a drill bit set against my joints. 'I have not quite finished digesting Nero's power, but I suppose it will have to do. He tastes like dried rat anyway.'

I was relieved to hear I'd interrupted Python's emperor-tasting. Perhaps this would make him slightly less impossible to defeat. On the other hand, I didn't like how unperturbed he sounded, how utterly confident.

Of course, I didn't look like much of a threat.

I nocked another arrow. 'Slither away, snake. While you still can.'

Python's eyes gleamed with amusement. 'Amazing. You *still* haven't learned humility? I wonder how you will taste. Like rat? Like god? They are similar enough, I suppose.'

He was *so* wrong. Not about gods tasting like rats . . . I wouldn't know. But I had learned *plenty* of humility. So much humility that now, facing my old nemesis, I was racked with self-doubt. I could not do this. What had I been thinking?

And yet, along with humility, I'd learned something else: getting humiliated is only the beginning, not the end. Sometimes you need a second shot, and a third, and a fourth.

I fired my arrow. This one hit Python in the face, skittering across his left eyelid and making him blink.

He hissed, raising his head until it towered twenty feet above me. 'Stop embarrassing yourself, Lester. I control

Delphi. I would have been content to rule the world through my puppets, the emperors, but you have helpfully cut out the middlemen. I have digested the power of the Triumvirate! Now I will digest –'

My third shot throat-punched him. It didn't pierce the skin. That would've been too much to hope for. But it hit with sufficient force to make him gag.

I sidestepped around piles of scales and bones. I jumped a narrow fissure so hot it steam-baked my crotch. I nocked another arrow as Python's form began to change. Rows of tiny leathery wings sprouted from his back. Two massive legs grew from his belly, lifting him up until he resembled a giant Komodo dragon.

'I see,' he grumbled. 'Won't go quietly. That's fine. We can make this hurt.'

He tilted his head, like a dog listening – an image that made me never want to own a dog. 'Ah . . . Delphi speaks. Would you like to know your future, Lester? It's very short.'

Green luminescent fumes thickened and swirled around him, filling the air with the acrid scent of rot. I watched, too horrified to move, as Python breathed in the spirit of Delphi, twisting and poisoning its ancient power until he spoke in a booming voice, his words carrying the inescapable weight of destiny: '*Apollo will fall* –'

'NO!' Rage filled my body. My arms steamed. My hands glowed. I fired my fourth arrow and pierced Python's hide just above his new right leg.

The monster stumbled, his concentration broken. Clouds of gas dissipated around him.

He hissed in pain, stomping his legs to make sure they still worked.

He roared, 'NEVER INTERRUPT A PROPHECY!'

Then he barrelled towards me like a hungry freight train.

I leaped to one side, somersaulting through a pile of carcasses as Python bit a chunk out of the cave floor where I'd been standing. Baseball-size debris rained down around me. One chunk hit the back of my head and nearly knocked me unconscious.

Python struck again. I'd been trying to string another shaft, but he was too fast. I jumped out of the way, landing on my bow and shattering my arrow in the process.

The cave was now a whirring factory of snake flesh – conveyor belts, shredder apparatuses, compactors and pistons, all made of Python's writhing body, every component ready to grind me into pulp. I scrambled to my feet and leaped over a section of the monster's body, narrowly avoiding a newly grown head that snapped at me from Python's side.

Given Python's strength and my own frailty, I should have died several times over. The only thing keeping me alive was my small size. Python was a bazooka; I was a housefly. He could easily kill me with one shot, but he had to catch me first.

'You heard your fate!' Python boomed. I could feel the cold presence of his massive head looming above me. '*Apollo will fall*. It's not much, but it's enough!'

He almost caught me in a coil of flesh, but I hopped out of the snare. My tap-dancing friend Lavinia Asimov would have been proud of my fancy footwork.

'You cannot escape your destiny!' Python gloated. 'I have spoken, so must it be!'

This demanded a witty comeback, but I was too busy gasping and wheezing.

I leaped onto Python's trunk and used it as a bridge to cross one of the fissures. I thought I was being clever until a random lizard foot sprouted next to me and raked my ankle with its claws. I screamed and stumbled, desperately grasping for any handhold as I slipped off the side of the reptile. I managed to grab a leathery wing, which flapped in protest, trying to shake me off. I got one foot on the rim of the fissure, then somehow hauled myself back to solid ground.

Bad news: my bow tumbled into the void.

I couldn't stop to mourn. My leg was on fire. My shoe was wet with my own blood. Naturally, those claws would be venomous. I'd probably just reduced my lifespan from a few minutes to a few fewer minutes. I limped towards the cavern wall and squeezed myself into a vertical crack no bigger than a coffin. (Oh, why did I have to make that comparison?)

I'd lost my best weapon. I had arrows but nothing to shoot them with. Whatever fits of godly power I was experiencing, they weren't consistent and they weren't enough. That left me with an out-of-tune ukulele and a rapidly deteriorating human body.

I wished my friends were here. I would have given anything for Meg's exploding tomato plants, or Nico's Stygian iron blade, or even a team of fast-running troglodytes to carry me around the cavern and screech insults at the giant tasty reptile.

But I was alone.

Wait. A faint tingle of hope ran through me. Not *quite* alone. I fumbled in my quiver and drew out Ye Olde Arrow of Dodona.

HOW DOETH WE, SIRRAH? The arrow's voice buzzed in my head.

'Doething great,' I wheezed. 'I gotteth him right where I wanteth him.'

THAT BAD? ZOUNDS!

'Where are you, Apollo?' Python roared. 'I can smell your blood!'

'Hear that, arrow?' I wheezed, delirious from exhaustion and the venom coursing through my veins. 'I forced him to call me Apollo!'

A GREAT VICTORY, intoned the arrow. *'TWOULD SEEM 'TIS ALMOST TIME.*

'What?' I asked. Its voice sounded unusually subdued, almost sad.

I SAID NOTHING.

'You did too.'

I DIDST NOT! WE MUST NEEDS FORMULATE A NEW PLAN. I SHALL GO RIGHT. THOU SHALT GO LEFT.

'Okay,' I agreed. 'Wait. That won't work. You don't have legs.'

'YOU CAN'T HIDE!' Python bellowed. 'YOU ARE NO GOD!'

This pronouncement hit me like a bucket of ice water. It didn't carry the weight of prophecy, but it was true nonetheless. At the moment, I wasn't sure *what* I was. I certainly wasn't my old godly self. I wasn't exactly Lester Papadopoulos, either. My flesh steamed. Pulses of light flickered under my skin, like the sun trying to break through storm clouds. When had that started?

I was between states, morphing as rapidly as Python himself. I was no god. I would never be the same old Apollo again. But, in this moment, I had the chance to decide what I would become, even if that new existence only lasted a few seconds.

The realization burned away my delirium.

'I won't hide,' I muttered. 'I won't cower. That's not who I will be.'

The arrow buzzed uneasily. *SO . . . WHAT IS THY PLAN?*

I grasped my ukulele by the fret board and held it aloft like a club. I raised the Arrow of Dodona in my other hand and burst from my hiding place. 'CHARGE!'

At the time, this seemed like a completely sane course of action.

If nothing else, it surprised Python.

I imagined what I must have looked like from his perspective: a raggedy teenaged boy with ripped clothes and cuts and contusions everywhere, limping along with one bloody foot, waving a stick and a four-stringed instrument and screaming like a lunatic.

I ran straight at his massive head, which was too high for me to reach. I started smashing my ukulele against his throat. 'Die!' *CLANG!* 'Die!' *TWANG!* 'Die!' *CRACK-SPROING!*

On the third strike, my ukulele shattered.

Python's flesh convulsed, but, rather than dying like a good snake, he wrapped a coil around my waist, almost gently, and raised me to the level of his face.

His lamp-like eyes were as large as I was. His fangs glistened. His breath smelled of long-decayed flesh.

'Enough now.' His voice turned calm and soothing. His eyes pulsed in synch with my heartbeat. 'You fought well. You should be proud. Now you can relax.'

I knew he was doing that old reptile hypnosis trick – paralysing the small mammal so it would be easier to swallow and digest. And, in the back of my mind, some cowardly part of me (Lester? Apollo? Was there a difference?) whispered, *Yes, relaxing would feel really good right now.*

I *had* done my best. Surely, Zeus would see that and be proud. Maybe he would send down a lightning bolt, blast Python into tiny pieces and save me!

As soon as I thought this, I realized how foolish it was. Zeus didn't work that way. He would not save me any more than Nero had saved Meg. I had to let go of that fantasy. I had to save myself.

I squirmed and fought. I still had my arms free and my hands full. I stabbed Python's coil with my broken fretboard so forcefully that it ripped his skin and stuck in his flesh like a massive splinter, green blood oozing from the wound.

He hissed, squeezing me tighter, pushing all the blood into my head until I feared I would blow my top like a cartoon oil well.

'Has anyone ever told you,' Python rasped, 'that you are annoying?'

I HATH, the Arrow of Dodona said in a melancholy tone. *A THOUSAND TIMES.*

I couldn't respond. I had no breath. It took all my remaining strength to keep my body from imploding under the pressure of Python's grip.

'Well.' Python sighed, his breath washing over me like the wind from a battlefield. 'No matter. We have reached the end, you and I.'

He squeezed harder, and my ribs began to crack.

34

Found my shot. Took it.

Forgot I was tied to it.

Down I go. Bye-bye.

I FOUGHT.

I squirmed.

I pounded on Python's skin with my tiny fist, then wriggled my ukulele thorn back and forth in the wound, hoping to make him so miserable he would drop me.

Instead, his giant glowing eyes simply watched, calm and satisfied, as my bones developed stress fractures I could hear in my inner ear. I was a submarine in the Mariana Trench. My rivets were popping.

DIEST THOU NOT! the Arrow of Dodona implored me. *THE TIME HAS COME!*

'Wh–?' I tried to wheeze out a question, but I had too little air in my lungs.

THE PROPHECY WHICH PYTHON SPAKE, said the arrow. *IF THOU MUST FALL, THEN SO YOU SHALL, BUT FIRST, USETH THOU ME.*

The arrow tilted in my hand, pointing towards Python's enormous face.

My thought process was muddled, what with my brain

exploding and all, but its meaning jabbed into me like a ukulele fretboard.

I can't, I thought. *No.*

THOU MUST. The arrow sounded resigned, determined. I thought about how many miles I had travelled with this small sliver of wood, and how little credence I'd usually given its words. I remembered what it had told me about it being cast out of Dodona – a small expendable branch from the ancient grove, a piece no one would miss.

I saw Jason's face. I saw Heloise, Crest, Money Maker, Don the Faun, Dakota – all those who had sacrificed themselves to get me here. Now my last companion was ready to pay the cost for my success – to have me do the one thing it had always told me never to do.

'No,' I croaked, possibly the last word I would ever be able to speak.

'What is that?' Python asked, thinking I had spoken to him. 'Does the little rat beg for mercy at the end?'

I opened my mouth, unable to answer. The monster's face loomed closer, anxious to savour my last sweet whimpers.

FARE THEE WELL, FRIEND, said the arrow. APOLLO WILL FALL, BUT APOLLO MUST RISE AGAIN.

With those last words, conveying all the power of his ancient grove, the arrow closed the reptile's prophecy. Python came within range, and with a sob of despair I jabbed the Arrow of Dodona up to its fletching in his enormous eye.

He roared in agony, lashing his head back and forth. His coils loosened just enough for me to wriggle free. I dropped, landing in a heap at the edge of a wide crevice.

My chest throbbed. Definitely broken ribs. Probably a broken heart. I had far exceeded the maximum recommended mileage for this Lester Papadopoulos body, but I had to keep going for the Arrow of Dodona. I hadeth to keepeth goingeth.

I struggled to my feet.

Python continued flailing, trying to dislodge the arrow from his eye. As a medical god, I could have told him that this would only make the pain worse. Seeing my old Shakespearean missile weapon sticking out of the serpent's head made me sad and furious and defiant. I sensed that the arrow's consciousness was gone. I hoped it had fled back to the Grove of Dodona and joined the millions of other whispering voices of the trees, but I feared it was simply no more. Its sacrifice had been real, and final.

Anger pumped through me. My mortal body steamed in earnest, bursts of light flashing under my skin. Nearby, I spotted Python's tail thrashing. Unlike the snake that had curled around the leontocephaline, *this* serpent had a beginning and an end. Behind me yawned the largest of the volcanic crevices. I knew what I had to do.

'PYTHON!' My voice shook the cavern. Stalactites crashed around us. I imagined, somewhere far above us, Greek villagers freezing in their tracks as my voice echoed from the ruins of the holy site, olive trees shuddering and losing their fruit.

The Lord of Delphi had awoken.

Python turned his remaining baleful eye on me. 'You will *not* live.'

'I'm fine with that,' I said. 'As long as you die, too.'

I tackled the monster's tail and dragged it towards the chasm.

'What are you doing?' he roared. 'Stop it, you idiot!'

With Python's tail in my arms, I leaped over the side.

My plan should not have worked. Given my puny mortal weight, I should have simply hung there like an air freshener from a rear-view mirror. But I was full of righteous fury. I planted my feet against the rock wall and pulled, dragging Python down as he howled and writhed. He tried to whip his tail around and throw me off, but my feet stayed firmly planted against the side of the chasm wall. My strength grew. My body shone with brilliant light. With one final defiant shout, I pulled my enemy past the point of no return. The bulk of his coils spilled into the crevasse.

The prophecy came true. Apollo fell, and Python fell with me.

Hesiod once wrote that a bronze anvil would take nine days to fall from Earth to Tartarus.

I suspect he used the word *nine* as shorthand for *I don't know exactly how long, but it would seem like a long, long time.*

Hesiod was right.

Python and I tumbled into the depths, flipping over one another, bouncing against walls, spinning from total darkness into the red light of lava veins and back again. Given the amount of damage my poor body took, it seems likely that I died somewhere along the way.

Yet I kept fighting. I had nothing left to wield as a weapon, so I used my fists and feet, punching the beast's

THE TOWER OF NERO   347

hide, kicking at every claw, wing or nascent head that sprouted from his body.

I was beyond pain. I was now in the realm of *extreme agony is the new feeling great*. I torqued myself in mid-air so that Python took the brunt of our collisions with the walls. We couldn't escape one another. Whenever we drifted apart, some force brought us back together again like marriage bonds.

The air pressure became crushing. My eyes bulged. The heat baked me like a batch of Sally Jackson's cookies, but still my body glowed and steamed, the arteries of light now closer to the surface, dividing me into a 3-D Apollo jigsaw puzzle.

The crevice walls opened around us, and we fell through the cold and gloomy air of Erebos – the realm of Hades. Python tried to sprout wings and fly away, but his pathetic bat appendages couldn't support his weight, especially with me clinging to his back, breaking his wings as soon as they formed.

'STOP IT!' Python growled. The Arrow of Dodona still bristled in his ruined eye. His face oozed green blood from a dozen places where I had kicked and punched him. 'I – HATE – YOU!'

Which just goes to show that even arch-enemies of four thousand years can still find something to agree on. With a great *KA-PHROOOOOM!* we hit water. Or not water . . . More like a roaring current of bone-chillingly cold grey acid.

The River Styx swept us downstream.

If you love category-five rapids on a river that can drown you, dissolve your skin and corrode your sense of self all at the same time, I highly recommend a giant serpent cruise on the Styx.

The river sapped my memories, my emotions, my will. It prised open the burning cracks in my Lester Papadopoulos shell, making me feel raw and unmade like a moulting dragonfly.

Even Python was not immune. He fought more sluggishly. He flailed and clawed to reach the shore, but I elbowed him in his one good eye, then kicked him in the gullet – anything to keep him in the water.

Not that I wanted to drown, but I knew Python would be much more dangerous on solid ground. Also, I did not like the idea of showing up on Hades's doorstep in my present condition. I could expect no warm welcome there.

I clung to Python's face, using the Arrow of Dodona's lifeless shaft like a rudder, steering the monster with tugs of torture. Python wailed and bellowed and thrashed. All around us, the Styx's rapids seemed to laugh at me. *You see? You broke a vow. And now I have you.*

I held on to my purpose. I remembered Meg McCaffrey's last order: *Come back to me, dummy.* Her face remained clear in my mind. She had been abandoned so many times, used so cruelly. I would not be another cause of grief for her. I knew who I was. I was her dummy.

Python and I tumbled through the grey torrent and then, without warning, shot off the edge of a waterfall. Again we fell, into even deeper oblivion.

All supernatural rivers eventually empty into Tartarus – the realm where primordial terrors dissolve and re-form, where monsters germinate on the continent-size body of Tartarus himself, slumbering in his eternal dream state.

We did not stop long enough for a selfie. We hurtled through the burning air and the spray of the abysmal water-fall as a kaleidoscope of images spun in and out of view: mountains of black bone like Titan scapulae; fleshy land-scapes dotted with blisters that popped to release glistening newborn drakons and gorgons; plumes of fire and black smoke spewing upward in darkly festive explosions.

We fell even further, into the Grand Canyon crevasse of this horror world – to the deepest point of the deepest realm of creation. Then we slammed into solid rock.

Wow, Apollo, you marvel. *How did you survive?*

I didn't.

By that point, I was no longer Lester Papadopoulos. I was not Apollo. I'm not sure who or what I was.

I rose to my feet – I don't know how – and found myself on a blade of obsidian, jutting over an endless churning sea of umber and violet. With a combination of horror and fas-cination, I realized I was standing on the brink of Chaos.

Below us churned the essence of everything: the great cosmic soup from which all else had spawned, the place where life first began to form and think, *Hey, I am separate from the rest of this soup!* One step off this ledge, and I would rejoin that soup. I would be utterly gone.

I examined my arms, which seemed to be in the process of disintegration. The flesh burned away like paper, leaving marbled lines of glowing golden light. I looked like one of those transparent anatomy dolls designed to illustrate the circulatory system. In the centre of my chest, subtler than the best MRI could capture, was a haze of roiling violet energy. My soul? My death? Whatever it was, the glow was getting stronger, the purple tint spreading through my form, reacting to the nearness of Chaos, working furiously to unknit the golden lines that held me together. That probably wasn't good . . .

Python lay beside me, his body also crumbling, his size drastically reduced. He was now only five times larger than me – like a prehistoric crocodile or constrictor, his shape a mixture of the two, his hide still rippling with half-formed heads, wings and claws. Impaled in his blind left eye, the Arrow of Dodona was still perfectly intact, not a bit of fletching out of place.

Python rose to his stubby feet. He stomped and howled. His body was coming apart, turning into chunks of reptile and light, and I must say I didn't like the new disco-crocodile look. He stumbled towards me, hissing and half-blind. 'Destroy you!'

I wanted to tell him to chill out. Chaos was way ahead of him. It was rapidly tearing apart our essences. We no longer had to fight. We could just sit on this obsidian spire and quietly crumble together. Python could cuddle up against me, look out over the vast expanse of Chaos, mutter *It's beautiful*, then evaporate into nothingness.

But the monster had other plans. He charged, bit me around the waist and barrelled forward, intent on pushing me into oblivion. I couldn't stop his momentum. I could only shuffle and twist so that when we hit the edge, Python tumbled over first. I clawed desperately at the rock, grabbing the rim as Python's full weight almost yanked me in half.

We hung there, suspended over the void by nothing but my trembling fingers, Python's maw clamped around my waist.

I could feel myself being torn in two, but I couldn't let go. I channelled all my remaining strength into my hands – the way I used to do when I played the lyre or the ukulele, when I needed to express a truth so deep it could only be communicated in music: the death of Jason Grace, the trials of Apollo, the love and respect I had for my young friend Meg McCaffrey.

Somehow, I managed to bend one leg. I kneed Python in the chin.

He grunted. I kneed him again, harder. Python groaned. He tried to say something, but his mouth was full of Apollo. I struck him once more, so hard I felt his lower jaw crack. He lost his grip and fell.

He had no final words – just a look of half-blind reptilian horror as he plummeted into Chaos and burst into a cloud of purple fizz.

I hung from the ledge, too exhausted to feel relief.

This was the end. Pulling myself up would be beyond my ability.

Then I heard a voice that confirmed my worst fears.

35

Hanging with my peeps,
Hanging by my fingertips,
It's the same, really.

'I TOLD YOU SO.'

I never doubted those would be the last words I heard.

Next to me, the goddess Styx floated over the void. Her purple-and-black dress might have been a plume of Chaos itself. Her hair drifted like an ink cloud around her beautiful, angry face.

I wasn't surprised that she could exist here so effortlessly, in a place where other gods feared to go. Along with being the keeper of sacred oaths, Styx was the embodiment of the River of Hate. And, as anyone can tell you, hatred is one of the most durable emotions, one of the last to fade into nonexistence.

I told you so. Of course she had. Months ago at Camp Half-Blood, I had made a rash oath. I'd sworn on the River Styx not to play music or use a bow until I was a god again. I'd reneged on both counts, and the goddess Styx had been dogging my progress ever since, sprinkling tragedy and destruction wherever I went. Now I was about to pay the final price – I would be cancelled.

I waited for Styx to prise my fingers from the obsidian ledge, then give me a raspberry as I plummeted into the soupy, amorphous destruction below.

To my surprise, Styx wasn't done talking.

'Have you learned?' she asked.

If I hadn't felt so weak, I might have laughed. I had learned, all right. I was *still* learning.

At that moment, I realized I'd been thinking about Styx the wrong way all these months. She hadn't put destruction in my path. I'd caused it myself. She hadn't got me into trouble. I *was* the trouble. She had merely called out my recklessness.

'Yes,' I said miserably. 'Too late, but I get it now.'

I expected no mercy. Certainly, I expected no help. My little finger slipped free of the ledge. Nine more until I fell.

Styx's dark eyes studied me. Her expression was not gloating, exactly. She looked more like a satisfied piano teacher whose six-year-old pupil had finally mastered 'Twinkle, Twinkle, Little Star'.

'Hold on to that, then,' she said.

'What, the rock?' I murmured. 'Or the lesson?'

Styx made a sound that did not belong at the brink of Chaos: she chuckled with genuine amusement.

'I suppose you'll have to decide.' With that, she dissolved into smoke, which drifted upward towards the airy climes of Erebos.

I wished I could fly like that. But, alas, even here, at the precipice of nonexistence, I was subject to gravity.

At least I had vanquished Python.

He would never rise again. I could die knowing that my friends were safe. The Oracles were restored. The future was still open for business.

So what if Apollo was erased from existence? Maybe Aphrodite was right. Eleven Olympians was plenty. Hephaestus could pitch this as a reality TV show: *Eleven Is Enough.* His streaming-service subscriptions would go through the roof.

Why couldn't I let go, then? I kept clinging to the edge with stubborn determination. My wayward pinky found its grip again. I had promised Meg I would return to her. I hadn't sworn it as an oath, but that didn't matter. If I said I would do it, I had to follow through.

Perhaps that was what Styx had been trying to teach me: it wasn't about how loudly you swore your oath, or what sacred words you used. It was about whether or not you meant it. And whether your promise was worth making.

Hold on, I told myself. *To both the rock and the lesson.*

My arms seemed to become more substantial. My body felt more *real*. The lines of light wove together until my form was a mesh of solid gold.

Was it just a last hopeful hallucination, or did I actually pull myself up?

My first surprise: I woke.

People who have been dissolved into Chaos typically don't do that.

Second surprise: my sister Artemis was leaning over me, her smile as bright as the harvest moon. 'Took you long enough,' she said.

I rose with a sob and hugged her tight. All my pain was gone. I felt perfect. I felt . . . I almost thought, *like myself again*, but I wasn't sure what that even meant any more.

I was a god again. For so long, my deepest desire had been to be restored. But instead of feeling elated I wept on my sister's shoulder. I felt like if I let go of Artemis, I would fall back into Chaos. Huge parts of my identity would shake loose, and I would never be able to find all the puzzle pieces.

'Whoa, there.' She patted my back awkwardly. 'Okay, little fella. You're all right now. You made it.'

She gently extricated herself from my arms. Not a cuddler, my sister, but she did allow me to hold her hands. Her stillness helped me stop trembling.

We were sitting together on a Greek-style sofa bed, in a white marble chamber with a columned terrace that opened onto a view of Olympus: the sprawling mountaintop city of the gods, high above Manhattan. The scent of jasmine and honeysuckle wafted in from the gardens. I heard the heavenly singing of the Nine Muses in the distance – probably their daily lunchtime concert in the agora. I really *was* back.

I examined myself. I wore nothing but a bedsheet from the waist down. My chest was bronze and perfectly sculpted. My muscular arms bore no scars or fiery lines glowing beneath the surface. I was gorgeous, which made me feel melancholy. I had worked hard for those scars and bruises. All the suffering my friends and I had been through . . .

My sister's words suddenly sank in: *Took you long enough.*

I choked on despair. 'How long?'

Artemis's silver eyes scanned my face, as if trying to determine what damage my time as a human had done to my mind. 'What do you mean?'

I knew immortals could not have panic attacks. Yet my chest constricted. The ichor in my heart pumped much too fast. I had no idea how long it had taken me to become a god again. I'd lost half a year from the time Zeus zapped me at the Parthenon to the time I plummeted to Manhattan as a mortal. For all I knew, my restorative siesta had taken years, decades, centuries. Everyone I'd known on Earth might be dead.

I could not *bear* that. 'How long was I out? What century is this?'

Artemis processed this question. Knowing her as well as I did, I gathered she was tempted to laugh, but hearing the degree of hurt in my voice, she kindly thought better of it.

'Not to worry, Brother,' she said. 'Since you fought Python, only two weeks have passed.'

Boreas the North Wind could not have exhaled more powerfully than I did.

I sat upright, throwing aside my sheet. 'But what about my friends? They'll think I'm dead!'

Artemis studiously regarded the ceiling. 'Not to worry. We – I – sent them clear omens of your success. They know you have ascended to Olympus again. Now, please, put on some clothing. I'm your sister, but I would not wish this sight on anyone.'

'Hmph.' I knew very well she was just teasing me. Godly bodies are expressions of perfection. That's why we appear naked in ancient statuary, because you simply do not cover up such flawlessness with clothing.

Nevertheless, her comment resonated with me. I felt awkward and uncomfortable in this form, as if I'd been given a Rolls-Royce to drive but no car insurance to go with it. I'd felt so much more comfortable in my economy-compact Lester.

'I, um . . . Yes.' I gazed around the room. 'Is there a closet, or –?'

Her laughter finally escaped. 'A closet. That's adorable. You can just wish yourself into clothes, Little Brother.'

'I . . . ah . . .' I knew she was right, but I felt so flustered I even ignored her *little brother* comment. It had been too long since I'd relied on my divine power. I feared I might try and fail. I might accidentally turn myself into a camel.

'Oh, fine,' Artemis said. 'Allow me.'

A wave of her hand, and suddenly I was wearing a knee-length silver dress – the kind my sister's followers wore – complete with thigh-laced sandals. I suspected I was also wearing a tiara.

'Um. Perhaps something less Huntery?'

'I think you look lovely.' Her mouth twitched at the corner. 'But very well.'

A flash of silver light, and I was dressed in a man's white chiton. Come to think of it, that piece of clothing was pretty much identical to a Hunter's gown. The sandals were the same. I seemed to be wearing a crown of laurels instead of a tiara, but those weren't very different, either. Conventions of gender were strange. But I decided that was a mystery for another time.

'Thank you,' I said.

She nodded. 'The others are waiting in the throne room. Are you ready?'

I shivered, though it should not have been possible for me to feel cold.

The others.

I remembered my dream of the throne room – the other Olympians gambling on my success or failure. I wondered how much money they'd lost.

What could I possibly say to them? I no longer felt like one of them. I *wasn't* one of them.

'In a moment,' I told my sister. 'Would you mind . . . ?'

She seemed to understand. 'I'll let you compose yourself. I'll tell them you'll be right in.' She kissed me lightly on the cheek. 'I *am* glad you're back. I hope I won't regret saying that.'

'Me, too,' I agreed.

She shimmered and vanished.

I took off the laurel wreath. I did not feel comfortable wearing such a symbol of victory. I ran my finger across the gilded leaves, thinking of Daphne, whom I had treated so horribly. Whether Aphrodite had cursed me or not, it was still my fault that the blameless naiad had turned herself into a laurel tree just to escape me.

I walked to the balcony. I set the wreath on the edge of the railing, then ran my hand across the hyacinth that grew along the lattice – another reminder of tragic love. My poor Hyacinthus. Had I *really* created these flowers to commemorate him, or just to wallow in my own grief and guilt? I found myself questioning many things I had done over the centuries. Strangely enough, this uneasiness felt somewhat reassuring.

I studied my smooth tan arms, wishing again that I had retained a few scars. Lester Papadopoulos had earned his cuts, bruises, broken ribs, blistered feet, acne . . . Well, perhaps not the acne. No one deserves that. But the rest had felt more like symbols of victory than laurels, and better commemorations of loss than hyacinths.

I had no great desire to be here in Olympus, my home that was not a home.

I wanted to see Meg again. I wanted to sit by the fire at Camp Half-Blood and sing ridiculous songs, or joke with the Roman demigods in the Camp Jupiter mess hall while platters of food flew over our heads and ghosts in glowing purple togas regaled us with tales of their former exploits.

But the world of demigods wasn't my place. I had been privileged to experience it, and I needed to remember it.

That didn't mean I couldn't go back to visit, though. But first I had to show myself to my family, such as they were. The gods awaited.

I turned and strode out of my room, trying to recall how the god Apollo walked.

36

Hooray! Yippee! Yay!
Apollo is in the house.
Hold your applause, please.

WHY SO BIG?

I'd never really thought about it before, but after six months away, the Olympians' throne room struck me as ridiculously huge. The interior could have housed an aircraft carrier. The great domed ceiling, spangled with constellations, could have nested all the largest cupolas ever created by humans. The roaring central hearth was just the right size for rotisserie-cooking a pickup truck. And, of course, the thrones themselves were each the size of a siege tower, designed for beings that were twenty feet tall.

As I hesitated on the threshold, awestruck by the massiveness of it all, I realized I was answering my own question. The point of going big was to make our occasional guests feel small.

We didn't often allow lesser beings to visit us, but, when we did, we enjoyed the way their jaws dropped, and how they had to crane their necks to see us properly.

If we then chose to come down from our thrones and shrink to mortal size, so we could pull these visitors aside and have a confidential chat, or give them a pat on the back, it seemed like we were doing something really special for them, descending to their level.

There was no reason the thrones couldn't have been human-size, but then we would have seemed too human (and we didn't like being reminded of the resemblance). Or *forty* feet tall, but that would have been too awkward – too much shouting to make ourselves heard. We'd need magnifying glasses to see our visitors.

We could've even made the thrones six inches tall. Personally, I would have loved to see that. A demigod hero straggles into our presence after some horrible quest, takes a knee before an assembly of miniature gods, and Zeus squeaks in a Mickey Mouse voice, *Welcome to Olympus!*

As I thought all this, it dawned on me that the gods' conversations had stopped. They had all turned to look at me standing in the doorway. The entire squad was here today, which only happened on special occasions: the solstice, Saturnalia, the World Cup.

I had a moment's panic. Did I even know how to turn twenty feet tall any more? Would they have to summon a booster seat for me?

I caught Artemis's eye. She nodded – either a message of encouragement, or a warning that if I didn't hurry up and enchant myself, she would help by turning me into a twenty-foot-tall camel in an evening gown.

That gave me just the shot of confidence I needed. I strode into the room. To my great relief, my stature grew with every step. Just the right size, I took my old throne, directly across the hearth from my sister, with Ares on my right and Hephaestus on my left.

I met the eyes of each god in turn.

You have heard of imposter syndrome? Everything in me screamed *I am a fake! I do not belong here!* Even after four thousand years of godhood, six months of mortal life had convinced me that I wasn't a true deity. Surely, these eleven Olympians would soon realize this unfortunate fact. Zeus would yell, *What have you done with the real Apollo?* Hephaestus would press a button on his gadget-encrusted chair. A trapdoor would open in the seat of my throne, and I would be flushed unceremoniously back to Manhattan.

Instead, Zeus simply studied me, his eyes stormy under his bushy black eyebrows. He'd chosen to dress traditionally today in a flowing white chiton, which was not a good look for him given the way he liked to manspread.

'You have returned,' he noted, supreme lord of stating the obvious.

'Yes, Father.' I wondered if the word *Father* sounded as bad as it tasted. I tried to control the bile rising inside me. I mustered a smile and scanned the other gods. 'So, who won the betting pool?'

Next to me, Hephaestus at least had the good manners to shift uncomfortably in his seat, though of course he was *always* uncomfortable. Athena shot a withering look at Hermes as if to say, *I told you that was a bad idea.*

'Hey, man,' Hermes said. 'That was just something to keep our nerves under control. We were worried about you!'

Ares snorted. 'Especially because of the way you were fumbling along down there. I'm surprised you lasted as long as you did.' His face turned red, as if he'd just realized he was speaking aloud. 'Uh . . . I mean, good job, man. You came through.'

'So you lost a bundle,' I summed up.

Ares cursed under his breath.

'Athena won the pot.' Hermes rubbed his back pocket, as if his wallet were still hurting.

'Really?' I asked.

Athena shrugged. 'Wisdom. It comes in handy.'

It should have been a commercial. The camera zooms in on Athena, who smiles at the screen as the promotional slogan appears below her: *Wisdom. It comes in handy.*

'So . . .' I spread my hands, signalling that I was ready to hear whatever: compliments, insults, constructive criticism. I had no idea what was on the agenda for this meeting, and I found I didn't much care.

On the other side of the room, Dionysus drummed his fingers on his leopard-skin-patterned armrests. Being the only god on the 'goddess side' of the assembly (long story), he and I often had staring contests or traded eye-rolls when our father got too long-winded. Dionysus was still in his slovenly Mr D guise, which annoyed Aphrodite, who sat next to him. I could tell from her body language that she wanted to squirm out of her Oscar de la Renta midi.

Given Dionysus's exile at Camp Half-Blood, he was rarely allowed to visit Olympus. When he did, he was usually careful not to speak unless spoken to. Today he surprised me.

'Well, I think you did a marvellous job,' he offered. 'I think, in your honour, *any* god who is currently being punished with a stint on Earth ought to be pardoned immediately –'

'No,' Zeus snapped.

Dionysus slumped back with a dejected sigh.

I couldn't blame him for trying. His punishment, like mine, seemed completely senseless and disproportionate. But Zeus worked in mysterious ways. We couldn't always know his plan. That was probably because he didn't *have* a plan.

Demeter had been weaving wheat stalks into new drought-resistant varieties, as she often did while listening to our deliberations, but now she set aside her basket. 'I agree with Dionysus. Apollo should be commended.'

Her smile was warm. Her golden hair rippled in an unseen breeze. I tried to spot any resemblance to her daughter Meg, but they were as different as a kernel and a husk. I decided I preferred the husk.

'He made a wonderful slave to my daughter,' Demeter continued. 'True, it took him a while to adjust, but I can forgive that. If any of you need a slave in the future for your demigod children, I recommend Apollo without hesitation.'

I hoped this was a joke. But Demeter, like the growing season, was not known for her sense of humour.

'Thanks?' I said.

She blew me a kiss.

Gods, Meg, I thought. *I am so, so sorry your mom is your mom.*

Queen Hera lifted her veil. As I'd seen in my dream, her eyes were red and swollen from crying, but when she spoke her tone was as hard as bronze.

She glared at her husband. 'At least Apollo *did* something.'

'Not this again,' Zeus rumbled.

'My chosen,' Hera said. 'Jason Grace. Your *son*. And you –'

'*I* didn't kill him, woman!' Zeus thundered. 'That was Caligula!'

'Yes,' Hera snapped. 'And at least Apollo grieved. At least *he* got vengeance.'

Wait . . . What was happening? Was my wicked stepmother defending me?

Much to my shock, when Hera met my eyes, her gaze wasn't hostile. She seemed to be looking for solidarity, *sympathy*, even. *You see what I have to deal with? Your father is horrible!*

In that moment, I felt a twinge of compassion for my stepmother for the first time in, oh, ever. Don't get me wrong. I still disliked her. But it occurred to me that being Hera might not be so easy, given who she was married to. In her place, I might have become a bit of an impossible meddler, too.

'Whatever the case,' Zeus grumbled, 'it does appear that after two weeks, Apollo's fix is permanent. Python is truly gone. The Oracles are free. The Fates are once again able to spin their thread without encumbrance.'

Those words settled over me like Vesuvian ashes.

The Fates' thread. How had I not considered this before? The three eternal sisters used their loom to spin the life-spans of both gods and mortals. They snipped the cord of destiny whenever it was time for someone to die. They were higher and greater than any Oracle. Greater even than the Olympians.

Apparently, Python's poison had done more than simply strangle prophecies. If he could interfere with the Fates' weaving as well, the reptile could have ended or prolonged lives as he saw fit. The implications were horrifying.

Something else struck me about Zeus's statement. He had said it *appeared* my fix was permanent. That implied Zeus wasn't sure. I suspected that when I fell to the edge of Chaos, Zeus had not been able to watch. There were limits to even *his* far sight. He did not know exactly what had happened, how I had defeated Python, how I'd come back from the brink. I caught a look from Athena, who nodded almost imperceptibly.

'Yes, Father,' I said. 'Python is gone. The Oracles are free. I hope that meets with your approval.'

Having spent time in Death Valley, I was confident that my tone was much, much drier.

Zeus stroked his beard as if pondering the future's endless possibilities. Poseidon stifled a yawn as if pondering how soon this meeting would end so he could get back to fly-fishing.

'I am satisfied,' Zeus pronounced.

The gods let out a collective sigh. As much as we pretended to be a council of twelve, in truth we were a tyranny. Zeus was less a benevolent father and more an iron-fisted leader with the biggest weapons and the ability to strip us of our immortality if we offended him.

Somehow, though, I didn't feel relieved to be off Zeus's hook. In fact, I had to stop myself from rolling my eyes.

'Super,' I said.

'Yes,' Zeus agreed. He cleared his throat awkwardly. 'Welcome back to godhood, my son. All has gone according to my plan. You have done admirably. You are forgiven and restored to your throne!'

There followed a smattering of polite applause from the other deities.

Artemis was the only one who looked genuinely happy. She even winked at me. Wow. It truly was a day for miracles.

'What's the first thing you'll do now that you're back?' Hermes asked. 'Smite some mortals? Maybe drive your sun chariot too close to the Earth and smoke the place?'

'Ooh, can I come?' Ares asked.

I gave them a guarded shrug. 'I think I may just visit some old friends.'

Dionysus nodded wistfully. 'The Nine Muses. Excellent choice.'

But those weren't the friends I had in mind.

'Well, then.' Zeus scanned the room, in case any of us wanted one last chance to grovel at his feet. 'Council is dismissed.'

The Olympians popped out of existence one after the other – back to whatever godly mischief they'd been managing. Artemis gave me a reassuring nod, then dissolved into silvery light.

That left only Zeus and me.

My father coughed into his fist. 'I know you think your punishment was harsh, Apollo.'

I did not answer. I tried my best to keep my expression polite and neutral.

'But you must understand,' Zeus continued, 'only *you* could have overthrown Python. Only *you* could have freed the Oracles. And you did it, as I expected. The suffering, the pain along the way . . . regrettable, but necessary. You have done me proud.'

Interesting how he put that: I had done *him* proud. I had been useful in making him look good. My heart did not melt. I did not feel that this was a warm-and-fuzzy reconciliation with my father. Let's be honest: some fathers don't deserve that. Some aren't capable of it.

I suppose I could have raged at him and called him bad names. We were alone. He probably expected it. Given his awkward self-consciousness at the moment, he might even have let me get away with it unpunished.

But it would not have changed him. It would not have made anything different between us.

You cannot change a tyrant by trying to out-ugly him. Meg could never have changed Nero, any more than I could change Zeus. I could only try to be different from him. Better. More . . . human. And to limit the time I spent around him to as little as possible.

I nodded. 'I understand, Father.'

Zeus seemed to understand that what *I* understood was not perhaps the same thing *he* understood, but he accepted the gesture, I suppose because he had little choice.

'Very well. So . . . welcome home.'

I rose from my throne. 'Thank you. Now, if you'll excuse me . . .'

I dissolved into golden light. There were several other places I'd rather be, and I intended to visit them all.

37

Burnt marshmallow bliss,
Pinochle, and strawberries.
Love you, Camp Half-Blood.

AS A GOD, I COULD SPLIT MYSELF INTO
multiple parts. I could exist in many different places at once.

Because of this, I can't tell you with absolute certainty
which of the following encounters came first. Read them in
any order you like. I was determined to see all my friends
again, no matter where they were, and give them equal
attention at roughly the same time.

First, though, I must mention my horses. No judgement,
please. I had missed them. Because they were immortal, they
did not need sustenance to survive. Nor did they absolutely
have to make their daily journey through the sky in order
to keep the sun going, thanks to all the other solar gods
out there, still powering the movements of the cosmos, and
that other thing called astrophysics. Still, I worried that my
horses hadn't been fed or taken out for exercise in at least
six months, perhaps a whole year, which tended to make
them grumpy. For reasons I shouldn't have to explain, you
don't want your sun being pulled across the sky by grumpy
horses.

I materialized at the entrance of the sun palace and

found that my valets had abandoned their posts. This happens when you don't pay them their gold drachma every day. I could barely push open the front door because months of mail had been shoved through the slot. Bills. Ad circulars. Credit card offers. Appeals for charities like Godwill and Dryads Without Borders. I suppose Hermes found it amusing to deliver me so much snail mail. I would have to have a talk with that guy.

I also hadn't put a stop to my automatic deliveries from the Amazons, so the portico was piled high with shipping boxes filled with toothpaste, laundry detergent, guitar strings, reams of blank tablature and coconut-scented suntan lotion.

Inside, the palace had reverted to its old Helios smell, as it did every time I was gone for an extended period. Its former owner had baked the place with the scent of Titan: pungent and saccharine, slightly reminiscent of Axe body spray. I'd have to open some windows and burn some sage.

A layer of dust had accumulated on my golden throne. Some jokers had written WASH ME on the back of the chair. Stupid venti, probably.

In the stables, my horses were glad to see me. They kicked at their stalls, blew fire and whinnied indignantly, as if to say, *Where the Hades have you been?*

I fed them their favourite gilded straw, then filled their nectar trough. I gave them each a good brushing and whispered sweet nothings in their ears until they stopped kicking me in the groin, which I took as a sign that they forgave me.

It felt good to do something so routine – something I'd done millions of times before. (Taking care of horses,

I mean. Not getting kicked in the groin.) I still didn't feel like my old self. I didn't really *want* to feel like my old self. But being in my stables felt much more comfortable and familiar than being on Olympus.

I split myself into separate Apollos and sent one of me on my daily ride across the sky. I was determined to give the world a regular day, to show everyone that I was back at the reins and feeling good. No solar flares, no droughts or wildfires today. Just Apollo being Apollo.

I hoped that this part of me would serve as my steady rudder, my grounding force, while I visited my other stops.

The welcome I received at Camp Half-Blood was uproarious and beautiful.

'LESTER!' the campers chanted. 'LESTER!'

'LESTER?!'

'LESTER!'

I had chosen to appear in my old Papadopoulos form. Why not my glowing perfect god bod? Or one of the Bangtan Boys, or Paul McCartney circa 1965? After complaining for so many months about my flabby, acne-spotted Lester meat sack, I now found that I felt at home in that form. When I'd first met Meg, she had assured me that Lester's appearance was perfectly normal. At the time, the notion had horrified me. Now I found it reassuring.

'Hello!' I cried, accepting group hugs that threatened to deteriorate into stampedes. 'Yes, it's me! Yep, I made it back to Olympus!'

Only two weeks had passed, but the newbie campers who had seemed so young and awkward when I first arrived now carried themselves like demigod veterans. Going through a major battle (sorry, 'field trip') will do that to you. Chiron looked enormously proud of his trainees – and of me, as if I were one of them.

'You did well, Apollo,' he said, gripping my shoulder like the affectionate father I'd never had. 'You are always welcome here at camp.'

Ugly weeping would not have been appropriate for a major Olympian god, so that's exactly what I did.

Kayla, Austin and I hugged each other and wept some more. I had to keep my godly powers firmly under control, or my joy and relief might have exploded in a firestorm of happiness and obliterated the whole valley.

I asked about Meg, but they told me she had already left. She'd gone back to Palm Springs, to her father's old home, with Luguselwa and her foster siblings from Nero's Imperial Household. The idea of Meg handling that volatile group of demigods with only the help of LuBeard the Pirate made me uneasy.

'Is she well?' I asked Austin.

He hesitated. 'Yeah. I mean . . .' His eyes were haunted, as if remembering the many things we'd all seen and done in Nero's tower. 'You know. She *will* be.'

I set aside my worries for the moment and continued making rounds among my friends. If they felt nervous that I was a god again, they hid it well. As for me, I made a conscious effort to stay cool, not to grow twenty feet tall or burst into golden flames every time I saw someone I liked.

I found Dionysus sitting glumly on the porch of the Big

House, sipping a Diet Coke. I sat down across from him at the pinochle table.

'Well,' he said with a sigh, 'it appears some of us do get happy endings.'

I think he was pleased for me, in his own way. At least, he tried to tamp down the bitterness in his voice. I couldn't blame him for feeling salty.

My punishment was over, yet his continued. A hundred years compared to my six months.

To be honest, though, I could no longer consider my time on Earth to have been a punishment. Terrible, tragic, nearly impossible . . . yes. But calling it a *punishment* gave Zeus too much credit. It had been a journey – an important one I made myself, with the help of my friends. I hoped . . . I *believed* that the grief and pain had shaped me into a better person. I had forged a more perfect Lester from the dregs of Apollo. I would not trade those experiences for anything. And if I had been told I had to be Lester for another hundred years . . . well, I could think of worse things. At least I wouldn't be expected to show up at the Olympian solstice meetings.

'You will have your happy ending, Brother,' I told Dionysus.

He studied me. 'You speak as the god of prophecy?'

'No.' I smiled. 'Just as someone with faith.'

'Surely not faith in our father's wisdom.'

I laughed. 'Faith in our ability to write our own stories, regardless of what the Fates throw at us. Faith that you will find a way to make wine out of your sour grapes.'

'How deep,' Dionysus muttered, though I detected a faint smile at the corners of his mouth. He gestured to his game table. 'Pinochle, perhaps? At that, at least, I know I can dominate you.'

I stayed with him that afternoon, and he won six games. He only cheated a little.

Before dinner, I teleported to the Grove of Dodona, deep within the camp's forest.

Just as before, the ancient trees whispered in a cacophony of voices – snatches of riddles and songs, bits of doggerel (some of it actually about dogs), recipes and weather reports, none of it making much sense. Brass wind chimes twisted in the branches, reflecting the evening light and catching every breeze.

'Hello!' I called. 'I came to thank you!'

The trees continued to whisper, ignoring my presence.

'You gave me the Arrow of Dodona as my guide!' I continued.

I detected a tittering of laughter among the trees.

'Without the arrow,' I said, 'my quest would have failed. It sacrificed itself to defeat Python. Truly, it was the greatest in all the grove!'

If the trees could have made a screechy rewind noise, I'm sure they would have. Their whispering died away. The brass chimes hung lifeless in the branches.

'Its wisdom was invaluable,' I said. 'Its sacrifice noble. It represented you with honour. I will certainly tell this grove's guardian, my grandmother Rhea, all about its great service. She will hear what you did – that when I needed aid, you sent your best.'

The trees began whispering again, more nervously this time. *Wait. Wait, we didn't . . . What?*

I teleported away before they could see me smile. I hoped that wherever its spirit was, my friend the arrow was having a laugh worthy of a Shakespearean comedy.

That night, after the campfire, I sat watching the embers burn down with Nico, Will and Rachel.

The boys sat comfortably next to each other, Will's arm around Nico's shoulder, as the son of Hades twirled a burnt marshmallow on a stick. Next to me, Rachel hugged her knees and stared contentedly at the stars, the dying fire reflecting in her red hair like a charging herd of *tauri silvestres*.

'Everything's working again,' she told me, tapping the side of her head. 'The visions are clear. I can paint. I've issued a couple of prophecies already. No more snake poison in my mind. Thank you.'

'I'm glad,' I said. 'And your parents' destroyed house?'

She laughed. 'Turned out to be a good thing. Before, my dad had wanted me to stay around here in the fall. Now, he says maybe it's a good idea if I do what I wanted to begin with. Gonna take a gap year in Paris to study art while they rebuild the house.'

'Oh, Paris!' Will said.

Rachel grinned. 'Right? But don't worry, I'll be back here next summer to dish out more oracular awesomeness.'

'And if we need you in the meantime,' Nico said, 'there's always shadow-travel.'

Will sighed. 'I'd love to think you're suggesting a date night in Paris, Mr Dark Lord. But you're still thinking about Tartarus, aren't you? Hoping for some prophetic guidance?'

Nico shrugged. 'Unfinished business . . .'

I frowned. It seemed like so long ago they had mentioned this to me – Nico's compulsion to explore the depths of Tartarus, the voice he had heard, calling for help.

I didn't want to open fresh wounds, but I asked as gently as I could, 'You're sure it's not . . . Jason?'

Nico picked at his blackened marshmallow. 'I won't lie. I've wondered about that. I've thought about trying to find Jason. But, no, this isn't about him.' He snuggled a little closer to Will. 'I have a sense that Jason made his choice. I wouldn't be honouring his sacrifice if I tried to undo it. With Hazel . . . She was just drifting in Asphodel. I could tell she wasn't supposed to be there. She *needed* to come back. With Jason, I have a feeling he's somewhere better now.'

'Like Elysium?' I wondered. 'Rebirth?'

'I was hoping you could tell me,' Nico admitted.

I shook my head. 'I'm afraid I'm clueless about after-death matters. But if it's not Jason you're thinking about . . . ?'

Nico twirled his s'more stick. 'When I was in Tartarus the first time, somebody helped me. And I – *we* left him down there. I can't stop thinking about him.'

'Should I be jealous?' Will asked.

'He's a Titan, dummy,' Nico said.

I sat up straight. 'A *Titan*?'

'Long story,' Nico said. 'But he's not a bad guy. He's . . . Well, I feel like I should look for him, see if I can figure out what happened. He might need my help. I don't like it when people are overlooked.'

Rachel bunched up her shoulders. 'Hades wouldn't mind you traipsing down to Tartarus?'

Nico laughed without humour. 'He's expressly forbidden it. After that business with the Doors of Death, he doesn't want anybody in Tartarus ever again. That's where the troglodytes come in. They can tunnel anywhere, even there. They can get us in and out safely.'

'*Safely* being a relative term,' Will noted, 'given that the whole idea is bonkers.'

I frowned. I still didn't like the idea of my sunshiny son skipping off into the land of monster nightmares. My recent tumble to the edge of Chaos had reminded me what a terrible travel destination it was. Then again, it wasn't my place to tell demigods what to do, especially those I loved the most. I didn't want to be that kind of god any more.

'I wish I could offer you help,' I said, 'but I'm afraid Tartarus is outside my jurisdiction.'

'It's okay, Dad,' Will said. 'You've done your part. No story ever ends, does it? It just leads into others.' He laced his fingers through Nico's. 'We'll handle whatever comes next. Together. With or without a prophecy –'

I swear I had nothing to do with it. I did not press a button on Rachel's back. I did not prearrange a surprise gift from Delphic Deliveries.

But as soon as Will said the word *prophecy*, Rachel went

rigid. She inhaled sharply. A green mist rose from the earth, swirling around her and coiling into her lungs. She tipped over sideways while Nico and Will lunged to catch her.

As for me, I scrambled away in a very ungodlike manner, my heart beating like a frightened Lester. I guess all that green gas reminded me too much of my recent quality time with Python.

By the time my panic subsided, the prophetic moment had passed. The gas had dissipated. Rachel lay comfortable on the ground, Will and Nico both standing over her with perturbed looks.

'Did you hear it?' Nico asked me. 'The prophecy she whispered?'

'I – I didn't,' I admitted. 'Probably better if . . . if I let you two figure this one out.'

Will nodded, resigned. 'Well, it didn't sound good.'

'No, I'm sure it didn't.' I looked down fondly at Rachel Dare. 'She's a wonderful Oracle.'

38

Carrots and muffins,
Sally's fresh-baked blue cookies.
I am so hungry.

THE WAYSTATION FELT SO DIFFERENT IN
the summer.

Emmie's rooftop garden was bursting at the seams with
tomatoes, peas, cabbage and watermelon. The great hall
was bursting at the seams with old friends.

The Hunters of Artemis were in residence, having taken
quite a beating on their most recent excursion to catch the
Teumessian Fox.

'That fox is murder,' said Reyna Avila Ramírez-
Arellano, rubbing her bruised neck. 'Led us right into a den
of werewolves, the little punk.'

'Ugh,' agreed Thalia Grace, pulling a werewolf tooth
out of her leather cuirass. 'TF spreads destruction everywhere he goes.'

'TF?' I asked.

'Easier than saying *Teumessian Fox* twenty times a day,'
Thalia told me. 'Anyway, the fox runs through a town and
stirs up every monster within twenty miles. Peoria is pretty
much in ruins.'

This sounded like a tragic loss, but I was more concerned with my Hunter buddies.

'Are you regretting your decision to join up?' I asked Reyna.

She grinned. 'Not for a minute. This is fun!'

Thalia punched her in the shoulder. 'Great Hunter, this one. I knew she would be. We'll get that fox one of these days.'

Emmie called to them from the kitchen to help with dinner, because the carrots weren't going to dice themselves. The two friends strode off together, laughing and sharing stories. It did my heart good to see them so happy, even if their version of fun was a never-ending foxhunt that destroyed large portions of the Midwest.

Jo was teaching Georgina, their daughter (and possibly mine, too), to forge weapons in the smithy. When Georgina saw me, she looked unexcited, as if we'd just parted a few minutes ago. 'You keep my doll?' she demanded.

'Ah . . .' I could have lied. I could have magically produced an exact likeness of the pipe-cleaner figure and said *Of course*. But the truth was that I had no idea where the little guy had ended up, perhaps in Delphi or Tartarus or Chaos? I told her the truth. 'Would you make me another one?'

Georgina thought about this. 'Nah.'

Then she went back to quenching hot blades with her mom.

The swordsman Lityerses seemed to be adjusting well. He was overseeing an 'elephant visitation programme' with Waystation resident Livia and Hannibal from Camp Jupiter. The two pachyderms were romping around together in the back lot, flirting by throwing medicine balls at each other.

After dinner, I got to visit with Leo Valdez, who had just straggled back home after a full day of community service. He was teaching homeless kids shop skills at a local shelter.

'That's amazing,' I said.

He grinned, biting off a chunk of Emmie's fresh-made buttermilk scones. 'Yeah. Bunch of kids like me, you know? They never had much. Least I can show them somebody cares. Plus, some of them are excellent mechanics.'

'Don't you need tools?' I asked. 'A shop?'

'Festus!' Leo said. 'A bronze dragon makes the best mobile shop. Most of the kids just see him as a truck, with the Mist and all, but a few of them . . . they know what's up.'

Jo passed by on her way to the griffin lofts and patted him on the shoulder. 'Doing good, this one. He's got potential.'

'Thanks, Mom,' Leo said.

Jo scoffed, but she looked pleased.

'And Calypso?' I asked Leo.

A flurry of emotions passed across his face – enough to tell me that Leo was more lovesick than ever over the former goddess, and things were still complicated.

'Yeah, she's good,' he said at last. 'I've never seen anyone actually *like* high school before. But the routine, the homework, the people . . . She ate it up. I guess it's just so different from being stuck on Ogygia.'

I nodded, though the idea of an ex-immortal liking high school didn't make much sense to me either. 'Where is she now?'

'Band camp.'

I stared. 'Excuse me?'

'She's a counsellor at a band camp,' Leo said. 'Like, for regular mortal kids who are practising music and stuff. I don't know. She's gone all summer.'

He shook his head, clearly worried, clearly missing her, perhaps having nightmares about all the hot clarinet-player counsellors Calypso might be hanging around with.

'It's all good,' he said, forcing a smile. 'You know, a little time apart to think. We'll make it work.'

Reyna passed by and heard the last part. 'Talking about Calypso? Yeah, I had to have a heart-to-heart with mi hermano here.' She squeezed Leo's shoulder. 'You don't call a young lady *mamacita*. You got to have more respect, entiendes?'

'I –' Leo looked ready to protest, then seemed to think better about it. 'Yeah, okay.'

Reyna smiled at me. 'Valdez grew up without his mom. Never learned these things. Now he's got two great foster moms and a big sister who isn't afraid to smack him when he gets out of line.' She flicked a finger playfully against his cheek.

'Ain't that the truth,' Leo muttered.

'Cheer up,' Reyna said. 'Calypso will come around. You're a doofus sometimes, Valdez, but you've got a heart of Imperial gold.'

Next stop: Camp Jupiter.

It did not surprise me that Hazel and Frank had become the most efficient and respected pair of praetors ever to run the Twelfth Legion. In record time they had inspired a rebuilding effort in New Rome, repaired all the damage from our battle against Tarquin and the two emperors, and started a recruitment drive with Lupa's wolves to bring in new demigods from the wild. At least twenty had arrived since I left, which made me wonder where they'd all been hiding, and how busy my fellow gods must have been in the last few decades to have so many children.

'We're going to install more barracks over there,' Hazel told me, as she and Frank gave me the five-denarius tour of the repaired camp. 'We've expanded the thermal baths, and we're constructing a victory arch on the main road into New Rome to commemorate our defeat of the emperors.' Her amber eyes flashed with excitement. 'It's going to be plated with gold. *Completely* over the top.'

Frank smiled. 'Yeah. As far as we can tell, Hazel's curse is officially broken. We did an augury at Pluto's shrine, and it came up favourable. She can summon jewels, precious metals . . . and use them or spend them now without causing *any* curses.'

'But we're not going to abuse that power,' Hazel hastened to add. 'We'll only use it to improve the camp and honour the gods. We're not going to buy any yachts or private aeroplanes or big golden necklaces with "H plus F 4Ever" diamond pendants, are we, Frank?'

Frank pouted. 'No. I guess not.'

Hazel ribbed him.

'No, definitely not,' Frank amended. 'That would be tacky.'

Frank still lumbered along like a friendly grizzly bear, but his posture seemed more relaxed, his mood more cheerful, as if it were starting to sink in that his destiny was no longer controlled by a small piece of firewood. For Frank Zhang, like the rest of us, the future was open for business.

He brightened. 'Oh, and check this out, Apollo!'

He swirled his purple praetor's cloak like he was about to turn into a vampire bat (which Frank was fully capable of doing). Instead, the cloak simply turned into an oversize sweater wrap. 'I figured it out!'

Hazel rolled her eyes. 'My sweet, sweet Frank. Could you please *not* with the sweater wrap?'

'What?' Frank protested. 'It's impenetrable *and* comfortable!'

Later that day, I visited my other friends. Lavinia Asimov had made good on her threat/promise to teach the Fifth Cohort to tap-dance. The unit was now feared and respected in the war games for their ability to form a testudo shield wall while doing the three-beat shuffle.

Tyson and Ella were happily back at work in their bookshop. The unicorns were still weaponized. The Jason Grace temple-expansion plan was still moving forward, with new shrines being added every week.

What did surprise me: Percy Jackson and Annabeth Chase had arrived and taken up residence in New Rome, giving them two months to adjust to their new environs before the fall semester of their freshman year in college.

'Architecture,' Annabeth said, her grey eyes as bright as her mother's. She said the word *architecture* as if it were the answer to all the world's problems. 'I'm going to focus on environmental design at UC Berkeley while dual-enrolling at New Rome University. By year three, I figure –'

'Whoa, there, Wise Girl,' Percy said. 'First you have

to help me get through freshman English. And math. And history.'

Annabeth's smile lit up the empty dorm room. 'Yeah, Seaweed Brain, I know. We'll take the basics together. But you *will* do your own homework.'

'Man,' Percy said, looking at me for commiseration. 'Homework.'

I was pleased to see them doing so well, but I agreed with him about homework. Gods never got it. We didn't want it. We just assigned it in the form of deadly quests.

'And your major?' I asked him.

'Yeah, uh . . . marine biology? Aquaculture? I dunno. I'll figure it out.'

'You're both staying here?' I gestured at the bunk beds. New Rome University may have been a college for demi-gods, but its dorm rooms were as basic and uninspired as any other university's.

'No.' Annabeth sounded offended. 'Have you seen the way this guy throws his dirty clothes around? Gross. Besides, dorms are required for all freshmen and they aren't co-ed. My roommate probably won't arrive until September.'

'Yeah.' Percy sighed. 'Meanwhile, I'll be all the way across campus in this empty boys' dormitory. Two whole blocks away.'

Annabeth swatted his arm. 'Besides, Apollo, our living arrangements are none of your business.'

I held up my hands in surrender. 'But you did travel across the country together to get here?'

'With Grover,' Percy said. 'It was great, just the three of us again. But, man, that road trip . . .'

'Kind of went sideways,' Annabeth agreed. 'And up, down and diagonal. But we made it here alive.'

I nodded. This was, after all, about the most that could be said for any demigod trip.

I thought about my own trip from Los Angeles to Camp Jupiter, escorting the coffin of Jason Grace. Percy and Annabeth both seemed to read my thoughts. Despite the happy days ahead of them, and the general spirit of optimism at Camp Jupiter, sadness still lingered, hovering and flickering at the corners of my vision like one of the camp's Lares.

'We found out when we arrived,' Percy said. 'I still can't . . .'

His voice caught. He looked down and picked at his palm.

'I cried myself sick,' Annabeth admitted. 'I still wish . . . I wish I'd been there for Piper. I hope she's doing okay.'

'Piper is a tough young lady,' I said. 'But yes . . . Jason. He was the best of us.'

No one argued with that.

'By the way,' I said, 'your mother is doing well, Percy. I just saw her and Paul. Your little sister is entirely too adorable. She never stops laughing.'

He brightened. 'I know, right? Estelle is awesome. I just miss my mom's baking.'

'I might be able to help with that.' As I had promised Sally Jackson, I teleported a plate of her fresh-baked blue cookies straight into my hands.

'Dude!' Percy stuffed a cookie in his mouth. His eyes rolled up in ecstasy. 'Apollo, you're the best. I take back almost everything I've said about you.'

'It's quite all right,' I assured him. 'Wait . . . what do you mean, *almost*?'

39

Two hundred and ten
Is a lot of haiku, but
I can do more if –
(*insert the sound of a god being strangled here*)

SPEAKING OF PIPER MCLEAN, I EMBAR-
rassed myself when I popped in to visit her.

It was a lovely summer night in Tahlequah, Oklahoma.
The stars were out by the millions and cicadas chirred in
the trees. Heat settled over the rolling hills. Fireflies glowed
in the grass.

I had willed myself to appear wherever Piper McLean
might be. I ended up standing on the flat roof of a mod-
est farmhouse – the McLean ancestral home. At the edge
of the roof, two people sat shoulder to shoulder, dark sil-
houettes facing away from me. One leaned over and kissed
the other.

I didn't mean to, but I was so flustered I flashed like
a camera light, inadvertently changing from Lester to my
adult Apollo form – toga, blond hair, muscles and all. The
two lovebirds turned to face me. Piper McLean was on the
left. On the right sat another young lady with short dark
hair and a rhinestone nose stud that winked in the darkness.

Piper unlaced her fingers from the other girl's. 'Wow, Apollo. Timing.'

'Er, sorry. I –'

'Who's this?' the other girl asked, taking in my bed-sheet clothing. 'Your dad has a boyfriend?'

I suppressed a yelp. Since Piper's dad was Tristan McLean, former A-list heartthrob of Hollywood, I was tempted to say *Not yet, but I'm willing to volunteer.* I didn't think Piper would appreciate that, though.

'Old family friend,' Piper said. 'Sorry, Shel. Would you excuse me a sec?'

'Uh. Sure.'

Piper got up, grabbed my arm and guided me to the far end of the roof. 'Hey. What's up?'

'I . . . Uh . . .' I had not been this tongue-tied since I'd been a full-time Lester Papadopoulos. 'I just wanted to check in, make sure you're doing okay. It seems you are?'

Piper gave me a hint of a smile. 'Well, early days.'

'You're in process,' I said, remembering what she had told me in California. Suddenly, much of what she and I had talked about started to make sense. Not being defined by Aphrodite's expectations. Or Hera's ideas of what a perfect couple looked like. Piper finding her own way, not the one people expected of her.

'Exactly,' she said.

'I'm happy for you.' And I was. In fact, it took effort for me not to glow like a giant firefly. 'Your dad?'

'Yeah, I mean . . . from Hollywood back to Tahlequah is a big change. But he seems like he's found some peace. We'll see. I heard you got back on Olympus. Congratulations.'

I wasn't sure if congratulations were in order, given my general restlessness and feelings of unworthiness, but I nodded. I told her what had happened with Nero. I told her about Jason's funeral.

She hugged her arms. In the starlight, her face looked as warm as bronze fresh from Hephaestus's anvil. 'That's good,' she said. 'I'm glad Camp Jupiter did right by him. You did right by him.'

'I don't know about that,' I said.

She laid her hand on my arm. 'You haven't forgotten. I can tell.'

She meant about being human, about honouring the sacrifices that had been made.

'No,' I said. 'I won't forget. The memory is part of me now.'

'Well, then, good. Now, if you'll excuse me . . .'

'What?'

She pointed back to her friend Shel.

'Oh, of course. Take care of yourself, Piper McLean.'

'You too, Apollo. And next time maybe give me a heads-up before popping in?'

I muttered something apologetic, but she had already turned to go – back to her new friend, her new life and the stars in the sky.

The last and hardest reunion . . . Meg McCaffrey.

A summer day in Palm Springs. The dry, blistering heat reminded me of the Burning Maze, but there was nothing malicious or magical about it. The desert simply got hot.

Aeithales, the former home of Dr Phillip McCaffrey, was an oasis of cool, verdant life. Tree limbs had grown to reshape the once fully man-made structure, making it even more impressive than it had been in Meg's childhood. Annabeth would have been blown away by the local dryads' environmental design. Windows had been replaced by layers of vines that opened and closed automatically for shade and cool, responding to the winds' smallest fluctuations. The greenhouses had been repaired and were now packed with rare specimens of plants from all around Southern California. Natural springs filled the cisterns and provided water for the gardens and a cooling system for the house.

I appeared in my old Lester form on the pathway from the house to the gardens and was almost skewered by the Meliai, Meg's personal troupe of seven super dryads.

'Halt!' they yelled in unison. 'Intruder!'

'It's just me!' I said, which didn't seem to help. 'Lester!' Still nothing. 'Meg's old, you know, servant.'

The Meliai lowered their spear points.

'Oh, yes,' said one.

'Servant of the Meg,' said another.

'The weak, insufficient one,' said a third. 'Before the Meg had *our* services.'

'I'll have you know I'm a full Olympian god now,' I protested.

The dryads did not look impressed.

'We will march you to the Meg,' one said. 'She will pass judgement. Double-time!'

They formed a phalanx around me and herded me up the path. I could have vanished or flown away or done any number of impressive things, but they had surprised me. I fell into my old Lester-ish habits and allowed myself to be force-marched to my old master.

We found her digging in the dirt alongside her former Nero family members – showing them how to transplant cactus saplings. I spotted Aemillia and Lucius, contentedly caring for their baby cacti. Even young Cassius was there, though how Meg had tracked him down, I had no idea. He was joking with one of the dryads, looking so relaxed I couldn't believe he was the same boy who had fled from Nero's tower.

Nearby, at the edge of a newly planted peach orchard, the karpos Peaches stood in all his diapered glory. (Oh, sure. He showed up *after* the danger had passed.) He was engaged in a heated conversation with a young female karpos whom I assumed was a native of the area. She looked much like Peaches himself, except she was covered in a fine layer of spines.

'Peaches,' Peaches told her.

'Prickly Pear!' the young lady rejoined.

'Peaches!'

'Prickly Pear!'

That seemed to be the extent of their argument. Perhaps it was about to devolve into a death match for local fruit supremacy. Or perhaps it was the beginning of the greatest love story ever to ripen. It was hard to tell with karpoi.

Meg did a double take when she saw me. Her face split in a grin. She wore her pink Sally Jackson dress, topped with a gardening hat that looked like a mushroom cap.

Despite the protection, her neck was turning red from the work outdoors.

'You're back,' she noted.

I smiled. 'You're sunburned.'

'Come here,' she ordered.

Her commands no longer held force, but I went to her anyway. She hugged me tight. She smelled like prickly pear and warm sand. I might have got a little teary-eyed.

'You guys keep at it,' she told her trainees. 'I'll be back.'

The former imperial children looked happy to comply. They actually seemed determined to garden, as if their sanity depended on it, which perhaps it did.

Meg took my hand and led me on a tour of the new estate, the Meliai still in our wake. She showed me the trailer where Herophile the Sibyl now lived when she wasn't working in town as a Tarot card reader and crystal healer. Meg boasted that the former Oracle was bringing in enough cash to cover all of Aeithales's expenses.

Our dryad friends Joshua and Aloe Vera were pleased to see me. They told me about their work travelling across Southern California, planting new dryads and doing their best to heal the damage from the droughts and wildfires. They had lots of work still to do, but things were looking up. Aloe followed us around for a while, lathering Meg's sunburnt shoulders with goo and chiding her.

Finally, we arrived in the house's main room, where Luguselwa was putting together a rocking chair. She'd been fitted with new mechanical hands, compliments, Meg told me, of the Hephaestus cabin at Camp Half-Blood.

'Hey, cellmate!' Lu grinned. She made a hand gesture that was usually not associated with friendly greeting. Then she cursed and shook her metal fingers until they opened into a proper wave. 'Sorry about that. These hands haven't quite been programmed right. Got a few kinks to work out.'

She got up and wrapped me in a bear hug. Her fingers splayed and started tickling me between the shoulder blades, but I decided this must be unintentional, as Lu didn't strike me as the tickle type.

'You look well,' I said, pulling away.

Lu laughed. 'I've got my Sapling here. I've got a home. I'm a regular old mortal again, and I wouldn't have it any other way.'

I stopped myself from saying Me, too. The thought made me melancholy. It would have been inconceivable to the old Apollo, but the idea of ageing in this lovely desert tree house, watching Meg grow into a strong and powerful woman . . . that didn't sound bad at all.

Lu must have picked up on my sadness. She gestured back to the rocking chair. 'Well, I'll let you two get on with the tour. Assembling this IKEA furniture is the toughest quest I've had in years.'

Meg took me out to the terrace as the afternoon sun sank behind the San Jacinto Mountains. My sun chariot would just now be heading towards home, the horses getting excited as they sensed the end of their journey. I would be joining them soon . . . reuniting with my other self, back at the Palace of the Sun.

I looked over at Meg, who was wiping a tear from her eye. 'You can't stay, I guess,' she said.

I took her hand. 'Dear Meg.'

We remained like that in silence for a while, watching the demigods work in the gardens below.

'Meg, you've done so much for me. For all of us. I . . . I promised to reward you when I became a god again.'

She started to speak, but I interrupted.

'No, wait,' I said. 'I understand that would cheapen our friendship. I cannot solve mortal problems with a snap of my fingers. I see that you don't want a reward. But you will always be my friend. And if you ever need me, even just to talk, I will be here.'

Her mouth twitched. 'Thanks. That's good. But . . . actually, I would be okay with a unicorn.'

She had done it again. She could still surprise me. I laughed, snapped my fingers, and a unicorn appeared on the hillside below us, whinnying and scratching the ground with its gold-and-pearl hooves.

She threw her arms around me. 'Thanks. You'll still be my friend, too, right?'

'As long as you'll still be mine,' I said.

She thought about this. 'Yeah. I can do that.'

I don't recall what else we talked about. The piano lessons I had promised her. Different varieties of succulents. The care and feeding of unicorns. I was just happy to be with her.

At last, as the sun went down, Meg seemed to understand it was time for me to leave.

'You'll come back?' she asked.

'Always,' I promised. 'The sun always comes back.'

———

So, dear reader, we have come to the end of my trials. You have followed me through five volumes of adventures and six months of pain and suffering. By my reckoning, you have read two hundred and ten of my haiku. Like Meg, you surely deserve a reward.

What would you accept? I am fresh out of unicorns. However, any time you take aim and prepare to fire your best shot, any time you seek to put your emotions into a song or poem, know that I am smiling on you. We are friends now.

Call on me. I will be there for you.

GUIDE TO APOLLO-SPEAK

Achilles   a Greek hero of the Trojan War who was killed by an arrow shot into his heel, his one vulnerable spot

Aelian   an early third-century-CE Roman author who wrote sensational stories about strange events and miraculous occurrences and was best known for his book *On the Nature of Animals*

Agrippina the Younger   an ambitious and bloodthirsty Roman empress who was Nero's mother; she was so domineering towards her son that he ordered her killed

ambrosia   a food of the gods that can heal demigods if eaten in small doses; it tastes like the user's favourite food

amphisbaena   a snake with a head at each end, born from the blood that dripped from Medusa's severed head

Anicetus   Nero's loyal servant, who carried out the order to kill Agrippina, Nero's mother

Aphrodite   Greek goddess of love and beauty. Roman form: Venus

Ares   the Greek god of war; the son of Zeus and Hera. Roman form: Mars

Artemis   the Greek goddess of the hunt and the moon; the daughter of Zeus and Leto, and the twin of Apollo. Roman form: Diana

Asclepius   the god of medicine; son of Apollo; his temple was the healing centre of Ancient Greece

Athena   the Greek goddess of wisdom. Roman form: Minerva

Athena Parthenos   a forty-foot-tall statue of the goddess Athena that was once the central figure in the Parthenon of Athens. It currently stands on Half-Blood Hill at Camp Half-Blood.

Bacchus   Roman god of wine and revelry; son of Jupiter. Greek form: Dionysus

Battle of Manhattan   the climactic final battle of the Second Titan War

Benito Mussolini   an Italian politician who became the leader of the National Fascist Party, a paramilitary organization. He ruled Italy from 1922 to 1943, first as a prime minister and then as a dictator.

boare   Latin equivalent of *boo*

Boreas   god of the North Wind

Caligula   the nickname of the third of Rome's emperors, Gaius Julius Caesar Augustus Germanicus, infamous for his cruelty and carnage during the four years he ruled, from 37 to 41 CE; he was assassinated by his own guard

Camp Half-Blood   the training ground for Greek demigods, located in Long Island, New York

Camp Jupiter   the training ground for Roman demigods, located in California, between the Oakland Hills and the Berkeley Hills

Celestial bronze   a powerful magical metal used to create weapons wielded by Greek gods and their demigod children

Celtic   relating to a group of Indo-European peoples identified by their cultural similarities and use of languages such as Irish, Scottish Gaelic, Welsh and others, including pre-Roman Gaulish

centaur   a race of creatures that is half human, half horse. They are excellent archers.

Chaos   the first primordial deity and the creator of the universe; a shapeless void below even the depths of Tartarus

Cistern   a refuge for dryads in Palm Springs, California

cohort   a group of legionnaires

Commodus   Lucius Aurelius Commodus was the son of Roman Emperor Marcus Aurelius; he became co-emperor when he was sixteen and emperor at eighteen, when his father died; he ruled from 177 to 192 CE and was megalomaniacal and corrupt; he considered himself the New Hercules and enjoyed killing animals and fighting gladiators at the Colosseum

Cumaean Sibyl   an Oracle of Apollo from Cumae who collected her prophetic instructions for averting disaster in nine volumes but destroyed six of them when trying to sell them to Tarquinius Superbus of Rome

Cyclops (Cyclopes, pl.)   a member of a primordial race of giants, each with a single eye in the middle of his or her forehead

cynocephalus (cynocephali, pl.)   a being with a human body and a dog's head

Daedalus   a Greek demigod, the son of Athena and inventor of many things, including the Labyrinth, where the Minotaur (part man, part bull) was kept

Dante   an Italian poet of the late Middle Ages who invented terza rima; author of *The Divine Comedy*, among other works

Daphne   a beautiful naiad who attracted Apollo's attention; she transformed into a laurel tree in order to escape him

Deimos   Greek god of fear

Demeter   the Greek goddess of agriculture; a daughter of the Titans Rhea and Kronos

denarius (denari, pl.)   a unit of Roman currency

Diana   the Roman goddess of the hunt and the moon; the daughter of Jupiter and Leto, and the twin of Apollo. Greek form: Artemis

Didyma   the oracular shrine to Apollo in Miletus, a port city on the western coast of modern-day Turkey

dimachaerus (dimachaeri, pl.)   a Roman gladiator trained to fight with two swords at once

Dionysus   Greek god of wine and revelry; the son of Zeus. Roman form: Bacchus

drachma   a unit of Ancient Greek currency

drakon   a gigantic yellow-and-green serpentlike monster, with frills around its neck, reptilian eyes and huge talons; it spits poison

dryad   a spirit (usually female) associated with a certain tree

Elysium   the paradise to which Greek heroes are sent when the gods grant them immortality

Erebos   the Greek primordial god of darkness; a place of darkness between Earth and Hades

fasces   a ceremonial axe wrapped in a bundle of thick wooden rods with its crescent-shaped blade projecting outwards; the ultimate symbol of authority in Ancient Rome; origin of the word *fascism*

Fates   three female personifications of destiny. They control the thread of life for every living thing from birth to death.

faun   a Roman forest god, part goat and part man

Fields of Punishment   the section of the Underworld where people who were evil during their lives are sent to face eternal punishment for their crimes after death

Gaia   the Greek earth goddess; wife of Ouranos; mother of the Titans, giants, Cyclopes and other monsters

Ganymede   a beautiful Trojan boy whom Zeus abducted to be cupbearer to the gods

Gaul   the name that Romans gave to the Celts and their territories

Germanus (Germani, pl.)   a bodyguard for the Roman Emperor from the Gaulish and Germanic tribal people who settled to the west of the Rhine river

glámon   the Ancient Greek equivalent of *dirty old man*

Golden Fleece   this hide from a gold-haired winged ram was a symbol of authority and kingship; it was guarded by a dragon and fire-breathing bulls; Jason was tasked with obtaining it, resulting in an epic quest. It now hangs on Thalia's tree at Camp Half-Blood to help strengthen the magical borders.

Greek fire   a magical, highly explosive, viscous green

liquid used as a weapon; one of the most dangerous sub-
stances on Earth

Grey Sisters Tempest, Anger and Wasp, a trio of old
women who share a single eye and a single tooth and
operate a taxi that serves the New York City area

griffin a flying creature that is part lion, part eagle

Grove of Dodona the site of the oldest Greek Oracle,
second only to Delphi in importance; the rustling of
trees in the grove provided answers to priests and priestesses who journeyed to the site. The grove is located
in Camp Half-Blood Forest and accessible only through
the myrmekes' lair.

Hades the Greek god of death and riches; ruler of the
Underworld. Roman form: Pluto

Harpocrates the god of silence

harpy a winged female creature that snatches things

Hecate goddess of magic and crossroads

Helios the Titan god of the sun; son of the Titan Hyperion
and the Titaness Theia

Hephaestus the Greek god of fire, including volcanic,
and of crafts and blacksmithing; the son of Zeus and
Hera, and married to Aphrodite. Roman form: Vulcan

Hera the Greek goddess of marriage; Zeus's wife and sister; Apollo's stepmother

Hermes Greek god of travellers; guide to spirits of the
dead; god of communication. Roman form: Mercury

Herophile the Oracle of Erythraea; she spouts prophecies
in the form of word puzzles

Hestia Greek goddess of the hearth

Hunters of Artemis a group of maidens loyal to Artemis

and gifted with hunting skills and eternal youth as long as they reject men for life

Hyacinthus   a Greek hero and Apollo's lover, who died while trying to impress Apollo with his discus skills

Icarus   the son of Daedalus, best known for flying too close to the sun while trying to escape the island of Crete by using metal-and-wax wings invented by his father; he died when he didn't heed his father's warnings

Imperial gold   a rare metal deadly to monsters, consecrated at the Pantheon; its existence was a closely guarded secret of the emperors

Julius Caesar   a Roman politician and general whose military accomplishments extended Rome's territory and ultimately led to a civil war that enabled him to assume control of the government in 49 BCE. He was declared 'dictator for life' and went on to institute social reforms that angered some powerful Romans. A group of senators conspired against him and assassinated him on 15 March, 44 BCE.

Jupiter   the Roman god of the sky and king of the gods. Greek form: Zeus

karpos (karpoi, pl.)   grain spirit; a child of Tartarus and Gaia

King Midas   a ruler who was famous for being able to turn everything he touched into gold, an ability granted by Dionysus

Koronis   one of Apollo's girlfriends, who fell in love with another man. A white raven Apollo had left to guard her informed him of the affair. Apollo was so angry at the raven for failing to peck out the man's eyes that he cursed the bird, scorching its feathers. Apollo sent his sister, Artemis, to kill Koronis, because he couldn't bring himself to do it.

Kronos   the Titan lord of time, evil and the harvest. He is the youngest but boldest and most devious of Gaia's children; he convinced several of his brothers to aid him in the murder of their father, Ouranos. He was also Percy Jackson's primary opponent. Roman form: Saturn

Labyrinth   an underground maze originally built on the island of Crete by the craftsman Daedalus to hold the Minotaur

Lar (Lares, pl.)   Roman house gods

leontocephaline   a being with the head of a lion and the body of a man entwined with a snake without a head or tail; created by Mithras, a Persian god, to protect his immortality

Leto   mother of Artemis and Apollo with Zeus; goddess of motherhood

Lugus   one of the major gods in ancient Celtic religion

Lupa   the wolf goddess, guardian spirit of Rome

Mars   the Roman god of war. Greek form: Ares

Marsyas   a satyr who lost to Apollo after challenging him in a musical contest, which led to Marsyas being flayed alive

Meliai   Greek nymphs of the ash tree, born of Gaia; they nurtured and raised Zeus in Crete

Mercury   Roman god of travellers; guide to spirits of the dead; god of communication. Greek form: Hermes

Minerva   the Roman goddess of wisdom. Greek form: Athena

Minoans   a Bronze Age civilization of Crete that flour-
ished from c. 3000 to 1100 BCE; their name comes from
King Minos

Minotaur   the half-man, half-bull son of King Minos of
Crete; the Minotaur was kept in the Labyrinth, where
he killed people who were sent in; he was finally defeated
by Theseus

Mist   a magical force that prevents mortals from seeing
gods, mythical creatures and supernatural occurrences
by replacing them with things the human mind can
comprehend

Mithras   a Persian god who was adopted by the Romans
and became the god of warriors; he created the
leontocephaline

Morpheus   the Titan who put all the mortals in New York
to sleep during the Battle of Manhattan

Mount Olympus   home of the Twelve Olympians

naiad   a female water spirit

nectar   a drink of the gods that can heal demigods

Nero   ruled as Roman Emperor from 54 to 58 CE; he had his
mother and his first wife put to death; many believe he
was responsible for setting a fire that gutted Rome, but
he blamed the Christians, whom he burned on crosses;
he built an extravagant new palace on the cleared land
and lost support when construction expenses forced
him to raise taxes; he committed suicide

New Rome   both the valley in which Camp Jupiter is
located and a city – a smaller, modern version of the
imperial city – where Roman demigods can go to live in
peace, study and retire

Nine Muses   goddesses who grant inspiration for and protect artistic creation and expression; daughters of Zeus and Mnemosyne; as children, they were taught by Apollo. Their names are: Clio, Euterpe, Thalia, Melpomene, Terpsichore, Erato, Polymnia, Ourania and Calliope.

nymph   a female deity who animates nature

omphalos   Greek for *navel of the world*; the nickname for Delphi, a spring that whispered the future to those who would listen

Oracle of Delphi   a speaker of the prophecies of Apollo

pandos (pandai, pl.)   a man with gigantic ears, eight fingers and toes, and a body covered with hair that starts out white and turns black with age

pegasus (pegasi, pl.)   a winged divine horse; sired by Poseidon, in his role as horse-god

Peleus   father of Achilles; his wedding to the sea nymph Thetis was well attended by the gods, and a disagreement between them at the event eventually led to the Trojan War; the guardian dragon at Camp Half-Blood is named after him

Persephone   the Greek goddess of springtime and vegetation; daughter of Zeus and Demeter; Hades fell in love with her and abducted her to the Underworld to become his wife and queen of the Underworld

Phaethon   the demigod son of Helios, Titan of the Sun; he accidentally scorched the Earth when he drove Helios's sun chariot, and Zeus killed him with lightning as a result

Pluto   the Roman god of death and ruler of the Underworld. Greek form: Hades

Poseidon   the Greek god of the sea; son of the Titans Kronos and Rhea, and the brother of Zeus and Hades. Roman form: Neptune

praetor   an elected Roman magistrate and commander of the army

Primordial Chaos   the first thing ever to exist; a void from which the first gods were produced

princeps   Latin for *first citizen* or *first in line*; the early Roman emperors adopted this title for themselves, and it came to mean *prince of Rome*

Pythia   the priestess of Apollo's prophecies; the name given to every Oracle of Delphi

Python   a monstrous serpent that Gaia appointed to guard the Oracle at Delphi

River Styx   the river that forms the boundary between Earth and the Underworld

roc   an enormous bird of prey

Sassanid gas   a chemical weapon the Persians used against the Romans in wartime

Saturnalia   an Ancient Roman festival held in December in honour of the god Saturn, the Roman equivalent of Kronos

satyr   a Greek forest god, part goat and part man

scusatemi   Italian for *excuse me*

shadow-travel   a form of transportation that allows creatures of the Underworld and children of Hades to use shadows to leap to any desired place on Earth or in the Underworld, although it makes the user extremely fatigued

Sibyl   a prophetess

sica (siccae, pl.)   a short, curved sword

Socrates   a Greek philosopher (c. 470–399 BCE) who had a profound influence on Western thought

Stygian iron   a magical metal forged in the River Styx, capable of absorbing the very essence of monsters and injuring mortals, gods, Titans and giants; has a significant effect on ghosts and creatures from the Underworld

Styx   a powerful water nymph; the eldest daughter of the sea Titan, Oceanus; goddess of the Underworld's most important river; goddess of hatred; the River Styx is named after her

Sutro Tower   a massive red-and-white transmission antenna in the San Francisco Bay Area where Harpocrates, the god of silence, was imprisoned by Commodus and Caligula

Tarquin   Lucius Tarquinius Superbus was the seventh and final king of Rome, reigning from 534 to 509 BCE, when, after a popular uprising, the Roman Republic was established

Tartarus   husband of Gaia; spirit of the abyss; father of the giants; the darkest pit in the Underworld, where monsters go when they are slain

taurus silvestris (tauri silvestres, pl.)   a forest bull with an impenetrable hide; ancestral enemy of the troglodytes

Terpsichore   Greek goddess of dance; one of the Nine Muses

terza rima   a form of verse consisting of three-line stanzas in which the first and third lines rhyme and the middle line rhymes with the first and third lines of the following stanza

testudo   a tortoise battle formation in which legionnaires put their shields together to form a barrier

Teumessian Fox   a gigantic fox sent by the Olympians to prey upon the children of Thebes; it is destined never to be caught

Thalia   the Muse of comedy

Three Graces   the three charities: Beauty, Mirth and Elegance; daughters of Zeus

Titans   a race of powerful Greek deities, descendants of Gaia and Ouranos, that ruled during the Golden Age and were overthrown by a race of younger gods, the Olympians

triumvirate   a political alliance formed by three parties

troglodytes   a race of subterranean humanoids who eat lizards and fight bulls

Trojan War   according to legend, the Trojan War was waged against the city of Troy by the Achaeans (Greeks) after Paris of Troy took Helen from her husband, Menelaus, king of Sparta

Trophonius   demigod son of Apollo, designer of Apollo's temple at Delphi and spirit of the dark Oracle; he decapitated his half brother Agamethus to avoid discovery after their raid on King Hyrieus's treasury

Troy   a pre-Roman city situated in modern-day Turkey; site of the Trojan War

Underworld   the kingdom of the dead, where souls go for eternity; ruled by Hades

ventus (**venti**, pl.)   storm spirits

Venus   the Roman goddess of love and beauty. Greek form: Aphrodite

Vnicornes Imperant   Latin for *Unicorns Rule*

Vulcan   the Roman god of fire, including volcanic, and of crafts and blacksmithing. Greek form: Hephaestus

Waystation   a place of refuge for demigods, peaceful monsters and Hunters of Artemis located above Union Station in Indianapolis, Indiana

Zeus   the Greek god of the sky and the king of the gods. Roman form: Jupiter

THE TRIALS OF APOLLO

GET AN EVEN CLOSER
LOOK AT APOLLO . . .

READ ON FOR

APOLLO SINGS
AND DANCES AND
SHOOTS PEOPLE

APOLLO SINGS AND DANCES
AND SHOOTS PEOPLE

YOU HAVE TO PITY APOLLO'S MOM.

Being pregnant is hard enough. (Not that I would know, but my mom has told me about a million times.) Apollo's mother, the Titan Leto, was pregnant with *twins*, and she couldn't go to the hospital when she went into labour. Instead she had to run for her life, rushing from island to island, pursued by a vengeful goddess and a giant snake.

Would it surprise you to learn that the whole thing was Zeus's fault?

Old Thunderbritches fell in love with Leto and convinced her it would be totally fine to have kids together.

'Hera will never find out!' he promised.

Zeus had told that lie to so many different women he probably even believed it.

Of course, Hera found out. She glared down from Mount Olympus at the beautiful pregnant Leto, who was glowing with health, sitting in a meadow and patting her swollen tummy, singing to her unborn children.

Hera grumbled to herself, 'How *dare* she be happy? Let's see how happy she is in *eternal pain!*' The Queen of Heaven spread her arms and addressed the entire earth below her. 'Hear me, world! Hear me, Mother Gaia! I forbid any land with roots in the earth to receive Leto when it is time for her to give birth. Any land that dares to oppose me, I will curse for all eternity! Leto will have no bed to lie in, no place to rest! She will be forced to wander without a place to give birth, she will stay pregnant and in labour forever, suffering for the crime of taking my husband! HAHAHA!'

Yeah, Hera was definitely channelling her inner Wicked Witch of the West that day. The ground rumbled. All the nature spirits on every land with roots in the earth promised not to help Leto. Now, you're wondering, why couldn't Leto just buy a boat and give birth at sea? Why couldn't she go underwater, or down into Erebos, or rent a helicopter and give birth one thousand feet in the air?

Near as I can figure, Hera included all that in the curse. She created an impossible situation, where Leto could only give birth on solid ground, but all solid ground was forbidden to accept her. Hera was tricky that way.

When Leto was seven months pregnant, she went into early labour.

'Oh, great,' she groaned. 'These kids aren't going to wait!'

She tried to lie down, but the earth shook. Trees burst into flame. Fissures opened in the ground, and Leto had to run for safety. No matter where she moved, she couldn't find a safe place to rest. She took a boat to another island, but the same thing happened. She tried a dozen different places all over Greece and beyond. In each spot, the nymphs refused to help her.

'Sorry,' they said. 'Hera will curse us for all eternity if we let you come ashore. You can't give birth on any land with roots in the earth.'

'But that means *every* land!' Leto protested.

'Yeah, that's the idea,' the nymphs told her.

Leto drifted from place to place, her body racked with pain, her unborn children getting more and more impatient. Leto felt like she'd swallowed an over-inflated beach ball and a couple of feral cats.

In desperation, she went to Delphi, which had once been her mother Phoebe's sacred place. Leto figured the Oracle would give her sanctuary.

Unfortunately, the Oracle's cave had been taken over by a giant snake called Python. Where did he come from? You'll love this. The word *python* is from the Greek *pytho*, which means *rotting*. The monster Python was born out of the festering, rotten slime left over from the great flood when Zeus drowned the world. Tasty!

Anyway, Python had moved into the area and told himself, *Hey, this is a nice cave. Lots of juicy mortals to eat!* Python proceeded to swallow the priests and the soothsayers and the pilgrims who came looking for aid. Then he coiled up for a nap.

When Leto visited, she was shocked to find a hundred-foot-long snake as thick as a school bus hanging out in her mother's favourite holy place.

'Who are you?' Leto demanded.

'I am Python,' said Python. 'And you must be breakfast.'

The snake lunged at her. Leto fled, but she looked so appetizing, being plump and pregnant and slow, that Python pursued her for miles. A couple of times he almost caught her. Leto barely made it back to her boat.

Where was Zeus this whole time? Hiding. Hera was in a royal snit, and Zeus didn't want to be the target of her wrath, so he let Leto take all the heat. Nice guy.

Leto kept sailing until finally she had a crazy idea. She asked the captain of her ship to sail for the island of Delos.

'But, my lady,' said the captain, 'Delos is a floating island! Nobody knows where it is from day to day.'

'JUST FIND IT!' Leto screamed. Labour pain made her eyes glow red with agony.

The captain gulped. 'One Delos, coming right up!'

Several nerve-racking days later, they found the place. It looked like a normal island – beaches, hills, trees, etc. – but Delos wasn't attached to the earth. It floated on the waves like a giant life-preserver, drifting around the Mediterranean, occasionally pinballing off other islands or running over unsuspecting whales.

As the ship got closer, Leto forced herself to stand at the bow. She was in so much pain she could hardly think, but she called out to the main nature spirit of the island: 'O great Delos, you alone can help me! Please let me come ashore and give birth on your island!'

The island rumbled. A voice echoed from the hills: 'Hera will be royally ticked off if I do that.'

'She can't hurt you!' Leto yelled. 'Her curse specified any land with roots in the earth. You don't have roots! Besides, once my children are born, they will protect you. *Two* Olympian gods on your side. Think about that. Delos will become their holy place. You will have great temples of your own. You can finally settle down in one spot. The tourism alone will make you millions!'

Delos thought about that. The island was tired of drifting around. The forest nymphs were getting seasick from constantly bobbing on the waves.

'All right,' said the voice. 'Come ashore.'

As soon as Leto found a spot to lie down, the whole world trembled with anticipation. It's not every day that two new Olympian gods are born. All the goddesses – except, of course, Hera – rushed to Leto's side to help her give birth.

Leto had two beautiful babies – a boy named Apollo and a girl named Artemis. They were born on the seventh day of the seventh month, when Leto was seven months pregnant, so their holy number was thirteen. (*Just kidding. It was seven.*)

Apollo wasted no time taking the spotlight. As soon as he'd tasted nectar from his baby bottle, he hopped out of his mother's arms, stood on his own two feet and grinned.

"Sup, folks?" he said. 'My name's Apollo, and I need a bow and arrows, stat! Also, a musical instrument would be good. Has anybody invented the lyre yet?'

The goddesses looked at each other in confusion. Even the Olympians were not used to grinning babies who spoke in complete sentences and demanded weapons.

'Erm, I've never heard of a lyre,' Demeter admitted.

In fact, the lyre would be invented later, but that's another story.

Apollo shrugged. 'Fine. A guitar will do. Or a ukulele. Just not a banjo, please. I don't do banjos.'

The goddesses rushed off to find what the kid wanted. Hephaestus made him a beautiful golden bow and a quiver of magic arrows. The best musical instrument they could come up with was a *keras*, which was like a trumpet.

By the time the goddesses returned to Delos, Apollo had grown so much he looked like a five-year-old, though he wasn't even one day old. He had long golden hair, a super-bronze tan and eyes that shone like the sun. He'd found himself a Greek robe woven from gold, so he was almost too flashy to look at.

He slung the bow and quiver over his shoulders and grabbed the keras. He played a beautiful melody on the trumpet, then began to sing a cappella.

'*Oh, I am Apollo, and I'm so cool! La-la-la, something that rhymes with cool!*'

Actually I have no idea what he sang, but he announced that he would be the god of archery and song and poetry. He also announced that he would become the god of prophecy, and interpret the will of Zeus and the words of the Oracle for all the poor little mortal peons.

When his song was finished, the goddesses clapped politely, though they still thought the whole scene was a little weird. The island of Delos rejoiced that it had a new patron god. Delos put down roots and anchored itself in the sea so that it wouldn't move around any more. The island covered itself with golden flowers in honour of the golden god Apollo. If you visit Delos today, you can still see those fields of wildflowers stretching out among the ruins, though thankfully Apollo doesn't play the trumpet there very often.

Apollo grew with super-speed. In about a week, he'd become a regular adult god, which meant he totally skipped school, got an honorary diploma and stopped ageing when he looked twenty-one years old. Then he stayed that way forever. Not a bad deal, if you ask me.

His first act was to avenge his mother for her pain and suffering while she was trying to find a place to give birth. Sadly, he couldn't destroy Hera, since she was the Queen of Heaven and all, but when he heard about the giant snake Python, who'd chased his mother out of Delphi, Apollo was enraged.

'Be right back,' he told Leto.

Apollo flew to Delphi (yes, he could fly) and called out Python.

'Yo, snake!'

Python opened his eyes. 'What do you want?'

'To sing you a song about my awesomeness!'

'Oh, please. Just kill me now.'

'Okay!' Apollo drew his bow and shot the snake between the eyes. *Then* he sang a song about his awesomeness. He threw the snake's body into a fissure below the cave, where it rotted eternally and spewed all kinds of cool odours.

Apollo took over the Oracle of Delphi. He welcomed back the priests and the pilgrims. Because the Oracle had once belonged to his grandmother, Phoebe, he was sometimes called Phoebus Apollo. The main priestess who told the future became known as the *Pythia*, after the snake Python. Or maybe she was called that because she spoke a bunch of rot. Anyway, she would get her prophecies straight from the god Apollo, and the lines would always be riddles or bad poetry, or both.

She dwelt in the cave where the snake had died. Usually she sat on a three-legged stool next to one of the big fissures that vented gross volcanic gas, which smelled of dead snakes. If you made an offering, the Pythia would tell your fortune or answer any question. That didn't mean you would understand the answer. If you did understand it, you probably wouldn't like it.

*

Apollo claimed his place among the Olympian gods, and even Hera didn't dare object. He just looked so . . . *godly*.

He was as tall and muscular and bronze as a *Baywatch* lifeguard. He kept his blond hair long, but tied back in a man bun so it didn't interfere with his archery. He sauntered around Olympus in his gleaming robes with his bow and arrow, winking at the ladies and high-fiving the dudes, or sometimes winking at the dudes and high-fiving the ladies. Apollo didn't care. He figured *everybody* loved him.

He was great with poetry and music . . . or, at least, some people liked it. Me, I'm more of a straight-ahead rock 'n' roll kind of guy, but whatever. Apollo was always popular at parties, because he could entertain you with songs, tell your fortune and even do cool trick shots with his bow, like intercepting a dozen ping-pong balls at once or shooting a wine cup off Dionysus's head.

Apollo also became the god of shepherds and cowherds. Why? You got me. Obviously Apollo liked premium cuts of meat. He raised the finest cattle in the world. *Everybody* wanted to steal them, but Apollo kept them under constant guard. If anybody got near his sacred herd, they were likely to start World War C (for cow).

When Apollo got mad, he didn't mess around. He could punish any mortal anywhere in the world simply by drawing his bow and firing. The arrow would arc through the sky and find its mark, no matter how far away. If Apollo was hanging out in Greece and some guy in Spain muttered, 'Apollo is stupid!' . . . *BAM!* One dead Spanish guy. The arrow would be invisible, too – so the other mortals would never know what hit him.

In Ancient Greece, anytime somebody dropped dead unexpectedly, they assumed Apollo had struck him down – maybe as a punishment, maybe as a reward for one of the guy's enemies.

Considering that, this is going to sound strange: Apollo was the god of healing. If you wanted plasters or aspirin, Apollo could help you out. But he also had power over plagues and epidemics. He could cure or kill off an entire army or a whole nation. If he got mad, he'd shoot a special arrow that exploded into a foul vapour and spread smallpox or black plague or anthrax. If a zombie apocalypse ever comes around, you'll know who to blame.

Apollo was the god of so many different things that even the Greeks got confused. They'd be like, 'Hmm, I forgot who the god of basket weaving is. Must be Apollo!'

Maybe that's why, later on, the Greeks and Romans started calling Apollo the god of the sun. That was actually Helios's job, but the mortals sort of forgot about Helios and decided to give Apollo the sun chariot instead. Since Apollo was all flashy and golden like the sun, it made sense.

In this book, though, let's not think of him as the sun god. The dude's got enough other stuff on his plate. Plus, the idea of Apollo driving the sun chariot freaks me out, 'cause you know he'd be talking on his cell phone most of the time with the radio cranked to max, the subwoofers rattling the whole chariot. He'd have his dark shades on and be checking out the ladies, like, *How you doing?*

Anyway, his symbols were the bow and arrow – no surprise. Later, when the lyre (like a small harp) was invented, that was his symbol, too.

The main thing to know about Apollo: never underestimate the guy. One day he might be the god of limericks and stupid earworm songs and first-aid classes. The next day he's the god of chemical weapons and world-destroying plagues. And you thought *Poseidon* had a split personality.

Apollo wouldn't kill you for no reason. He just didn't need much of a reason.

Example: one time his mom, Leto, was coming to see him at Delphi. Along the way she got harassed by a giant named Tityos. I know. Terrible name, Tityos. Nothing I can do about that.

Anyway, Tityos was a nasty piece of work. He was one of Zeus's most monstrous kids. His mom was your typical mortal princess, Elara, but when she was pregnant Zeus had the brilliant idea of hiding her from Hera by sticking her in an underground cave. Something about the cave vapours made Elara's unborn child grow ugly and so huge that his mom's body simply couldn't contain him. It's a little disgusting, but . . . well, *KA-BLAM!* Elara died. However, the child kept growing until the entire cave became his incubation chamber. Then Gaia, good old Dirt Face herself, decided to be Tityos's surrogate mom. She completed his training in the Dark Side. When Tityos finally emerged from the earth, he looked less like the son of Zeus and more like the son of Frankenstein's monster.

Anyway, Hera got hold of him and figured she could use this giant to get her long-awaited revenge on Leto.

'Hey, Tityos,' Hera said to him one day.

'Blood!' Tityos screamed. 'Meat and blood!'

'Yes,' Hera said. 'Those are very nice. But how about a pretty wife for you, too?'

'Meat!'

'Okay. Maybe later. A woman will be walking this way soon, heading to Delphi. She just *loves* it when big strong giants try to abduct her and drag her to their underground lair. Interested?'

Tityos scratched his massive head. 'Blood?'

'Why, certainly.' Hera smiled. 'If she resists, shed all the blood you want!'

Tityos agreed, so Hera gave him a cookie for good behaviour and left him lying in wait on the road to Delphi. Soon Leto came along, and Tityos leaped out to grab her.

Thanks to her experience with Python, Leto had had a lot of practice running away from monsters, and this time she wasn't pregnant. She dodged the giant and took off full-speed for Delphi.

'Hey, son?' she yelled. 'A little help back here?'

Apollo heard his mother's call. He grabbed his bow and fired. *THWACK*. Tityos bit the dirt with a golden arrow straight through his heart.

But that revenge was too quick for Apollo. He went down to see Hades in the Underworld and said, 'This guy Tityos . . . I guess he still counts as a mortal demigod. Not sure. Anyway, if his spirit shows up, torture him for me. Something cool . . . like Zeus did with Prometheus. Except not with an eagle. Maybe vultures or something.'

'Vultures or something?' Hades asked.

'Yeah! Perfect!'

Hades must not have been feeling very creative, because he followed Apollo's suggestion exactly. When the spirit of Tityos turned up, the giant was convicted of assaulting Leto. He was sent to the Fields of Punishment, where he was chained down, given a regenerating liver and cut open so that vultures could feast on it forever. (I think Prometheus filed a copyright infringement suit later on.)

Another time, Apollo avenged an insult by committing mass murder. That seems fair, right? The queen of Thebes, a lady named Niobe, had fourteen kids – seven boys and seven girls. The children were all healthy and attractive and made good grades in school, so Niobe was always bragging about them. You've probably met moms like that. You say, 'Yeah, I scored a goal in the football game last night.' And she says, 'Oh, that's nice. All fourteen of my children are the *captains* of their teams, and they make straight As and can play the violin.' And you just want to smack her.

Well, Niobe was *that* lady. One day the city of Thebes had a festival in honour of Leto. The priests were praising the Titan for being so beautiful and courageous and giving birth to not one but *two* amazing gods, Apollo and Artemis. As the prayers were going on and on, Queen Niobe couldn't stand it any more.

'Oh, that's not so special!' she said to the audience. 'I don't think Leto's any more beautiful or courageous than *I* am. Besides, she only had two children. I had *fourteen* amazing children!'

O-o-o-o-kay. Bad move.

Halfway across the world, Apollo and Artemis heard the insult and came flying with their bows at the ready.

They descended on Thebes and a wave of terror spread across the city. Everyone turned to stone except for the queen and her family.

'Proud of your kids?' Apollo bellowed. 'Maybe we need to put things in perspective for you.'

He shot seven golden arrows and murdered all of Niobe's sons on the spot. Artemis shot down all seven of the daughters. Niobe's husband, the king, wailed in outrage, drew his sword and charged at Apollo, so the god struck him down, too.

Niobe's heart was shattered. She fled to a mountain in Asia Minor – the country we call Turkey – and wept for years and years, until finally she turned to rock. The Greeks used to visit the spot on Mount Sipylus where a weathered sandstone figure of a woman stood, water seeping from its eyes. Maybe she's still there.

As for her dead family, they weren't buried for nine days. The bodies just lay in the streets of Thebes, attracting flies and getting grosser and more, um, *python*, while the rest of the townspeople were frozen as statues.

Finally, Zeus took pity on Thebes. He unfroze the people and allowed them to bury the royal family. Nobody in Thebes ever insulted Leto again, but I'm pretty sure Apollo and Artemis weren't very popular there, either.

And *still* Apollo could find new and horrifying ways to punish people.

The most horrible thing he did was to the satyr Marsyas.

This goat-legged dude lived in Phrygia, over in Asia Minor, kind of near the spot where Niobe turned to stone. One day Marsyas was trotting along the riverbank, minding his own business, when he spotted a strange instrument lying in the grass. It happened to be the flute Athena had made – the very first one in the world. Maybe you remember that the other goddesses teased her about the way she looked when she played it, so she threw it off Olympus and swore that anyone who played it would suffer a terrible fate.

Well, poor Marsyas didn't know that. It wasn't like Athena had put a warning label on it. The satyr picked up the flute and began to play. Since it had been filled with the breath of a goddess, the flute sounded amazing. In no time, Marsyas had mastered the fingering and was playing so beautifully that all the nature nymphs for miles around came to hear him.

Pretty soon he was signing autographs. He scored six number-one hits on *Billboard*. His YouTube channel attracted seven million followers, and his first album went platinum in Asia Minor.

Okay, maybe I'm exaggerating. But he got popular for his music. His fame spread.

Apollo didn't like that. He only had *five* number-one hits on *Billboard*. He didn't want some stupid satyr on the cover of *Rolling Stone* when it should have been him.

Apollo came down to Phrygia and floated invisibly above the crowd that had gathered to hear Marsyas play. The guy was good, no question. That made Apollo even angrier.

He waited and listened, knowing it was only a matter of time . . .

Soon enough, a starry-eyed nymph in the front row screamed, 'Marsyas, you're the new Apollo!'

The praise went right to Marsyas's head. He winked at the nymph. 'Thanks, babe. But, seriously, whose music do you like better – Apollo's or *mine*!'

The crowd cheered wildly – until Apollo appeared on stage in a blaze of golden light. Everyone went absolutely silent.

'What a great question, Marsyas!' Apollo cried. 'Was that a challenge? 'Cause it sounded like a challenge.'

'Uh . . . Lord Apollo . . . I didn't – I wasn't –'

'A *music contest*, you say?' Apollo grinned ear to ear. 'I accept! We'll let the crowd choose who is better and, just to make things interesting, the winner can do *whatever he wants* to the loser – demand any price, inflict any punishment! How does that strike you?'

Marsyas turned pale, but the crowd cheered and hollered in approval. Funny how quickly a flute concert can turn into a public execution.

Marsyas didn't have much choice, so he played the best he could. His flute music brought tears to the nymphs' eyes. The satyrs in the audience cried, held torches in the air and bleated like baby goats.

Apollo followed with a song on his lyre (which had been invented by this time). He strummed and sang and did a blazing extended solo. The girls in the front row fainted. The audience roared enthusiastically.

It was impossible to tell who had won the contest. Both musicians were equally talented.

'Well . . .' Apollo scratched his head. 'Tiebreaker, then. Let's see who can do the best *trick* playing.'

Marsyas blinked. '*Trick* playing?'

'Sure, you know. Fancy moves! Showmanship! Can you do *this*!'

Apollo put his lyre behind his head and played a tune

without even looking at the strings. The crowd went nuts. Apollo windmilled his arms. He slid across the stage on his knees while shredding sixteenth notes, then hit the reverb button on his lyre and leaped into the mosh pit, ripping out a solo as the crowd pushed him back onto the stage.

The applause died down after about an hour. Apollo grinned at Marsyas. 'Can you do that?'

'With a flute?' Marsyas cried. 'Of course not! That's not fair!'

'Then I win!' Apollo said. 'I have just the punishment for you. See, Marsyas, you think you're special, but you're a fad. *I'll* be famous forever. I'm immortal. You? All glitter, no gold. Scratch the surface, and you're just another mortal satyr – flesh and blood. I'm going to prove that to the crowd.'

Marsyas backed up. His mouth tasted like python slime. 'Lord Apollo, let me apologize for –'

'I'm going to flay you alive!' Apollo said cheerfully. 'I'm going to remove your skin, so we can all see what's underneath!'

Grossed out yet?

Yeah. It was pretty horrible.

Marsyas suffered a grisly death just because he dared to make music as good as Apollo's. The satyr's body was buried in a cave near the site of the music contest, and his blood became a river that gushed down the side of the hill.

Apollo made the cover of *Rolling Stone*. From his smiling face, you'd never guess the guy sewed curtains out of satyr skin.

*

Final thing about Apollo: he was a confirmed bachelor and a real ladies' man. Hey, a mass-murdering psychopath who plays the lyre? It doesn't get much more charming than that!

According to some stories, he dated each of the Nine Muses – the goddesses who oversaw different kinds of art, like tragedy, comedy, docudrama and whatever. Apollo couldn't decide between them. They were all too lovely; so he vowed never to marry, just date around.

Only once was he tempted to break that promise. He fell in love and got his heart broken – and it was his own fault.

One afternoon Apollo happened to be walking through the palace at Mount Olympus when he ran across Eros, Aphrodite's son. The hitman of love was sitting on a window ledge restringing his bow. The kid looked so young, his bow so tiny, that Apollo burst out laughing.

'Oh my gods!' Apollo wiped a tear from his eye. 'You call that a *bow*! Those arrows look like darts. How can you *hit* anything?'

Eros was seething inside, but he managed a smile. 'I do all right.'

'*This* is a bow, kid!' Apollo pulled out his own golden longbow, made by Hephaestus. 'My enemies tremble when they see me coming. I can destroy anyone with a single arrow from any distance! You . . . well, I suppose you'd be a fearsome gerbil hunter.'

Apollo strode off, still laughing.

Eros gritted his teeth. He muttered to himself, 'We'll see

about that, Mr Big Shot. Maybe you can bring down your enemies, but I can bring down *you*.'

The next morning, Apollo was walking by the riverside in Thessaly, just playing his lyre and enjoying the sunshine, when Eros shot an arrow straight into Apollo's heart.

By chance, a naiad was bathing nearby – one of the daughters of the local river spirit. Her name was Daphne. By anybody's standards, Daphne was beautiful. Most naiads were. But the moment Apollo saw her he thought she was even hotter than Aphrodite. All the other women he'd dated suddenly seemed like complete losers. Apollo decided he *had* to marry Daphne.

Sadly, like a lot of smart nymphs, Daphne had long ago sworn off dating gods, because bad things happened to their girlfriends. Not all the time, maybe. Just, like, 99.9 percent of the time.

'Hey!' Apollo called out. 'What's your name?'

Daphne leaped out of the water and wrapped herself in her robe. 'I'm – I'm Daphne. Please, go away.'

'Oh, Daphne Please-Go-Away,' Apollo said, 'I love you! Marry me, and I will make you the happiest naiad in the universe.'

'No.'

'I insist! Come; let me kiss you. I will prove my affection and . . . Hey, where are you going?'

Daphne ran.

Apollo was fast, but Daphne was faster. Apollo was burdened with his bow and his lyre and he was dazed with love, so he kept stopping to compose new haiku in her honour.

Eventually, though, Daphne began to tire. She reached a cliff that looked out over a canyon. Apollo climbed the slope behind her. There was no way Daphne could double back.

That left her with two options: leap to her death, or agree to marry Apollo. Hearing him spout love poetry, she thought leaping off the cliff sounded pretty good.

In desperation, she tried one last thing: 'O Gaia, protector of all nature spirits, hear me! Save me from becoming this god's girlfriend!'

Gaia took pity on Daphne. Just as Apollo reached the cliff and threw his arms around the naiad, Daphne changed into a laurel tree. Apollo found himself hugging a tree trunk, caressing arms that had turned into branches, running his hands through hair that had become leaves.

Apollo sobbed in despair. 'Oh, beautiful naiad! I will never forget you. You were my one true love. You should have been my wife! I failed to win your love, but from now until the end of time you will be a symbol of victory. Your leaves shall adorn my head, and I will totally start a new fashion trend!'

That's why you'll often see pictures of Greeks and Romans wearing laurel wreaths on their heads. Apollo made it stylish. Laurels became a sign of honour. If you won a contest or a sporting event, you got to wear laurels. If you conquered an enemy nation, more laurels! If you got tired of doing amazing deeds and you had enough wreaths to stuff a mattress, you could retire and rest on your laurels!

All because Apollo bragged about his big fancy golden bow.

Eros had the last laugh, but, generally speaking, Apollo was right to brag. He *was* the best archer in the world. Only one person was as good as he was, maybe even better.

That would be his sister Artemis. If you want to read about her, fine. But, guys – be on your best behaviour. I'm warning you now: Artemis doesn't have a sense of humour.

Have you gone on all the quests?

Fought all the monsters?

Done all the world-saving?

Discover the complete collection of adventures
from genius storyteller Rick Riordan . . .

THE WORLD OF PERCY JACKSON

PERCY JACKSON

THE GREEK GODS ARE ALIVE AND KICKING!

Percy is having a pretty ordinary day, until he learns he's the son
of Poseidon, god of the sea. Now he must travel to Camp Half-Blood –
a secret base dedicated to the training of young demigods.

There are missions to complete, monsters to defeat and a whole lot
of universe to save. Welcome to the world of Percy Jackson . . .

HEROES OF OLYMPUS

THOUGHT THE PERCY JACKSON ADVENTURES WERE OVER? YOU COULDN'T BE MORE WRONG . . .

Sometimes a handful of half-bloods isn't quite enough to save humanity. Sometimes you need a whole lot more.

Introducing Jason, Piper and Leo.

Along with Percy Jackson and his friends, they must team up to stop a new and powerful threat from destroying the world.

THE TRIALS OF APOLLO

PERCY JACKSON AND THE DEMIGODS HAVE TRIED SAVING HUMANITY. NOW IT'S TIME FOR A GOD TO HAVE A GO . . .

Bad news for the god Apollo – he's been banished to Earth, stuck in the body of a teenage boy.

Help from Percy Jackson is at hand, but if Apollo wants to regain his godly form, there will be harrowing trials to face and a trio of Roman emperors to defeat.

IT'S NOT JUST PERCY JACKSON AND FRIENDS SAVING THE WORLD.

Discover a whole new host of heroes, villains and gods . . .

THE GODS OF ANCIENT EGYPT ARE FAR FROM DEAD AND BURIED . . .

Since their mother's death, siblings Carter and
Sadie Kane have become near strangers.

Until one night their brilliant Egyptologist father unleashes the
Egyptian god Set, who banishes him to oblivion.

Now only Carter and Sadie can save the day, as they travel
the globe and battle the gods of Ancient Egypt.

1. THE RED PYRAMID
2. THE THRONE OF FIRE
3. THE SERPENT'S SHADOW

THE VIKING MYTHS ARE TRUE. THOR IS REAL.
THE GODS OF ASGARD ARE PREPARING FOR WAR . . .

Magnus Chase has been killed in battle with a fire giant, resurrected in Valhalla
and chosen to be a warrior of the Norse god Odin.

He's had better days.

Now the gods of Asgard are readying themselves for Ragnarok –
the Norse doomsday – and Magnus has a leading role . . .

1. MAGNUS CHASE AND THE SWORD OF SUMMER
2. MAGNUS CHASE AND THE HAMMER OF THOR
3. MAGNUS CHASE AND THE SHIP OF THE DEAD

WANT MORE FROM YOUR FAVOURITE HEROES AND GODS?

Discover training manuals, character guides, short stories and so much more . . .

THE WORLD OF PERCY JACKSON

Diaries of your favourite heroes, files on the scariest monsters, and an in-depth guide to Camp Half-Blood. It's all here.

THE DEMIGOD FILES

THE DEMIGOD DIARIES

CAMP HALF-BLOOD CONFIDENTIAL

PERCY JACKSON AND THE GREEK GODS

PERCY JACKSON AND THE GREEK HEROES

THE TRIALS OF APOLLO

Find out what's really behind all the strange things happening in Camp Jupiter through Claudia's journal entries. Warning: secrets will be uncovered.

CAMP JUPITER CLASSIFIED

THE KANE CHRONICLES

These companion guides and incredible short stories give readers the inside scoop on the Kane Chronicles.

THE KANE CHRONICLES SURVIVAL GUIDE

BROOKLYN HOUSE MAGICIAN'S MANUAL

DEMIGODS AND MAGICIANS: THREE STORIES FROM THE WORLD OF PERCY JACKSON AND THE KANE CHRONICLES

MAGNUS CHASE

Travel the Nine Worlds with your favourite characters and enjoy the ultimate companion guide to Magnus Chase and the gods of Asgard.

HOTEL VALHALLA GUIDE TO THE NORSE WORLDS

9 FROM THE NINE WORLDS

ABOUT THE AUTHOR

RICK RIORDAN, dubbed 'storyteller of the gods' by *Publishers Weekly*, is the author of five *New York Times* number-one bestselling middle-grade series with millions of copies sold throughout the world: Percy Jackson, the Heroes of Olympus and the Trials of Apollo, based on Greek and Roman mythology; the Kane Chronicles, based on Egyptian mythology; and Magnus Chase, based on Norse mythology. His Greek myth collections, *Percy Jackson and the Greek Gods* and *Percy Jackson and the Greek Heroes*, were *New York Times* number-one bestsellers as well.

Rick lives in Boston, Massachusetts, with his wife and two sons.

Follow him on Twitter @camphalfblood.
To learn more about him and his books, visit:

www.rickriordan.co.uk